MW00928754

RUINS OF THE GALAXY
BLACK LABYRINTH

CHRISTOPHER HOPPER
J.N. CHANEY

VARIANT
PUBLICATIONS

LAS VEGAS, NV · NEW YORK, NV

CONNECT WITH J.N. CHANEY

Join the conversation and get updates in the Facebook group called "JN Chaney's Renegade Readers." This is a hotspot where readers come together and share their lives and interests, discuss the series, and speak directly to J.N. Chaney and his co-authors.

https://www.facebook.com/groups/jnchaneyreaders/

He also post updates, official art, and other awesome stuff on his website and you can also follow him on Instagram, Facebook, and Twitter.

For email updates about new releases, as well as exclusive promotions, visit his website and enter your email address.

https://www.jnchaney.com/ruins-of-the-galaxy-subscribe

Enjoying the series? Help others discover the *Ruins of the Galaxy* series by leaving a review on Amazon.

CONNECT WITH CHRISTOPHER HOPPER

Wondering when the next Ruins book is dropping on print or audio?

Want the latest news on custom merch and exclusive promos?

Then visit the Ruins launch center today and sign up. Just head to the web address below.

https://upbeat-innovator-9021.ck.page/00c66d6b44

CONTENTS

JOIN THE RUINS TRIBE

Visit **ruinsofthegalaxy.com** today and join the tribe. Once there, you can sign up for our reader group, join our Facebook community, and find us on Twitter and Instagram.

If you'd like to email us with comments or questions, we respond to all emails sent to ruinsofthegalaxy@gmail.com, and love to hear from our readers.

See you in the Ruins!

PREVIOUSLY

Last Time in Ruins of the Galaxy Book 4: Void Horizon...

AFTER DEFEATING a Paragon recon force in the Novian city of Itheliana, Magnus and his Gladio Umbra returned to their shuttles with a prisoner in tow—one Captain Nos Kil, the right-hand enforcer for Lord Moldark. But their departure was cut short by a surprise Talon attack. However, the squadron's assault failed, and Magnus found himself in charge of a second prisoner—famed ace Talon pilot Ricio Longo.

Once in detention abroad Azelon's Spire, the two prisoners turned out to be both boons and banes while under interrogation. For his part, Nos Kil nearly killed Magnus after provoking him over their shared past. Meanwhile, Ricio provided valuable information about Moldark and the Paragon's activities. The new intel prompted Magnus and his team to contemplate an assault on Worru, the Luma homeworld. As the group formulated a plan to rescue Valerie's mother, Elder Willowood, Piper was discovered alone in Nos Kil's cell block, the fallout of which has strained her relationship with Magnus for reasons connected to his dark past.

The Worru mission began with Magnus garnering the support of Republic Marine Corps Colonel Caldwell. Once employed, the task force advanced on Elders Hall and freed Willowood as well as several dozen Luma hostages. But their escape was hindered, first by the shocking appearance of reanimated Luma corpses and then by Master So-Elku's Blue Guard.

The mission's final phase pitted the Gladio Umbra against Captain Forbes and a company of Republic Marines. Eventually, Magnus led his unit back to the shuttles, but not before the team suffered their most significant loss yet. In an attempt to protect her from a rocket strike, Magnus inadvertently pushed Valerie Stone into oncoming enemy fire. Her tragic loss sent Piper into an explosive emotional and metaphysical state, one that not only wiped out the remaining company of Marines but also caused her to vanish.

Faced with the choice of searching for Piper or saving the Gladio Umbra and Luma hostages, Magnus was forced to make the hard decision to leave Piper behind. Their escape would have been for nothing, however, had it not been for

Ricio's sudden appearance flying Azelon's newly revealed starfighter—the Novian Fang.

Now, bruised and in search of a way forward, our heroes contemplate their next steps in recovering the most powerful child in the galaxy. The only problem is that no one knows where Piper Stone is.

PROLOGUE

"ORDER ALL SHIPS TO hold their fire," David Seaman said from his captain's chair aboard the Super Dreadnaught *Solera Fortuna*.

"Yes, Commodore," replied his communications officer.

"And tell the *Ardent Eclipse* to lower their aft shields to thirty percent."

"Right away."

The comms officer went to work while Seaman's Flag Captain, Lani DiAntora, leaned into his ear. "Commodore, what do you intend to do here?"

In the short time that Seaman had known the woman, he'd found her to be inquisitive, analytical, and unafraid of senior officers—three things that tended to keep junior officers from being promoted. But she was also Sekmit, which meant these attributes were characteristic of their species, making them both trusted advisers and, at times, incredibly frustrating companions.

"*Voknareth ilphin nockfarock,*" Seaman replied in his best Jujari accent.

DiAntora tilted her head and twitched her feline-like nose. "Never surrender?"

"Never back down," he corrected. "Especially when the kill is sure, so the saying goes."

DiAntora stood upright and reviewed *Ardent Eclipse's* position as it fled from a Jujari Pride-class Battleship named *Behold the Glory of Mwadim Pethroga's Victorious Might.* The *Ardent* had already suffered severe damage, putting most of the Battlecruiser's 2,000-plus sailors at risk. Ordering the vessel to lower its shields further was a death sentence. But the *Ardent* was also fleeing toward the safety of First Fleet.

"You intend to lure them in," DiAntora said. Her cat-shaped ears flicked once, poking out of her human-like head of blonde hair.

"I do. Once they're in range of our quad cannons, and too close to deploy countermeasures against our torpedoes, I want you to fire on it from our port side."

"Aye-aye, Commodore." Then, barely above the noise in the bridge, she said, "A well-conceived tactic—using the Jujari's ambitions against them." Seaman smiled at her appraisal. While he didn't need it, and she would be out of line to give it without being asked, he liked knowing they were on the same page.

Seaman watched as the *Ardent's* shield status dropped to

thirty percent. If the ship's commander survived this engagement, Seaman would be sure to submit his name for an award —if the Paragon did such things. With so much rapid change, it was hard to know what policies and traditions remained in effect and what had been abandoned.

As soon as the *Victorious Might* detected the shield drop, it began pummeling the *Ardent* with heavy artillery fire. Within seconds, the shields had been reduced to nothing, and blaster rounds chewed into the ship's aft. The first salvo alone took out both starboard engines. The massive exhaust cones blew apart, showering the *Ardent's* hull with chunks of debris.

Unspent reactor energy cascaded over the tail in purple and white flames, bursting with charges of electrical power. Seaman knew that if the ship's crew didn't get the reactor core's output under control, the *Ardent* wouldn't succumb to a Jujari attack—it would detonate from a containment breach.

Fortunately, the hemorrhage tapered off, but not before more blaster fire took out the port-side engines.

"Commodore, the *Ardent* is reporting complete aft engine failure," the comms officer said. "They're requesting permission to raise shields."

"Negative." Seaman stood. "Tell them to stand down and continue drifting."

"Yes, Commodore."

"Cutting it close, aren't you?" DiAntora asked, keeping her voice just soft enough that the rest of the bridge crew wouldn't hear. Seaman hated that she knew the right volume level to speak her mind without making it look like she was questioning his authority. She'd been at her job far longer than he'd been at his, and she seemed to be letting it go to her head.

"Life support is still nominal," Seaman said with his hands behind his back. He was confident in his plan, and he didn't need a Sekmit or anyone else questioning him at such a critical juncture—he didn't care how long she'd been a Captain. "More importantly, however, the *Victorious Might* is still not committed. It will be, though."

DiAntora purred—but whether in resignation or disagreement, Seaman could not tell. Only time with her at his side would give him the ability to know what she was thinking without speaking. And if they survived this, he'd enjoy getting to know her. Seaman always had a thing for Sekmit despite the stigmas that surrounded inter-species relationships. But if these recent days proved anything, it was that progressive thought was lauded, and the old ways were dying.

Seaman's recent promotion from Captain and Director of Strategic Fighter Command to Commodore of First Fleet had come as a surprise, especially given that it was a field promotion. Then again, the Paragon was anything but predictable. Hell, it had only existed for the better part of a few weeks. But apparently both First and Second Fleet's admirals had resigned their posts, and Fleet Admiral Brighton had insisted that the vacancies be filled by "those competent officers loyal to Lord Moldark."

The Republic Navy would never have sanctioned such a unilateral move—not without approval from Capriana—

which made saying yes to Brighton even easier, as this was indeed a once in a lifetime opportunity. With no other flag officers over First Fleet, his new rank as Commodore gave him command of not only his own Super Dreadnaught, but all ten carriers and dozens of support vessels.

The *Victorious Might* continued to track after the wounded *Ardent*, moving closer and closer into the target window. With the shields down, the Jujari ship fired torpedoes into the *Ardent's* aft, blowing away vast sections of the Battlecruiser's stern. But most of these were engineering sections, and Seaman had already ordered the commander to move his sailors amidships.

"Just a little bit more," Seaman said to himself.

"Commodore, Captain Milhorn is hailing again, asking for permission to—"

"Belay that, Ensign. Tell them to remain as they are."

"Aye-aye, sir."

"You do realize that if this fails, you'll be charged with gross negligence and dereliction of duty, responsible for willfully placing over 2,000 sailors in harm's way."

"And when it works, XO?" Seaman turned to look at her, staring into her deep green eyes. "What then?"

The Sekmit swallowed, narrowing her eyes at the main holo display. "We will have achieved a significant blow against the remaining Jujari forces over Oorajee. And we will be another step closer to their surrender."

Seaman smiled, pulled up a ship's schematic in a new holo window, and spoke in a calm, even tone. "As you will recall,

Ardent is a Growler-class Battlecruiser. They were overbuilt in the stern in order to compensate for the drive core advances made around the turn of the century. As long as the captain keeps his sailors ahead of the reactor core bulkheads, which he has, that ship can lose up to thirty-five percent of its stern mass and still keep the crew alive, still return fire, still raise shields, and still maintain basic thrust-vector steerage." He turned to face her. "Do you still think I'm being reckless?" DiAntora opened her mouth, but Seaman raised a finger. "That was rhetorical, Captain."

"Understood. You wouldn't have liked my answer anyway."

Suddenly, Seaman noticed that the *Victorious Might's* bow crossed the target window's plane—the enemy was within range, and no amount of maneuvering could get them out in time.

"Tell the *Ardent* to raise shields." He looked at DiAntora. "Open fire!"

DiAntora relayed the commands to weapons and engineering, and within seconds, *Solera Fortuna's* port side was ablaze in blaster fire and torpedo flames. The weapons fire crossed above Oorajee's stratosphere and assailed the enemy Battleship. Shields held against the first few seconds of blaster fire, dispersing the energy over huge spherical shells. But Seaman wasn't commanding a squadron of Talons—this was a Super Dreadnaught, a ship feared in every section of the quadrant.

Within seconds, the Battlecruiser's shields were knocked

away, allowing the quad cannons and auto turrets to rake the hull. As small plumes of fire erupted along the ship's port side, torpedoes found their targets, blowing up defense towers and sensor arrays. The second wave of torpedoes took out critical life support junctions, communications nodes, and power relay stations. The *Victorious Might* purged fire into hard vacuum. While the flames were snuffed out as soon as any combustible fuel was spent, the long trails of debris were flung into forever in all directions.

"It's working," DiAntora said as if she still couldn't believe it.

"No, Captain. It *worked*," Seaman said, feeling quite pleased with himself. The *Victorious Might* attempted to veer away from the assault, but another Paragon Dreadnaught was prepared to head it off. Seaman turned to DiAntora, sensing he may have gloated in a way that might harm any future they had together. "Though, I feel it worth noting that I take your reservations as wise council and not…" He considered the right word. "Skepticism."

She flicked her tail one time and nodded at him. "As it was intended."

Seaman nodded and then looked to the holo display. But, for the life of him, he couldn't figure out what DiAntora meant by "it." Wise counsel? Or skepticism?

"Sir," the sensors officer said. "I'm detecting a vector change among the Sypeurlion ships."

"How many?" Seaman asked.

"Fleetwide. They appear to be slowing, Admiral."

Seaman glanced at DiAntora. The change in momentum was a good sign, and—based on the subtle smile she gave him—she knew it too. In war, alliances could flip in a heartbeat, all at the drop of a credit chip. If you were on the winner's side, the odds were in your favor, and taking risks usually meant big payouts. But when fortune favored the enemy—or, *Fortuna*, Seaman thought with a wry twinge in the corner of his lips—all bets were off, even among the strongest of friends. He'd seen allegiances crumble before, and he was witnessing it once again, or so he thought. The Jujari's loss of the *Victorious Might* was more than just a blow to their own forces—it was a blow to the faith the Sypeurlion had in them. Probably the Dim-Telok too.

"Let's press our new advantage," Seaman said to his captain. "The Jujari's surrender is imminent. Let's make sure no Sypeurlion ever thinks about aiding them again."

"Right away," DiAntora replied and walked toward the navigation and weapons officers.

Seaman sucked in a deep breath through his nose and pursed his lips. He'd always dreamed of helming a flagship, and now that he'd been given a chance, he felt as though his childhood dreams had been realized. With his recent streak of minor victories, and now this significant win, Seaman felt as though he belonged here at the helm. And it felt good. While Lord Moldark hadn't conveyed all of the ways he intended to restore order to the galaxy, Seaman felt confident that he would play a critical role in the redemptive process. Forcing the Jujari to surrender and hopefully join the Republic was only the beginning.

"Commodore," said the comms officer. "Incoming message from Admiral Brighton."

"On screen," Seaman said.

The Fleet Admiral's bust appeared, outfitted in the Paragon's new naval suit adorned with three white stripes across the left breast. "Commodore Seaman, congratulations on taking out *Pethroga's Victorious Might*. Well done."

"Thank you, sir."

"I am relaying new objectives to you now."

Seaman hesitated. "I don't think that will be necessary, Brighton. We have detected what we believe is a Sypeurlion retreat and think it wise to press our—"

"Your new objectives should be on display now."

The smaller missions objectives window floated to the main screens right side, sitting a meter forward. Running down the column was a list of all the remaining Jujari ships.

"I—I'm not sure I understand," Seaman said.

Brighton's left eye twitched ever so slightly—enough that Seaman noticed. Either the man was not used to a Commodore talking back and saw this as insubordination, or —Seaman's thoughts wandered—*or Brighton was insecure about the orders himself*. Seaman almost felt ashamed for this second conclusion, but he couldn't avoid his conscience.

"I am ordering you to destroy all the remaining Jujari vessels, Commodore. What don't you understand about that?"

Seaman swallowed. *Destroy all the remaining vessels?* "Admiral

Brighton, sir, the enemy fleet is withering away as we speak. Meanwhile, we have a chance to engage the allied ships and make a lasting statement."

"The remaining Jujari ships, Commodore," Brighton said with a crisp tone.

Seaman hesitated. He didn't want to jeopardize his newfound command—*but this?* "You're—you're asking me to annihilate a crippled foe on the verge of surrender?"

"There will be no surrender."

"But you can't be sure about that. They have little left that threatens—"

"I don't think you understand what Lord Moldark wishes, Commodore." Brighton leaned in, and, once again, Seaman felt as if the other man was trying to convince himself of his own words. "Even if the Jujari offer a surrender, it will not be acknowledged."

"Not be acknowledged?"

Brighton hesitated, seeming to study Seaman's face. "Is there a problem?"

"With all due respect, sir, this violates the Valdaiga Accords and the Naval Rules of Engagement."

"And yet you are commanding a Paragon flagship, are you not?"

"I am."

"And we are charged with the sacred duty of bringing order to chaos, of righting terrible wrongs. And this power has been granted to us by the highest echelons of the Republic, which transcend all previous standards." Brighton seemed to be gaining confidence as he spoke, now lowering his voice into a more contrite tone. "Commodore Seaman, you have before you the tremendous opportunity to defeat our greatest enemy once and for all. I think it is not a stretch to say that future generations will look back on your actions today and call you a hero."

Seaman didn't know what to say to Brighton. All his life, Seaman had been trained to kill on a large scale, setting up battlefields and giving orders. He'd become a master of strategic warfare, adept at commanding forces large and small, as today's victories illustrated. But with it came a great responsibility, one that recognized the sizable power that lay beneath each touch of a data pad, every press of a button. It was the power to wipe out life, to end uprisings, to destroy ships, and cities, and worlds. With the responsibility came rules—rules that helped keep the power from getting out of control.

But the rules had been removed, and the power was writhing, searching to swallow order, like a Fathroni sand snake slithering just under the desert's surface. At first, the disturbance in the dune seemed like nothing more than the work of a gentle breeze, but another few seconds and the entire dune became unstable, frothed up into a frenzied sand trap that could swallow a light freighter in seconds. Seaman felt his heartbeat quicken as the sand snake's body swirled under the ground beneath his feet.

Suddenly, blaster fire struck *Solera Fortuna's* front shields. The ship shuddered, snapping Seaman from his thoughts.

"Sir," DiAntora yelled. "We're taking heavy fire from a Sypeurlion vessel."

"Bring us around to bearing 125 mark 240," Seaman ordered. "Auxiliary power to forward shields, return fire."

"Commodore," Brighton said, his voice stern. "What is going on?"

"We are taking fire from a Sypeurlion ship," Seaman replied, noting the strange hopefulness in his voice. Seaman was about to sign off when the Brighton's channel cut out. He looked back toward the communications console and saw DiAntora standing over the ensign with her paw pressed firmly on the primary data pane.

"Oops," she said with a shrug of a shoulder.

1

MAGNUS ADJUSTED his body in his captain's chair, assuaging the soreness in his muscles and joints. Nos Kil had given him quite the beating, and Magnus was still mending from both Azelon and TO-96's surgeries and his new flesh. Still, he had a job to do. And since sleeping was difficult—being plagued by nightmares about Valerie's death and fears regarding Piper's whereabouts—Magnus knew there was no better place to be than in the *Spire's* bridge addressing his command team.

Awen and Willowood stood arm-in-arm, their puffy eyes evidence that they were still mourning Valerie's loss and Piper's disappearance. Abimbola stood beside them, flanked by Berouth and Colonel Caldwell, followed by Titus, Zoll, and Bliss. The Jujari representatives included Rohoar, Saladin, and Czyz, each still wearing their Novian armor chest plates. Ezo and Sootriman leaned on one another while Saasarr looked over their shoulders.

The newest face, of course, was Ricio's. The man had helped save their lives as they escaped Worru, and he deserved to be here. The other two men who deserved to be here were Flow and Cheeks, but their lingering aversion to Jujari made it impossible for Magnus to allow them in this meeting. He'd fill them in later, but it still pained him not have them by his side.

Magnus opened by greeting everyone and recognizing their unit's losses—Andocs, Haney, and Valerie. The last one made him catch his breath. He knew he wasn't the only one either. So he encouraged everyone to take the time they needed to grieve, especially while time was on their side, due to the time dilation in between metaspace and protospace.

Then Magnus turned to the tasks at hand, reminding everyone that they were at war. "The galaxy's going to splick, and we're the ones who've volunteered to stop it. So, until this thing is over, we all face it the same way—together and with courage."

Despite forlorn looks on several faces, Magnus knew his team would pull together. They *had* to. *Hell,* you *have to, Magnus,* he reminded himself.

Magnus cleared his throat then looked around the room. "I need a SITREP on our current position in metaspace, as well as points of concern as we look to move forward with…"

With what?

Magnus hadn't even thought about what was next. Valerie's death and Piper's disappearance had so consumed the few waking minutes of his consciousness that he realized he hadn't planned much past the assault on Worru.

"With stopping Moldark and So-Elku," Magnus said, finishing the sentence. Those were general terms, of course, but at least they pointed the way forward.

"OTF," Colonel Caldwell said in reply. Those who knew the Marine expression repeated it back.

"And as we move forward with finding Piper," Awen suddenly interjected. Hearing those words made Magnus's heart skip a beat. He thanked Awen silently, grateful that someone else had inserted the mission point in the conversation. "I'm sorry, I just—"

"It's all good." Magnus raised a hand to calm her. "Do you have any idea where she is?"

Awen turned to Willowood. The older woman's shoulders raised and lowered. "I'm afraid not, Magnus. She has concealed herself in ways that even I don't know how to penetrate. Piper will only be seen when she wants to be seen."

Magnus ran his tongue along the front of his teeth. His gums were sore from his fight with Nos Kil—*the traitor*. Magnus recalled the recording of Nos Kil's conversation with Piper, and the memory of it made Magnus sick to his stomach. He swallowed, willing the bile to stay down, then asked, "Is her location something you can keep working on?"

"Of course," Awen said. "Granted, it's harder to search for her from here in metaspace. The closer we are to Worru, the easier we can find her."

"If she's still on the planet," Magnus said.

Awen looked from Magnus to Willowood and back. "What do you mean, still on the planet? You think So-Elku took her somewhere?"

Magnus shook his head. "I reviewed the footage from her conversation with Nos Kil." Suddenly, Magnus felt the room shift. He guessed that either everyone had already seen the footage or that no one had. "In it, she confessed to having discovered a new ability."

"Moving things within the Unity," Awen said, her eyes focused somewhere else.

"Yes. You knew?"

"I suspected."

Magnus thought back to past conversations with Awen, where she alluded to Piper's powers. Awen hadn't been specific, of course, but there'd been something there, something just beneath the surface. Magnus wanted to be mad with her for not telling him sooner, or for her not figuring it out. But he knew the feelings were just his frustrations coming out. The situation was not Awen's fault. If anything, it was his.

"And do you think that is what she has done?" Abimbola asked. "Has she moved somewhere else?"

"It might explain why we can't detect her," Willowood replied. "Though, as Awen said, we are very far away from her. Again, until she wants to be found, I suspect we will search in vain. Still, I will remain vigilant."

That was not the kind of intel Magnus liked. He wanted something firm, something that would help narrow options and focus on a concise course of action. But with Piper being anywhere in the galaxy—even in metaspace for all they knew —securing Piper was quickly becoming less of an actionable objective than he wanted. Instead, she would be a side goal, one they may or may not ever actualize. And that pissed him off.

"What else do we have?" Magnus asked.

"Piper managed to imprison So-Elku," Awen said. "But there's no way to know how long that will last. He's grown more powerful with the knowledge he gleaned from the codex."

"And the codex itself?" Magnus said. "Did it survive the…?"

The what? he asked himself. He meant to say something about Piper's explosion of power but found himself at a loss for words.

"Yes, it survived," Awen said, sparing Magnus. "And I have possession of the volume. Willowood and I hope to leverage it, with Azelon's help, to train the Luma in the Novian ways."

"Good," Magnus said, reflecting positively on the win. *Maybe it will help them find Piper sooner too*, he thought. "Any idea what So-Elku's up to? What he'll do next?"

Ezo raised a hand. "Can we talk about those corpses coming to life in the catacombs? Because that freaked Ezo right out. Anyone else?"

Several people nodded, including Magnus. He didn't mind admitting that he'd been rattled, having never seen anything like it. But if So-Elku had power over the dead, who knew what he'd use it for in the future.

"I can speak to that, Ezo." Willowood took a step forward. "It seems that So-Elku has already leveraged much of what he's learned from the codex. His study of it began shortly upon returning from an expedition that I now know was to Ithnor Ithelia in metaspace." Willowood acknowledged Awen in a way that suggested the two had debriefed while Magnus had been recovering.

"So-Elku explained that he'd garnered a new token of power," Willowood said. "One that would rival anything in the galaxy. He demanded allegiance from those who wished to join him in his ultimate pursuit of peace. But when many asked for clarification, So-Elku became enraged and dismissed the meeting.

"Over the next few days, many of the elders had a chance to formulate objections to So-Elku's violent pursuit of peace. Conversely, others took the time to redouble their support of So-Elku, perhaps sensing the power he'd acquired. When the council reconvened, the clash between the two factions turned hostile. So-Elku, however, anticipated the confrontation and seized those who opposed him, locking them in the catacombs. I learned of this by those who joined me in the tombs. I had already been placed there following my attempts to help Awen escape.

"As for the living dead that you encountered, I can only guess that So-Elku's new powers in the Unity—those dealing with the Foundation and the Nexus, of which I am still learning about from Awen—enabled him to reanimate the bodies of the mystics for nefarious purposes. Beyond that, I cannot tell you exactly how he summoned the corpses."

Awen stepped forward to stand equal with Willowood. "As far as what he's planning next, we suspect So-Elku will continue with his campaign to rally the Luma to his side and attempt peace by force."

"And yet he's the bad guy, and we're not," Titus said. The phrase seemed intended for himself, but all eyes turned toward him. "Peace by force. Isn't that what we're doing too? Don't get me wrong, this guy's a lunatic, and he needs to be stopped. But if we're talking about the way to restore peace to the galaxy, shouldn't we at least admit that we're trying to bring peace by force too?"

"Ezo thinks that's a load of splick," the former smuggler said.

But it was Caldwell who raised his hand and insisted that Titus be allowed to continue.

"I'm just saying I think we need to define what makes us different before we go sending more rounds downrange," Titus said. "'Cause it might just lead to more bloodshed if we don't."

"He's got a point," Caldwell added. "Not to be too sanctimonious here, but we oughta be clear about what makes our motives different from everyone else's. If not, we'll get neck deep in splick faster than a senator caught sleeping with his sister."

"This is the Jujari way," Rohoar said suddenly.

"Sleeping with your sisters?" Ezo asked. "Explains a lot."

"No." Rohoar sneered. "This way of peace by force, this is how we have maintained control over our lands. This the Jujari way." The giant hyena-like warrior lowered his head. "But surely it is not the Novian way of our ancestors, nor that of the Gladio Umbra."

"I can affirm this assertion," Azelon interjected. "Though it is worth noting that creating new peace is not always the same as maintaining existing peace."

"I'm not following," Dutch said.

"Peace sought any other way but through peaceful means poisons the root," Rohoar replied. "But sometimes force is required to spare lives until sustainable peace is achieved, especially in the most hostile of contexts. We Jujari have suffered much from violence with no goal of sustainable peace. Worse still, the poison of ill-won peace still stains our paws."

Magnus scratched his chin, recognizing just how much the Repub had in common with the Jujari on this point. Pursuing peace through necessary conflict was the only way Magnus knew. The Republic's military existed to exercise force against those deemed a threat to galactic peace. And while he despised So-Elku, Magnus at least felt that he understood some of what the leader was after—*if* he was indeed honest about his desires for peace and not the pursuit of some personal oligarchy. If order could not be sought through non-violent means, then it must be secured through conflict. Perhaps the Luma leader had more in common with the

Republic than he cared to admit. And that gave Magnus pause for concern.

Magnus had no illusions that the Repub had lost its way after three hundred years. Not entirely, of course. The will of the people would keep such things from happening. At least he hoped it would. But as conflicts became more complex, and backroom deals formed new alliances, which then spurred new threats, Magnus knew corners had been cut. Promises had been broken. And the Repub's military might had been used in ways that its originators never intended.

Such things were kept from the public, of course. The senate had a way of assuaging the anxieties of the Corps and the populace by downplaying questionable ethics. But now Magnus wondered what kind of navy could allow someone like Admiral Kane to become Moldark without anyone trying to stop him. He wondered about a senate that could commute the life sentence of a monster like Nos Kil so they could use him on their enemies and an unsuspecting child like Piper. And he wondered about a Marine Corps that could turn its back on a decorated veteran and accuse him of treason.

Something had come undone. Something deep within the machine. And it had to be stopped.

Sadly, Magnus knew that peace would not bring peace. His past conversations with Awen bubbled to mind, the ones about finding alternative ways for conflict resolution. But there would be no stopping these foes without aggression, without force. Which was ironic, because in his attempt to thwart these particular enemies, he feared becoming just like them.

"It seems we all want to use peace to justify force," Magnus said after a moment. "I suppose the only way we keep ourselves from sliding into the abyss is reminding ourselves why we do this. And by deciding what we want the end to look like."

Sootriman spoke next. "You mean, who's going to be in charge when all this is done?"

Magnus nodded. "Essentially. Yes."

"Do you honestly think we can know that this far out?" Ezo asked.

Magnus looked around the room. Everyone seemed to wear uncertain faces, which is how he felt too. "In a word? No. For all I know, there won't be anything left to lead by the time this is over."

"Magnus," Awen chided.

"I'm just saying. I think it's too soon to tell."

"I agree," Caldwell replied. "But if we can at least say that the various factions represented in this room have within themselves something worth salvaging, then we have something to fight for. The Repub, for example, isn't all bad. I know plenty of good men and women who have given everything for the preservation of peace, bucketheads and politicians alike. Likewise, I spent the last year on Worru. I've met my share of Luma who would keep a Marine's blaster from firing faster than a mother walking in on her teenage son doing—"

"We got the picture, colonel," Magnus said, trying to suppress some laughter.

"And the Jujari are not truly out for blood," Awen said.

"At least not all of us," Rohoar amended, giving the Elonian what seemed to be the Jujari version of a wink. "But I thank you for the honorable consideration."

"So what you're saying is that we're fighting to return things to some semblance of what they once were," Sootriman said.

Magnus nodded. "That seems like the best-case scenario. If not, then we're talking chaos, aren't we? Hundreds of years of treaties blown to ribbons. Whole systems without governance. If we don't try to salvage some of the existing systems —if we can't at least see the good in the roots, then what are we fighting for?" For some reason, Magnus found himself looking at Awen when he said this. He knew it wasn't everything she'd want him to say. But it was a start. "Plus, none of us are smart enough to create a new governing body."

"Speak for yourself," Ezo said.

"But sir," TO-96 said, raising a hand. "You failed to pay your taxes and file your divorce notice. Your competency in the civic realm would be questionable at best."

"Ouch," Dutch exclaimed. "Slammed by your own bot."

"How does that feel?" Bliss asked.

Ezo blushed but was quick to reply, "Better than getting shot in the ass."

Magnus smiled as he recalled the incident where Bliss got hit in the rear during their escape from the Grand Arielina.

He cleared his throat and decided to change directions. "Do we believe there is any further link between So-Elku and Moldark?" Magnus asked.

It was Ricio's turn to step forward. "I don't know this So-Elku character, but as I've explained to Magnus, Moldark's intentions seem to be somewhat different."

"In what way?" Sootriman asked.

"For one, he doesn't mention peace. All his talk is about elimination. About destruction."

"Against the Jujari?" Sootriman said.

"That's just it. Based on the war between the Repub and the Jujari, you'd think so."

Sootriman folded her arms. "But you suspect something different."

Ricio nodded. "I do. And for reasons I can't fully explain. What little I've seen of the man, something seems to possess him, to drive him like a mad man toward some inexorable end."

"Layman's terms please, jockey," Dutch said.

"Inevitable. Unstoppable." Ricio looked around the room. "I think he wants to bring it all down."

Ricio's words made the room sag as if something heavy had just been draped over everyone's shoulders. If having a wayward mystic bent on using otherworldly forces to bring supposed peace to the galaxy wasn't enough, it seemed the cosmos also had a maniacal tyrant set on destroying whatever he could and using the Republic fleets to do so.

"We're going to need help," Caldwell said, breaking the long silence.

"Any suggestions, colonel?" Magnus asked.

"My best idea is to try rallying any Marines loyal to the Corps's original mandate."

"Ensure peace in the galaxy," Magnus finished.

"OTF," Bliss said.

Caldwell grunted in assent.

"And how do we go about doing that exactly?" Ricio asked.

The colonel gnawed the unlit cigar, moving it from one corner of his mouth to the other. "Well, I'm still working on that. But my first action would be to address those under my direct command."

"You mean the Marines who got wiped out in Plumeria?" Abimbola asked.

"Easy, Bimby," Magnus said with a raised hand. The team didn't need any infighting.

"Not all of them got wiped," Dutch added. "Many in the remaining two companies survived whatever Piper did."

"And you think they'd be worth talking to?" Sootriman asked. "The last bunch didn't seem too keen to hear you out."

The colonel nodded. "That last scenario certainly was a splick show, I agree. But under the right circumstances, I think they'd at least consider what I have to say. It's not gonna be easy, and I'll invite plenty of danger in the process. But at my age? You get more comfortable with certain things, and dying is one of them." Caldwell looked around the room, withdrew a lighter, and lit the end of his cigar. The flame disappeared inside the tobacco several times as thick white smoke got sucked up toward the ceiling. When the cigar was sufficiently stoked, Caldwell pulled it from his mouth and blew out. "The way I see it, I'd rather die for this than anything else on the table. Wouldn't you?"

Magnus was grateful for the colonel's perspective and the scent of the cigar's tobacco. It reminded him of long nights around a campfire after firefights. He'd spent many an evening listening to his COs discuss strategies and share war stories. The old guard knew how to lead under pressure—to take fire and keep everything from going sideways. Which meant Caldwell knew how to throw his weight around to steer the ship in the captain's direction. In this case, Magnus was the captain, and his heart swelled as everyone around the circle began to nod their heads in consent.

"So you're implying that we head back to Worru so you can attempt to persuade some of your Marines?" Awen asked.

"I'm not implying *you* head anywhere, ma'am. But I am saying I should go back."

"If some of us did go, it would give Awen and me more time to search for Piper locally," Willowood said. "Assuming she's planetside."

"Azie," Magnus said. "Can you give me the statistical likelihood that someone detects our ship and the quantum tunnel?"

"It is infinitesimal, sir," Azelon replied. "Given the Republic's current technologies, the void horizon is undetectable.

Therefore, it would take an enemy vessel accidentally passing through it and physically ramming into us to alert enemy sensors of the *Spire's* presence."

While Magnus was somewhat comforted by Azelon's words, he worried that she was only using TO-96's database on current Repub tech. She had no files on Paragon tech—at least that Magnus knew of. Something told him that Moldark had more tricks up his sleeve than any of them bargained for.

"But So-Elku found the *Spire*," Titus said and crossed his arms. "At least enough to free Nos Kil and Ricio here. Who's to say he can't do that again?"

"I hadn't anticipated that he would do that," Awen said. "I should have guessed he might try to locate our ship and harm us. So that's my fault. But he won't be that lucky again. We've constructed a shield in the Unity." Awen looked at Magnus. "While you were recovering."

"A shield?" Ezo asked. "As in something to keep us out of view?"

"Precisely." Awen brushed a few strands of hair behind her pointed ear. "Like with Azelon's cloaking abilities for a physical ship, we'll be hidden from sight within the Unity, both here and in protospace. That's the hope anyway. We can't anticipate his every move, especially now that he has access to the other realms of the Unity. But we can at least implement safeguards."

"The shield we've fashioned will also let us know when he's trying to find us," Willowood added. "It's one more preventative measure."

"I like preventative measures," Magnus said. "Anyone have anything else pertinent before we get underway?"

Sootriman raised her hand. "If we need reinforcements, I'd like to return to Ki Nar Four with Ezo, Saasarr, and TO-96, if you can spare them, and see what we can drum up. It might not be much, but it will at least be something. Maybe get word to some others in the outlying systems too."

Magnus nodded in agreement. "I'm all for it if you trust them. The way I see it—"

"Ah, splick," Ricio blurted out.

Magnus glanced at the pilot. "Everything alright there, commander?"

"No." Ricio shook his head. "No, it's not. I just remembered something."

"You leave a roast in the oven too long, jockey?" Abimbola asked.

But Ricio wasn't laughing. The man seemed genuinely rattled about something. "I can't believe I didn't remember this. I'm... sorry."

"Remember what, Ricio?"

"Nos Kil. He tried sending a transmission. Just before we left the brig."

"He what?" Awen asked with as much surprise as Magnus felt.

"Azië," Magnus said, turning to the bot. "Can you confirm this?"

Azelon's head cocked sideways as her subroutines did whatever computing they needed to do. Finally, she said, "I'm sorry, Magnus, but I have no record of any transmission being sent during the prisoners' escape."

"Are you lying to us, small flying human?" Rohoar asked as he took a step toward Ricio.

"No. I promise." Ricio looked to Magnus. "Maybe it got wiped from her data drive. Or maybe he hacked the logs. I don't know. But I do know he tried sending something. He even made me step out of the room for it."

"And you did not try to listen in?" Rohoar's hackles stood up, betraying his irritation. "Jujari have ears to let us hear very far away."

"Well, if you haven't noticed, my fine furry friend, humans don't have giant flycatchers like you. And second, I didn't exactly know I was going to betray the Repub yet, so I didn't think there was a reason. Plus, you saw that guy, right?"

"So you have no idea what Nos Kil said?" Magnus asked, trying to keep things on task.

"Again, no. But he did mention it was a report of sorts."

"Splick." Magnus ran a hand over his face. He was tired, and still in a lot of pain despite all the nanobots he guessed were creeping through his body. "Azie, I need a better explanation of what you think happened. If he gave up information about the ship or its crew..."

"Again, sir, I am sorry to report that I have no additional information to provide."

"But I thought you said your systems were fully restored? Don't you have any footage from the control room? No transmission logs?"

"I do not have cameras in the control room, sir. That is where the brig's security cameras are ported *to*. And, as I said, no data logs indicate any outgoing traffic. However, my systems may not be as fully restored as I previously thought. That, or Commander Ricio's suspicions of Nos Kil hacking the logs could be accurate."

"He could do that?" Ezo asked. "Ezo does not believe that oversized Bludervian dimdish had the wherewithal to outsmart Novian technology."

"We forget one more element," Willowood said.

"So-Elku," Awen replied.

Willowood nodded. "Whatever he did to the *Spire* could have altered Azelon's systems enough to mask activity in the brig, even unintentionally."

"Dammit," Magnus said, feeling his head start to spin a little. He needed sleep. But he also knew he had a job to do. "We can't know what we don't have a record of, so we need to suspect the worst."

"Which is?" Awen asked.

"That Moldark has intel on the *Spire* and any crew he came in contact with."

"Which includes Piper," Awen said.

Magnus closed his eyes. "Which includes Piper, yes. And more importantly, it includes the *Spire's* last known position over Worru."

"Then we need a new quantum tunnel," Zoll suggested. "The time dilation will give us the cushion we need to get it done."

"But where?" Dutch replied. "I mean, we still need to get back to Worru for the colonel, and if we put it any further away from Ki Nar Far, Sootriman will be too long in getting there and back."

"Don't worry about us," Ezo said. "Ezo knows just the ship to use. Focus on what's best for the colonel and the *Spire*."

"We proceed as planned, but we do so quickly and carefully," Magnus said. "Even if Moldark has actionable intel, it will still take time to organize a search party, and something tells me he already has his hands full with the Jujari resistance."

"La-raah," Rohoar exclaimed with his chest puffed out.

Magnus smiled at the Jujari, then looked around the bridge. "We'll jump back to Worru. But Azie, I need you to put us somewhere different, in case Moldark decides to get curious."

"As you wish, sir."

"Once there, Sootriman and her team will head to Ki Nar Four, while the colonel and I head to the surface along with Awen and Willowood."

"Now hold on just a minute there, son," Caldwell interjected. "You're in no shape to be heading back down there."

"I'm with the colonel on this one," Awen added.

"Thank you both for your concern," Magnus said. "But that's not being realistic."

"Realistic?" Awen put her hands on her hips.

Magnus leveled his eyes at the colonel. "What are you gonna say when your captains ask you for proof about all this, sir?" There was an awkward pause as the colonel worked his cigar in mouth. "And how hard do you wanna work at defending your actions against your own unit back there? The way I see it, you need someone a bit deeper in this splick hole to talk about just how bad it really is, to explain why we had to do what we did." When the colonel didn't respond right away, Magnus leaned back in his captain's chair. "Plus, the way I see it, the only thing more convincing than a Caldwell is a Magnus, and it's about time I throw my grandfather's name around on purpose, wouldn't you say, Colonel?"

Caldwell took several puffs on his cigar and let the smoke seep from his mouth and nose, swirling up and over his grey mustache. "You're a stubborn-ass son of a bitch, Adonis."

"Just taking after you, colonel."

Caldwell chuckled.

"I'll get rest when I can," Magnus added. Then he turned to Awen and Willowood. "Your job is to look for Piper. You won't have much time, and I don't want you leaving the ship unless you clear it with me first, copy?"

Awen nodded, but she seemed reluctant. Probably just pissed at him for not staying put and resting here on the *Spire*.

"Then I think we have a plan. I'm not interested in a vote because, truthfully, I'm too damn tired to argue it through. But if you disagree with this line of thinking, I need to know right now."

To a person, everyone in the room stayed silent, including the bots. Magnus felt relieved to know that at least one thing was going right.

"Alright then," he said, pushing himself up from his chair. "The rest of you debrief your platoons and square away your equipment if you haven't already. Dutch, I want you instituting daily PT and anything else you want to do to ensure battle readiness. Connect with Rohoar to make sure its comprehensive for everyone. Abimbola, Titus, work with Azelon on refitting armament and keeping everyone well fed. And Ricio?"

"Yes, sir?"

"Since you're the first human with any flight experience on a Jujari fighter, I want you to come up with a plan to train new pilots. If the colonel ends up doing what the colonel does best, then I think you're going to get some recruits, and I want you prepared. Work with Azelon to make it happen."

"Roger that, sir."

"Good." Magnus nodded and looked around the bridge. "Thank you. All of you. For being a part of this. It seems that…" The right words alluded him. But he had to find them —for their sake as much as his own. "It seems that we're in this too far to back out now. The only way through is forward. I don't know what we'll find in the dark, but I want to be standing next to you when we find it. Dominate…"

"Liberate," they responded as one.

Magnus took a deep breath and reflected on just how much he appreciated everyone in the room. It was an honor to serve with them, and he doubted he'd ever have the right words to express how he felt.

2

IT WOULDN'T BE LONG before the Jujari were crushed. A few more days. Maybe a week at most. *But either way,* Moldark told himself, *the end is near.*

The panoramic windowplex wall in his quarters offered a stunning view of the ongoing space battle as hundreds of starships jockeyed for position in a fight to the death. Some ships lumbered through the open void, engaged on all sides, while others ran close to Oorajee's gravity well, engines straining to keep them from sinking in-atmosphere. Fighters dodged one another, streaking in and out of cover behind the giant battleships. And all the while blaster fire flashed against the void's expanse just as the colors glinted against Moldark's all-black eyes.

A small comms chime interrupted his revelry. Moldark

looked at the display on his chair's arm to see the call was from the bridge. He swiped the channel open and watched as Admiral Brighton's head and torso floated a meter in front of the chair.

"Admiral Brighton," Moldark said.

"My lord. You've received an encoded transmission."

"From?"

"Unknown. Though it appears to originate from an unidentified vessel somewhere in the Wyndorian system."

Moldark raised an eyebrow. "Worru?"

"We can't confirm that, but I—"

"Forward it to me."

"Right away, my lord."

Moldark closed the channel, and Brighton's holographic body blinked out. A moment later, a trill alerted Moldark to the incoming message. The metadata showed that it was pre-recorded, timestamped from four days prior. Someone had sent the transmission in haste with no exact recipient defined, or there had been subspace interference.

Curious, Moldark opened the message and was prompted for a passphrase and a voiceprint match. The holo display projected a security window that read:

The Paragon…

This message was from one of his own. But he had no one on Worru at present. All forces there were either Republic or Luma—neither of which were on speaking terms with him. Moldark touched the red button in the holo display, then said, "Of perfect rule."

"Answer verified. Voiceprint accepted," said a feminine voice. "Begin encoded transmission."

Suddenly, a bust of Nos Kil hovered in front of Moldark. The trooper was bare chested, covered in dried blood, and missing one eye. Moldark sensed this scene would have disturbed Kane or any of the other humans. Instead, Moldark felt only mild pity for the man.

"My lord," Nos Kil began. "I don't have much time. The mission on Ithnor Itheliana was unsuccessful. A small but well-armed force attacked us, led by a former colleague of mine, a Marine named Adonis Magnus. His transcript is readily available on TACNET.

"Somehow Magnus's team has managed to obtain an alien vessel, I'm guessing from the Novia Minoosh, though it's in far better condition than anything we found when we were there. They also have someone you might be very interested in—that senator's daughter you've been looking for, Piper Stone. They've taken another prisoner too, one of the pilots you sent to check in on us."

Nos Kil looked off-camera and snapped his fingers at someone. "What's your name again, jockey?"

Moldark heard someone in the background say, "Longo."

"Longo," Nos Kil repeated, back on the camera. "Not that great of a jockey if you ask me. I'm sending the ship's coordinates with this transmission in the off chance that Longo and I are unsuccessful in taking the ship. With any luck, you'll be able to engage these rebels before they skip out of the system. Nos Kil, out."

Nos Kil's image vanished, and a set of coordinates along with a star chart took its place. Just as Moldark suspected, the ship was over Worru, or at least it had been at the time of Nos Kil's transmission. Moldark suspected that the rebels were long gone by now, and Nos Kil with them. The Marine would have sent a real-time update by now if he had succeeded in taking the enemy's ship.

Nos Kil had been a good asset. Violent but competent. And one not easily replaced, especially knowing that he had some connection to this Marine named Magnus. But replaced he would be. For, in the end, the Republic and its species of humans and other lifeforms only satisfied Moldark's meta-objective—annihilation. So what did it matter that Nos Kil was terminated earlier than Moldark desired? Ultimately, Nos Kil and the rest of his kin would be exterminated like the disease their species was to this galaxy. The humans consumed without care just as the Novia had consumed without care, and Moldark would cleanse the stars of them both.

The more critical detail to Nos Kil's transmission was that he'd seen Piper. Hearing him speak her name stirred Moldark. It was the closest he'd been to finding Kane's progeny since the Bull Wraith lost the senator's crew. Still, the girl remained just out of arm's reach, and Moldark would need her for the next phase of his plans. Especially now that the quantum tunnel had been closed, or at least that's what Moldark suspected.

The quantum tunnel was seven days away from Worru via subspace—less if a ship had a subspace modulator. Granted, it could have taken Nos Kil that much time to escape, but given his particular set of skills, Moldark doubted that very much. More likely, the enemy's ship had emerged from a new void horizon somewhere near Worru, which meant they'd closed the first. At least that's what he would have done.

"Brighton," Moldark said over comms, summoning the admiral.

The man's head and chest appeared in the holo projection again. "Yes, my lord."

"Have the *Peregrine* readied at once. And I want two battle-cruisers and escorts to be resupplied and ready to depart the system. Make sure there is a battalion of Paragon Marines at my disposal as well."

Brighton hesitated, squinting through the feed. "You're planning to pull these ships from the conflict, my lord?"

"A new goal has presented itself that needs my attention, yes."

"Of course, my lord. But might I suggest—"

"You may suggest nothing, Admiral. My orders stand. Maintain pressure on the Jujari fleet but give me the ships that you deem temporarily nonessential. Also, I want a scout vessel sent to the quantum tunnel's last known coordinates."

"As you command, my lord. As for your destination?"

Moldark steepled his fingers and turned his chair back toward the space battle. "Worru."

3

"You're awfully quiet," Willowood said, taking a seat beside Awen in the shuttle's crew compartment. The crash couches were designed to fit Jujari-sized Novia Minoosh bodies, naturally, which meant humans—and Elonians in particular—considered the furniture to be unusually luxurious. If Awen hadn't been so anxious about finding Piper, she could easily see herself taking a nap in such an all-consuming chair.

"Just thinking," Awen replied, pleased to see Willowood join her.

A moment of silence passed between the two of them, then Willowood pointed out the starboard-side window causing the bangle bracelets on her wrist to chime together. "I never get tired of that. Seeing Worru from above, I mean."

Awen turned to follow Willowood's hand to the space-view of the Luma homeworld. "Neither do I." She paused, then added, "It's a lot safer than viewing it from down below."

Awen felt her mentor's eyes move to her face. "You're still thinking about the accident. Valerie and Piper."

"Of course I am," Awen replied, more abruptly than she meant to. "Forgive me."

"No need to apologize." Willowood patted the top of Awen's hand. "So am I."

"But how do you do it? I mean, you seem so calm, so assured of everything."

The elder woman smiled. "Then I'm a good actress."

"Right. But it's more than that for you. On the inside, I mean. You're calm on the inside."

"What are my other options, dear?"

"You could be freaking out," Awen said, her nerves causing her to laugh. "Like me."

Willowood laughed with Awen a little and squeezed her hand. "Can you control it?"

"Control my nerves?"

"No, no. *It*, the world around you, the things others are doing. Can you control them?"

"Of course not."

"So your brain knows that. But your heart doesn't."

"Then how do I send my heart the message?"

The older woman smiled and looked back out the window. "One of the things I've always loved most about you is that you believe you can fix the galaxy."

"You say that like it's a bad thing."

"Far from it. Though it is somewhat naive."

Awen wanted to be hurt, but she knew the woman was too wise to resort to personal insults. "Naive?"

"Among other things, yes."

"Other things? Like what?"

"Arrogant, narcissistic—"

"Whoa, whoa." Awen put her hands up. "I'm good with naive. But I need you to explain."

Willowood thought for a moment. "Tell me, Awen, has anyone been able to fix you when you were broken?"

"Fix me?"

The older woman nodded. "Through a sheer force of will, has anyone ever been able to make you change your course without you first consenting yourself?"

Awen knew better than to reply to such a question without giving it thought. She looked out the window as the shuttle neared Worru's atmosphere. "No, I suppose not."

"Which means that people are people."

Awen looked back at Willowood and repeated the line to the older woman as if saying it would magically elicit more information.

"Sure," Willowood replied. "People do what people want to do, and no matter how we might want them to choose differently, in the end, they live and die by their own decisions. If we are resistant to change, and to wise counsel, then we are naive, proud, and self-serving."

"Thanks, Dr. Willowood."

"Wait until you get my bill." Willowood removed her hand from Awen's and sat back. "Your heart cares so deeply for people that you *want* them to choose what's right."

"And that's wrong?"

"No. That's beautiful. But what is wrong is expecting your will to change theirs. That creates anxiety in you *and* them."

"Then why try? Why do any of this?"

"Because you must do what you believe is right for you. If others want to follow you, that is their decision. And if they don't?"

"It's still their decision too," Awen replied. She took a deep breath and blew some strands of hair away from her face. "To follow me."

Willowood snapped her head toward Awen. "Says who?"

"Says... I don't know. The cosmos."

"So you're the one deciding what's best for everyone now?"

"I didn't mean it like that."

"Sure you did."

Awen opened her mouth to reply but thought better of it.

"We all think our way is the right way," Willowood said, closing her eyes. "Or else we wouldn't be choosing it. And if we don't think the things we're doing are the best, then shame on us for not being authentic with ourselves."

"So you're saying I just stop trying to change everyone and worry about myself?"

"I'm saying you should sit back and enjoy these giant crash couches because they really are glorious."

Awen smiled at Willowood even though the older woman's eyes were closed. Then she settled back and sank into the cushions. "You miss her, don't you?"

"Valerie? Yes. Especially considering how little time we had together. But I let my daughter go a long time ago, Awen. She's been making her own choices and living by them just fine ever since. I did my part. And she lived her life, making every decision count right up to the last one."

"The last one?" Awen sat up and looked at Willowood. "You mean choosing to fight against those Republic troopers?"

But Willowood shook her head, eyes still closed. "No. I mean, her choice to save others."

"I don't follow."

Willow opened her eyes. "Have you gone back yet? To the firefight in the docking bay below the shuttles?"

Willowood was talking about calling the episode back from within the Unity. It was less like time travel and more like reviewing a holo movie in detail. And it also wasn't something most practitioners could manage without a great deal of experience. But Awen's new powers within the Unity had made such things far more manageable. Again, not time travel, but it felt pretty close to it.

"I'll take your silence to mean you haven't," Willowood said. "Which I understand. No one wants to revisit that tragedy. But were you to, you'd notice that Valerie made one final decision that cost her everything."

"Let me." Awen held up a hand and closed her eyes.

"You don't have to. I can tell you."

"Please," Awen said, already on her way back to the fire-fight. "I need to."

From within the Unity, Awen summoned the strength of the Nexus, which united all things, and saw the docking bay appear. Unlike her natural memory that clouded details and created generalities, the Unity's memory was perfect—at least when informed by the Nexus. The troopers were so real she could reach out and touch them. The sounds shook her belly, and the flashes of blaster fire made her wince. Even the smoke in the air and the odors of burning flesh and armor seemed real, pulling her back into the moment with unimaginable speed.

But this wasn't just a memory she was seeing. This was the actual event indelibly imprinted on the cosmos's ethereal fabric. There was no changing this, and to see it was to revisit what actually transpired.

Awen sped the scene forward as if she were advancing a holo movie to a desired location. She saw the image of her own body grab Piper and hoist her up the shuttle's loading ramp. Then a blast of light from across the bay caused her to pause the scene. The rocket from a trooper's shoulder-mounted weapon was frozen two meters from its tube, while blaster bolts hovered in midair.

Awen floated around the scene like a spirit, looking at the light reflecting off visors and dancing in terrified eyes. She passed through clouds thick with debris and mourned the soulless corpses of the dead as they fell to the ground. Then she found Magnus whose eyes recognized the incoming rocket. And beside him, Valerie, who had no idea she was experiencing her last seconds of life.

With a lump stuck in her throat, Awen moved the scene forward. The rocket trailed a white plume of spent accelerant as it careened toward Magnus. Then he pushed Valerie aside like a rag doll. Her personal shield took several rounds before the final blaster bolt went straight through her helmet. Awen could feel hot tears streaming down her cheeks as her mortal body sat beside Willowood. Then Valerie's lifeless body slammed against the ground and slid to a halt.

"This is so hard to watch," Awen said at last. "I didn't see—"

"Her last act?"

"Magnus tries to save her, but she gets hit by enemy blaster fire." Awen swallowed, trying to keep from throwing up.

"Look more closely."

Awen moved the scene back again to where the blaster bolts drained Valerie's shield. Her body was sideways, but her feet were still on the ground. Awen began playing the scene again, but slow, as if frame by frame on a holo display. That's when Awen noticed Valerie's body push off the ground—by her own two legs. Her hands thrust up, taking her further than Magnus's push would have sent her, and put her head directly into the path of the blaster rounds that killed her. She must've have seen the troopers aim and thrown herself into their line of fire—on purpose.

"She…" Awen swallowed again. The image made her cry. "She moved toward those blaster rounds."

"And who is behind her? Who else is in the line of fire?"

Awen moved her view until she could follow the bolts' trajectories. Beyond it, past Valerie's head, she saw herself. And she saw Piper.

The emotion was too much. Awen sobbed and broke her connection with her second sight. Instantly, she felt Willowood's arms around her. "There, there, my child."

"She saved us."

Willowood released Awen and wiped some tears off the younger woman's cheek. "And now you know. It wasn't Magnus or anyone else who killed Valerie. She chose. She gave her life for others."

"Magnus needs to know this."

"And I think I know just the person to tell him."

Awen nodded, wiping her nose on her sleeve. She hated crying. Normally. But it was right to do now. In fact, this had been the most she'd truly grieved for Valerie since she died. And it felt right. To be here with Willowood. To reflect on the value of sacrifice.

"You can't change people, Awen. And you can't make them do what you want them to. The most you can offer is your presence. You were there for my daughter, and she was there for you. That is the most anyone can offer."

AWEN AND WILLOWOOD sat there for several minutes as the shuttle started plowing through Worru's atmosphere, entering the planet on its dark side. Nolan was at the controls, with Magnus and Colonel Caldwell seated beside him, so Awen knew entry would be okay. Still, this part of flying was always the worst. She thought about grabbing the vomit bag in the seatback but then realized she was on an alien vessel. For all she knew, the Novia Minoosh didn't even have regurgitation reflexes.

When the violent shuddering subsided and Awen could see Plumeria's nightlights dotting the distant continent, she looked back at Willowood.

"What is it, my child?" the elderly woman asked.

"I went forward in time," Awen said without preamble. But she had a feeling Willowood wouldn't need context.

"In the Unity."

Awen nodded.

"I see." Willowood seemed to search Awen's face, trying to divine the reason for this sudden sharing of information. "And?"

"And... I saw Piper."

"A reflection of Piper," Willowood added.

"But it was her. And she... she was with—"

"Awen, you mustn't allow—"

"She was with Moldark." Awen placed a hand on her chest. "I saw her. Standing beside him."

"Awen, please."

"No, you have to know."

"I already know."

Awen caught her breath and looked at Willowood. "But how? You don't have a connection to—"

"To the Nexus?" Willowood smiled out of the corner of the side of her mouth. "Just because I'm old doesn't mean I'm incompetent, you know."

"I didn't mean that. I just meant—"

"I know what you meant, dear. And you're right to be surprised. No, I didn't have access to So-Elku's beloved codex, nor to your wonderful discoveries in metaspace. But might I remind you that the Unity is still the Unity with or without a name. It doesn't need us to call it something, just like we don't always need books to discover its many mysteries."

Awen blinked a few times. "So you're saying you already knew about the Foundation? About the Nexus?"

"Not by those names," she replied, shrugging. "But we knew there was more to the Unity than we Luma taught in observances."

"So-Elku knew too?"

"Oh no. He was far too consumed with leading the order to delve into the deeper side of things. It was only a few of us who had such time on our hands."

"Amazing."

"Hardly. We were old and bored. The only other options were sex and Antaran backdraw, and that gets old quick."

"The sex?"

"No, the card game."

"Ah." Awen chuckled. "Good to know."

"Anyway, back to what you saw. You still have ears for the words of an old lady?"

"I mean, now that you say sex doesn't get old…"

Willowood patted Awen on the hand again. "What you saw was a reflection, and you must understand the difference."

"Between…?"

"What could be and what will be."

"So you're saying the Unity shows what could be?"

Willowood nodded. "Perhaps it is even likely, what you saw. But that doesn't mean it is what will be, and that's a critical distinction. Nor does it show what will happen next."

"What do you mean, next?"

"Well," Willowood said, adjusting the harness around her robes. "Did you see Piper turn around and clock Moldark in the face with the butt of a blaster rifle?"

Awen huffed a blast of air out her nostrils. "No."

"And did you see her hijack a shuttle and zip back to the *Spire* all on her own?"

"Of course not."

"Then neither does the Unity. It presents reflections of the most likely outcomes, not actual outcomes. It also can't account for the greatest variable of all."

"What's that?"

"You," Willowood said, pushing a finger into Awen's sternum. "While you may not have power over others, the one thing you do have power over is yourself. And don't you forget it."

"I won't with your fingernail in my chest." Awen rubbed the spot. "But, thanks."

"No need to thank me. It's my job." Willowood sat back, closing her eyes. "You can change the future by deciding to change yourself."

Awen studied the older woman's face and wiry grey hair for a minute. She was so grateful to be reunited with her and only wished that Valerie and Piper could be here right now too.

"We'll find her, you know," Willowood said.

"Find her?"

"Piper." Willowood cracked an eye open. "We'll find her. She can't hide forever. And she wants you whether she knows it or not."

"I'm not so sure about that."

"Every girl needs her mother," Willowood said, closing her eyes again. "And if she can't have her mother, then she'll take the next best thing. And, child?"

"Yes?"

"You're the only next best thing she'll ever need."

4

GETTING onto the Worru was easier than Magnus had suspected. But with half the city's planetary defenses in shambles and the Repub Talon squadrons obliterated—no small thanks to Ricio—Magnus should have guessed that entering Plumeria's airspace would have been uneventful. Plus, the city seemed immersed in the chaos of rebuilding as fast as it could. *Nothing like the rich and powerful swooping in to revive the galaxy's seat of peace*, Magnus noted to himself.

All the activity made it easy for Cyril and Azelon to steal a Repub ident from one of the many ships coming and going since the raid. Since the so-called rebels were purported to be long gone, at least according to what Cyril gleaned from all the comms traffic, no one suspected that an alien ship alleging to be a cargo hauler had landed in docking bay twenty-four.

Nor had they reason to believe the vessel was offloading anything but maintenance workers and supplies.

"As well as muck and junk, junk and muck removal, ya know?" Cyril had said when outlining the details of his code slicing. "Sir, but that's your order to call, sir."

Magnus had thanked him and made a mental note of just how handy Cyril's skills were.

"I want you both staying put," Magnus said to Awen and Willowood. "Nolan, if you encounter any trouble that the ladies don't feel up to handling, I want you up and out of here, no questions asked. You copy?"

"I read you, sir."

"Good." He looked at Awen. "And if you find her, report to me first. We don't need any stunts. We do this by the book."

"It almost sounds like you care for me," Awen replied with a quirky grin.

"I'm serious." Magnus didn't have time to play around.

"By the book," Awen said.

"Monitor comms and vitals. If you lose connection with us, or we don't report in—"

"Or our hearts stop beating," Caldwell interjected.

Magnus gave him a sour look. "Or our vitals flatline, you get your asses out of here."

"I'll get it done," Nolan said.

"Stay on your guard, Magnus," Awen said, her voice filled with concern. "The Luma, they're crafty. For all I know, So-Elku has people looking for interlopers as we speak. Just— watch your back. Promise?"

"Promise." Magnus turned to the colonel. "You ready?"

"Like a cooling pad on a fat lady's ass."

"Where the hell do you come up with these things?"

"Read it on a cereal box." Caldwell looked at Awen and spoke to her behind his hand. "I really didn't."

"Be safe, Colonel," Awen said. "And take care of this one for me, would you?"

"Wouldn't dream of letting you down."

Magnus and Caldwell activated their Novian armor's chameleon mode while Nolan doused the cargo bay's lights. The ramp opened, half-hidden in the docking bay's muted lights, and the two gladias jogged down to the tarmac, signaling Nolan to close it as soon as they were clear.

"Garrison's less than one klick from here," Caldwell said.

"Looks like we're headed south," Magnus replied.

"Captain Forbes's quarters are on post. He won't be in bed yet if I know him. Bit of a night owl."

"Copy that."

The two men moved at a light run, their suit's servo-assist doing half the work for them. It was just after midnight local time, late enough for people to be off the streets, but not so late that windows were black. While Magnus and Caldwell didn't plan on killing anyone, they still chose to carry their NOV1s. And if things got *really* out of hand? *Let's hope it doesn't come to that*, Magnus reminded himself. *For everyone's sake.*

The former Marines ran unhindered through the streets, stopping only occasionally to let a hover skiff pass or to avoid a couple walking down the sidewalk. Their suits made detection almost impossible in these conditions, but still, Magnus didn't want to take any chances.

The only hiccup came when a drunk man emerged from a cantina and threw a beer bottle at a stray cat less than a meter from Magnus's feet. Bits of glass and ale splashed against his suit, causing the drunk man and the cat to step back. To them, Magnus imagined, it must have looked like the beer was floating in midair, and the bits of glass were changing directions without cause. Fortunately, the only one of them able to figure out what they were seeing was the cat, who darted away. The drunk man, on the other hand, swore at the air and stumbled back into the cantina.

"That was close," said the colonel.

"Yeah. Can you imagine trying to get the smell of cat urine off this suit?"

"Smartass."

"And I owe it all to the Corps."

GETTING on post was probably the easiest part of the entire mission. Magnus had never thought about it, but who in all of Plumeria would want to mess with the Republic's garrison of trained killers? Even with the "bad" parts of the city taken into account, Worru's capital had the lowest crime rate in the quadrant. *Hell, probably the whole galaxy. That is unless you count the crime going on in the Grand Arielina.*

Caldwell led Magnus through the front gate, around some

administration buildings, and then up a street toward the officer's housing. Again, their suits allowed them to make good
time and travel without so much as a whisper through the
warm midnight air. Magnus almost said that this was too easy
but thought better of it. The last thing either of them needed
was for someone to jinx the op.

"That's his residence there," Caldwell said.

"Wife? Kids?" Magnus hesitated. "Cat?"

"None of the above. Spends most of his time reading,
from what he tells me. Smart man, this one. So stay sharp."
Caldwell slowed to a stop and studied the house. The only
light came from the rear of the house, casting soft shadows
through a wooden fence. "Well, he also likes to spend time in
the dirt."

"Gardener?"

"Something like that. Come on."

The pair of them walked along the side of the house,
passed silently through the gate, and emerged into Forbes's
backyard. If it could be called a backyard. Magnus studied
the space in awe, marveling at streams of flowers cascading
down rock walls and beside small waterfalls. A stone path
meandered between trees and led to a swimming pool shaped
like some forgotten lagoon deep in a lush jungle. Lights
washed up the sides of old-growth trees, while birds roosted in
their bows.

"You sure this guy's a Marine?" Magnus asked, taking in
the scene. "I think he missed his calling."

"He's got a lot of extra time on his hands."

"Yeah, cause he's clearly a slacker."

"Man's efficient as the day is long. I'm just glad he was late to the party the other night. I would have hated to put him down."

"Especially if he was your gardener."

"He is, too. Well, was."

"Never pictured you as the gardener type," Magnus said.

"Why do you think I had Mr. Green Thumbs here manage it for me? Mystics, man." Caldwell turned toward the house. "Up there."

Magnus looked up three tiers to see a man sitting in a lawn chair reading on a data pad. He held a drink in one hand and wore shorts and a t-shirt, his feet bare. His black hair was tight on the sides and swooped across his brow. The guy looked like a damn movie star.

"Slow and steady on the steps," Caldwell said. "Guy's a bit of a crack shot too."

"You think he's packing something in those shorts?"

"He most certainly is." Magnus heard the smile in the colonel's voice.

"Mystics, next thing you're going to tell me he cooks, paints, and has a lifetime membership at the Capriana Altitude Club."

Caldwell turned toward Magnus but didn't say anything.

"You're splicing me," Magnus said.

"Nope."

"And you're sure he's not married?" Magnus thought

better of the question. "Never mind. If he were married, he'd never have time for the rest of this."

"We have a winner."

Caldwell led the way up the first set of steps. They'd barely made it up the second when a step under Magnus's foot creaked.

"Son of a—"

Forbes's hand was up and holding a blaster pistol before Magnus could finish the sentence.

"Bitch."

Forbes's brown eyes searched his picture-perfect backyard, straining to see through the path lighting and shadows cast by the greenery. Meanwhile, Magnus stood extremely still, aware only of his suit's soft hum traveling up the base of his spine.

Satisfied that nothing was there, Forbes placed his blaster on the lawn table beside him and went back to his reading.

"Guy's a little wound up," Magnus offered.

"Wouldn't you be? He just saw half his battalion get laid waste."

Magnus sighed. "Fair enough."

"Watch your step." Caldwell proceeded up the steps again, and Magnus moved even more cautiously. By the time they ascended to the top level, Forbes seemed none the wiser, engrossed in his reading material and sipping from his snifter of amber liquid. The fact that Magnus could be this close and still not have the man suspect them was a true marvel and testament to Novian tech. Magnus made another mental note, this time to thank Azie for her engineering skills.

"We tackle him on three," Caldwell said. "Barracks style."

"Just—tackle him?"

"One..."

"Oh, splick. We're actually doing this."

"Two..."

"You going high or low?"

"Three..."

Caldwell dove at the unsuspecting man, knocking him back and out of his lawn chair. The snifter shattered, and the data pad went flying. Magnus dove as well, pinning the man's legs to the deck. "He's a strong son of a bitch," Magnus yelled, trying to stay on top of the wiggling captive.

"Forbes," Caldwell said over external speakers. "Settle down, Forbes. It's the colonel. It's me, Caldwell."

If Forbes recognized the colonel's voice, he didn't show it. Instead, the captain bucked and twisted as if his life depended on it. Caldwell struggled to keep the man pinned down, but Forbes managed to wrest an arm free and swung in the air. When his hand struck against the colonel's shoulder plate, Forbes cursed and recoiled in shock.

"Forbes," Caldwell yelled again, and once more, the captain threw another wild punch at the air. This time, Magnus heard a bone crack as the captain's fist crashed against the colonel's helmet.

"Forbes! Stand down!"

Magnus saw the man wince against the speaker's volume; any more of this and they'd wake the neighbors. Suddenly, Caldwell deactivated chameleon mode. Forbes's eyes went wide. But now he could see a target to fight and began tussling with the colonel even more.

"The hell with this," Magnus said, then he struck Forbes in the head with the butt of his NOV1. The man jerked and then went still.

"Dammit, Magnus," Caldwell said, sliding off Forbes's limp body. "Now we're going to have to wait."

"Better than having him break his other hand against your thick head. And next time, can we consult before you go and do something crazy like that?"

"Mystics, but it felt good, didn't it?"

Magnus chuckled. "Like bootcamp?"

"Like bootcamp."

FORBES SAT SLUMPED in one of his kitchen chairs as Magnus finished stirring salt and cleaning solution together in a glass. He'd rested his NOV1 and helmet on the dining room table for effect—he guessed the alien weaponry might help his case with Forbes in a minute—while Caldwell stood to one side with his arms crossed.

"You ready?" Magnus asked.

The colonel nodded.

Magnus placed the glass under Forbes's nose. It took less than a second for the improvised smelling salts to do their work, causing Forbes to jerk his head back. He blinked several times as he struggled to orient himself. "Who... who the hell are you?" Then his eyes locked on Caldwell's face. "Colonel?"

"In the flesh."

Then Forbes turned to Magnus. "And who the hell are you?"

"Name's Adonis Magnus."

Forbes jerked back again, eyes still blinking. "Magnus? As in General Atticus Magnus?"

"Am I that ugly?"

"Splick," Forbes said, grabbing the back of his neck. "What the hell is this about? They said you were dead, colonel."

"Nice to see you too, Forbes," Caldwell said.

"Yeah, right. I'm the one who got hit in the head. Bad."

"That was my call, not his," Magnus said. "You put up a good fight there, captain."

"Well, it's not every day you get assaulted by things you can't see. Gonna have a headache for a week."

"It'll wear off soon." Magnus lied. He'd probably given Forbes a major concussion—wouldn't know until the medics took a look. Hell, Magnus was surprised the smelling salt idea even worked.

"You guys scared the splick out of me. What the hell is going on? And how'd you sneak up on me like that?"

"Is that Gundonium bratch?" Caldwell asked, pointing to the bottle on the other end of the table.

"Single malt," Forbes replied. "You gonna butt-strike that too, Magnus?"

Magnus grinned. "Hell no. It's way more valuable than you."

"Better pour three new glasses," Caldwell said, turning to Forbes. "'Cause your headache's about to get a lot worse."

—————

To HIS CREDIT, Forbes listened attentively as Caldwell and Magnus outlined the quadrant's precarious predicament. From Moldark's seizure of the fleets to So-Elku's power trip to the discovery of the Novia Minoosh and the existence of quantum space continuums, Magnus made sure to cover all the major topics while keeping an eye on the clock. The conversation accelerated as the subject changed to the fire-fight from a few days earlier.

"So that was you fighting against Charlie and Delta company?" Forbes asked, pouring himself another finger of bratch.

Caldwell eyed the bottle. "You do know you're not gonna pass inspection tomorrow morning, right?"

Forbes shot the liquid and sucked air through his teeth. "Something tells me I won't be doing PT in the morning, colonel."

That was the first thing Forbes said that gave Magnus any indication of what he was feeling. And unless Forbes meant he would die trying to keep the two intruders from leaving his home alive, the phrase boded well. At least he hoped so—Caldwell still had to answer the question.

"That was us fighting against the two companies, yes," the Colonel replied.

Forbes put his glass down. "Mystics, Colonel. You know how many of our men you killed? *My* men?"

"The colonel didn't kill a single one," Magnus said. Both heads turned to look at Magnus.

"And how's that?" Forbes asked.

"He was the one using non-lethal force. Wish I'd thought of it first."

"Well, isn't that rainbows and avacots. You coulda told that to the rest of your team."

Magnus sighed. "If that would've gotten us out of there without casualties, I would have."

"You sure about that, *Lieutenant*? 'Cause it sure as hell seems like you had a lot of fun with your fancy guns and armor there." Forbes nodded at the NOV1 and helmet on the table.

Magnus sat back. He wasn't going to win this argument by force of will. Hell, there wasn't an argument to win. And wasn't that the problem with fighting? War was making the best of a thousand horrible situations gone sideways with lives on the line and little to no time to think it through. "I'm sorry."

Forbes face filled with the coldness of a CO who'd need-lessly lost Marines. "You're sorry."

Magnus nodded, looking at the bratch in his glass. "What happened back there? Those are the kinds of moments that never leave you—the kind that haunt your sleep until the day you die. And part of me will never be able to forgive myself for it. And so, for them, and for your loss, I'm deeply sorry.

"The other part of me, though? The part that had to get my people to safety, that decided to keep evil people from murdering the innocent? That part isn't sorry at all. Because that's the mission. Your Marines and my gladia? They signed up to die. But the people that *Luma bastard* put down? And the innocent lives Moldark wants to take out? They haven't signed up to die. So I'm going to do whatever it takes to fight for them and complete the mission."

Forbes seemed to consider Magnus's words for a while, then asked, "What about the company of marines that got wiped out? We cleaned up a lot of boys in that docking bay."

"Now that—that was different," Magnus said.

"That was a little girl," Caldwell replied.

Forbes looked like he was about to choke on the liquor. "You wanna run that by me again?"

"It was a child named Piper," Magnus said, sparing the colonel the reply. Magnus gave the captain a summarized version of Piper's background, leading up to her energy explosion in the bay.

"And you're saying she's been missing ever since?" Forbes asked.

Magnus nodded, swirling the last of the amber liquid in his glass. "We have reason to believe she's still here on Worru. Got some teammates checking on that now."

Caldwell finished the last of his drink and looked at Forbes. "Well, cappy? What'll it be?"

Forbes thought for a moment and looked up from his empty glass. "It's crazy. All of it. I think you're both out of your mysticsdamned minds. And even if I believed it all, there's no way I could communicate it with two companies of Marines and still mobilize them on such a short timeline. They wouldn't believe it. Hell, I hardly believe it." Forbes studied Caldwell's face before taking a deep breath. "But I don't have to believe the whole story. I just need to believe you, Colonel."

Magnus couldn't read Forbes at all. Just when Magnus thought the captain was going one way, the man juked. So until Forbes came around and said it straight, Magnus couldn't be sure. Talking to this man was like talking to a blasted politician.

"I don't like what happened to my men back there. And I'm not getting over that quickly. Don't know that I ever will. Like you said, Magnus, some things just haunt you into hell." Forbes paused, then looked at the colonel. "I once told you that I'd follow you to hell and back. I meant it then, and I mean it now. I guess I didn't plan on hell looking so damn strange."

"So you're in?" Magnus asked, unable to support the suspense any longer.

"Hell, yes," Forbes replied. "Bastards wanna screw around with power at other people's expense? You can bet I'm going to help you land a fistful of hurt on them."

Magnus offered up his hand, elbow on the table.

Forbes clasped it. "OTF."

"OTF," Magnus replied, the old mantra coming to his lips faster than he would have liked. "Now I say Dominate, and you say Liberate."

Forbes cocked an eyebrow but didn't seem opposed to the idea.

"Dominate," Magnus said, holding the man's unblinking eyes.

"Liberate." Forbes released Magnus's hand. "Has a nice ring to it."

"So how are we getting two companies off this planet without raising suspicions?" Magnus asked.

"Easier than you'd think," Forbes answered. "Command still hasn't assigned a new battalion commander, and with all the recovery operations still underway, ships have been coming and going faster than Plumeria's space traffic control can track."

"So you're in charge?" Caldwell asked.

Forbes nodded. "First few hours I've had to myself in four days. 'Til you showed up and ruined it. And by the sounds of it, I won't have any more peace and quiet for quite a while." Forbes capped the bottle and slid it away. "But who needs peace and quiet anyway?

"I've got two rifle companies and a support company under my command, along with a few attachments from other battalions, including some navy jockeys."

"We could use them too," Magnus said. "But what about ships?"

"I've got ships coming out my ass," Forbes said with a

chuckle. "Seems the whole sector is interested in what you all did here. Guess you might say that's how I know."

"That we're telling the truth?" Magnus asked.

"That what you're doing is important and that you're going to need all the support you can get. Two Alvera-class transports will get everyone off-planet. Give me three hours?"

"You've got two," Caldwell said.

Magnus pushed the bottle back toward Forbes. "And I'd say bring the bratch. You might want it before this is all over."

Suddenly, an alert chimed from Magnus's helmet. He met the colonel's eyes for a split second before transferring the comm alert to his bioteknia eyes with the audio ported through bone induction. "Go for Magnus."

An image of Awen appeared in his vision. By the looks of it, she was still in the shuttle, which was a good thing. "Magnus, I think we found her."

His heart skipped a beat. "Where? Here?"

Awen nodded. "We're pretty sure she's in the Grand Arielina."

"The Grand—you're kidding me."

"I wish I was."

"You think he's captured her?"

"I don't know what I think. But that's not the worst of it. Azelon said eight Paragon warships just jumped into the system."

Caldwell nodded at Magnus. "What's wrong, son?"

"We've got company."

"Magnus," Awen said, regaining his attention. "You know what this means?"

"We're not gonna have time to look for her." He could already see the tears welling in her eyes. "We'll come back. We'll get her."

Awen didn't reply. Willowood appeared beside Awen and put an arm around her. "It's not the time, child," the older woman said. "But it will come."

"We're almost done here," Magnus said.

"And?" Willowood asked.

"And it looks like Azelon better make room for a few more guests on the *Spire*. Tell Nolan to warm up the shuttle."

"Will do," Awen replied.

Magnus terminated the call and looked at Forbes. "Timeline just bumped up, Captain. You've got an hour." Forbes looked like he was about to reply when a chime rang at the front door. "You expecting someone?"

Based on the look Forbes gave them both, the answer was no. "You?" Forbes asked in reply.

"It's too late for dinner and too early for breakfast," Magnus said.

"But never too late to whoop ass," Caldwell added as he pulled his V from its holster and racked a charge.

5

"You smell that, 'Six?" Ezo asked as he rubbed his hands across the top of his captain's chair in *Geronimo Nine*. The heavily modified Katana-class light freighter sat inside the *Spire*, occupying a large hangar bay beside a long line of Novia Fangs.

"Iron oxide and cleaning astringents, sir," the bot replied with a nod. "Yes, I am detecting those."

"No. The smell of home."

TO-96 turned. Ezo knew if the bot could have expressed a puzzled look, he would have. "I don't believe I'm familiar with that smell, sir."

"It's a metaphor, 'Six." Ezo sniffed the leather seat back and moved around to sit down. His body made the chair squeak, and then he reached for the flight yoke. "Mystics, it feels good to be back."

"It feels exactly as it did before," TO-96 remarked as he sat in the co-pilot chair. "I am beginning to think that you're suffering the effects of nostalgia, sir."

"You could say that."

"Will you smell me with such fondness when my structural composition degrades?"

Ezo glanced as his co-pilot. "Smell you?"

"Yes. If I project the odors of iron oxide and cleaning astringents, will you make a metaphor about me?"

Ezo chuckled. "Sure, 'Six."

"And what will the metaphor be?"

"I suppose that all depends." Ezo's fingers danced over several instrument panels, summoning the ship from slumber.

"On what, sir?"

"On how I feel about you when you're a derelict."

"I see. I trust I will be a satisfactory derelict worthy of a nostalgic metaphor."

"Don't we all." Ezo brought the ship's systems online one by one. "Are you gonna help me run the pre-flight check, or are you just gonna sit there and pine about your obituary?"

"I hope you compare me to a warm beach," TO-96 said, assisting Ezo with the startup sequence and pre-flight checklist.

Ezo passed and looked sideways. "A warm beach?"

"My first records with you are in Caledonia. If you said that *Geronimo Nine* reminds you of home, then that is the home I wish to be remembered by."

Ezo swiped holo-screens left and right, ordering them to

compliment his field of view out the cockpit window. "You know, 'Six, you can be surprisingly sentimental."

"Is that a desired trait to have in a companion?"

"You could say that. Just don't go overboard with it."

"Like smelling the seats of your starship, sir?"

Ezo glared at his bot. "Stay focused on pre-flight."

"As you wish, sir."

"What's this about beaches?" Sootriman asked as she walked onto the ship's bridge.

"I wish to be remembered as a beach," TO-96 said before Ezo could respond.

Sootriman's eyebrows went up. "Is that so."

"It's a long story," Ezo said.

"On the contrary," the bot replied. "The dialogue transpired over a matter of—"

"It's a long story, and we don't have the time for it." Ezo looked back at Sootriman. "You and Saasarr ready to shove off?"

"The gear is stowed, and we're ready to go."

"Great." Ezo activated the ramp closing sequence and began transferring all systems to internal power, disconnecting from the *Spire's* infrastructure. "'Six, what do we need from Azelon to get out of here?"

"Nothing, Ezo," Azelon said from speakers in the console.

Ezo sat back in surprise and patted his thighs. "Ezo keeps forgetting you seem to be everywhere at once."

"It is a characteristic all humanoids from your universe

seem to forget. In any case, I am opening your bay's blast doors now."

Ezo's heart skipped a beat as the thin crack on the hangar bay's doors appeared through the cockpit's window, revealing the void's starry expanse. The thrill of open space, of destinations unknown, always invigorated him. And now that he was back behind *Geronimo's* helm, the galaxy was at his disposal. Well—almost. They had a job to do first. But he wondered how much longer this conflict would last before he could get back to his life of roaming the galaxy. Alone.

No, not alone, Ezo corrected himself. He glanced over his shoulder at Sootriman. He had her to think about now.

As if prompted by his inner thoughts, Sootriman placed her hand on his shoulder. They'd been through so much together. And after almost losing her—*twice*—Ezo couldn't imagine being without her. Then again, she'd never liked the starfaring lifestyle. She'd barely been able to leave her family behind on Caledonia. But she did, to be with him. And maybe she'd be willing to do that again. To leave Ki Nar Four and venture off into the outer reaches of the galaxy. *When this is all over,* Ezo reminded himself. *Gotta survive it first.*

"Atmospheric force field is at 100% and holding," Azelon said. "You are clear for departure."

"Roger that, Azelon," Ezo replied. "Take us out, 'Six. Nice and slow."

"Affirmative." TO-96 activated *Geronimo's* vertical thrusters, and Ezo's stomach fluttered. The ship rumbled as the landing gear retracted, locking in place within the hull.

Then, as smoothly as a dancer entering stage-right, TO-96 moved the ship through the force field and into the vacuum of space.

"Safe travels, Ezo," Azelon said. "We're awaiting your safe return."

"And we await safely returning to you," TO-96 replied.

Ezo looked at his bot. "I don't know what is with you two, 'Six." Then, back to Azelon, he said, "We'll see you soon, *Spire*. Ezo out."

THE TRIP to Ki Nar Four took one day via subspace. It would have been faster had Ezo taken one of Azelon's shuttles equipped with the Novian equivalent of a subspace modulator on it. But the slower speed was worth showing up in *Geronimo Nine*. In fact, they had to or else risk blowing the whole point of coming this way, which was to recruit reliable people for the Gladio Umbra.

Sootriman did not want to tip their hand too soon regarding the nature of the mission volunteers would be asked to join. One look at a Novian ship, and everyone would see credit symbols and fat accounts. Trying to keep those kinds of leeches happy would be an uphill battle, especially when they learned they weren't being paid.

No, what the team needed were those who saw the big picture, those who realized that the galaxy was going to splick, as Magnus had started saying, and would risk their lives to keep it from happening. The reward, for those on Sootriman's planet, was staying alive to rip someone off another day. Therefore, showing up in *Geronimo Nine* meant the queen was back in town, so everyone had better straighten up. Plus, Sootriman had some very particular people she wanted to recruit, but that was all she would say.

Ezo brought the ship into a docking bay reserved for Sootriman and powered down everything but life-support and drive core subroutines. He wanted to be able to move fast if the need arose.

"What's the plan?" Ezo asked as he, Sootriman, TO-96, and Saasarr readied themselves in the main cargo hold. They'd traded their Novian armor for more normal garments that Azelon had helped manufacture—all but TO-96. He couldn't exactly swap out the telecolos emulation compound on his plating. Instead, Ezo gave him a cloak to cover up the expensive looking patina.

Saasarr recovered most of his Reptalon armor but wore a new black bodysuit, courtesy of Azelon. The garment's woven fibers were said to be stronger than Saasarr's original and needed to be laundered less frequently too—always a plus for a Reptalon.

Sootriman donned a luxurious red dress that she'd designed with Azelon. The open back closed at the small of her back, and gave way to a wide train that expanded outward to sweep the floor. Meanwhile, her ample cleavage and the front of her long legs were on display for all to see—

few allusions to her well-endowed figure left to the imagination.

For his part, Ezo had requested his old floor-length leather coat back but agreed to a new thick-collared knit shirt and black cargo pants and boots. He holstered his Novian V pistol on his right hip and his Supra 945 on a shoulder holster under his left armpit. "Stay in the shadows and keep out of sight?" Ezo asked Sootriman.

Sootriman shook her head from beneath a white travel cloak that she fastened around her neck. "I need a show."

"A show?" Saasarr repeated.

"I want everyone knowing that I've survived Moldark's attack on me and my inner circle. I want the city to know I'm untouchable."

"But Sootriman, you're not," TO-96 said. Saasarr hissed at the bot.

"Saasarr, that's enough." Sootriman raised a hand at the Reptalon, then turned to TO-96. "I know that, and you know that. But they don't need to know that."

"A display of defiance," the bot said, beginning to surmise the woman's intent. "To bolster your image among the common folk."

"Common folk?" Ezo asked.

"Piper gave me some suggested reading, volumes which were not previously in my database."

"Let me guess," Ezo said. "Fantasy?"

"I believe that is the colloquial category, yes."

Sootriman smiled. "It's less about bolstering my image

81

and more about good marketing, Tee-Oh. But that's the basic idea."

"Might I be allowed to lead the way then?" TO-96 asked. "A queen deserves a herald."

Ezo and Sootriman exchanged playful looks before Sootriman said, "I don't see why not."

"You got something in mind, 'Six?" Ezo asked.

"I think I can froth some milk into cream, yes."

"Froth what?" Ezo gave Sootriman a bemused look while Saasarr glared at the robot in confusion.

"Beat an egg quickly," the bot added to clarify.

"You mean whip something up?" Ezo said.

"Precisely. You know—metaphor."

"Come on," Sootriman said. "Lead the way, oh magnanimous milk frother. My peasants await."

FOUR FIGURES EMERGED from the docking complex and into the crisp night air, turning toward the heart of Gangil, Ki Nar Four's capital floating city. The planet's volcanic activity, some twenty-thousand kilometers below, reflected against the clouds that hovered above the city, casting it in a dirty amber hue. Chimney stacks and industrial vents spewed exhaust into the atmosphere in an eternal attempt to keep the city aloft, held in safety far above the planet's lethal mix of gases.

TO-96 wasted no time in moving out in front of the group while Ezo and Saasarr flanked Sootriman. Within another block, the bot stepped into the middle of the street, which made several skiffs blare their horns at him. But as he pointed his weaponized forearms at them from beneath his cloak, they quickly veered away—though still sending vulgar gestures and comments at him.

"Trying to make new friends?" Ezo asked the bot.

"Follow me," TO-96 said, motioning everyone to follow him into the middle of the street.

Ezo shrugged at Sootriman, then said, "After you."

"No," Saasarr said. "After me." The lizard-man stepped out in front of Sootriman and raised his hand at another hover skiff that didn't seem to mind running people over. But when the driver saw the Reptalon, his eyes went wide. The skiff veered into a food cart, knocking its contents onto the filth-ridden sidewalk.

Sootriman followed after Saasarr with Ezo picking up the rear. As soon as TO-96 saw the three walking toward him, he turned his attention back down the street. He raised one hand toward the sky and fired three micro-rockets, the white tails of which braided around one another until the projectiles detonated with sequential *booms*. A warning klaxon bellowed from TO-96's chest, followed by the near-deafening sound of his voice.

"Attention, common folk of Gangil. To all those lurking in the shadows of iniquity and pondering their demise at the hands of the merciless plagues…"

"Merciless plagues?" Ezo asked Sootriman. "What kind of books was Piper into?"

"Shhh," Sootriman said. "I want to see where this is going."

Already, the bot had people's attention. Heads turned, and conversations died down. Shop owners stopped their transactions, and drivers slowed their vehicles.

"Yes, you, pitiful miscreants and sycophants, doomed in your perilous plights to beat the ground with tool and trowel, condemned to the meager existence of those cursed with the—"

"'Six," Ezo hissed. "We want them to be enamored with her, not stone us."

"I am simply trying to make them see their current state as being below that of Sootriman's," TO-96 replied.

"I think you made your point. Move it along."

TO-96 resumed his loud proclamation to his not so doting masses. "Behold! The quadrant's guiding light and the mystery of virginity, the stable boy's fancy and the flame of fabulous fantasies, I give you the conquering mistress of the assassin's blade and blaster, quenched at the illustrious sight of her gaze, the one, the only, *Sootrimaaaan, Queen of Ki Nar Fouuuur!*"

As TO-96's voice expanded, reverberating off buildings to a crescendo, he fired off six more micro-rockets, and this time they detonated with an incendiary shower of sparks. People screamed at the sound, ducking for cover. Then, just as Sootriman pulled her hood back, rear-facing LEDs on the bot's head popped on, bathing Sootriman's body in white light. Her white cloak and red dress shimmered in the bot's lights—*the damn things actually sparkled.*

Ezo was a breath away from scolding TO-96 when someone along the sidewalk started clapping. Ezo spun to see a bedraggled old coot inside a bodega step out of the doorway. Then the man put two dirty fingers in his mouth and whistled. Within seconds, dozens of people were clapping—and then hundreds. Faces poked out of windows, and drivers stepped out of their vehicles. All up and down the main street leading to her den, Sootriman had a veritable sea of adoring fans showering her with praise.

"Son of a bitch," Ezo said with his hands on his hips.

Sootriman glanced at Ezo. "I like him."

THE PARADE CONTINUED to Sootriman's domed headquarters in the middle of the city. By the time Ezo and the others reached the burned-out main entrance, the streets were full of people celebrating their beloved leader's momentous—if not slightly melodramatic—return.

"Thank you," Sootriman said, waving to the cheering crowds. She repeated herself several times, touching her chest in appreciation, then waving again.

"There's a point to all this, right?" Ezo asked, yelling above the din.

"Relax, husband," she said, still waving and smiling. "It's coming."

Ezo turned away from the crowds. He rubbed his forehead, wondering how much longer this might go on. When he thought the praise might die, a chant began to pulse in the air.

"Soo-tri-maan! Soo-tri-maan!" the people cried, pounding fists against whatever they could hit. The sound was almost deafening. Ezo almost let his impatience get the best of him when someone tugged on his sleeve.

"Are you with her?" the man yelled.

Not expecting the question, Ezo did his best to nod.

"You're one lucky son of a dimdish," the man replied, then slapped Ezo on the back.

Ezo stepped away from the man, eyeing him. Then he looked at Sootriman, and then at all the people cheering for her. This woman, his wife, was—well, she was adored. Why he'd never seen this sooner, he didn't know. But these people, *her* people, actually loved her. *And why shouldn't they?* he asked himself.

Sootriman was, after all, the most remarkable woman he'd ever known. Hell, she was the greatest woman in the galaxy as far as he was concerned. And like her parents, Sootriman was born to rule, next in a royal line of benevolent leaders. Granted, reigning over Caledonia was a far cry from the criminally rogue world of Ki Nar Four. But if barely surviving the wars with the Akuda had taught Sootriman anything, Ezo figured it was how to handle herself around a bunch of bloodsucking scum bags hellbent on eviscerating her. And scumbags of Ki Nar Four loved her for it.

Why Ezo had never seen Sootriman in this light, he didn't

know. Perhaps, like many things in life, he'd just taken her for granted. But seeing her in front of her people like this was— *well, it's pretty incredible*, he thought. So he smiled. And then he clapped for her and stepped down into the masses to see how it felt—to see her through their eyes. And she was beautiful.

———

"ALL THAT TO SAY, I have a mission for some of you," Soot-riman said. She'd been speaking for almost five minutes, using TO-96's audio system as a public address system. His speakers projected the sound detected from her in-ear comm so that her voice traveled over the masses and echoed off the buildings. Not that she needed much help—the people were dead quiet. Right up until she gave them something to cheer about.

"Granted, it is not for the faint of heart," Sootriman said. "Nor is it for those looking to turn a profit. Some might even find themselves staring down the barrel of a blaster before it's through."

"Wouldn't be the first time," someone yelled from the audience. Several people laughed.

Sootriman nodded in appreciation. "Even so, you'll be placing your life in jeopardy in ways you can't possibly imagine."

"Anything for you, our queen!" someone else screamed. The words were met with several shouts of affirmation and more applause. Sootriman let the cheers linger before raising a hand to silence everyone.

"Be that as it may, know that what we face in the coming days is not like anything we've encountered before. The quadrant is under assault from the same people who attacked Ki Nar Four, killed many who you knew, and tried to kill me. These forces also threaten peaceful systems and planets—rogue or otherwise. And Ki Nar Four will not be excluded if our enemies have their way. If you have kin and a home that cannot afford your absence, I do not think less of you for staying here. But if you feel worthy of a great task, then join me.

"My bot here will take your applications in order of appearance and make them known to me until we have filled out our roster. We will depart again in three days' time with all those who make the cut. The rest of you, pray to the mystics for our success and safe return."

Sootriman paused and looked over the crowds. Ezo thought he saw a tear glisten in her eye but couldn't be sure. *She loves them*, he thought, surprised by the tenderness of her affection. *The warlord actually loves them.*

"Thank you, everyone. Dominate, liberate."

There was a momentary pause as the crowd seemed to consider how to respond to Sootirman's words. Then, something magical happened—something that Ezo would never have imagined in a hundred years. The sea of faces, stretching from left to right and down the streets that stemmed away from Sootriman's den like spokes from a wheel hub, raised their voices and yelled, "Dominate, liberate!"

Having never heard the mantra of the Gladio Umbra

before—at least as far as Ezo knew—the people took to the phrase with unusual affinity. It wasn't like they were an army of disciplined troopers, drilled in call and response by red-faced instructors. No, these were convicts and enemies of various states around the sector. These were people whose luck had run out elsewhere, the galaxy's refuse. But they were also survivors. And they reminded Ezo of Abimbola's Marauders, and of those who lived in the Dregs of Oorajee. People like that would fight if given a chance—fight until they won, or died trying.

Sootriman spun on a heel, cloak and dress billowing in TO-96's lights. Then she fled from the crowd and disappeared into her den's blackened entry tunnel. Ezo followed her while Saasarr stood guard beside TO-96, the bot already ordering people to calm down as he tried to take their applications. Ezo listened to the crowd chant Sootriman's name as he followed their queen into the depths of her burned out home.

6

"YOU MIGHT WANT TO TAKE COVER," Forbes said from beside his still-closed front door. Magnus and Caldwell had their pistols drawn and helmets on while the captain looked at the exterior camera's holo feed. "A hundred credits says they already see us."

Magnus nodded at Caldwell. The two split up and covered the door from different angles. Then Forbes activated his camera and addressed the four Luma Elders outside.

"Good evening, Captain Forbes," said the foremost figure, dressed in the Order's signature robes.

"I'm pretty sure it's the morning," Forbes replied. "And since you woke me up, I'm not sure it's all that good."

"We are sorry to disturb you, sir, but we have reason to believe there are two fugitives on your property."

"Fugitives?"

"That's correct. We are here to take the people in question into custody and escort them to holding."

"Who issued the order?"

"The order comes by way of Master So-Elku, sir. And in case you need reminding, you are here at the pleasure of the Order."

"No," Forbes replied. "I'm standing on sovereign Republic territory granted through the mutually agreed upon terms of the Valdaiga Accords. So if Master So-Elku wishes to convey orders, he'll do so through the proper channels."

"Master So-Elku has been unable to reach Colonel Caldwell since the firefight, and you are the highest-ranking survivor, are you not?"

"The Order can file a complaint with me in the morning. I'm going back to sleep."

The Luma's tone grew more stern. "Captain Forbes, I'm afraid we must insist on searching the premises. We have reason to believe you are harboring traitors to both the Order and the Republic."

"Well, that escalated quickly. Still, you can file a complaint through my office in the morning."

"We are under orders to search your home with or without your consent."

"You do know you've just threatened a Galactic Republic Marine Corps officer on sovereign soil."

"If you see our presence as a threat, that is up to you. However, we will enter the premises by force if you refuse to let us in peacefully."

"I'm pretty sure a Margonian merrel rat crawled up his butt and died with its teeth stuck in his colon," Caldwell said from in the kitchen. "Let's end this."

"Who was that?" the Luma asked.

"Your mom," Forbes replied. "And she wants you to back away from the door, or else this is going to end poorly for you."

"Is that a threat, captain?"

"No," Forbes said. "But this is. Door, open."

Forbes's automated home security system immediately opened the front door. The panels weren't even fully separated when Forbes fired a blaster bolt from his MC99 and struck the first Luma in the torso. But the shot seemed to wrap around the Luma as if surging around a personal force field.

"Splick!" Forbes yelled as he dove from the doorway in time to avoid a blast of energy that shot through the house and out the back wall. Debris sprinkled down on Magnus as he leaned out from a pillar and fired two three-shot bursts with his V at the first Luma. Again, a force field displaced the bolts.

The Luma's attention shifted toward Magnus. Aware he was the new target, Magnus ducked just as the pillar broke apart a few centimeters above his head with a loud *crack*. Magnus looked across the hallway to see Forbes roll into a kneeling position and aim his rifle across the path of the threshold.

"Switching to NOV1," Magnus said to Caldwell.

"With you," Caldwell replied.

Magnus stowed his pistol and pulled his rifle from his back. The weapon's holo sights lit up, paired with his helmet and bioteknia eyes, and registered a full charge. Then, without looking around the corner, Magnus poked the weapon's barrel around the pillar and sighted in on the leading Luma. The man took two steps into the house and raised his hands as if to block any incoming fire.

Blue blaster bolts from three different positions erupted from inside the house and struck the Luma in a hail of lightning. Forbes's MC99 chewed into the man's knees while Caldwell and Magnus's fire pounded his chest. But again, the withering assault seemed to do little to stop the advancing man or the three behind him.

"Splick," Magnus yelled as he pulled back behind the pillar just in time for the second Luma to send a bolt of energy whizzing by his head. The blast struck a glass wall that looked onto the back deck, blowing it into a thousand pieces.

Magnus had never fired the NOV1 on its highest setting before, but he figured now was as good a time as any—these Luma had survived the recent raid and were no doubt some of So-Elku's best.

He moved his weapon's fire rate to the maximum setting. A magazine discharge warning alerted him that a sustained burst of more than three seconds would drain his current magazine. He dismissed the sign, turned back toward the first Luma, and squeezed the trigger.

The NOV1 punched Magnus's shoulder like a mad Boresian taursar and screamed like a banshee. Not even his helmet's noise suppression system could combat the sound pressure level the weapon produced. Magnus yelled in reply as if his voice could fight back the weapon's terrible noise in his ears. The weapon sent a blistering 3,000 rounds per second into the lead Luma's midsection. The man's force field gave way, and then he exploded in a shower of light—flesh flash-incinerated.

The blaster rounds that passed through the victim struck the second Luma in the chest. The man suffered a similar fate, unable to avoid the alien weapon's sustained barrage. His shield sent the first nano-seconds of energy flinging off into the street. But the remaining blaster bolts punched through and shredded his torso until only a pair of legs and mutilated hips remained. The limbs toppled to the ground while the remaining two Luma disappeared from the doorway.

"Mystics, Magnus," Forbes yelled from in his living room, hands covering his ears. His voice was hoarse, and Magnus realized the man hadn't had any hearing protection. "What the hell was that?"

Magnus thought of switching to external speakers to give a snarky reply, but there was no time. Plus, Forbes wouldn't be able to hear him anyway—the man probably needed ear surgery.

"I'm tracking one moving around the west side of the house," Caldwell said. "The other's looking to flank us through a window."

"I'll take the one out back," Magnus replied. "You and Forbes take the peeping tom."

"Copy that."

"Forbes is going to need hand signals. Pretty sure he's deaf."

"Dammit."

Magnus switched out to his second magazine and lowered his NOV1s fire rate by 50%. While the weapon's max rate had done the job, it had spent too much energy. He wouldn't be able to sustain that level of output if the firefight dragged on. Plus, he wouldn't have the enemies stacked up again—that had been lucky.

With the glass wall shattered, Magnus stepped through it and onto the back deck. His thermal imaging showed the third Luma tracking along the home's west side, which meant Magnus needed to find cover across the pool. From there, he could hit the enemy in the rear when the Luma addressed the house.

Magnus ran through a cluster of ferns, skirted the far right side of the pool, and took a position behind a tall stone water-fall. While he doubted it changed much for the Luma, Magnus activated his suit's chameleon mode. There was something to be said for feeling safe—whether or not you were. Magnus also noticed several lights coming on in the adjacent homes. He even saw silhouettes appear in second-story windows as Forbes's neighbors looked to see what was happening. *The good*, Magnus thought—if there was any good to be had—*is that we were on a Marine Corps post*. Where civilians would retreat from the sound of weapons fire, Marines would advance—*even in their damn underwear.*

A beat later, the third Luma appeared around the side of the house. For whatever reason, the man was focused on looking for a way into the home and failed to notice Magnus. *Hell yeah.* Magnus locked onto the mystic's chest, slowed his heart, and squeezed the trigger.

At the same instant, flashes of light and sound erupted from inside the house, forcing more glass out of the ground floor's windows. The event made Magnus's target duck a split second before the NOV1's rounds hit. Instead, the blaster fire chewed a hole through the home's siding the size of a spaceball.

Immediately, the Luma turned to face the direction of fire and launched an energy blast at Magnus. He ducked just in time for the waterfall to explode, sending chunks of stone high into the air. Water vaporized into steam, and rocks pelted the garden and pool from above.

Magnus was back on the offensive, firing at the Luma as the man raced across the deck and toward another one of Forbes's handmade rock formations. But then more flashes of light and belches of weapons fire erupted from inside the home. Magnus could see Caldwell's thermal image pivot, firing a withering stream of NOV1 bolts at the fourth Luma who dashed through the house. The bolts traveled straight through the home and projected into the neighborhood. Collateral damage with their new high-powered weapons was a genuine threat.

Magnus was about ready to warn Caldwell when another blast of energy detonated the remainder of his cover. The resulting explosion knocked him backward and into a cluster of small shrubs. He thrashed about and then dove into a mulch bed just as another Luma blast scorched the greenery. He rolled to one knee, aimed at the thermal image beside the pool, and fired.

This time, the rounds found their mark. They punched a hole in the shield and drilled into the Luma's chest. In less than a second, the rounds eviscerated the victim. But Magnus's stream of fire drifted up the man's chest until his head vanished in a blaze of light. When Magnus released the trigger, the Luma's halved body fell into the pool with a splash.

"House clear," Caldwell said over comms. The colonel had taken out the last Luma with a point-blank round to the head—at least that's how Magnus interpreted the wide splatter of gore against one wall. The mess showed up as yellow, green, and red IR splotches in his HUD, while the corpse was missing the rear section of its skull.

"Backyard clear," Magnus replied loudly, stepping out to examine the floating corpse.

"House clear," Forbes yelled loud enough that Magnus's sensors picked him up. "I think we got them all."

"Affirmative," Caldwell said over externals.

"You're gonna have to speak up, Colonel. I can't hear you."

Magnus noticed the street in front of the house start to fill with emergency lights. "Well," Magnus said to Caldwell. "Looks like Forbes is gonna have an easier time mobilizing his units than we thought."

"Which is our sign to get lost," Caldwell said.

"Copy that."

"Captain," Caldwell said with his index finger raised. "Wheels up in one hour!"

Forbes nodded and slung his MC99 under his arm. "One hour! See you in the sky!"

7

So-Elku knocked on Piper's door. "It's So-Elku."

"I know," Piper said.

"May I come in?"

The little girl hesitated. "Sure."

So-Elku turned the handle of the old wooden door and pushed. The staff chambers of Brookside Manor maintained the ancient-style rooms, complete with hinged doors and sliding windows. There was something quaint about these quarters that So-Elku liked, something that spoke of a simpler time before the Order could afford more expensive technologies. It also spoke of the Luma's rich legacy, one that had been around long before he'd arrived. And, now that So-Elku had Piper, one that would carry on long after his death.

Piper sat on the large raised bed with her knees tucked to her chest. She'd traded the Novian power suit for the traditional robes of the Luma, opting for the green and black fabrics that signified her as an apprentice to the Luma Master. That had pleased So-Elku deeply.

The girl didn't bother to look So-Elku in the face. Instead, she seemed preoccupied with the bird songs filling the lush gardens behind the Grand Arielina. The open window let in the fragrant scents of blooming plumeria flowers as well as the undertones of damp soil and bark.

"Is your room to your liking?" So-Elku asked.

Piper nodded, still looking out the window. "The bed is soft."

"I'm glad to hear that." So-Elku moved to look down at the garden. "It's a lovely day outside. Wouldn't you rather go for a walk?"

"I thought you told me to stay in here?" Piper scrunched up her nose. "You said it wasn't safe."

"That was before." So-Elku waved a hand. "The city has been restored to order."

"You mean, my..." The girl hesitated on what to call Awen and the others.

"The rebels."

Piper nodded. "They've been killed?"

So-Elku raised an eyebrow, surprised by how fast the child went to the most fatalistic outcome. "They've been driven off and won't bother you anymore. Especially Magnus."

"Don't say his name, please."

"My apologies, Piper. I was only trying to comfort you."

"Don't say it, though."

"I won't." So-Elku looked back at the garden, motioning toward it with a hand. "Shall we?"

Piper sighed, then moved her legs and slid off the bed. "It would be a shame to waste such a beautiful day by remaining inside."

"Wise words."

"Eh. It's what my…" Again, Piper faltered, this time—So-Elku guessed—in naming her recently deceased mother.

"Your mother." So-Elku made a show of sighing more deeply than he needed to. "Her loss is devastating, I must admit."

Piper looked down at her slippered feet, then back at So-Elku. "Are we going for a walk or what?"

So-Elku and Piper moved along the stone paths that meandered under the leafy canopies. Sunlight filtered down in blotches, playing on Piper's golden hair and sullen features. Despite the beautiful birdsongs, which seemed to entice her out of her misery, she kept her hands folded, head down, and feet moving one after the other.

"I do wish you'd find your way out of all that sadness, Piper," So-Elku said as they rounded a turn to face a lily pond. "At least for a moment, anyway. Is it not beautiful here?"

"Yes, sir."

"Please, please, child. Call me master."

"Yes, master."

"That's better. Now, what could I do to cheer you up?" He tapped his chin and looked down at Piper. But the girl didn't respond. So he knelt at the edge of the pond. "You know, you're not in your power suit anymore, Piper."

"I know."

"And I believe that the premise of our arrangement here is that I would help you discover who you are, free of limitations."

She looked up and wrinkled her nose at him. "The premniss?"

"Premise. The…" He tapped his chin again, then extended his finger as if having an idea. "The main reason we've agreed to work together. Would you like to begin?"

Piper took a step away from the pond and lowered her head. "I don't know."

"Why, Piper. Whatever is the matter, child?"

"Last time I went into the Unity without my suit, I almost hurt people. Like I did before."

"Piper, I need you to listen very carefully to me. Are you listening?" She nodded. "Good. You cannot hurt me."

Her eyes darted up to his. "I can't?"

He shook his head. "I won't let it happen."

"But how? Not even shydoh Awen could stop me."

"Shydoh Awen?"

"Sorry. That's our word for master. In the Gladio Umbra, I mean."

"I see. Would it be easier for you if you called me shydoh, then?"

Piper shrugged. "Maybe."

"Shydoh So-Elku then. I like the sound of that."

"Me too."

"And what you like, I like." He pointed toward the pond. "Come here, child." Then he had another thought, knowing Awen wouldn't have had the girl call her shydoh without a student term. "And what did Awen call you?"

"Piper."

So-Elku smiled. "No. I mean, if you called her shydoh, what term did she use for you?"

"Doma," Piper said, taking a step toward So-Elku.

So-Elku repeated the word, trying it out. "Then that's what I'll call you. Come, doma. Look."

Piper moved toward the pool until she was even with So-Elku. He pointed into the clear waters. "What do you see?"

"A lily pond with some fish in it."

"As do I. Tranquil, yes?"

Piper bit her lip. "What's trank-will mean?"

"Calm. Peaceful."

"Okay."

"But in the end, what is it really?"

"What's trank-will?" Piper asked, looking at So-Elku for the first time.

"No, what is the pond? The fish? The lilies?"

"I... don't get what you mean."

"I mean, what composes it all? What makes it what it is?"

"Mole—mo'mecueles?"

"Molecules. Good. And what are the molecules made of?"

Piper thought for a second. "Atoms?"

"And the atoms?"

Piper shrugged. "Smaller stuff?"

So-Elku smiled. "Yes, smaller stuff. Would you like me to show you?"

"Show me?" Piper looked between the pond and So-Elku. "The smaller things?"

He nodded, then he scooped up a handful of water and let it slide out of his palm, slipping between his fingers. "Shall we?"

FROM WITHIN THE UNITY, So-Elku marveled at Piper's presence. While little more than a waif in physical form, the girl's ethereal footprint was that of a giant. He figured there was more potential energy in her than any Luma he'd ever known —himself included.

Piper's power wasn't new to him, of course. He'd noticed her strength during their confrontation in the Unity. How could he not? The child was as mighty as she was majestic. But she lacked precision, evident in her lack of discipline. *The hapless snares of youth*, he noted to himself.

"The lily pond itself is merely a manifestation," So-Elku said, looking down at the pool.

"A manifestation?" Piper asked.

So-Elku studied the girl's face and realized an illustration was in order. "When the wind blows, do you see the breeze? Or do you see its effect on the leaves it touches?"

"I see the leaves move."

"Good. That is the same as—"

"Unless I'm in the Unity. Then I can see the wind just fine."

"Yes. But I'm talking about with your natural eyes."

"But we aren't using our natural eyes right now."

"I know that. This is an illustration to help you see."

"But I can see fine."

"To *understand*," So-Elku said.

"Understand what I don't see? But I can see everything in the Unity just fine, can't I?"

So-Elku took a breath. "Yes, in the Unity. The wind was meant as an illustration to explain the word manifestation, nothing more."

"I still don't get what it has to do with the pond."

"The wind is—" So-Elku bit his lower lip. *Patience, So-Elku.* He suddenly remembered how long it had been since he'd spoken with a child for any length of time. There was a reason the Order only took young people in their late teens. "Forget the wind. Look at the pond."

"I can see the wind blowing on its surface."

"Yes." So-Elku nodded his head absently, then arrested himself. "I mean, no. Forget the wind, Piper."

"But you said—"

"Forget the wind," So-Elku said with a sharp wave of his hand.

Piper recoiled as blonde wisps of hair closed over her face.

"I'm sorry, doma." So-Elku lowered his head and softened his tone. "Forgive my impatience."

"But you're mad at me."

He looked in her eyes and smiled. "Mystics, no, my child. I simply... I'm mad at myself. For not being the teacher you deserve."

"Shydoh Awen says we should not be mad with ourselves, but treat ourselves gently."

So-Elku clenched his teeth for a second before speaking again. "And Shydoh Awen is right, on that point. I promise not to be mad with myself anymore."

"You should tell yourself that you're sorry."

"I should what?"

"You know. Say sorry to yourself. Apologize."

"Piper, we don't have time for this."

Piper put her hands on her hips. "Apologize."

The Luma master blinked twice, then looked down at the pond. He saw his reflection in the water, then said, "I'm sorry."

"I'm sorry, So-Elku," Piper said with the corrective air of a school teacher.

"I'm sorry, *So-Elku*."

"For?"

So-Elku looked up from the pool. "Piper, we really—"

"For what? You have to say what you're apologizing for, or it doesn't mean anything."

This was not going as he'd planned. He sighed and then looked back at his reflection in the pool. "I'm sorry, So-Elku, for being mad at you."

"And?"

Great mystics of antiquity. This child was getting on his nerves faster than he cared to admit. No wonder few people wanted to commit to working with children: they were downright infuriating. "And I'll do my best to never let it happen again?"

"Are you asking me, or telling yourself?" Piper said. "She pointed to the pool.

"And I'll do my best to never let it happen again," So-Elku said to his reflection. When he looked back at Piper, she gave him a satisfied look and took her hands off her hips. "Can we get back to the pool now?"

"Sure."

"So, the pool and the fish and everything that composes them are connected through space and time in the Nexus. You know of it."

"Of course. That's how I trapped you before."

"Quite so, quite so." He studied the waters again. "But unlike shydoh Awen, I bid you venture into the Nexus unbridled." Piper blinked at him. "You're going to be free to do whatever you want in the Nexus."

"You use a lot of fancy words, shydoh."

"I consider myself informed."

"So, you want me to follow the pool back to the Nexus?"

"Not quite, my child. I want you to use the Nexus to discover the pool."

"But I see it fine. I don't need to discover it."

"Yes, that's true, you do see it. But you see it with your second sight much like a bee sees a flower. But do you know how the flower's stem sees the flower?"

"Stems don't have eyes."

Again, So-Elku took a controlled breath before continuing. "But pretend they do."

"But they don't."

"Pretend."

Again, Piper took a step back.

So-Elku repeated himself more gently. "Let's just imagine that they do, for fun."

"Like a game?"

"Like a game, exactly."

"Well, if a flower's stem has make-believe eyes, I guess it sees the flower a lot differently than a bee. It's not gonna want to make honey from it."

"Quite so. What is it interested in?"

"Feeding it with water, maybe?"

"Excellent. And where does the moisture come from?"

"I said water."

"That's what moisture is."

"Oh."

"And where does it come from?"

"From the ground, silly."

"This is like the Nexus then," So-Elku said, holding his hand over the water. "When you look at the pond, you see water and fish and bubbles and all manner of things. But when the Nexus sees the pond, it even sees the atoms that compose it."

"And even the smaller stuff?"

"Even the smaller stuff, yes. Would you like to see what the Nexus sees?"

"The smaller stuff?"

"That's what I implied, yes."

"Sure."

So-Elku stepped into the pool. Piper took his offered hand and joined him, the water going just over her knees. "Now, I want you to get close and sense the Nexus without going *to* the Nexus."

"Huh?"

So-Elku was tiring of the tedious explanations. *How had Awen managed to teach this little* thing *so much?* He imagined throwing himself off a tall building were he to endure days on end of this sort of exchange. "The Nexus. Sense it, but don't go to it."

"Sense it?" she asked.

"Yes."

"But don't go down to it."

"Correct."

Piper's eyes darted around the pool. "From right here."

"Precisely." When she hesitated longer than he had the

patience for, he decided to try and employ yet another word picture. "Think of it as a scent."

"The scent of what?"

"Well, what smells do you like?"

"Warm bread."

So-Elku smiled. "That is a wonderful smell, yes. Now, when you're standing outside and smell warm bread, what do you think?"

"I want to eat it."

"Yes, which means what?"

"Which means I'm hungry."

"Yes, but—"

"And it will taste so good with melted butter."

"Yes, but go back to the smell. If you smell warm bread, it means that..." So-Elku moved his hand in a circular motion, trying to summon the answer out of her.

"That... I'm hungry?"

So-Elku shook his head but continued waving his hand.

"That I'm smelling warm bread..."

"Which is coming from?"

"From... from someone who's making it?"

"Yes!" So-Elku clapped his hands in celebration of the small victory. Piper smiled at his exuberance, apparently pleased. "So the scent leads to somewhere else."

"Oh, so you're saying that I can smell the Nexus from the pond."

"In a manner of speaking, yes. But unlike the bread analogy, we're not going to find the baker and the bread shop.

We're going to stay right here and look more closely at the smell."

"You can't see smells."

"It's an analogy, Piper."

"Doma."

"Excuse me?"

"You're supposed to call me doma, not Piper."

Was she always this much of a handful? he wondered. "Do you want me to teach you something interesting or not?"

Piper withdrew again. "I was just trying to point out that you called me the wrong thing."

For what felt like the hundredth time, So-Elku took a deep breath, steadied himself, and cleared his mind. "Thank you for the correction, doma."

"You're welcome."

"Now, shall we see what we can see?"

"Sure," she said, winking with one of her big blue eyes.

"Focus, doma," So-Elku said, lifting his palm to each side of her head like blinders. Piper straightened her back and then closed her eyes. "I want you to feel the Nexus flowing up and into the lily pond, feeding it, surrounding it, sustaining it. Can you sense it?"

"I... yes, I think so."

"Good. Now, follow that feeling, not—"

"Not down to the Nexus. I got it, shydoh."

So-Elku nodded. *Perhaps she's not entirely hopeless after all.* "Instead, dwell within it. Exist within it. Feel yourself merging with the energy and becoming a part of it."

"Like this?"

Suddenly, a blast of energy knocked So-Elku off his feet—not just within the Unity but outside of it. The wave was so powerful that it dislodged him from his second sight and forced him out of the ethereal realm. He lay on his back, ears and head ringing, and squinted as he got his bearings. When he could focus, he saw Piper hovering above the pool—*no, where the pool had been*. There was only a shallow pit in the ground. Instead, the water, the fish, the lilies, algae, all of it circled Piper. Her hands were lifted as if controlling the movements of everything within the lily pond, fingers flowing in rhythm with the Nexus's power.

"That's marvelous, Piper," So-Elku said, aware that his voice freely betrayed the wonder he felt inside. He touched the back of his head and then saw blood on his fingertips, barely aware of the injury. He looked back at the girl. "Now, now—can you feel deeper? Can you sense that there is more to explore?"

"Uh-huh," Piper said. "Should I?"

So-Elku braced himself, still out of breath. "Yes."

The next demonstration of power came not as a blast but as a rumble that made the pebbles on the stone path pop off the ground in fits. So-Elku steadied himself, hands on the ground, body vibrating. He glanced around the garden and noticed the tree limbs quivering and the flower beds shaking. The birds had gone silent too.

Then So-Elku witnessed something he never imagined

possible. The matter surrounding Piper began to spread apart.

At first, the change was subtle, as if the floating pool of water and all its contents were blurry. So-Elku thought to rub his eyes save for the fact that Piper herself wasn't blurry; unlike everything else in the garden, she was utterly still. Then separation became more noticeable as droplets of water began separating from one another. The fish too began pulling apart—not in a violent way that suggested their death. So-Elku imagined they were still very much alive. Instead, it was as if the fish had been separated on a fundamental level, their life force present, but their composition exposed.

The pool and its contents suddenly began to expand— matter pulled apart in a swirling display of colored light. So-Elku hadn't the slightest idea how any molecular bonds remained intact. By all accounts, this act should have released cataclysmic levels of energy. Instead, the pool's components broke down into some infinitesimal level that defied understanding. The light and matter spread out over the garden like the helical star cloud of a distant nebula. So-Elku felt as though he was gazing into eternity itself as the cascade of light swirled above him.

"Magnificent," he said, barely able to speak the word. Tears rolled down his cheeks, and he found himself hardly able to breathe.

"I see it," Piper said at last. "I see it all."

"Yes. Mystics yes, you do, my child."

"It's beautiful."

This time So-Elku couldn't respond. He was shaking in ecstasy. There was no precedent for what he was witnessing. Piper made whatever thresholds So-Elku had crossed look elementary at best and unmentionable at worst. This was a display of power no Luma had ever seen, and may never see again.

"I can see more," Piper said after a moment.

"More?" *What more was there to see?*

"I see a path leading up to this moment," Piper continued. "And paths leading away. They're like trails for all the things that make up the pond."

Mystics, was she seeing time? It wasn't unheard of for Luma to traverse limited aspects of time. But to see the routes of matter itself? It defied explanation. No wonder the girl had been given a suit to regulate her abilities.

Seeing Piper like this, So-Elku knew he'd been right to secure her for his plans. What force existed that could withstand her? That could rival her? But not just for his sake—for hers too. She owed it to herself to be a part of the galaxy's future. She might not see it today, of course, but she would arrive at it soon enough—*if she is adequately guided. Everyone needs guidance*, he reminded himself, *lest they fail to see what is right in front of them.* And guide her he would.

So-Elku struggled to prop himself up on his elbows. Then, as he sought to gain control of his voice, he said, "Now bring it back. Slowly. Let everything be rejoined as it once was."

Piper seemed to acknowledge his instructions with a nod though it was hard to make her body out amidst the brilliant lights. She moved her hands up and down as if they played on the winds of the universe. At once, the helical expanse began to collapse. The light folded in on itself—atoms fused, particles rejoined, and the droplets of water merged just as the fish and the lilies took shape once again. And then, the whole scene descended back into the pit until the waters lapped against the pool's stone edges.

When Piper looked up, water still above her knees, she let out a giggle. "That was super awesome," she said, looking all around.

So-Elku smiled, thinking of what was to come. "You don't know the half of it, my child."

8

"WE'RE JUMPING IN-SYSTEM NOW, my lord," said the *Peregrine's* captain.

Moldark couldn't remember the man's name. Ellis perhaps. But why bother with names when this quadrant's organizations had given everyone ranks. *Pathetic.* "Thank you, Captain," Moldark replied. "I'll be up momentarily. Begin scanning the coordinates I gave you for ships."

"As you command, my lord."

Moldark closed out the channel and stared at the mirror in his quarters. Kane's body was deteriorating faster than expected. Apparently, human physiology was weaker than he first surmised. "The decrepit species," he said, seething the words through pointed teeth. Spittle landed on the mirror and ran down his black eyes and scabbed skin. He would need more sustenance, and more frequently if he was to stay bound with this… *this thing.*

Finding hosts was a troublesome affair, and building a reputation that allowed for adequate manipulation of the infrastructure even more so. But Moldark wouldn't be without some measure of convenience should Kane's body fail him. There was always Admiral Brighton, Captain Seaman, and several other notable leaders within the Paragon who would suit his purposes. Plus, they'd already surrendered enough to his mind-crafting that taking control would be far less of a hassle than it had been with Kane.

But Wendell Kane served another purpose, one far more critical than strategic leadership within the quadrant's ruling military arm. Kane was seed-bearer to *her*—progeny of the Unity. That the fates would have granted him such a find was proof that he was to silence the pitiful cries of mortal life.

He feared, however, that the seed had been tampered with, that she had been caught up with those who resisted the Paragon and the Republic. Perhaps even So-Elku meddled with her—steward of the Unity for this pithy sector of a forsaken universe. And she was close—he could feel it. Coaxing her to join him, however, may present his greatest obstacle yet. But he would find a way—he *must*. He needed the child if he was going to accomplish his plans.

For all Moldark's powers as an Elemental, he could not commune with the Unity. That was reserved for mortals, and he scorned them for it more than ever. Likewise, he despised them for finding freedom from their meager existence through death. They lived but the span of a vapor before blinking out of existence. Meanwhile, he was cursed to roam the cosmos with no hope of rest. None, that is, unless he were to vanquish his foes and eradicate life until the universes were quiet once more. The Republic and its amalgamation of species were not the first victims to suffer his relentless pursuit of his mortal enemies. And they would not be the last.

"WHAT HAVE YOU FOUND?" Moldark said upon entering the ship's bridge. A few other crew members occupied workstations throughout the dimly lit space, their faces illuminated by the glow of holo displays and button-strewn consoles.

"We have identified dozens of Republic ships coming and going from Worru, my lord. But none of them match the description or location you provided."

Moldark's teeth pricked his tongue, and he instantly tasted Kane's blood. The ship was most likely gone, as he suspected. But if the scout vessel he'd sent to the quantum tunnel's location returned with a negative report, then he knew the rebels and their new void horizon wouldn't be far. "No matter," Moldark said, sucking the blood across his teeth. "Keep scanning. If you discover anything out of the ordinary, let me know."

"Surrounding the reconstruction efforts?"

Moldark had turned away but stopped to look back at the captain. "What reconstruction efforts?"

"In the capital city, my lord." The captain paused, but when Moldark didn't say anything, he added, "There seems to have been a sizable ground conflict in the capital city."

"Show me. Ellis, is it?"

"Yes, my lord. As you wish." The captain called his sensors officer to attention and ordered images to the main viewing window. Within seconds, live orbital views of Plumeria populated the *Peregrine's* bridge, each sub-window showing details of the destruction. Hundreds of black blisters pockmarked the roads with gashes that streaked away from their epicenters. Buildings crumbled into street corners, and wreckage from blown-up vehicles made certain side-streets impassable. He even thought he saw the remains of starfighters littered throughout the city. That, along with the decimated planetary defense batteries, meant a significant conflict had played out here not more than a few days ago—perhaps even around the time that Nos Kil had sent his transmission.

"There," Moldark said, pointing to a particular docking bay. "Zoom in and clarify." The sensors officer followed Moldark's orders and brought up the image of the bay.

Moldark felt Kane's heart skip a beat. "She was there."

"Who was, my lord?" Ellis asked.

But Moldark barely heard the man's question. The girl had been in that hangar bay—he could feel it. He didn't need second sight to see there had been a release of power, one so strong that its marks would never leave that place. Hundreds of lives had been snuffed out at that moment. Which meant…

"She's becoming herself."

"My lord?" Ellis asked from beside him.

Moldark eyed the man curiously. He seemed unusually pliable. Perhaps he would make a good underling. Or a good meal, Moldark couldn't decide. "Hail the planet," he said. "I want to speak to So-Elku, Master of the Luma."

"As you wish, my lord."

The comms officer went into motion, making the necessary contact with Plumeria and eventually getting through to the Grand Arielina and Elders Hall.

"I have Master So-Elku, Captain."

Ellis was about to say something, but Moldark said, "Bring him up."

The comms officer complied, and a holo feed of So-Elku stood before Moldark at the front of the bridge. He seemed to be standing in a garden of sorts, though the background details were washed out.

"Fleet Admiral Kane," So-Elku said. "To what do I owe the displeasure of this unsolicited communication? I see you are in-system and without invitation."

"Come now, Luma master, is my presence here really all that unwelcome?"

So-Elku seemed to consider this for a moment before saying, "Considering the scope of our last encounter, I should think so. Unless, of course, you've come to make amends."

Moldark placed his hands behind his back and ignored

the statement. "It seems you have been visited by some misfortune as of late."

"If by misfortune you mean your own presence, then I heartily agree."

"Our sensors are detecting quite the skirmish in your city's center."

"And what business is this of the Republic's?" So-Elku asked, clearly unaware of the Paragon as a name.

"I was hoping you could tell me that, seeing as how you have become such close friends with them."

If So-Elku was put off guard by the words, Moldark could not tell. The man was as slippery as a Limerian nethermander in a sewer. *No wonder he's at home with the Nine*, Moldark remarked to himself. Not that he had any experience with Limerian amphibians, but Kane did.

"Admiral Kane," So-Elku said after a short pause. "Unless you have official business with the Luma, I suggest you leave the system before we are forced to prevail upon the Galactic Republic."

"And yet, it seems you've already conferred with them enough as it is." Moldark thought he saw the Luma's eye twitch. "Be that as it may, I won't leave the system. In fact, it's come to my attention that you and I have some unfinished business to attend to."

"I must warn you that any attempt to land on Worru will be met with force," So-Elku said.

"Not very becoming of a peace-minded Luma master."

"We render peace to those who wish to make it with us.

You, however, have ulterior motives, ones which we will take every measure to thwart. I can assure you, Admiral, that we will thwart you."

"And I can assure you, Luma, that based on my review of your planetary defenses, you are in no shape to be making threats against me." Moldark was about to continue when he saw someone walk behind So-Elku. A child. A female child with blonde hair dressed in green and black robes. She'd been there for only an instant, but it was enough. It was *her*.

"Admiral, I must insist that—"

"Terminate," Moldark ordered the comms officer, and the woman wasted no time in closing the channel. Then he turned to Captain Ellis, spitting as he spoke. "Order the *Valiant* to prepare an away team, four platoons. Departure in ten minutes. We're landing in Plumeria, and I want every weapon we have on civilian targets. Is that clear?"

"Yes, my lord," Ellis said, wiping blood from his cheek. "Consider it done."

9

"How we looking?" Magnus asked as he ripped off his helmet and threw it into a crash couch. Awen and Willowood turned to greet him and Caldwell while Nolan reviewed the data on several holo screens.

"You're late," Awen said, hands on her hips.

"We ran into some trouble."

"What kind of trouble?"

"Nothing we couldn't handle, Miss Awen," Caldwell said. He looked at Nolan and repeated Magnus's initial question.

"The good news is that no one's questioned our ship ident and security clearance yet. So as long as we move slow and steady, and the towers don't get curious about our ship's visual presence, we should be good."

"And the bad news?"

"Paragon ships just landed, ten bays down."

"Splick." Magnus looked at Caldwell. "This is gonna be closer than we thought."

"I'm afraid it's worse than that," Nolan added. "According to Ricio, Moldark's personal ship is called the *Peregrine*."

"Why the hell do I care about… *Splick*. It's here, isn't it."

Nolan nodded. "Like I said, ten bays down. And if his accompanying transports are full, like I suspect they are, then he has a small company of troopers along for the ride."

Magnus looked at Caldwell, then said, "One look at this ship, and they'll know something's up."

"Agreed," the colonel replied. "Let me check in with Forbes—see where he's at." Caldwell stepped out of the bridge and started shouting in his comm.

"Why are you shouting?" Awen redirected the question to Magnus. "Why's he shouting."

"Long story. Listen, how's Piper?"

"It's hard to say, but I think she's okay."

Magnus ran a hand over his face. "And you couldn't speak with her or anything?"

Awen shook her head. "It isn't like a comms system, Magnus. We felt her presence. That's all."

"Well, at least she's alive, right?"

"Yes." Awen put a hand on his chest. "Let me remind you of what you just told me: we'll come back for her."

Magnus sighed. "Right." But Magnus couldn't suppress the sense of dread he felt growing in his gut. "You think Moldark's come for her?"

"Piper?" Awen looked away. "It crossed my mind, yes."

"Dammit." The whole scenario felt like a Junlithkin chess match where the adversary was always two steps ahead and loved catching opponents with their pants around their ankles. "Bend over."

"Excuse me?" Awen pulled her head back.

"Not you. Well, yeah, you. And me. All of us, I guess."

"Easy, Magnus." She sighed and searched his eyes. "If there's one thing I know, Piper can handle herself."

"How can you even say that? She's so…"

"Young?"

"I was gonna say naive. She was carrying around a damned stuffed animal up until a few months ago."

"A stuffed animal that was keeping her powers from harming everyone around her."

Magnus eyed Awen curiously. "You're saying her powers are going to keep her safe? But didn't we stuff her in a power suit to do the same thing as that ratty corgachirp?"

"We did. But that's just it. Willowood and I detected her only because—"

"You don't think she's wearing it anymore."

Awen nodded.

"So she's a loose blaster waiting to go off."

"And even with the suit, you saw what she did down here."

Magnus's mind went back to the two companies of dead Repub Marines scattered out the docking bay doors and into Plumeria's streets. He thought about the civilian casualties as well—the untold numbers of people who'd perished within the safety of their own homes. "Mystics," he whispered.

"I don't know what decisions her little girl brain is going to make," Awen said. "I'll give you that. But I do know that if anyone tries to harm her, well... let's just say they'll never know what hit them."

"Forbes is still half-deaf, but he's ready for departure," Caldwell said, stepping back inside the bridge. "He has an idea on how to get us out of here too."

THE FIRST ALVERA-CLASS transport rumbled overhead as Magnus and the others looked up at it through the shuttle's cockpit window. The behemoth was so low that its monstrous repulsor engines shook everything within a kilometer, blasting the city with sustained waves of energy. Forbes's idea for concealment from the Paragon meant making a dash from the hangar and slipping between the two transports. It would require deft piloting, but Magnus felt Nolan would be up for it —at least he hoped so. There wasn't a lot of margin for error.

The ship wasn't halfway passed when Nolan said, "Hold on!"

The former navy pilot raised the Novian shuttle out of the docking bay faster than regulations permitted, barely missing the far side's top edge. Awen clutched Magnus's bicep as the momentum forced everyone back in their crash couches.

Magnus watched as the Alvera-class ship stretched out in

front of them, only to be followed tightly by the second transport. A small gap of maybe three-hundred meters appeared between the stern of the first ship and the bow of the latter—a hole Nolan flew toward with a little too much speed.

"You sure you got this?" Magnus asked, tightening his sphincter out of reflex. The shuttle closed so fast on the first transport that Magnus was sure they'd strike it. His vision tunneled on the two large engine cones that propelled the ship forward. As the energy wakes threatened to tear the shuttle apart, Magnus heard his voice rise in pitch. "Nolan?"

Just before a fiery ion explosion consumed the shuttles, Nolan spun the craft around and applied full throttle. The movement threw the passengers sideways and then shoved them into their seats. Magnus felt his vision darken as the G-forces skyrocketed. He grunted, forcing blood to stay in his head, willing himself to remain conscious.

The crash couches shook so hard Magnus was sure they'd rip from the deck. Out of the cockpit window, he saw the second transport's nose. He couldn't tell if Nolan was trying to crash into the stern of the first or impale them on the bow of the second. Then, just when the thought of death had firmly planted itself in Magnus's head, the shuttle spun around again and faced the first transport's tail. Nolan cut the throttle, and all was silent save for the gentle thrum of repulsor engines from the transport ahead. The shuttle was in perfect alignment with both ships, floating along as if on parade.

"All set," Nolan said with a calm voice, spinning around. "Smooth sailing from here on out."

"You're one crazy bastard," Magnus said, examining their position in the sensors screen. "Next time, how about engaging the dampeners?"

"But where's the fun in that?"

The words had barely left his mouth when something else left Awen's. Projectile vomit splashed into Nolan's lap.

"Sorry," Awen said, covering her mouth.

"You know what, Nolan? Never mind about the dampeners." Magnus helped Awen unbuckle. "This is way more fun."

NOLAN LED the convoy back to the quantum tunnel while Magnus briefed Captain Forbes on what to expect during the crossing. Since Magnus's Novian shuttle was built to withstand the cataclysmic forces placed on its crew, the feeling of dying every time they went through the void horizon was minimized. Forbes, on the other hand, wouldn't be so lucky. Magnus had thought about calling the *Spire* back, but it would have been too risky with the Paragon ships in orbit over Worru. Plus, he kinda felt every Marine needed to have a near-death experience at least once in their careers, and as far as he was concerned, these Marines—the new ones who'd been called in to help fight with the Gladio Umbra —were due.

Forbes thanked Magnus for the briefing and said he'd forward it down the chain of command.

"Why are you smiling?" Awen asked Magnus when he'd closed the channel.

"I'm not smiling."

"Yeah, you are."

Magnus looked at her. "I mean, wouldn't you love to see an entire transport of Marines get sick at the same time?"

"You're a bad man," Awen said.

"Once was enough for me," Nolan said, pointing to the fresh pair of crew shorts he sported. "And she wasn't even a Marine."

Awen laughed and shook her head. "I'm so sorry, Nolan, but you kinda earned it."

"I hear that," Nolan replied. "Still, Magnus is right. What I wouldn't give to be a fly on that wall."

"I can accommodate that request," Azelon suddenly said over comms.

"Come again, Azie?" Magnus said, stepping toward the central flight console.

"I have gained access to both transports' security systems, which includes onboard cameras. If you would like to view the common crew holds, I can send the feeds directly to your shuttle."

Magnus looked at Awen. "No... that's—"

Awen shrugged, and the edges of her lips curled into a devilish smile. "Send it over, Azie."

Magnus stared at Awen. "Look who's the bad person now."

AFTER ALL FOUR of them watched a few hundred hardened Marines puke on one another, Colonel Caldwell hailed Captain Forbes. "Everyone make it across okay, Forbes?"

"The word 'okay' may not be the best description," the captain hollered back. "But we're all accounted for. We'll be a little while in cleaning up."

"Understood. Consider this your official welcome to meta-space, captain."

Forbes chuckled. "If this is the welcome, I hate to see the goodbye."

"It's a bitch. Listen, don't waste too much time cleaning up. There are bots for that. Plus, you're not gonna need the Repub armor anyway."

"We get the fancy stuff like you, colonel?"

"Eventually. It's gonna take some time to manufacture. We'll keep the Repub weapons and armor in case we need them later. But for now, let's just get everyone into some clean clothes and square your quarters away."

"Copy that."

"Caldwell out."

When the older man spun from the co-pilot chair, Magnus waved him back into the crew compartment. "A word, colonel?"

"Of course."

Caldwell followed Magnus to the compartment's rear, just before the cargo bay. They sat facing one another on either side of the aisle.

"We're gonna need to restructure," Magnus said. "I think you realize that by now too."

"The Gladio Umbra, you mean?" Caldwell nodded. "The units are about to grow by a factor of seven or eight, I gather. Doesn't even count whatever reinforcements Sootriman and Mr. Third-Person can rustle up."

"Ezo," Magnus said.

"Right."

"It's gonna be a lot to handle—reorganization, integration, training."

"Sure the hell is," Caldwell said.

"We're talking some serious oversight."

"We are."

Magnus rubbed the back of his neck. "Oversight that requires training and experience I don't have."

"But with the right guidance, you'll figure it out, son."

Magnus shook his head. "No, colonel. I won't. I don't have the time to learn it all, and the galaxy's safety isn't gonna sit around and wait."

Caldwell looked stone-faced at Magnus. "Splick, son. You're not suggesting that—"

"I sure as hell am."

Caldwell reached into a pocket inside his chest plate and pulled out a half-smoked cigar. He stuck it under his tobacco-stained mustache and studied Magnus's face with hard eyes. A long minute passed in total silence, one that felt more like an hour.

Magnus honestly couldn't decide which way the colonel was going to go. The old man was sure to stay on in some capacity, which was all well and good. But Magnus knew he needed the colonel at the helm, not as a grunt. Magnus couldn't lead what the Gladio Umbra was about to turn into —a battalion. Give him a platoon and a firefight, and he knew where to be and when. But a battalion? Hell, there was a reason gifted men and women spent a decade learning how to command a unit this size. Without the colonel, Magnus knew he was screwed. And he hoped the colonel knew it too.

"You do you know Plumeria was my retirement, right?" The colonel asked.

Magnus sat back. He had him. "Probably would've given you a house next to So-Elku too. Damn shame."

"Damn shame," Caldwell repeated, chewing on his cigar. "But I gave that up, and now I'm stuck here with you. And if I'm stuck here with you, I don't really wanna be running around in firefights, bustin' my balls. I'm getting too old for that splick. Have you seen my knees lately?"

"I don't even know how you're still standing, colonel."

"Hell if I know." The older man chuckled, then squared with Magnus. "Listen, son. You're a damn fine Marine and an even better man. Maybe the best I've ever known. So if you want me on latrine duty, I'll scrub every alien ass pot in the quadrant for you, if that's what helps you save the day."

"Not to discount your offer, but like you told Forbes, we've got bots for that. Where I really need you is at the top. The Gladio Umbra needs a battalion commander. Mystics know I can't do that. But you can. So *that's* where I need you."

The colonel removed his cigar and put his hand up. "Then I'll give you my last breath, Adonis. Dominate."

Magnus clasped the old man's thick hand. "Liberate."

10

Ezo and Sootriman had been cleaning the burnt-out den for almost an hour when Saasarr appeared at the entrance. The Reptalon looked around and gave what Ezo assumed was an impressed look, but it seemed more like a disgusted sneer.

"Well done, my queen," Saasarr said.

"No small thanks to the bots Ezo conscripted," she replied, pointing to Ezo. Again, Saasarr gave him the same impressed look—*or is* that *the sneer of disgust?* He couldn't tell. Either way, he waved from a pile of soot-covered metal that he'd been stacking.

Thanks to the small fleet of service bots, most of the light fixtures had been repaired, the floors scrubbed, and the walls were well on their way to taking on some semblance of their former states. The ceilings, however, would take longer. The grand garments that once billowed through the dome's upper reaches would also need replacing, but those would come in time. *If we make it back*, Ezo noted to himself.

The bots had also done an efficient job of collecting and itemizing the debris and tidying up. Their help was especially useful with the corpses, a task which neither Sootriman or Ezo could handle emotionally. Moldark's massacre had been even more gratuitous than Ezo first thought. After all, the last time he'd been in the den was with Awen and TO-96, and they hadn't come to itemize the dead. But now, picking through the rubble in an attempt to bring the hall back to life, the atrocity's impact hit Ezo hard—Sootriman even more so.

"Would you like to see the first applicants?" Saasarr asked.

"Yes," Sootriman replied. "How many do you have so far?"

"Several hundred, my queen."

Sootriman looked at Ezo. "It's as you suspected."

Ezo gave her an astonished look. "Of course it is. All of them adore you, in case you hadn't noticed."

Sootriman waved off the compliment—*one genuinely paid*, Ezo noted to himself. "But not all of them are suited to fight. Which is why we must interview them."

"You do realize that's going to take more than the day we allotted, don't you?" Ezo asked.

"If Saasarr may speak," the Reptalon said, and Sootriman waved her hand. "The robot man has already filtered the current applicants according to what he thinks is the best fit for us."

"You see?" Sootriman said, glancing at Ezo. "That should

expedite things nicely. Send them, Saasarr. And then come by my side. In case things get… interesting."

Saasarr gave another one of his half smiles and left the den.

"Ezo can't tell if your pet likes him or wants to eat him," Ezo said as he wiped his hands on a cloth.

"Probably both," Sootriman said. She ascended her dais and double-checked the chair's cleanliness before sitting down. "And he's not my pet. You know I hate when you call him that."

"Pet, slave, indentured servant—it's all the same to Ezo."

"Why do you do that?"

"Do what?" Ezo asked, stuffing the cloth inside his pants pocket.

"Talk about yourself with me in the third person?"

"Ezo doesn't do…" He shrugged. "Apparently, he does."

"And yet you don't do it with Tee-Oh."

"That's because he…"

"He what? He's always been faithful to you? Always stuck it out no matter what?"

"Ezo doesn't mean to. It's just that…" Ezo's mouth worked to find words like a fish probing the water.

"I wasn't the one who left you, husband. You know that, right?"

Ezo looked down at his calloused soot-stained hands. "No, you didn't leave Ezo." He sighed, then corrected the statement. "You didn't leave *me*. I suppose it's because I was the one who left you. And I'm ashamed of it."

"Well, get over it."

Ezo snapped his head up at her. "What?"

"Get over it—talking in the third person. Others might think it's endearing or whatever. But don't do it with me. And stop calling Saasarr bad names. He's a person and a fine protector. And if neither works for you, I'll cut your tongue out."

Ezo raised his hands in defense. "I got it. I got it." He was spared any further punishment by the sudden appearance of twelve people at the den's entrance. Saasarr strode out in front and then turned around to face the newcomers.

"I present to you the Mistress of Caledonia, Queen of Khimere, and the Warlord of Ki Nar Four, Sootriman." He bowed as he backed away, hissing at the few guests who didn't bow along with him.

"Come forward," Sootriman said.

The twelve people who crossed the newly swept floor were unusual in a Dregs of Oorajee sort of way. Their clothing was a patchwork of plate armor and fabrics gathered from around the galaxy. But rather than a sign of poverty, as many emoted on this rusted out floating dung heap, these people wore it as a badge of honor. In fact, if Ezo didn't know better, he'd say these people were leaders of some kind. And they looked ready for a fight.

Ezo felt his trigger finger twitch as Sootriman stood from her battered throne and descended the dais. A man stepped out from the group's center and meet Sootriman. He wore a burgundy cloak over one shoulder, a black Repub-style chest plate, and a beige pair of cargo pants with heavy black boots. On his head, he wore a style of black beret that Ezo couldn't quite place.

Sootriman and the interloper stood less than a meter apart, and Ezo felt the overwhelming urge to pull his Supra from his holster.

"How dare you show your face here," Sootriman said, her tone seething with hatred.

"And miss an opportunity to gloat?" the man replied. "I wouldn't dream of it."

"Yeah? Well, maybe you should do more dreaming and less drinking." The two opponents scowled at one another. Ezo was sure this was about to be a one-sided blood bath. Suddenly, Sootriman embraced the man, welcoming him with a wide smile. "It's good to see you, Phineas."

"And you, my lord queen," the man replied. "We feared you were lost."

"I almost was, were it not for some help from friends." Sootriman looked at Ezo and gestured for him to join her. "Husband, this is Phineas Barlow, magistrate of Kildower."

"You can just call me Phineas."

"But magistrate?" Ezo said, shaking the man's hand.

"You think all the floating cities govern themselves?" Phineas asked.

"Come to think of it, Ezo had never given it much thought."

"Offworlders," someone else muttered.

"All Ki Nar Four's floating cities have magistrates," Soot-riman said to Ezo. "Save mine, of course."

"Naturally," Ezo said. "So… you two are friends?"

"Well," Phineas said, stifling laughter. "If you call losing your favorite skiff in a bad hand of Antaran backdraw friendship—"

"Which I do," Sootriman said.

"Then, yeah. And I'm gonna win that skiff back, queen. Don't go making any mods to it."

"Too late," Sootriman said. "It's pink now."

"Pink?" Phineas looked confused. "But, you hate pink."

"I do, yes. But my cats don't."

"Son of a bitch. You know I'm allergic!"

Sootriman shrugged. "Whoops." She called down the hall to the Reptalon. "Saasarr, tell Tee-Oh we have enough applicants for today. We'll be in touch with the others if we need them."

"Yes, your highness."

Ezo dipped his head to catch Sootriman's eye, then leaned in toward her ear. "*These* are the particular people you were trying to get the attention of?"

"You're very perceptive," she whispered.

"So what was with all the fanfare and speech giving?"

Sootriman smiled. "It worked, didn't it?"

"You went through all that just to get them here?"

"Hardly. I sent them a message before we entered subspace. As Tee-Oh suggested, *all that* will help my magistrates when it comes time to solicit the common folk for their help, should they need it."

"Would it have hurt to let Ezo—let *me* in on it?"

Sootriman pulled away and looked Ezo in the eyes. "There's something to be said for being a woman of mystery, don't you think?"

SOOTRIMAN LED everyone up a private staircase to a portico that overlooked Gangil's southern sector. The covered deck was far enough away from the den's main rooms that it escaped Moldark's savagery. A canopy made of billowing fabric played in the evening breeze while hanging lanterns bathed the low-slung chairs and communal tables in soft light.

Ezo, Sootriman, and the twelve magistrates reclined in friendly conversation, drinks in hand, while Saasarr and TO-96 stood watch. Not that anyone dared ambush the gathering. After all, Sootriman had just defied the harbinger of death and returned victoriously—at least as far as the citizens of Gangil were concerned. Furthermore, Ezo suspected the magistrates had not ventured from their respective haunts unaccompanied. He guessed their position was safeguarded by several snipers whose keen eyes searched the shadows for would-be assassins.

"If I could have your attention," Sootriman said. "Your attention, please."

The various side conversations died down, and everyone turned to Sootriman.

"I want to thank you for coming tonight. I know many of you had far more important affairs to deal with than attending to my request for a meeting."

"Boris still needs a bath," someone offered, which brought on a round of laughter made easier by the drinks.

"When doesn't he?" Sootriman added. Then she raised her glass that held two fingers of an aged bottle of bratch she'd kept in a private liquor cabinet. "A toast. To warm baths and bread."

"Warm baths and bread," the gathering echoed, clinking glasses then downing the strong drink.

When the chuckling died down, Sootriman sat back and put her glass on the table. "The fact is, I need your help. *We* need your help." She looked at Ezo, then Saasarr and TO-96. "It seems trouble has come to the galaxy. And while we all pride ourselves in staying out of the affairs of others, it seems I have been pulled into a fight much more significant than my own cares and concerns.

"Granted, you may not find yourself in the same place once you hear everything I have to say. You may wish to resign yourself to your current affairs just as they are, and bid me farewell. I will not condemn you. But know that it may very well be the last time we speak together."

"Is it so bad, this trouble you speak of?" asked the oldest looking man in the group. He sported a long grey beard and a gold ring in one eyebrow. His question and Sootriman's words seemed to lower everyone's mood.

"It is, Dieddelwolf. And then some." Sootriman threw the rest of her drink back and then struck the table with her empty glass. "Tee-Oh?"

"Yes?" said the bot.

"Another round of drinks."

"As you wish, my lady."

NEARLY AN HOUR HAD PASSED when Sootriman finished her story. She recounted the events she'd lived through since Moldark ransacked her den and slaughtered the members of her court. To their credit, the magistrates listened without so much as a burp. They were, to put it mildly, transfixed by her account. Whether or not they'd risk their lives for the sake of a little girl, some misguided Luma, and the Galactic Republic most of them despised, that was another story.

Just as Ezo suspected, one of the first people to speak was a woman who went by the name Chloe. Her short red hair flipped out from under a black Repub officer's cap, and she had a Sypeurlion admiral's jacket buttoned up with a tie around her waist. How the woman got either officer's garments piqued Ezo's interest.

"That's a fine story, your highness, and I'm certainly sorry for the hardships you've endured, but am I the only one here who thinks you're about ready to ask us to help get involved in a war that doesn't concern us?" Chloe looked around at everyone as if to gauge their response. At least two others nodded in agreement and turned to Sootriman. It seemed Ezo's wife had a bit of convincing to do before the night was out.

"A fair question," Sootriman replied. "Whether or not this fight is of your concern is entirely up to you. And your decision will not affect my view of your allegiance. I would never ask you to risk your life for something you don't believe in."

"So you *are* going to ask us then," Chloe said.

"I wouldn't be here if I wasn't. The rest of the Gladio Umbra are gathering forces and preparing to try and stop Moldark and So-Elku as we speak. And I must leave by morning to rejoin them."

"So what's the pitch, Sootriman?"

Sootriman stared at Chloe. Ezo guessed she would be the hardest sell. Something about the Repub and Sypeurlion items she wore told Ezo that the woman had taken out their former owners herself, and most likely at a high cost. She wasn't going to fight unless it was personal.

"The pitch is you all lend whatever fighters you can. We supply training, armament, food, transport, and plenty of targets, you supply the bodies. When it's all over, you retain your warriors and whatever new tech they're carrying."

"When it's all over, meaning if we survive," Chloe said. She leaned back in her chair and gave Sootriman a smug look. "I dunno, my queen. Feels like this war is going to be more hassle than it's worth."

If Chloe's stalwart demeanor phased Sootriman, she didn't show it. "It might. And you might die. Mystics, I've already stared death down twice. But if it's not your trouble now, something tells me it might be soon enough."

Dieddelwolf leaned in. "You think this Moldark is coming to our system?"

"I think he's coming to every system," Sootriman said. "It might not be today or tomorrow. But we're dealing with someone, with some*thing* the likes of which I've never seen. It's only a matter of time before he's done with the Republic. He has command of all three fleets."

"That's enough firepower to clear the sector," Borris said.

Dieddelwolf shook his head. "No, that's enough firepower to clear the quadrant. If the Jujari, Sypeurlion, and Dim-Telok are eliminated, there's nothing to stop him."

"Exactly," Sootriman said, her eyes searching their faces. A whole minute passed without a word spoken. A lonely dog howled in the distance, and a cantina fight spilled into a street, punctuated by the sound of breaking glass.

"Fifteen years, no taxes," Chloe said at last.

Ezo watched Sootriman's face brighten ever so slightly. "You know we can't operate without subsidies. The cities will fall out of the sky. Five years, tax-free."

"Ten." Chloe leaned across the table and spat in her hand. "And not a year less."

Sootriman seemed to consider the offer, but Ezo guessed the savvy businesswoman had already made up her mind. The truth was, she probably would have taken no taxes for life. But why give away more than was needed to make the deal? The galaxy may be a mess but credits were still credits. Sootriman spit in her hand, reached across the table, and grasped Chloe's hand. "Done."

HAVING CONCLUDED THEIR OFFICIAL BUSINESS, Sootriman dismissed her magistrates but welcomed them to stay the night if they wished. The den had more than enough accommodations in its sub-platform chambers—more space that Moldark had failed to defile.

When they were alone again, Ezo joined Sootriman at the portico's far end where she reclined on an amply cushioned tech chair. "I think that went rather well," Ezo said, mindful of using his real name. He sat down beside her and handed her a fresh drink.

"Thanks," she replied, taking a sip from the offered glass. "They're good people."

"Wasn't sure about that Chloe, though."

"She's been through a lot and doesn't like to waste her time with other people's wars."

"Understandable. But I suppose there's more to the story with her." Ezo waited to see if Sootriman would share. But when his wife didn't offer anything, Ezo said, "Like how she got those officer's clothes."

"As with most of the people on this planet, she wears what she kills."

"So she killed a Repub officer and a Sypeurlion admiral? I've gotta hear about this."

"Not my story to tell, love." Sootriman took another sip. "Maybe you can ask her one day. But fair warning."

"Oh?"

"Be ready for her to throw something. Most likely at you."

"Noted. Thanks." Ezo took another sip of the bratch and tried to enjoy the stillness of the night. "You think they're getting some more people to join?"

"I suspect they'll get us some fresh faces, yes," Sootriman replied. "Tee-Oh's little spectacle will help see to that. Of what quality and talents, well, that remains to be seen. At best, Magnus will have some new fighters to train. At worst…"

"Azelon will have some deckhands and galley rats."

"Precisely." Sootriman winked at Ezo.

"So, you think it was worth the trip out here?"

"I do. But there's one more thing I need to do."

"And what's that?"

"Would you mind summoning Saasarr for me?"

"Saasarr?" Ezo looked back toward the doorway expecting to see the Reptalon but realized he was securing the den's main gate. "Sure. We going somewhere?"

"No, love. He's the one I need to speak with."

Ezo hesitated. "As in, the one last thing you need to do?"

Sootriman nodded.

"And I suppose you're not going to tell me what it's about."

"Not yet, anyway."

"And why not?"

She shrugged and took another sip of her drink. "Because if it doesn't work out, I don't want you included among those who'll have their throats cut."

"And I'm absolutely okay with that."

11

PIPER SAT up and flicked on her bedside light. Her hands were clammy, and her nightgown was soaked. She'd had the dream again—the one where Magnus rescued her.

She looked around the bedroom as her brain tried to make sense of where she was. The old lamp's warm glow illuminated wooden furniture, a thick rug, and heavy curtains drawn over a window. The room smelled like old people and dust.

That's when the reality of her present circumstances came rushing back. She was in Plumeria, on Worru, and Shydoh So-Elku's newest doma.

Piper slid off the tall bed and landed on the rug, then she shuffled to the curtains. She pulled the left side back to reveal a clear sky filled with stars. The sight of tiny orbs sent a chill down her spine. It was as if they called to her, inviting her to leave. *This place*, she imagined them saying, *is not your home*.

The word "home" made Piper's heart flutter. She hadn't thought about being home for a long time. Well, that was, until the *nightmare* she'd just relived. Being back in her family's apartment on Capriana had felt wonderful. She could imagine her father's voice as he made morning holo calls from the dining room table. She could hear her mother singing in the shower. And Talisman was clutched tightly in her arm as she played a game on her holo pad.

And then the pain came. The city was destroyed, and Piper was left to wander the streets—lost and alone. But that was when Magnus came, appearing from the wreckage to rescue her.

"No," Piper said aloud, stepping away from the window. The curtain caressed her face as she moved toward a chair in the room's corner. "He's not a rescuer. He's a murderer."

Tears welled in her eyes as she thought about her mother. As hard as she tried, she couldn't forget her mother's dead body with her helmet split in two. Piper wept, wishing she had Talisman to hold.

Just then, another memory filled her mind, that of her father's burial. She sat with her mother as the hot sands of Oorajee stung her face. That day was so painful, rivaled only by the night her mother died. She remembered sneaking a few glimpses as Magnus buried her daddy beside his emergency pod, digging a grave in the sand with a Repub helmet.

Another shiver went down Piper's back, this time making her arms prickle. She was cold—cold and alone. And she was homesick.

So-Elku insisted that she was where she belonged. "You're home now," he'd said. They walked back to her quarters after the day's exercise in the lily pond, her arm through his. Her new shydoh assured her that she was in the right place. But, somehow, she didn't agree. She didn't feel like she was in the right place, and this wasn't home.

Then again, where was home?

Her father and mother were dead, and the only people she felt comfortable with were long gone—although *comfortable* wasn't the right word anymore. Not after what Magnus had done.

Which made her wonder a new thought: How could Awen be friends with someone like Magnus? Deep in her heart, Piper didn't believe Awen was bad. If anything, Magnus had blinded her just like he'd blinded Piper. *But is Awen really so impercip—percep—imperceptive?*

Suddenly, a feeling of guilt overshadowed the over-whelming feeling of being homesick. Piper pulled her legs up to her chest as another shiver went through her body. She felt ashamed for thinking that Awen wasn't smart enough to see through Magnus's deceit. She was, after all, a famed Luma and co-leader of the Gladio Umbra. She would have sensed Magnus's evil motives just like she had sensed—

Piper shook.

Just like Awen had sensed So-Elku's.

But she was wrong about the Luma Master. He wasn't bad. Maybe just misunderstood. Like she was. None of Piper's friends back in school got her. They'd made fun of her gifts. They called her a demon and said she didn't fit in. She'd wanted a second chance with them. She'd wanted to show them that she wasn't a freak and that her powers were beautiful. But they'd made up their minds—just like Awen had made up her mind against So-Elku.

After all, he'd asked Piper for a second chance. Wouldn't she be a hippalotaderm if she didn't give him one? *No, not a hippalotaderm. A hippa—hippacrat.* Something like that.

But working with So-Elku gave Piper an icky feeling. Taking off her power suit didn't feel right, especially after Awen had gone to such great lengths to make it for her. And her mother had been so enamored with it too. Piper remembered seeing it for the first time on the stone altar in the temple on Neith Tearness. The memory made her warm inside and pushed back the cold.

Then, an even more puzzling thought struck Piper. If So-Elku truly needed a second chance, why hadn't Awen given him one? And, more importantly, why hadn't her grandmother? After all, both women had known him for a long time—Awen almost as long as Piper had been alive if her math was right, and her grandmother for... well, for however old she and So-Elku were, she guessed.

This begged even more questions that Piper didn't feel up

to answering. Had her grandmother already given So-Elku some second chances? Had Awen? Her former shydoh wasn't exactly the mean type. Sure, Piper had seen Awen be cross, but that was only when Piper did something really dangerous. Or stupid. Or both.

In fact, Piper couldn't think of a time where Awen was not at least willing to see something through someone else's eyes—even Magnus's. And those two were about as opposite as people could be. Awen wanted peace, and Magnus wanted to blow things up. Well, he wanted to stop bad people from doing bad things. But still, the ways Awen and Magnus wanted to get things done seemed really different—at least until they formed the Gladio Umbra and started working together. That was when they traded what was best for themselves with what was best for everyone. At least, that's how Piper imagined it.

Suddenly, Piper had a memory of So-Elku's face as she stood in the lily pond after the day's exercise. But the image was fuzzy, and she knew she needed to see it more clearly—to *feel* it more deeply. That's when she remembered the new ability she'd discovered while flowing through the atoms of the lily pond: she'd been able to look back in time. Or something like that.

Born from a desire to see So-Elku's face in the garden, maybe even to hear his thoughts, Piper slipped into her second sight and summoned the Nexus's power. The forces that connected all things in the Unity flowed through her—or, rather, she flowed through them. Piper felt herself leap across steps in time like she was jumping from one stone to another in a beautiful river. She glanced into the shimmering waves of light and spotted the events of her day as easily as if she were watching a holo movie of her life. The moments rippled beneath the surface, inviting her to view each one and savor the past.

But Piper was not here to marvel at her newfound ability nor play with her memories *frivis—vivious—frivolously*. She had a job to do. So she leaped from stone to stone until she saw herself in the lily pond a moment after she'd returned the scene to normal.

"That was super awesome," Piper saw herself say. Then she looked at So-Elku.

"You don't know the half of it, my child," he replied.

Right there! she thought.

Piper stopped the scene in the Unity, using the Nexus to hold it in place. She drew close to the man's face and studied it. He had a strange look in his eyes—a greedy look. Like he wanted something that he'd never been able to have before, and he was looking at Piper.

No, she corrected herself, *he was looking* through *me*.

It was like So-Elku wanted what Piper had—her powers. After all, Piper knew she was more powerful than him. She could feel it. But two were always better than one, *which is why I need him, right?* she reasoned. *Being a team is why we need each other*.

But if that were true, why didn't her grandmother need

So-Elku? Why didn't Awen want to work with him to achieve peace? Piper wondered what made So-Elku so different than the two women, and why they all couldn't work to achieve the same things. Wasn't their goal the same?

Suddenly, Piper had an adult thought—a complicated and kind of confusing adult thought. *Their goal might be the same,* she said to herself, *but the way they want to get to it is not.*

Any warmth Piper had felt before disappeared. She snapped out of the Unity and found herself back on the old chair. Then she squeezed her knees tighter as the room seemed to close in on her. Piper wanted to run—wanted to get out of this place. But to where? She had no family left, and Awen had probably gone back to metaspace.

For the first time in her life, Piper truly felt alone. She curled up on the chair in her soaked nightgown and started to cry.

———

A SLIVER of sunlight irritated Piper's eyelid. She tried to squint it away, but the beam was persistent. It nagged at her until she moved her head some centimeters out of the way. After a few minutes, the warm glow had caught up with her eyelid again, tickling her eyelashes. She smiled and then turned away from the sunlight. She opened her eyes and found herself in the chair in the corner of her room. The sun shone through the narrow slit in the heavy drapes, carving a path along the rug to her. She'd fallen asleep after the nightmare and all the grownup type thinking she'd done. It was hard work.

Piper stretched and yawned and then shuffled back to the big fluffy bed. It still smelled like old people, but she was cold, and the covers looked warm and inviting.

As she nestled back in to try and get a little bit more sleep, her thoughts drifted back to what she'd thought about in the middle of the night. She rolled over and then went back as she tried to dismiss the images and feelings. Being a grownup was hard, and she felt like she'd put herself in a very grownup position way before she was supposed to. Worse still, she didn't know how to get out. She needed an escape.

Just then, Piper remembered the holo call So-Elku had taken when they were in the garden together. The man on the other end seemed very scary looking. *Now, Piper, that's mean*, she thought, correcting herself with a teacher-like tone. Rather than tell herself she was sorry for the judgment, Piper revised her assessment of the man in the black uniform with the scarred bald head and black eyes. *He's just different from me, that's all.*

And yet, the funny thing was, there was something about him that wasn't so different. In fact, there was something about the man that seemed familiar. Why, Piper had no idea. She'd never seen him before in her life. And yet she felt like she knew him, or maybe that she was supposed to know him. Like a long-lost friend who you hadn't seen in decades. Of course, Piper had no idea what decades felt like—she'd barely made it to one decade. Which reminded her: *Isn't my birthday soon?* But the thought of celebrating without her mother and father made Piper want to cry again, and she'd done enough of that for one day.

The man in the holo call said he was coming to visit So-Elku, and that gave Piper an idea.

12

Moldark heard So-Elku's voice coming from inside Elder's Hall long before he saw the Luma Master. "Let him in, let him in," So-Elku said with an exasperated tone. The guards who stood at the doors barring Moldark's way seemed confused. They looked at one another, then back in So-Elku's direction, before returning their gaze to Moldark.

"Your master seems insistent," Moldark said. "Of course, if you'd like to double-check with him, we'll wait here." He gestured behind him to the four platoons of Paragon troopers with weapons held across their chests.

"For the love of all the mystics, what are you waiting for?" So-Elku said again.

The guards, still appearing unsure as to why their commander would allow such an audience, begrudgingly stepped aside. Moldark nodded at them and then stepped through the half-open doorway, his entourage following close behind.

"Admiral Kane," So-Elku said with no attempt to hide his blatant disgust. The Luma leader stood in the circular room's center with his arms crossed. Far fewer elders surrounded him than during their last meeting in this place.

Moldark made a show of looking around as he approached So-Elku. "Where is everyone? I seem to recall there being more to your court than this."

"What do you want, Kane?"

"That's it?" Moldark turned and looked up to the domed ceiling above. His troopers spread out and encircled So-Elku and his Luma. "Where is the hospitality? Where is the peace-filled plea of entreaty? I thought the Order of Luma extended more of a welcome than—well, than *this*." Moldark flung his hands up and sneered at So-Elku.

"The Order does when the audience merits it," replied So-Elku.

"Merits it?" Moldark continued to turn, taking in the hall. "And does not the lord of the Paragon merit it?"

So-Elku squinted at the title, just as Moldark suspected he would. "Lord of what?"

The dark lord snapped back to look at So-Elku. "The Paragon, the reign of perfect rule, that which has supplanted your feeble Republic."

"I have no more allegiance to the Galactic Republic than—"

Moldark hissed at So-Elku. "Lying is unbecoming, Master Luma. You should know this."

"And your presence is unbecoming."

"Yes, especially considering that I am still alive."

So-Elku hesitated. "What do you want?"

"Ah, ah, ah. You must give an account for your transgressions against me." Moldark walked toward So-Elku and began circling him. The other elders did not attempt to stop him, no doubt remembering what Moldark did to the last man who'd tried.

"Whatever are you talking about?" So-Elku said, eyes darting to follow Moldark's route.

"You and I, we had a deal. You were to eliminate the Circle of Nine. Instead, what did you do?" So-Elku did not reply, so Moldark pressed him again. "What did you do, So-Elku?" Again, the Luma failed to respond. "No? Then I will proclaim your shortcomings to the cosmos. You betrayed me. You aligned yourself with them, gave them information, and attempted to thwart *me*—Moldark."

"Who?"

"Silence!" Moldark reached out and touched So-Elku's soul—not enough to suck him dry, but enough to make the man stiffen. "Do you deny your betrayal, human seed?"

So-Elku stood on his toes, chin raised. Veins bulged in his neck as he struggled to breath. "I—do—not."

"There now," Moldark said, releasing the man.

So-Elku collapsed to the ground and gasped for breath.

"You see? Truth-telling has its rewards, though it will not

spare you for long. For when I am done with the Jujari, I will turn my eyes toward Capriana, and then here to Worru. Your species and all those like you deserve extinction, Luma Master. And I won't stop until I've made it so."

"You are deranged, Kane," So-Elku said between coughs. "You're a menace and must be stopped. The Nine will see to it."

"A menace?" Moldark's eyes widened. "And still with this Kane business." He *tsk'd* the Luma Master and squatted in front of him. Then, placing a finger beneath his chin, he raised the man's head. "Do you really think I'm a menace, Luma Master? Is that what you see when you look at me in your beloved Unity? A menace? Because I can assure you, I am far worse."

Moldark reached out to three Luma elders and drank. The mortals writhed, and their shrieks added to the satisfaction he took in draining energy from their souls.

So-Elku's face shook as he stared into Moldark's eyes, wincing as the men's bones clattered to the marble floor. Moldark marveled at just how many bones the human body contained, never realizing the scope until they came to a rest in a jumble on the ground, half-hidden by the men's robes.

Moldark stretched his neck and then looked at the remaining elders. They were petrified, faces betraying a level of terror that Moldark found... *fitting*.

"If you've come to kill me, be done with it," So-Elku said, lowering his head.

"Kill you?" Moldark tilted his head. "Perhaps I will."

"That isn't why you've come?"

"No, but we can amend that."

So-Elku squinted at Moldark. "Then what do you want?"

"I want *her*."

"Her?" So-Elku's eyes snapped up. "I—I don't know what you're talking about."

"He means me," said a small voice from across the hall.

"Piper, stay back," So-Elku cried.

Moldark looked across the room and saw Piper standing by herself near a small doorway. So-Elku made to protest again, but Moldark exerted some energy and sent So-Elku to the ground in a spasm. "Come here, child. Don't be afraid."

"I'm not afraid of you," she replied, but the look on her face seemed to say otherwise.

Moldark tilted his head back and forth as his eyes searched the tiny human's body. He could feel the power emanating from her. Wave upon wave, her life force washed over him beyond any he'd ever sensed before, second only to the Norxük, of course. How this human had come by such power was beyond him. But he had found her—at long last, he'd finally found her.

"Release him," she said, pointing to So-Elku.

Moldark turned to examine the man writhing on the marble floor. "Why?"

"Or else I won't go with you," she said. "That is what you want, isn't it?"

"I have come to take you, yes."

"Then release him, and I'll go with you."

Suddenly, from somewhere deep within, Moldark felt his elemental presence lurch. It was as if some otherworldly force bumped into him, contending for his soul's place of preeminence. In his mortal body, Moldark felt as if he might wretch —an annoying human function which he despised. But internally, the discomfort was even more considerable. Then, without the ability to stop it, a voice came from his mouth— one he hadn't heard in quite some time.

"Is it really you?" the voice asked.

Piper scrunched up her nose, peering at Moldark with some measure of confusion.

No, Moldark said within. *You will not speak!*

But Kane's will pushed around him and even made Moldark kneel, hand extended toward the child. "Piper, I'm your—"

No! Moldark ordered within. *You have no permission.* Suddenly, Moldark yanked control from Kane and forced his body off the floor with a violent jerk. Piper let out a tiny yelp and jumped back.

"Come with me, child," Moldark said, back in control once more.

"Release him," she said, more forcefully this time.

"But he has kept you against your will and sought to kill your kin."

"But he does not deserve to die," Piper replied.

"Curse your kind," Moldark spat. "You all deserve to die."

"Still, release him, or I will not go with you."

Moldark knew better than to threaten the child. She could stop him if she wanted—or worse. But whether or not she knew such things was a different story. He suspected that if she knew about her powers, he wouldn't be negotiating with her. But since she was, it was probably best to abide by her wishes. For now, anyway. "As you wish."

Moldark released So-Elku from his leash. The man gagged, vomited, and then cried as he took in terrific lungfuls of air. *Pathetic, sniveling fool*, Moldark thought.

"Thank you," Piper said.

"Now we go," Moldark replied.

"Yes. Now we can go."

———

"You want my help for something, don't you," the girl said.

She marched beside him as they walked through the vaulted hallway leading out of the Grand Arielina with Moldark's four platoons following close behind them. "You are perceptive, child," Moldark replied. "I do."

"Then I have one more condition before I agree."

Moldark looked down at her. "You used it to free So-Elku."

"No one said I only had one."

"There are no more conditions. Come."

"No," Piper said. She stopped and folded her arms. The troopers halted as their armor smacked together.

Surely this infernal being knew her powers were strong or else she would not test Moldark like this. He seethed within but knew better than to push this child too far. At least, not yet. "What is it?"

"I wish you to give me a ship."

"A ship?"

"Yeah."

Moldark's lip curled. "Why do you want a ship?"

"When we're done doing whatever you want, I want a ship. No questions questioned."

"I think you mean no questions asked."

"Nope. The way I said it."

"No questions questioned?"

"Yup."

Moldark knew the mortal child would most likely not survive the plans he had for her. And if she did, well, he'd execute her himself. But he remained curious about whatever her goal was, so he'd let the bargaining continue. It may even work in his favor—if she intended to do what he suspected she did. "And what do you intend to do with this ship?"

"That's my business," she replied.

"But it's my ship."

"You need help doing something, and I need a ship. If you can't agree to that, then there's no deal."

Moldark made a show of looking around in frustration. "Fine," he said at last. "You have yourself a deal. Now, can we please continue to the transports?" He gestured outside toward the shuttles waiting beyond the front courtyard.

"Do you swear it?"

"Swear what?"

"Swear that you'll give me a ship?"

Moldark rolled his neck, trying to relieve the tension building in his shoulders. "I swear it."

"On your ancestors' graves?"

Moldark eyed the child with some level of curiosity. This was a strange custom.

She put out a hand as if offering him some invisible trinket. "Swear your eternal soul to be bound to their graves, or else I'm not getting on your shuttle out there."

"I swear it," Moldark said at last. "Now, can we go?"

"Sure." Piper turned down the long carpet and headed for the door without him.

WITH THE CHILD stowed in his private quarters, Moldark proceeded to the *Peregrine's* bridge. The main holo screen displayed an image of Worru from orbit. Moldark resisted the urge to incinerate the capital city and bury So-Elku forever, because he knew the child would sense it. He needed her to believe in Admiral Kane—to believe that he was good. *All in due time*, he thought to himself.

Captain Ellis greeted him with a salute. "Your lordship, I have information for you pertaining to—"

"I'm not interested." Moldark waved a hand at the man. "Take us out of the system."

"But sir, it's about the Republic ships we saw departing."

Perhaps he was interested, at least tentatively. "Speak."

"Our sensors detected the two troop transports leave orbit and then vanish."

"A subspace jump, Captain."

"That's just it, my lord. There was no jump signature and no wake pattern."

Moldark narrowed his eyes at the captain.

"I know, sir," Ellis said, seeming to sense Moldark's reservations. "I triple checked the data personally to make sure it was accurate. And still all sensors show that—"

"They entered a void horizon."

"Yes, my lord."

"What were the coordinates?"

Ellis waved at someone behind the navigation console, and a few seconds later, a star chart filled the main holo screen. "Here, my lord. On the other side of the planet adjacent to us."

"What are you up to?" Moldark whispered. He puzzled over why the Republic might be colluding with the rebels. Was this So-Elku's doing? But the more he thought about it, the more Moldark realized such a partnership seemed unlikely. For if something official had been sanctioned, more than two troop transports would have left the planet. Plus, he'd taken possession of the child. If Moldark played this right, he might get everything he wanted all at once, and that thought made him smile.

"Leave it," Moldark said to Ellis.

"But, my lord—"

"We have what we need," Moldark spat. "Return to the *Labyrinth*."

Ellis saluted. "As you have commanded, my lord."

13

MAGNUS CROUCHED behind four fire teams of ex-Marines as they fired their new NOV1s downrange. The men took cover behind burnt-out skiffs, clad in their newly manufactured Novian armor, only without the luxury of chameleon mode—at least not yet. The teams sent blaster bolts downrange in steady waves, firing on a well-armed enemy. Explosions erupted in the distance as the powerful sounds of destruction echoed off the skyscrapers and seemed to shake sand from the pale clouds.

The city-scape was a replica of Oosafar, and one Magnus had fought through before. It was accurate right down to the odor of urine and soured milk—scents that the helmets ported into the armor's air filters. But instead of fighting Tawnhack, Selskirt, or Clawnip, his new gladia were shooting at Repub Marines clad in black Mark V armor. Three white stripes over their left-side pauldron designated them as Paragon troopers. The enemy was well-fortified behind gun nests that they'd set up ahead of time. The emplacements ran along the sidewalks with a few atop the lower buildings. Likewise, they used vehicle-mounted M109 twin-barrel blasters, a MUT50, 50mm ultra torrent tri-reticulating blaster, and a 70mm RBMB—Really Big Missile Battery.

The old man certainly isn't going easy on them, Magnus thought to himself.

There was a break in the enemy's return fire, so the squad leader ordered his units to advance. Troopers crouched low and then peeled away from the skiffs, covered by their peers. But the enemy read the field too, targeting the exposed fighters as they moved down the road. A man dashing for a shipping container had his legs blown out from beneath him. He flipped once in the air, and then his chest slammed into the pavement with a loud *crack*. A second man took a blaster bolt to the shoulder that spun his body in a complete circle before he fell. And a third trooper fell forward from a gutshot, only to be blown backward by a secondary headshot.

Still, the squad leader pushed the advance, and the majority of his gladia made it to their next position behind a weathered concrete half-wall. Blaster fire whizzed overhead as the leader gave orders. Magnus smelled the sharp scent of burnt ozone, an odor that made the hair on the back of his neck stand up. He waited to see what the team might try, forcing old battlefield memories to stay buried—they had a pesky way of making him micromanage certain scenarios.

Suddenly, the squads dispersed into nearby buildings, and none too soon: a 70mm missile from **RBMB** streaked down the street, leaving a white plume of expended fuel in its wake. The half-wall exploded in a spray of fire and rock just as the last gladia left the structure's cover. The concussion shook the nearby buildings and knocked two gladia to the ground. But they scrambled to their feet and joined the forces advancing into the premises.

As the squad split up, Magnus switched his helmet's **HUD** to merge thermal imaging with sensor relay tracking. One squad returned to the streets where they took cover behind various obstructions lining the sidewalks. Another squad cleared a row of buildings, using interior doors between structures as a means of advancing toward the enemy. The third and final fire team—having absorbed the sole survivor of the fourth fire team—advanced along the rooftops.

The street-level squad drew the enemy's fire and kept the more massive weapons busy. They continued to dive in and out of the buildings to avoid the heavy ordinance. Missiles blew considerable holes in several structures while the M109 raked the sidewalks.

Inside the buildings, the second fire team made good time in clearing rooms and moving toward the intersection. The heaviest pocket of resistance came from three Paragon Marines who'd taken cover inside a Jujari kitchen. The enemy sent streams of blaster fire through the doorway, pinning the gladias down. But it wasn't long before someone tossed a variable output detonator into the room. The explosion was enough to remove the threat but not enough to cause a cave-in, which would have resulted in the squad taking the long way around—wasting precious time.

The third fire team made the fastest time, moving unobstructed across the building tops. Three of the four gladias took sniper positions along the street while the fourth stayed back to call out targets and watch for enemy fire. The setup was good, Magnus thought. But as he checked the time on the master clock, he guessed the unit wouldn't reach their objective in time. And he wasn't the only one either.

"Pick up the pace," Forbes bellowed from some unseen perch. "You're burning through time like you're on vacation!"

The captain's words added a new level of intensity to the squad's movements, causing them to make a few critical errors. One came in the form of a gladia popping onto a sidewalk without looking downrange first. The blaster bolt that killed him struck him in the helmet and flipped his body backward like a rag doll. Another gladia, this one on the roof, failed to hear the spotter call out an incoming missile—he was too preoccupied with a perfect shot on the M109 gunner. And the shot would have been a kill shot too, had the missile not blown a crater in the parapet the gladia hid behind. His body flew backward, landed, and then was sucked down the hole in the crumbling roof. He screamed until his simulated vital readouts muted his comm.

The remaining members of the squad pressed forward as Forbes began counting down the seconds. Several more gladias went down, some walking into enemy fire in hasty attempts to beat the clock.

"That's time," Forbes said. "End simulation."

Instantly, the Jujari landscape vanished and the hard-light emitters powered down, easing anyone on elevated positions back to ground level. All sixteen gladia collected themselves. Half got off the hangar bay floor and stretched their bodies, some rotating shoulders or favoring one leg over the other. The other half stowed their NOV1s and removed their helmets.

Forbes ordered the squad to fall in and make a circle around him. "Better than last time," the captain said, taking off his helmet. "But still not what it needs to be." Then Forbes went through the evolution's after-action review, covering three positives and three points for improvement. The captain's keen insights gave the gladia plenty to think about as the squad reset the simulation and prepped to rerun it.

Magnus caught Forbes's eye and waved him over. The two men stepped out of the enclosed combat-simulation environment, allowing the squad to get into position. "What do you think about the ECSE?" Magnus asked.

"Never seen anything like it," Forbes replied, his black hair matted down with sweat. "Sure beats the board and brick sets the Repub cobs together."

"Makes for believable combat scenarios," Magnus added.

"You can say that again. I have three guys who need medical attention from the hard-light emitters."

"Nothing motivates you to keep your head down like

pain."

"I feel that," Forbes said, rubbing the back of his neck.

"And the new armor and weapons?" Magnus asked.

"Gonna take some getting used to, but in a good way. This tech blows ours out of the water."

"And you're only running simulated rounds at 10% of the weapon's fire rate. Wait until you see it in action."

"I already did." Forbes pointed to his ears. "Remember?"

Magnus laughed. "Sorry about that."

"Payback's a bitch."

Over the last three days, Forbes had undergone cellular reconstruction therapy for his blown-out eardrums. He'd used the downtime to brief his team leaders and prep them for command within the newly restructured Gladio Umbra. The men in this simulation were those who would oversee platoons in Forbes's Taursar Company, the newly created rifle company under Colonel Caldwell's command.

"Azelon should have manufacturing done on the rest of your company's equipment within the next few days," Magnus said. "The colonel will let you know when your platoons can outfit in the armory."

"Sounds good. They're still getting briefed on this whole scenario anyway."

"How are they taking it?"

"Better than I expected. Then again, they *are* on an alien ship being briefed by *the* Colonel Caldwell and Lieutenant Magnus. Kinda hard to ignore that sales pitch."

"Worked on you too, it seems."

"And then someone went and blew out my ears."

Magnus chuckled again. "Not living that one down anytime soon, am I."

"Not a chance, Lieutenant." Forbes paused, and his smile disappeared. "So you've really asked the colonel to take over your spot leading the Gladio Umbra?"

"Wouldn't you?"

Forbes shrugged. "Hell yeah. But then again, I've never built a force of resistance fighters made up of several different species to take on the Galactic Republic."

"And the Luma," Magnus reminded him.

"And the Luma."

"The way I see it, I need someone who knows what they're doing, and I don't have enough time to learn it myself," Magnus said. "Who better to lead it than a seasoned veteran?"

"That kind of attitude is what gets guys promoted, you know."

"I don't need any more of that," Magnus said with a smile.

"So, where does that leave you?"

"I'm in charge of Granther Company, like before."

"And you're at home there," Forbes stated.

"Sure am. The old man says he has an idea to re-task it as a special operations unit, which I can run like a Recon platoon. Colonel says he wants to fill it out with some of the original members, calling them elites based on their expertise and experience. We'll see what he has up his sleeve."

"Aren't you fancy."

"Well, you still outrank me, Captain."

"And don't you forget it."

"I have a feeling you won't let me."

"Damn straight." Forbes brought his helmet around like he was about to put it back on. "I'm gonna get going. But Magnus?"

"Yeah?"

"Thanks for bringing us along for the ride."

"Thanks for saying yes. The alternative was I'd have to kill you."

"Like you'd have gotten a shot off."

"I had you dead to rights in your dining room," Magnus protested.

"Your weapon was on the table, Lieutenant."

Magnus gave Forbes a confused look. "And?"

"Mine was under it." Forbes covered his head, nodded at Magnus, and stepped back into the ECSE.

OVER THE LAST FEW DAYS, Colonel Caldwell had turned one of the *Spire's* largest conference rooms into his new battalion headquarters. He'd brought in several workstations for secretaries and administrators, and even asked Azelon if he could push two walls out to expand the room's capacity. The Novian AI was only too happy to comply, giving the colonel whatever he needed and making her share of recommendations.

By the time Magnus checked back on the colonel, dozens of holo displays filled with charts, personnel rosters, equipment profiles, and ship schematics lined the walls. Three administrative assistants hovered over glowing tabletops, and another pair of operators monitored data streams. Meanwhile, Azelon stood beside the colonel, lost in conversation about something above Magnus's pay grade.

The site made Magnus's heart swell. He'd been right to do this—to ask the colonel to take the lead. There was simply no way Magnus would have known where to start, let alone how to organize everything that was happening here. *And we're not even engaged with the enemy yet*, he noted.

But something else stood out to Magnus. The colonel looked different. Something had changed in the man's face. His eyes were alert, and he was—*smiling*—well, at least as much as a colonel could. But the man had a spring in his step again.

Magnus understood then. Caldwell wasn't deskbound on some peacekeeping mission on Worru, nor was he stuck babysitting a company of troopers in a remote non-action scenario. No, he was back in the thick of it, organizing resources for war. Where the blinking charts and number streams would have overwhelmed lesser Marines, Caldwell seemed like he was loving every second. *He's like a new man*, Magnus reasoned.

Suddenly, the colonel noticed Magnus and invited him toward the central black mapping table that took up a large portion of the room.

"Looks like you've made yourself at home, Colonel," Magnus said.

"It's hard not to with all new toys," the colonel replied with a smile. "Let me show you what we've got."

Magnus joined Caldwell and Azelon as the conference room lights dimmed. The other administrators quieted down as the colonel filled the tabletop with a three-dimensional schematic of the *Spire*. Then, from various sections of the ship, charts emerged to show troop rosters, supply lists, and various mission readiness status indicators.

"Holy hell," Magnus said. "You... you did all this in the last few days?"

"Wasn't all me, son. Miss Smarty Pants here made herself a damn fine addition to my admin team."

"Again, Colonel, my designation is Azelon."

"Which is why I call you Smarty Pants."

"And yet pants are neither items I wear nor are they sentient, so they are incapable of intelligence. I regret to say that don't follow your logic, sir."

"Probably best you try not to, Azie," Magnus replied.

The bot tilted her head and then nodded at Magnus. "Very well, Magnus."

The colonel pulled up a master list and expanded it. "We'll start here at the top. The Gladio Umbra now has seven companies, which include your special units company, two rifle companies, a support and intel company, a starfighter attack air wing, naval operations, and last but not least, your mystics."

Magnus whistled in appreciation. "Can you go through it all with me?"

"I thought you'd never ask, son." Caldwell started with Granther Company, which caused a section near the ship's bridge to glow. A smaller window came forward and listed twenty-six names in five sections. "You're leading Granther Company's first and only platoon right now. You've got yourself five teams ranging from Alpha to Echo. Each one consists of a Jujari, a rifleman, a mystic, a sniper, and a combination medic and demolition specialist."

"And the thinking behind it?"

"Turns out those damn hyenas have a pack ability."

"Something like a sixth sense in the Unity," Azelon added.

"Right," Caldwell said. "Allows them to sense each other and communicate emotionally. I figured that if there's one on each team, you've got yourself an extra layer of communication if something goes south."

"Well I just learned something new."

"Me too, son. Again, Smarty Pants here brought the attribute to my attention."

Azelon looked at Magnus as if to protest the nickname, but Magnus gave her a look that suggested she'd better stay quiet.

"I've given you Rohoar, Saladin, Cyzy, Longchamps, and Grahban for Jujari," Caldwell said. "For riflemen, there's Abimbola, Titus, Zoll, Bliss, and Robillard. They'll also act as your team leaders."

"Copy that." Magnus's eyes scanned the lists. "I see Awen

here listed as a mystic. But who are Nídira, Wish, Telwin, and Findermith?"

"Additions from Willowood's people," Caldwell said. "She said they were the best, so I figured you should take them."

"I'm grateful."

"For snipers, you've got Silk, Dutch, Reimer, Bettger, and Jaffrey."

"Nice. And the demo and medics?"

"Doc Campbell, Nubs, Rix, Dozer, and Handley."

"Nubs? A medic?" Magnus's eyebrows went up. "Kid's missing more than one finger."

"Abimbola vouched for him. Said he's got plenty of med training. But—yeah—he's gonna be more demo than surgeon."

Magnus chuckled. "Sounds about right."

"Next, you have Taursar Company."

"That's Forbes," Magnus said, noting the series of glowing hangar bays allotted to the captain.

Caldwell nodded. "Three fifty-man platoons. Followed by Hedgebore Company with another three platoons, led by Lieutenant Nelson." Another row of hangar bays glowed.

"Nelson's one of your former LTs?"

"He's *still* one my LTs, just a different insignia." Caldwell gave Magnus a crooked smile. "Next up is Drambull Company under Azelon's supervision." A large section near the ship's aft illuminated. "This is our support and intel company. First Platoon is under Cyril's command."

"Couldn't make a better choice for intel," Magnus noted.

"So I hear. Haven't met the kid yet, but Smarty Pants says he's got the right stuff."

"Yes," Azelon said. "As I informed the colonel, Cyril has demonstrated a high degree of—"

"I'm familiar with Cyril's code slicing abilities. Let's keep going."

Caldwell nodded. "Second Platoon is a logistics unit lead by Abimbola's righthand man, Berouth."

"Another good choice," Magnus said.

"And Third Platoon is a fighter support unit lead by our old pal Gilder."

"The guy can fix anything."

"So I hear. I'm attaching Third Platoon to Fang Company. Since all our forces are based on the *Spire*, it makes sense to spread Gilder's units out over all three squadrons until we have more numbers. If and when we do, I'll reallocate units to squadrons directly."

"Tell me about Fang Company."

"This is where TO-96 comes in, sir," Azelon said.

Magnus couldn't be sure, but it seemed like the bot spoke about TO-96 with some measure of pride. "Lay it on me, Azie."

"Lay what on you, sir?"

Magnus closed his eyes and let out a small laugh. "Tell me about TO-96 and his unit's composition."

"Ah, I see. *Laying it on someone* is a turn of phrase for expounding on a given topic."

Magnus chuckled. "Be sure to explain that to Awen next

time you see her."

Azelon perked up. "Duly noted, sir. Thank you for the action item."

"You're an evil son of a bitch," Caldwell whispered to Magnus.

"Ain't it grand?"

"As I was about to say, TO-96 will be overseeing Fang Company, which is composed of three squadrons: Red, Gold, and Blue," the bot said. "Each squadron is comprised of fourteen Novian Fangs—as you may have guessed from the aptly termed company name. The squadrons will be commanded by Mr. Ricio, Mr. Nolan, and Mr. Ezo, respectively. Ricio has already begun training new pilots recommended to him from Captain Forbes's and Lieutenant Nelson's Marine companies. It seems there were some air wing candidates in their ranks already."

"How convenient," Magnus said.

"As well as serendipitous, fortuitous, auspicious, providential, and charming," the bot added.

"Charming?"

Azelon eyed Magnus with a robotic look of suspicion. "Is it not charming, sir?"

Magnus smiled. "I suppose it depends on your definition. And given your cheerful optimism, I'd say charming works just fine."

"Thank you, sir."

"Additionally, Mr. Ricio will act as a field commander under TO-96, given his familiarity with naval combat. Were he not such an experienced pilot, I would have him relieve TO-96 altogether, but Ricio is far too valuable in the cockpit to retain him on the *Spire*."

"Raptor Company is our naval operations unit," Caldwell said. The bridge and its surrounding deck illuminated. "Azelon will lead this unit, naturally. I've designated Command and Fire Support divisions, with your two boys Flow and Cheeks in the latter. As per your request, there are no Jujari in that company."

"Thank you, Colonel," Magnus said with a grateful tone. "Appreciated."

"I might be running the show, but you still gave me the budget, son."

"Money talks."

"And always will," Caldwell said with a wink.

"What about this last unit—Paladia Company?"

"Willowood tells me it has some special meaning to the Luma," Caldwell said. "This unit organization is all her doing too." The colonel pulled up a window attached to a section in the *Spire's* belly. "The company has forty mystics recovered from the Luma we rescued in the catacombs. They're broken into three cadres of fourteen, fourteen, and twelve."

"And Awen didn't want to join her?" Magnus asked, his voice rising further than he'd intended it to.

Caldwell shook his head. "I put her with Willowood at first, but she insisted on being with you. And might I say that while she looks small, well… she's a fierce one."

"Tell me something I don't know."

Azelon's eyes lit up. "Are you aware of advanced interpolation architecture that governs the outer—"

"It was a rhetorical statement," Magnus said. It was uncanny how many of TO-96's mannerisms she'd picked up.

The bot's shoulders shrugged. "I see."

Magnus looked back at Caldwell. "What about Sootriman and Saasarr?"

"Well"—Caldwell moved his cigar to the other corner of his mouth—"I figured the mistress of Ki Nar Four might like to lead her people if she recruits any from that mystic's forsaken back-world. Hell if I'll know what to do with them."

"Fair enough. And I'm guessing that includes the Reptalon?"

Caldwell nodded. "Not saying I can't implement the lizard somewhere, but until I hear back from her, there's no sense organizing around what I don't know."

"Fair enough." Magnus looked to Azelon. "Any word from them?"

"Not yet, sir. But Awen has only just recently left to create a new quantum tunnel for them and close the existing one over Worru. That said, *Geronimo Nine's* transponder is still active. Its latest ping placed it on Ki Nar Four. With the time dilation, it may be another day or two before we hear from them."

"Understood." Magnus changed topics. "How are weapons and armor coming along?"

"I'll let Smarty Pants answer that one," Caldwell said.

"I have completed manufacturing enough weapons and

armor to get the two rifle companies operational," Azelon said.

"That's about what I told Forbes already," Magnus replied.

"Says she's got a few additional surprises for us too," the colonel added.

"I like the sound of that." Magnus turned to Azleon. "What about the NBTI?"

"I will begin adapting your forces when you command."

"How long will it take to integrate everyone?"

"Barring any additional biologics added by Sootriman, I will be able to update your entire force in 9.2813 days common."

"Thanks for the specificity, Azie."

"My pleasure, sir."

Caldwell removed his cigar. "An NBT—what now?"

"Novia biotech interface. It allows us to take advantage of some additional features on the Novian weapons."

"As well as the Fangs," Azelon added. "It also increases the armor's efficiency and life-support capabilities. Additionally, it allows every gladia to be integrated with the Novia Defense Architecture, or NDA, since TO-96 tells me how you love your acronyms."

"Don't tell me that she's gotta drill into our brains or some such splick," Caldwell said.

"The NBTI does require minor physical modifications, Colonel," Azelon replied. "But I can assure you that the invasion is both minimal and reversible."

"Do I need it to do my job?"

"That depends on how efficiently you would like to interface with your units, Colonel."

"I think that's a yes, sir," Magnus said.

"Mysticsdammit," the colonel said as he shoved his cigar back in his mouth.

"How about the Fangs?" Magnus asked, changing topics. "Are they in production too?"

"I already have three squadrons in inventory," Azelon said. "Ricio is checking them out as we speak."

"How *charming*." Magnus noticed Azelon's eyes warm at the word. The truth was, Magnus felt pretty warm himself. He couldn't have been happier about how everything was going—and all thanks to having an incredible team. It seemed just a few short months ago that he was alone with Awen, fighting their way through Oorajee. Now, he had a starship, a battalion, and people he could trust. Maybe their efforts to stop Moldark and So-Elku wouldn't be in vain after all. Granted, there was still plenty of work to be done. *But at least now*, Magnus thought, *we have a chance.*

Magnus put a hand on Caldwell's shoulder and then gestured at the holo display with the *Spire's* schematic and the Gladio Umbra's new roster. "Thank you, colonel. For all of this."

"You're welcome." Caldwell turned to Magnus and shook his hand. "And thank *you* for giving an old man another chance to kick some ass."

14

"END SIMULATION," Magnus said and removed his helmet. The hard-light emitters cycled down, and the streets of Capriana disappeared.

"Nice audible with the left flank idea," Dutch said to Rohoar as the system lowered her to the ground. She'd been perched in a blown-out fifth-story window in an office building, sniping Paragon troopers holed up in a corner restaurant.

"I smelled fresh meat in my helmet," Rohoar said, licking his lips. "And I was hungry. So they seemed like a good target."

"Well, it worked."

"And what is this audible you speak of?" Rohoar asked.

Dutch wrinkled her forehead at him in disbelief. "You don't watch spaceball? A play called on the fly?"

"If you are referring to how I gave Abimbola the idea for

the flanking maneuver through the use of my voice and his ear, then I understand. Also, there were no flies in this simulation, nor any spaceballs."

"Good grief," Dutch said.

"Okay, Granther Company," Magnus said, trying to get everyone's attention. "Bring it in."

Magnus's platoon of five teams had been running evolutions for the last four days straight. They'd taken breaks for meals and a few hours of sleep each night. But otherwise, they'd been on their deck's ECSE nonstop. Not that Magnus was complaining. Since Caldwell had restructured Granther Company, Magnus had been keen on getting as much time with his gladias in their new fire team composition as he could. And the work was paying off.

"You looked good out there," Magnus said. "You worked well as teams and as a platoon."

"Yeah," Robillard, Echo Team's rifleman, said. "And Handley even decided to run a little today."

"That's 'cause you kept poking me in the ass with your weapon," Handley replied. "What were you hoping to find up there?"

"Couldn't tell ya," Robillard replied. "Your butt was too fat to see past."

"And you enjoyed the view, didn't you?"

"Save it for later," Magnus said amidst a round of laughter. When everyone quieted down, he asked, "What do you think of the new NBTI addition?"

"Makes it easier to see each other," Zoll said, standing with Charlie Team. "And gives us a better comm control."

"Right," Magnus said, nodding. "What else?"

"Navigation seemed improved," Dozer offered from Delta Team.

"And targeting," Silk added, tapping the top of her new sniper rifle.

Azelon had invited Silk to assist in the weapon's design. She even helped name it, much to Magnus's surprise. The extended range blaster had been dubbed the CK360. "Confirmed kills all around," Silk said with a wide grin when she'd handed Magnus the first production model. It was twice the length of the NOV1, but almost half the weight. And while it was considerably slower than the NOV1's blistering 3,000 round-per-second maximum fire rate, it was twice as powerful. The CK360 delivered a whopping two megajoules of energy to targets up to nine kilometers away with less than 5% energy degradation. That, combined with its NBTI controlled sight and target tracking feature, made it the most formidable long-range infantry weapon on any battlefield in the quadrant.

"You had some excellent *confirmed kills* out there, Silk," Magnus said, using the weapon's namesake on purpose.

"Thank you, sir."

Dutch raised a hand. "When will Azelon let us use the multi-target fire effect mode?"

"Hell yeah," Rix echoed. "I wanna see this gimbaled barrel in action."

"Soon enough," Magnus answered. "We don't want anyone getting lazy out here."

"Tell that to Handley," Robillard said.

"I swear to mystics," Handley replied. "I'm gonna pound your damned teeth in so hard you'll be pooping dental floss for a week."

Everyone laughed when Magnus noticed the colonel step into the hangar bay along with Ricio. Caldwell waved Magnus over. "Let's take ten minutes to hydrate and stretch," Magnus ordered. "And Robillard?"

"Yeah?"

"You've got some dental floss hanging out the back of your suit."

"ANY UPDATE FROM AWEN?" Magnus asked the colonel.

"Said she opened the new tunnel for *Geronimo*. Sootriman's inbound, and it looks like she'll be arriving within the hour."

"And is the warlord of Ki Nar Four saying what she's bringing with her?"

"Negative," Caldwell replied. "Communication through the void horizon is limited to her transponder's beacon."

Magnus nodded. Subspace communication was hard enough as it was; he guessed inter-universal connectivity was even more temperamental.

"And how are things here?" the colonel asked, pointing to Granther Company.

"We're getting there," Magnus said. "Someone decided to change up the fire team composition on me, so…"

"I thought you might like the challenge."

"Yeah, 'cause that's just what I need right now." Magnus laughed and then shook his head. "But it's gonna be good, Colonel. The special teams structure is letting everyone's best rise to the surface. Just gotta work on building trust and communication."

"Like any good marriage," Ricio added.

"I wouldn't know," Magnus replied. "But I'll take your word for it. How are things with you?"

Ricio gave Magnus a devilish grin. "Excellent, Lieutenant."

"Really?"

"I thought the Fang was pretty good before, back when I helped rescue your asses on Worru…"

"Here he goes again," Magnus said, looking at Caldwell.

"Aces," Caldwell said. "Go figure."

Ricio smiled, undeterred. "But now with the biotech interface"—he whistled—"there's no weapons platform that can compete with it."

"That good, huh?" Magnus turned to Caldwell. "See? Look what happens when you let Azelon drill into your head."

Caldwell shook his head. "All in due time, son."

Magnus looked back at Ricio. "And your pilots?"

"They're doing well. A few have some previous flying experience, but most don't."

"That's gotta be rough," Magnus offered.

"Actually, you'd be surprised. Flying a Fang with the NBTI isn't like flying any other platform. So if you've never flown before, you have an advantage of sorts."

"No bad habits to break," Magnus said.

"Exactly. Azelon and I get to train them from the ground up. Of course, we won't be fully operational until TO-96 and Ezo get back, but that won't be long by the sounds of it."

"Sounds like everything's coming together, Colonel," Magnus said.

The old man spun in a cigar in his mouth. "Ee-yuht. Gonna be one hell of a fighting force when all's said and done. Couple more months to get the kinks worked out, and then a year before its smooth sailing."

Magnus eyed the colonel. "You do realize that timeline is—"

"A pipe dream, son. Of course, I do. What, do you think I popped out of my old lady's victory canal yesterday?"

"Victory canal?" Ricio asked, eyes wide.

"Nah," the colonel said to his point. "I just like to imagine how good it'd be if we did this the right way, not the necessary way. We might not be the most well-oiled machine when all is said and done, but we'll be ready to spank any limp-dick numbnut who points a gun at us."

"I'm still stuck on *victory canal*," Ricio said, looking at Magnus. "Anyone?"

"You get used to his one-liners," Magnus said.

"Somehow, I don't believe you."

A notification from Azelon interrupted their conversation.

Magnus saw it pop up in his bioteknia eyes, so he raised a finger at Caldwell and Ricio. "It's Azelon." He accepted the incoming comm request. "Go for Magnus."

"Lieutenant, I see the Colonel with you," Azelon said.

"He is."

"Forgive me using you as a passthrough but—"

"But until he lets you drill a hole in his head"—Magnus glared at Caldwell—"you can't speak with him directly and need to use me as your dummy."

Caldwell chewed on his cigar in irritation but said nothing.

"I wasn't going to put it so harshly, sir," Azelon replied. "But, essentially, yes."

"I read you. Whaddya got for us?"

"Sootriman, Ezo, and TO-96 have entered the system on *Geronimo Nine*."

Magnus repeated the information to Caldwell and Ricio. "And what about Saasarr?" he asked Azelon.

"He does not appear to be on the vessel, Lieutenant. Sootriman indicated that the Reptalon has been employed on another mission of her bidding."

"Fair enough." Magnus hesitated. "Any other ships with her?"

"Negative, sir. That's something she wishes to tell you about in person."

"Bad news then."

"What bad news?" Caldwell asked. But Magnus held up a

hand, and then made a motion with his finger like a drill bit going into the colonel's temple. Caldwell batted it away.

"I don't believe it is bad news, no," Azelon said. "Rather, her activity requires additional time to bring about the intended result. I believe you call it delayed gratification, in your parlance."

"I like it when you talk dirty to me, Azie."

"Talk dirty, sir?"

"Eh—talk to Awen about that too."

"Very well, Lieutenant."

"Also, I want to know the moment Awen gets back from Ithnor Ithelia. I need her training with Alpha Team."

"Understood."

"Anything else?"

"Negative. Azelon out."

"Magnus out."

"So, Sootriman's back," Caldwell said. "What'd she bring me?"

"Nothing yet," Magnus said. "But she's got something coming."

Caldwell gave an approving nod. "I like a woman who knows how to keep things interesting."

"If anyone knows how to do that, it's Sootriman." Magnus glanced at Ricio. "Time for you to get ready to receive your new company commander and squadron leader."

15

"ARE YOU COMFORTABLE, CHILD?" Moldark asked as he stepped into her quarters. Granted, the space was nothing more than a glorified cargo hold adjacent to his own converted observation deck. But he wanted her kept as close to him as possible while still providing the necessary separation humans seemed to require.

"It smells funny in here," Piper replied. She seemed to take refuge behind a blanket that she clutched in her hands.

"My apologies. I can have that addressed."

"And the bed isn't very comfortable."

"I will have my—"

"And the lights are too bright when they're all on, and too dark when they're all off. A night light would be nice."

He caught her eye. "Anything else?"

"I'm hungry," she said, looking away.

How this species tolerated raising their offspring was a mystery to Moldark. He'd just as soon devour the child than suffer her grating list of needs.

"I will have some food brought to you."

"Good food?"

Moldark's eyes twitched. "Is not all food meant for nourishment and therefore good?"

"You talk funny."

"What's wrong with the way I speak?"

"You use big words."

Moldark sighed. "Are we finished here?"

"Well, you're the one who asked to come in, so why are you asking me?"

The child was getting on his nerves, and they hadn't even been on the *Labyrinth* an hour. "Come with me."

Moldark turned from the doorway and moved toward his chair atop the dais. He looked out at the waning conflict with the Jujari and waited for the child. But she was slow in coming. She peered out of her quarters and blinked at him. The look on her face was a strange mix of fear and insubordination. He returned to the sight of starships at war and waited several moments until he heard the patter of small feet.

"Are those Jujari ships?" Piper asked, nearing the window.

Moldark nodded. "You recognize them?"

"Rohoar's looked like that," she replied. "He's my friend."

"And you're not scared of him, a Jujari?"

"Why?"

Moldark found her reply curious. The humans seemed to have an ages old hatred for the beasts born from an irrational fear of teeth and claws. "Because they are terrifying to you, are they not?"

"Terrifying?" Piper wrinkled her nose. "If you mean scary, no. Their teeth are sharp. But the rest of them is fluffy."

"Fluffy?"

Piper looked up at Moldark. "You've never petted one?"

"I can't say that I have, no."

"You should. They're nice." But then Piper seemed to grow concerned as her eyes examined the conflict. "Are you… are you blowing them up?"

Moldark realized that, given the child's unexpected love for the Novian descendants, answering the question truthfully may circumvent his goals. Subsequently, a new strategy presented itself. It was risky, and she might not be ready. But how would he know unless he tried? "I'm not blowing them up, no. But the Republic is."

"The Galactic Republic?"

"You've heard of them?"

"Of course." Piper's eyes seemed to grow distant. "My daddy was a senator."

"Then you know how much they hated the Jujari."

Piper nodded. "But aren't you part of the Republic? This is a navy ship, right?"

"I've actually been trying to stop the Republic."

"Stop them? From what?"

Moldark raised a hand toward the windowplex wall. "This. From killing the Jujari."

Piper squinted at him, and he feared she wasn't buying his claim. It was time to see what she could do. "You don't believe me?"

She shook her head.

"Very well." Moldark turned to face her and folded his arms. "You're a strong child. Stronger than anyone else you know."

Piper mimicked his posture and folded her arms. "Maybe."

"But you've been learning how to use your powers. In the Unity, that is."

"Maybe."

"So why don't you help them?" He pointed to the Jujari fleet.

"Help them?"

Moldark nodded.

"You... want me to try and help them? But I thought you were—"

"Trying to hurt them? I already told you, I want to stop the Republic." There was just enough truth to his lie that if she searched his mind—if she *could* search his mind—she might believe him.

"So, you want me to help them?"

"I could use the assistance."

"And that's why you brought me here?"

Moldark nodded. "My secret has been revealed."

Piper looked back at the battle playing out over Oorajee. "But what can I do?"

Moldark wondered if she was ready—if she knew the extent of her abilities. Of course, he was guessing. But what he sensed left little doubt in his mind that the child was able to do everything he supposed. And if not now, then soon. "Move them."

"What?"

Moldark turned and nodded at the ships. "Move one of the ships. Take it far away from here."

"But that's… I don't think—"

"You know you're able to. To move things in the Unity."

Piper bit her lower lip. "Yes. But not a starship."

"And why not?"

"They're too big."

"I suppose they are." Moldark nodded, then lowered his voice. "If only there were a way to open a gateway to another place. To the *other* universe…"

"You know about metaspace?"

Moldark smiled to himself, but then cleared his face. "Of course, child. It's beautiful there, isn't it?"

Piper gave a tiny nod. She eyed Moldark. "You've been there?"

"And I hope to go back very soon." *There was a price to pay for keeping children in the dark*, Moldark thought. The Elonian and her Marine partner had not told this girl as much as she needed to know, which made his job more manageable. "But for now, I feel the Jujari are the priority.

Imagine how safe they'd be if they could escape from all this?"

"They'd be safe in metaspace."

"And I agree, child. If only there were a way to get them there."

"There is. But only Awen knows how to…"

"To what?"

"I shouldn't tell you."

"You're right. We should never share our secrets with strangers." He waited, watching ship to ship blaster fire flash across the void's deep blackness. He tapped a finger on his arm, biding his time.

"Only Awen knows how to use the quantum tunnel machine."

Moldark turned, careful to keep his tone nonplussed. "The quantum tunnel machine?"

"Yeah, the thing that opens and closes the tunnels. But…"

"But what?"

"I don't think she needs the machine. Well, I mean, *she* needs the machine. But I don't think I do."

And there it is, Moldark said to himself with a grin. So she could open tears between the universes—at least, *she* suspected she could, and that was all that mattered. *Powerful indeed.* "You think that's something you could do?"

Piper looked away from the battle. "Maybe. I've never tried."

"It never hurts to try." That was a lie, of course. Tampering with a void horizon was perhaps the most dangerous exploit in the cosmos. It had taken the Novia Minoosh a million lives to do it, and a thousand years to perfect it. But even if the child died trying, what was it to him? He had an eternity to find another way to annihilate his enemy.

"Still," Piper said. "I don't think I should trust you."

This was an unfortunate turn, but one Moldark was prepared for. The child was right to mistrust him, of course. And he gave her credit for her perceptiveness—at least the little she'd shown. If she knew what was good for her, she would throw herself into the void and spare herself the coming pain. But humans had an irrational fear of death, and it made them weak. It also made them predictable.

Moldark closed his eyes and summoned his strength. It would take immense focus to let Kane surface without allowing him to regain control of his mortal body. Even though the man's power had waned, Kane's desperation had increased. So if Moldark wasn't careful, Kane would usurp him.

"I suppose you're right," Moldark said, opening his eyes. "But would you trust family?"

Piper turned, then looked over her shoulder to search the room.

"Not there," Moldark said. "Here."

Piper looked up at him in confusion. "I don't understand."

"Nor do I expect you to." Moldark allowed Kane to step forward and kneel. The man's presence drew near, but Moldark would control his speech. He couldn't let things get out of hand, not now, and not with Piper. "But I trust you'll feel it's true with your heart."

"Your... your voice." Piper narrowed her eyes as she looked into Moldark's. "It sounds... better."

Curse this child. She would think it an improvement.

"It sounds familiar."

"Like your mother's, perhaps?"

Piper straightened her arms, but then raised a hand to hold her elbow. "Maybe. Yes, perhaps like hers, but different. Because you're a man."

"And I am also your grandfather."

Piper's face didn't register the information right away. Her blank eyes reflected flashes of blaster fire as her tiny chest rose up and down. "You're my mother's father?"

Moldark nodded, keeping Kane close enough that Piper might sense him, but far enough away that the damned admiral didn't lunge out and embrace the girl. *Sentimental fool.* "It's the whole reason I wanted you here."

"You're my grandfather."

"Yes."

"You were married to Willowood."

"Yes."

"And you had Valerie together."

Are all human children this interceptive? "Yes, child. All of it, yes."

"Well then"—Piper extended her hand—"pleased to meet you, Mr. Admiral, sir."

Moldark looked down at the offered hand, recognizing the

human custom. Meanwhile, Kane desired to hug the child, and perhaps push her away and get her to safety—*the fool. There is nowhere safe now.* Moldark took her hand and shook it. "Please, call me…" What should she call him? "Just call me grandfather."

"I always wondered who you were. My grandfather, I mean."

"And I…" Moldark gave Kane more room than he wanted, but he had to. Only the mortal would know what to say to his offspring, and Moldark couldn't afford to scare her away. Not now. "I always wondered who you were too."

"Yeah. So, where've you been all my life?"

"Here," Moldark said. "Onboard ships bound for all parts of the quadrant."

Piper shifted on her feet and bit her lip.

Sensing the child wanted to say something more, he asked, "What is it?"

"Did you, ya know, ever wanna meet me?"

Kane's presence bucked inside Moldark. "Yes, of course."

"Then, if you've always wondered who I was, and you're a grown-up who can do whatever they want to do, why didn't you come meet me?"

"That's a complicated question."

"Then under complicated it."

Moldark eyed her. "You mean, make it less complicated?"

"Uh-huh."

Moldark allowed Kane's memories to help formulate a

believable response. "The work I do here, it's very important and requires that I stay far away from family."

"So, it was more important than meeting me?"

"That's not what I meant."

"But that's what it sounded like to me."

Moldark felt Kane squirm. This interaction was infuriating, and Moldark wanted it to end. But, again, necessity demanded otherwise. "Sometimes, in order to protect things that are important to you, you must do things that take you far away from them. Have you ever... have you ever loved something deeply?"

"My mother," Piper said. "And my father."

"And if they were ever in harm's way, would you try and do something to keep them from getting hurt? Maybe even something that you didn't want to do?"

"They're both dead."

Kane's life-force grew still, leaving Moldark in the awkward place of not having anything to say. Piper stared at him as water started filling her eyes and running down her cheeks. The child was leaking. Finally, Kane offered a reply—a simple one, but a reply nonetheless. "I'm so sorry to hear that."

"Yeah. So am I." Piper wiped her face with the back of her hand and then sniffed. "Did you know my mother well?"

"Not as well as I would have liked, no." The conversation was becoming too tedious for Moldark. Kane and Piper had made their connection—now it was time to leverage it.

"You would have liked her. She was an amazing person. My favorite person."

"I can only imagine."

Enough! Moldark scolded Kane and shoved his presence away. "Piper, would you try to open a tunnel in the void? Would you do it for me?"

"Your voice is scary again," Piper replied. "What's the matter with it?"

What would Kane say? "It's… because I'm fighting the coldness."

Piper winced. "You mean, you're fighting a cold?"

"Yes."

"Okay, well… I still don't—"

"If you could have done something to save your father and mother, would you have?"

"I don't like that question."

"And yet it stays before you. Would you have?"

Piper shook her head. "I… I don't want—"

"Because you have the chance to save other people's families now. You have an opportunity to preserve their souls. Right here, right now."

Piper opened her mouth again, but no words came out.

"Piper, I can't bring my daughter back. You can't bring your mother back. But we can save someone else's. Would you do it for them?"

Again, Piper wiped more water from her face. Then she took a deep breath that made her lower lip flutter. "I will try."

"Good. Very good. Let us see what happens when you try."

Suddenly, the door to Moldark's deck opened. He looked up to see Brighton enter, leading several Marines. "What is the meaning of this?"

"I'm sorry, my lord," Brighton said. "You have an urgent request." Brighton's eyes darted to the girl, and he hesitated. "But she needs to…"

Moldark sensed his admiral's fear and then looked down at Piper. Whatever this was about, Brighton didn't think it was appropriate for the child. And, seeing as how Moldark needed her to be as calm as possible for what he wanted her to do, he decided to entertain Brighton's implied suggestion. "Child, why don't you wait back in your room."

"But I want to—"

"No arguing." Moldark raised a finger toward her quarters. "Go. This meeting isn't for you. But I'll come get you when it's over."

"Yes, grandfather."

Moldark waited until Piper padded down the stairs, crossed the room, and closed the door behind her before addressing Brighton again. "Now, what is the meaning of this?" He'd barely said the words when a trooper behind Brighton threw him to the ground. The Marine raised a blaster and fired, striking Moldark in the side.

16

AWEN THANKED the shuttle pilot and then disembarked. The moment she stepped into the hangar bay, she heard a soft chime from the overhead speakers followed by a familiar voice.

"Welcome, Awen," Azelon said. "Please see Magnus on deck nine, section four."

"Not yet, Azelon." Awen headed across the bay to the exit, reminding herself to schedule an appointment to have the NBTI installed. "I need to speak with Willowood first."

"But Awen, I am under direct orders to have you check in with Magnus upon your arrival."

"And I will, but I need to speak with Willowood first. This isn't up for negotiation."

"I must insist that—"

"I said, this isn't up for negotiation, Azelon. Lead me to Willowood."

There was a brief pause before Azelon finally said, "As you wish."

Once Awen left the hangar, lines illuminated on the glossy white floor in the nearest corridor, indicating the path to Willowood. Awen felt terrible that she was purposefully ignoring Magnus's orders, but she needed to speak with Willowood first; not doing so would be a waste of time for everyone. Plus, she knew Magnus would want accurate information on Piper.

Awen followed Azelon's route through the *Spire*, sometimes walking, sometimes jogging. She trusted her senses in the Unity, but she needed confirmation, and Willowood was the only person who could answer her question—*questions*, Awen corrected herself.

When at last she arrived outside a hangar bay in the ship's belly, Azelon's voice came through the speakers overhead. "Willowood is inside. However, she is conducting a training session with the cadres of Paladia Company. Are you sure you wish to interrupt her?"

"Open the doors, Azelon."

"Very well."

The two metal panels slid apart to reveal three-dozen gladias in Novian power suits. They were arranged in neat rows, standing atop a butte that looked over a broad desert plain. Two setting suns glowed pink on the horizon, and the sounds of coyotes yipped in the distance.

Each gladia progressed through choreographed Li-Loré forms—hands and feet glowing in the fading light. And on the far side, Willowood called out positions as each gladia moved in smooth, fluid motions.

"Veneethima," Willowood said, her voice carrying over the plateau and disappearing into the evening air. The mystics moved as one, hands rotating, forelegs rising. "Sidronima." Again, the mystics adjusted, extending one arm and squatting low. "Ti nin."

The group lunged left, hands to the ground, every member saying, "Eeee…"

"Rah," Willowood said.

The group punctuated the extended vowel sound with "Rah!" and leaped into the air, executing a 180-degree spin. When they landed, their feet and hands touched the stone, bodies crouched.

"Doquin," Willowood said. All gladias extended one leg behind them, keeping the knee and toe a few centimeters off the ground. Then, when Willowood gave the final instruction, the entire company leaped into the air, each person executing a backflip. Thirty some-odd balls of light surged down their extended legs and shot skyward, joining the stars in orbit above.

Awen marveled at the sight and momentarily forgot why she'd come. A pang of jealousy beat in her chest. During observances on Worru, she'd been overlooked when the elders selected pupils to learn Li-Loré. "Your love for the Jujari and their customs dictated that you be trained elsewhere," she was told. And so she went the route of an emissary. But she'd watched the Li-Loré classes practice whenever she could. The artform mesmerized her in ways she couldn't explain. And now that Willowood was on the *Spire* teaching the ancient practice to students, Awen would miss the opportunity yet again. Instead, she would serve under Magnus in Granther Company—or at least that was how she viewed the order packet that Colonel Caldwell had sent the day before.

Awen coughed into her hand, hoping to try and get Willowood's attention. The older woman smiled as she turned toward Awen. Then she clapped twice. "Good work, every-one. We'll resume in the morning. End simulation."

The high desert scene vanished, and the lower hangar bay's dark gray surfaces and painted insignias reappeared. Willowood walked through her mystics and spread her arms. "Hello, my dear." Then she hesitated. "Something the matter?"

"Can we talk?" Awen asked.

The older woman narrowed her eyes. "Of course. There's a small—"

"No." Awen glanced around and then stepped to the hangar bay's corner. "There's no time."

Willowood followed Awen. "What is it?"

"I sensed Piper."

"While you were in Ithnor Ithelia?"

Awen nodded. "When I went to close the tunnel over Worru, I sensed her."

"As we already knew."

Again, Awen nodded, but more slowly. "Only this time, she was leaving."

"You think she's on the move?"

"I know so," Awen said. "I was able to see her. On a ship."

"You think she's been captured?"

"No." Awen took a breath. "I think—I think she *chose* to go with Kane. But I just don't understand why she would do that?"

The older woman's face fell, and she looked aside. "So she has found her grandfather."

It felt as though all the air had been sucked out of the room. "What?" Awen could hardly believe the words she'd heard. "Are you saying that—that Kane is Valerie's father?"

"It's more than that," Willowood replied. "He was my husband."

"You were married?"

Willowood nodded.

"To Admiral Kane?"

"Quite happily, too. Once."

Awen blinked, then noticed that she was holding her breath. She let out a puff of air and found herself repeating the facts. "You were married to Kane."

Willowood nodded.

"And Valerie was your daughter—I mean, both of yours."

"Yes, child."

"So that makes Piper…"

"As I said, that makes Piper Admiral Wendell Kane's granddaughter. Quite significant to think about."

"I—yeah—well, significant is—I mean—"

"Steady." Willowood placed a hand on Awen's shoulder. "You need to sit?"

"I just—maybe." Awen put a hand on a nearby cargo crate and leaned against it, putting her other hand to her head. "This is no small thing."

"No, it's not."

Awen glanced at Willowood. "And you didn't think to tell me or anyone else sooner?"

"First off, it wasn't mine to tell."

"How in mystic's name is it *not* yours to tell? He was your husband."

"And Valerie's father."

"So?"

"Did she ever bring it up to you?"

Awen was about to answer hastily but thought better of it. She searched her memoirs for any conversation about Kane's identity in relationship to Valerie. "No, but she—"

"She what?"

"She—" Awen worked her mouth for more words than where there. "She never said anything about it."

"Then she didn't deem it pertinent to you, and you're just going to have to trust her judgment there."

"But what about you?"

"What about me?"

"You never thought to tell me?"

Willowood sighed. "That marriage was long ago, and a lot has changed since then. Had I felt it would have impacted our cause, I would have shared it."

"But it *has* impacted our cause," Awen said as the tone of her voice rose. She didn't want to be disrespectful, but Willowood seemed short sighted on this point. "Kane—Moldark—*whoever*—he went after Piper *because* she is his—*your*—granddaughter. And if he told her as much, that would be one reason why she left with him, don't you think?" Awen stared at Willowood, waiting for a reply, wondering if she'd spoken out of turn.

Awen could feel the heat in her face. Perhaps she was just frustrated that Valerie had never said anything about this in all their time together. There had been plenty of opportunities. But now Awen guessed she'd never know why, and it was unfair to take out her frustration on Willowood. "I'm sorry. Forgive me."

Finally, the older woman nodded. "You're right, child. I was wrong to keep it from you, and I'm sorry. I suppose—well, I don't know what I supposed. Sometimes you try to bury the past so much that you fail to see how it's impacting your present."

"I understand, and I forgive you." Awen felt grateful that her words of correction weren't out of line. It took a strong woman to admit when she was wrong, and Willowood proved once again just how wise she was. Still, it didn't explain Valerie's behavior. "But why wouldn't Valerie tell me?"

"I can only speculate, but I wonder if both Kane and I are cause for her silence."

"How so?"

Willowood's eyes seemed to look past Awen, gazing upon a distant time. "While our marriage started beautifully enough, it did not end so. He wanted the navy, and I wanted the Luma."

Awen's thoughts went to Magnus. She could appreciate the tension that Willowood and Kane must have endured.

"And when Valerie showed no signs of being a true blood, well, Wendell took that as a sign from the cosmos that I should renounce my allegiances, abandon my desire to serve in the Order, and dedicate myself to being a mother while he went off to protect the galaxy."

"But you didn't, did you."

Willowood shook her head. "I was stubborn back then." She placed a hand on Awen's forearm. "Far more than I am now, even. I insisted that our daughter should not be raised in the ways of war and that we commit ourselves to the Order's teachings as a family."

"And that went over even less well," Awen said.

"He was furious. He'd always had an angry soul—I suppose it's what made him a good military man. But the anger eventually turned into violence, directed against anyone or anything he didn't like."

"Including you."

Willowood nodded. There was so much sadness in her eyes. "He refused to let Valerie come with me."

"Because she wasn't a true blood."

Again, Willowood nodded. "And because I refused to fight him further. He was so…"

Willowood clearly struggled to finish the sentence, and Awen could only imagine the pain she'd been through—verbally, emotionally, and physically. For Willowood to have abandoned her child, Kane must've been—*a monster*, was all Awen could think to say.

Awen covered Willowood's hand. "So, he raised her…"

The older woman gave a sad smiled, grateful for the hard conversation's change in direction. "As much as a navy captain can. Boarding schools did the majority of it. And the rest, well, you probably know. Marine, medic, doctor, senator's wife, and—"

"And the mother of the greatest true blood the galaxy has ever seen."

Willowood's eyes were still distant. "And, my, how brightly she doth gleam, outshining them all."

"Is that Demworth?" Awen asked as she thought back to her Luma literature studies.

"Samperson," Willowood corrected, her eyes coming back to the present. "I may have dated him once."

"You dated T.R. Samperson?"

"Don't get sidetracked, dear. That's a story for another day."

"But, I mean—"

"Tell me what you saw with Piper."

"Right." Awen shook the idea of Willowood dating one of

the great poets from the last century from her head. "She was with Kane. I mean, Moldark."

Willowood's eyes lit up. "Prisoner?"

"I don't think so. She didn't seem like she was in distress."

"Then we can safely assume two things."

"Which are?"

"She went willingly, for one. And that Kane is still in his body somewhere."

"You think that's why Piper went with him?"

"Hard to say. The last I knew, Valerie had kept her father's identity a secret from the child. In fact, as her father moved up the ranks in the navy, they had less and less contact—to the point that Valerie asked me to help her shield much of her activity."

"What do you mean?"

Willowood pursed her lips. "Well, take the ship they flew from Capriana, for example."

"You mean the one Magnus went to rescue?"

The older woman nodded. "Word had spread that war might be coming to the capital, and Darin and Valerie wanted to get clear. Piper had been having nightmares about the city being destroyed too. So for her mental and emotional health, they decided to get as far away as possible."

"And you helped get them off the planet, and kept their movements concealed."

Willowood nodded. "For a while, anyway."

"But how? You'd either have to know someone wealthy or..." Awen studied Willowood's face.

"Or be wealthy myself?" The older woman gave Awen a sly grin. "I said I was a Luma—I never said I was poor. But in the end, Kane still found them."

"And he's been hunting Piper ever since," Awen said in conclusion.

"We must assume as much."

"But why?"

"Because you and I both know her potential."

"Yeah, but what does Kane want with her?"

Willowood shook her head. "Not Kane. At least not anymore."

"Moldark."

"Yes. If there's anything left of Kane, Piper has no doubt seen it—or at least a shadow of it. I believe he's genuinely interested in meeting her."

"Because they'd never met before?"

"That's right. Valerie didn't want Piper to know either of us."

"She didn't?"

"At least not until she was older. I think my daughter feared that if Piper met me, the girl would want to become a Luma."

"And Valerie didn't want that."

"Of course not. She saw what my obsession did to me."

"And she didn't want her to meet her grandfather and become a slave to the Republic war machine either."

Willowood scrunched up her nose the same way Piper did. "Family can be a complicated thing, can't it."

"Tell me something I don't know."

"So you think Moldark exploited Kane's bloodline to get to Piper?" Awen pushed some strands of hair behind her ear. "But that seems crazy to me."

"What does?"

"That whatever Moldark is—I mean, at his core, beyond Kane—that he would not only take over a man of immense military and political power, but also one in the lineage of a magnificently powerful true blood." Even as Awen finished speaking the sentence, she felt her stomach churn. She looked up at Willowood. "You don't think it was an accident, do you."

Willowood sighed. "I don't know what Moldark is, and I don't know what he wants ultimately, but based on everything I've learned in the last few days, I fear it's for the worst. And I think Moldark chose my ex-husband very carefully. Again, I don't know what or how, but *it*—that thing within Wendell, as you say—it chose deliberately. And it's co-opted both him and Piper for its evil purposes."

"Mystics—which are?"

"I already told you, I don't know."

"But if you had to guess?"

Willowood sighed. "To take over the Republic."

Awen studied Willowood's features. "You don't really believe that though, do you?"

"My child, I've already told you, I don't—"

"What does your gut say, Willowood?" Awen knew she was being more forceful than etiquette allowed, but this was no time for tiptoeing around the facts. Deep in her heart, Awen already felt she had her answer, but she wanted to see if Willowood thought it too. If she didn't, then Awen figured she must be overthinking everything. But if she did, well, then things were worse than everyone feared.

"My gut says Moldark is out for blood," Willowood replied, her voice barely above a whisper.

"As in?"

"As in, he wants to kill everything alive. Everywhere. And he'll use every tool at his disposal."

"Including a little girl."

"Including Piper, yes."

Awen stood up straight. "We've got to tell Magnus. Let's go."

17

MOLDARK LOOKED down at the blaster wound in his side. The shot would have put down a regular human—one without an Elemental in it. Kane, therefore, was supremely fortunate to be playing host, or else he would have been dead. *The weakling.*

Alternatively, the blaster shot had a different effect on Moldark than what the Marine who shot him probably anticipated. Rather than slay him, the blaster bolt fed him. Not like a human soul did, of course—there was more sustenance in just one of them than a megajoule of electrical energy. But it did invigorate him, providing a renewed sense of alertness.

The wound itself would need to be healed, but that was easy enough to do. *Later,* he noted. First, he had an audience to attend to. These Marines had given him no warning— they'd made no threat. Instead, they'd simply come to assassinate him. So he would give them what they'd come for. *Death.*

Moldark looked up from the blast hole and then stared at the shooter's helmet. In the split second before Moldark reacted, he wondered if the man was unsure what to make of a target that didn't fall. Aided by his ethereal power, Moldark leaped into the air and sailed above the Marines just as they fired into the space he'd been standing a split second before. *The fools.* He figured that someone would have already made an attempt on his life. The fact that it was so long in coming was further evidence that this race needed to be extinguished —slow, incompetent, and unable to forge their own way in the universe without taking from other species.

He could practically hear their gasps as they tracked him through the air with their blasters. When he landed in the middle of the Marines, they turned inward, apparently unsure if they should fire due to the threat their crossfire posed to each other. *How courteous of them.* But their hesitation evaporated as they opened fire again.

In a fraction of a second, Moldark stretched his soul out and touched a shooter in the chest. The man's soul bucked but then gave way, flowing into Moldark. There was no time to enjoy this feeding—he yanked on the man's life force. The victim screamed so loudly that Moldark could hear it, even despite the Marine's helmet. With the trooper drained of life, Moldark dashed the dust-filled suit of armor against the next closest man. That Marine jerked away from the collision, seemingly shocked by the near-instantaneous disappearance of his companion.

Suddenly, Moldark felt a warning behind him, coming

from a Marine who'd recovered from his initial surprise at Moldark's speed. Moldark leaned aside as a blaster bolt zipped over his shoulder. The shot had been meant for his head and sped through the gap in the circle made by the first slain Marine.

Spinning on his heel, Moldark reached out an invisible tentacle and latched onto the offending trooper. "How unfortunate that you missed," Moldark said. He could tell the man was trying to say something back, but there was no sound. And, there was no time—Moldark was moving faster than they could think.

Like a child might flick something around at the end of a stick, Moldark threw the Marine right and left, bashing him into the men on each side. The first blow snapped the tethered man's neck, killing him instantly. But his body was still useful as a weapon. So Moldark flailed him around like a mace, knocking four more Marines to the floor. One downed man tried to climb back up, but Moldark pummeled him with the corpse and bashed him twice more into the floor.

It was a waste of soul energy—what he was doing now. Breaking their bodies so quickly meant their life force had the opportunity to dissipate into the ether, never to be recaptured for himself. But there was still half the kill team left, and he already felt full enough as it was. A little waste from time to time wasn't a bad thing, so long as it suited the big picture.

Moldark released the Marine he'd used as a club and then turned to a new victim, this one aiming a weapon at Kane's left side. Moldark grabbed the man's blaster and yanked it forward, pulling the man off balance. Then, just as fast, Moldark wrenched the weapon from the man's hands, spun him around, and used him as a shield. The next blaster rounds blew holes in the man's armor as Moldark turned and pushed toward two Marines emptying their magazines. The shield-man's body spasmed in Moldark's hands as he drove into the oncoming fire.

By the time he was near enough to the gun-wielding Marines, Moldark tossed the body and then connected to the two men at the same time. He took no pleasure in their deaths, but he didn't let their life force go to waste either. Drawing energy in as fast as he could, the Marines' armor clattered to the ground in a second.

With just three men left and Brighton writhing on the floor, Moldark extended his hands and moved toward the nearest Marine. The man fired but Moldark raised a hand and absorbed the three rounds into his palm. He was so nourished that Kane's skin hardly felt damaged. Instead, the current flowed into Moldark and—as before—rejuvenated him. *As if I needed something more*, he noted with a grin.

Using the same extended hand, Moldark reached around the blaster and latched onto the Marine's wrist. Then he connected his soul to the man's life force and found the place where the trooper's mind controlled his hand—an easy enough feat. Moldark turned the man's arm toward the other Marines while stepping behind the new host body and then forced the man to squeeze the trigger.

Blaster fire crisscrossed the room. Moldark fired into the

remaining two Marines, taking the first out with a neck-shot just beneath the helmet's brim, and the other with four rounds through the chest plate. But they'd returned fire before their deaths, striking their brother in arms several times in the chest and head. *The reckless idiots.*

When the other two men fell, Moldark released his hold on the Marine and allowed him to join the rest on the ground. The room was still, save for Brighton, who lay with his arms covering his head.

"Get up, Brighton," Moldark said.

"It's—it's over?"

Moldark sighed. "Yes. It's over. Now, to your feet."

"Yes, my lord."

As the man stood, Moldark could see a dark stain surrounding his hips and pants. Curious, he reached out and touched the clothing. Brighton winced but did not pull away. The fabric was wet, and Moldark's fingers smelled like urine.

"You are afraid," Moldark said.

Brighton shook his head at first, then changed directions. "Scared only for your fate, my lord."

"You lie."

"It's true," Brighton protested loudly. "I swear it."

"Then why didn't you try and stop them?"

"I—" Brighton's darted around. "I didn't know, I swear it. Or else I would have."

Moldark stepped in close. "You had no idea about their attempt to assassinate me?"

"No. Before the mystics, no. They pulled me from the

head and then marched me here at gunpoint. Said they had to speak with you and that it was a matter of utmost importance. An emergency. That it all, I swear to you."

Moldark sniffed the air—sniffed Brighton's soul. The man was telling the truth. "Any idea who ordered the hit?"

"No, my lord. I suspect some commanders in the two other fleets, but nothing concrete."

Moldark eyed Brighton a moment longer.

"I swear, my lord!"

"Very well. Get this cleaned up immediately, then return to the bridge. I have pressing work to finish."

"As you wish, my lord."

"And change your clothes, Brighton. You stink."

"Yes, my lord. I will."

Moldark turned around to walk toward Piper's room when he heard a moan from one of the Marines. He glanced at a suit of armor and noted a hint of movement. *One remained alive?* Moldark looked at Brighton, who merely shrugged. Then he walked to the survivor and bent down, motioning Brighton to join him.

"Remove his helmet," Moldark said to the fleet admiral. Brighton nodded, then moved around, undid the chin strap, and pulled the cover for the Marine's head.

Blood seeped from the man's nose and mouth, and burn marks laced his neck. He had precious few moments to live. "Who sent you?" Moldark asked. But the man only groaned. Moldark repeated his question more forcefully. "Who sent you?" Again, the man seemed in too much pain to reply.

When Moldark snapped his fingers in front of the Marine's face, the man's eyes focused then went wide with fear. The victim sputtered blood and tried to push himself away.

"I have no time for this," Moldark said. He summoned his strength and exerted his will upon the Marine. Doing so this quickly would kill the host, he knew, but the man was dying anyway, so it mattered little—even a hint of who was behind this assassination attempt might be useful. Moldark was the dominant force in the Marine's psyche, so he asked his question one final time, slowly. "Who sent you?"

The Marine trembled, still fighting, still resisting, even to the end. But it was impossible to resist an Elemental—the choices were submission or death.

"Nine," the Marine said, and then his face went blank.

Moldark stood, staring down at the body as if it had been cursed. He felt anger boil in his soul. No—it was stronger than anger. It was rage. "They double-cross me yet again."

"My lord?" Brighton asked, stepping back.

Moldark turned on his fleet admiral. "There will be consequences, Brighton. Painful ones. Ones they will regret only so long as they're alive to witness them."

"Of course, my lord."

For the first time in a long time, a new desire was forming in Moldark's mind—one that quite surprised him. He'd been focused on avenging his people for so long that all other goals failed to rival it. But now—now he had another goal. Not a rival, per se, but one he considered duly important. And, if the circumstances presented themselves, one he would entertain without hesitation.

"The bodies, the clutter"—Moldark gestured blindly to the floor—"I want it all gone, now."

"Right away, my lord."

Then Moldark headed for Piper's door.

18

THE FIRST MEETING with the Gladio Umbra's company commanders made Magnus feel awkward. It wasn't that he didn't want to be in the meeting, or even that he disliked those present. Instead, he missed seeing the faces of the people who'd gotten the team this far—who'd helped keep them alive.

But Magnus understood the nature of leadership and the ever-changing needs of a growing unit. To say that the Gladio Umbra had grown would be an understatement. Further, to say that it could continue to function healthily under its previous leadership structure would have been a fallacy. He, of all people, knew that unit success rose and fell on sound leadership. Without it, their efforts would fall short, and the galaxy could not afford that. A new structure must be employed—but it didn't mean he couldn't miss the past.

Colonel Caldwell led the meeting from the far end of a second conference room table that he'd commandeered from Azelon's inventory of endless rooms and tables. Around it sat Captain Forbes, leader of Taursar Company, and Lieutenant Nelson, leader of Hedgebor Company, both rifle units. Azelon was present for both support and intel with Drambull Company and naval operations with Raptor Company, while TO-96 lead Fang Company. And finally, Master Willowood, who sat at the table's far end, commanded the mystic-filled Paladia Company. No other members of the Gladio Umbra's ever-expanding ranks were allowed in this meeting.

"Thank you for breaking from your training evolutions to meet on such short notice," the colonel said, standing with his hands behind his back. He wore the standard attire of the *Spire's* crew, a white bodysuit with pale blue trim. The colonel had managed to keep off most of the weight that other men his age carried—a result of daily PT and attention to his diet. Still, he had a slight belly that protruded from the bodysuit in a way that suggested Azelon might want to look into alternative clothing styles for the less physically fit among the crew.

"It has come to our attention that a missing member of our team has been located," Caldwell said. "Forbes and Nelson, I know that neither of you have met Piper, but you're aware of her relationship to Senator Darin Stone, and, more importantly, her giftedness in the Unity."

The two company commanders nodded.

"Willowood, would you care to take it from here?"

"Thank you, Colonel." Willowood rose from her chair

and addressed the room. "During Awen's most recent use of the quantum tunnel generator on Ithnor Itheliana, she detected Piper's presence aboard a vessel leaving the Wyndo-rian system."

"Do we know what type of vessel?" Forbes asked.

"We do," Magnus said. "A Paragon ship named the *Peregrine*."

"According to Ricio's account, that is Moldark's personal ship," TO-96 said.

"Awen confirmed that Piper was indeed in Moldark's care." Willowood looked around the table. "She also did not sense that Piper was in distress."

"So, she went willingly?" Nelson asked.

"We believe so."

"And why do you think the girl would go willingly?" Forbes asked.

Caldwell answered for Willowood. "There are several plausible explanations—"

"But the most probable one is that Piper knew Admiral Kane was her grandfather."

Forbes stared at Willowood, dumbfounded. It was the same look Magnus had given Awen and the old woman when they'd told him as much. "Ho—ly splick. Are you saying Kane is—"

"My ex-husband?" Willowood nodded. "Yes."

Caldwell looked like he was about to say something, but Willowood kept going. "If it's any consolation, I recognize that it was wrong to keep the information from you."

Willowood let her eyes linger on Magnus. "For that, I'm sorry. It was a mistake, and I have myself to blame for the reasons why."

Awen seemed about to speak up, but the older woman raised a hand before continuing. "As for why Valerie never said anything, I can only speculate. If she did not wish her father's identity to be known, then she had a good reason for it. Unfortunately for us, we will never know the answer, nor do I believe it is something we need anyway. The curtain has been pulled back, and we will let Valerie rest in peace."

"The most important question now," Caldwell interjected, "is how are we going to rescue Piper?"

"OTF." Forbes pounded a fist on the table. Magnus liked that the man seemed all in with his new commission to the Gladio Umbra. "You have a plan, Colonel?"

"Negative. I only learned about Piper's whereabouts moments before I called you all here. This meeting is to determine whether or not we proceed with a rescue mission, and if so, what it looks like."

"May I offer an observation, sir?" TO-96 asked.

"Go ahead, Brass Balls."

TO-96 hesitated. "Brass Balls, sir?"

"Here we go." Magnus grinned at TO-96.

"I'm afraid I do not understand the reference, at least as it pertains to me."

The colonel smiled past the cigar and pointed to the bot's weaponized forearms. "You pack some heavy firepower for a bot. And I saw you put yourself in harm's way to protect lives on Worru. Then, you volunteer to command a company of starfighters that you've never flown before. And now you're offering suggestions to a Republic Marine Battalion Commander. Tell me, have you ever made a military suggestion to a colonel before?"

"No, sir."

"And are you afraid in any way?"

"Afraid?" TO-96 tilted his head slightly. "Sir, I'm incapable of experiencing fear."

"Damn straight," the colonel replied. "And, therefore, Brass Balls."

TO-96 looked at Magnus, presumably for an explanation. But Magnus shrugged. "The nickname makes sense, 'Six. You're gonna have to roll with it."

"Roll with Brass Balls," TO-96 said. "That is a very clever pun, sir. Though the exact implication of the colonel's meaning still eludes me."

Caldwell rapped his knuckles on the table and fixed his eyes on the bot. "Your suggestion?"

"My apologies, sir. If our larger mission is to thwart Moldark, and a potential mission is rescuing Piper from Moldark, it seems there is a certain fortuitous nature regarding the two objectives."

"I believe the word you're looking for is charming," Azelon said, and then gave the colonel a robotic wink.

The commander chuckled and scratched his eyebrow. "You're suggesting we utilize one to accomplish the other."

"I don't see the harm in trying."

"And how would you propose we take out Moldark?"

"Assuming the *Peregrine* has returned to the *Black Labyrinth*, then that places Piper with Moldark on his command ship. If we find her, we find him. My calculations suggest that the opportunity to eliminate Moldark increases exponentially as we close on Piper's position."

"So you're suggesting we hit the *Black Labyrinth*, grab the girl, and take out Moldark if he's hanging around," Forbes said.

"Without your prolific use of colloquialisms, yes—that's what I'm suggesting."

"The bot really does have brass balls," Nelson said to Forbes. "Now I need me a pair."

"All right," Caldwell said, raising a hand to quiet the laughter. "I think the bot makes a good point. However, I feel that one objective does not necessarily beget the other. A rescue operation is not the same as an assault, and we don't have the time, training, or resources to conduct the later, at least not without taking heavy losses. That said, I do think that whatever team goes after Piper will have the opportunity to take a shot at Moldark, and that shouldn't be overlooked in its importance. It is not, however, the prime objective. Do I make myself clear?"

Everyone nodded.

"You're thinking up something, aren't you, Colonel," Magnus stated.

Caldwell rocked back in his chair and rolled his cigar in his fingers. "We have Granther Company make a low-profile insertion onto the ship, locate and extract the girl, and then get the hell out."

"I like the sound of that," Magnus said. "The teams will be up for it."

Azelon raised a hand. "There are several obstacles to your plan, colonel. Not the least of which is getting the members of Magnus's unit onto the *Labyrinth* in the first place. According to TO-96's documentation on your typical special operations procedures, we'll need to work through target-analysis, mission-planning, equipment-staging, and rehearsal —the latter of which I don't foresee anyone having time for."

"And that's exactly why you're here, Smarty Pants," Cald-well said. "Because we're not going anywhere until we come up with something blaster proof—for the girl's sake and yours, Magnus."

Magnus cracked his knuckles. "Let's do this."

19

PIPER HEARD strange sounds outside her room. First, there were blaster shots and people running around. Then what sounded like muted screams and lots of heavy things falling on the floor. She'd thought about stepping into the Unity to see what was going on, but her grandfather had said the meeting wasn't for her. And, in case it was something bad or scary—which is what it sounded like—she thought better of looking. Plus, her grandfather might get mad if he found out she'd disobeyed him, so she stayed curled up on her bed.

It was several minutes before he came to get her. "Piper? Are you there?"

"Uh-huh," she said over the door's intercom. "Is it okay to come out now?"

"Yes, child. My meeting is over."

Piper slid off her bed, walked across the room, and

touched the keypad to open the door. Her grandfather smiled and then gestured back toward his chair at the top of the platform. But Piper looked around him to where the men had stood. They were all gone. The only thing she could see was a strange blackish powder along the floor like someone hadn't swept or dusted in a while.

"Shall we continue?"

PIPER KNEW metaspace was just beyond the veil—she could feel it. She stood in a forest-wrapped clearing deep in the Foundation's wilderness. The sunlight caressed her face as she looked up at a wall of water. It flowed from a rock outcrop twenty meters overhead and stretched nearly as wide. But unlike any other waterfall she'd seen, which pooled in a broad basin, this one disappeared into a slit in the ground ideally suited to capture the liquid sheet.

The cascading wall glimmered in the light, inviting Piper toward it. But as she neared the gap in the grass-covered stone ground, she was careful to keep her toes from slipping into the space. For, down there, she did not sense the Foundation, nor any realms of the Nexus. Instead, she sensed—nothing. Oblivion. The eternal vastness of the void. Whatever this place was, wherever she'd journeyed to in her attempt to give her grandfather his quantum tunnel to metaspace, it was unlike anything she'd seen—beautiful, but also dangerous.

"What do you see?" asked a voice from beside her physical

body. It belonged to her grandfather. The voice echoed through the trees like rocks grating on one another, and she didn't like it very much. But Piper's mother had sometimes said that a little girl's voice was irritating too, so she tried to give her grandfather the benefit of the doubt.

Piper also knew that her grandfather wasn't right. There was another presence with him, something dark and mean. She saw it hover around him—within him. When his voice was nicer, that was when the spirit stepped back a little. But when his voice was scratchier, like it was now, the spirit blocked her grandfather's presence. She wondered if she could help him when all this was over—after she helped him rescue the Jujari.

"I see a waterfall," Piper replied at last, using her physical body's mouth to communicate with her grandfather. He stood over her as she lay on the floor in his big observation deck with the huge window. He'd placed a pillow under her head, which she thought was very kind of him.

"Why a waterfall?"

Piper looked into the forest as if doing so would help her grandfather hear her better, but she realized it didn't matter—he couldn't see or hear the waterfall anyway. "It's what the wall looks like between the two universes."

"I was picturing something more dramatic," her grandfather replied.

"I don't know what that means."

"Never mind. What are you going to do next?"

Piper looked back at the waterfall and crossed her arms.

"I don't know yet. I need to think about it. And please stop talking. You're distracting me."

She studied the water as it flowed off the outcrop and fell into the wide slit. She knew that going around it would only place her on the backside of the falls, not on the other side of the universe. That was the whole point of going *through* something and not just around it.

But the falls felt dangerous, and the emptiness below even more dangerous. She could practically hear Awen telling her to step away from the gap now—warning her not to get any closer to the water. But Awen wasn't here now. And Awen hadn't been asked to help the Jujari escape. This was Piper's job—it was *her* chance to be a grownup and do something important. If So-Elku had tried to help her recognize who she was without the restraints of her power suit, then this was her chance to do something about it, to show the cosmos who she really was.

Still, fear of the unknown tugged on her heart. She looked back and forth between the water and the gap. The falls shot down into inky blackness, disappearing into infinity. It was a long way down. And there was just enough space that a small person, like her, could fall through. If she wasn't careful, Piper knew she might plummet into the pit.

But she would be careful. And she would be strong. Piper summoned her resolve, looked down at her hand, and extended her fingers toward the shimmering wall of water. She noticed how her fingers trembled more the closer they got. Small droplets of water formed on the tiny hairs on the back of her hand. They were cold. And heavy. In fact, the more moisture that gathered on her fingers, the harder it was to hold her arm up.

Piper suddenly wondered if the rest of the waterfall was heavy like this. She glanced past her toes and into the endless blackness beneath her. The waterfall's sound grew louder, and she could no longer hear her heartbeat in her ears.

The waterfall slapped her hand, soaking it in a heavy spray. Piper's chest felt like it might explode. All she could imagine was the waterfall grabbing onto her hand and pulling her down. But she had to try. She had to help the Jujari get to safety. And she had to get a ship to return to Awen and Willowood.

In a panic, Piper leaned forward and pushed her hand into the cascade. For a split second, she thought she was through and figured she'd passed the test. But the force of the heavy water latched onto her fingers and jerked her torso over.

Piper screamed, feeling herself teeter on the edge of forever. She thrust her hands to the sides and willed herself to keep from falling over. But the water droplets on her hand were still too heavy, forcing her to lose her balance. She thought of taking flight, but somehow she knew the moisture would not let her. There would be no avoiding the fall into the abyss unless she left the Unity. *Now.*

Piper sat up on her grandfather's floor and gasped. The fear of falling, the fear of losing control—they gripped her chest as if they were real things that could physically hurt her.

She began batting at her chest, trying to get the emotions off her. Then she reached out and touched the floor to make sure she wasn't falling.

And she wasn't. She was safe now, sitting beneath her grandfather's strange black eyes.

"Were you successful?" he asked.

"No," she replied, feeling the pain of disappointment flood her heart. "I'm sorry."

"What happened?" He sounded frustrated.

"It was too strong for me."

"Maybe you weren't trying hard enough."

His words stung, and tears started to well up in her eyes. "I suppose I could try harder, yes. But…"

"But what?" Her grandfather repeated himself. Only this time, he changed his tone to something softer and less scratchy. "What's the matter, child?" He knelt beside her and placed a hand on her shoulder. The fear and disappointment didn't leave, but at least Piper didn't feel so alone.

"The waterfall was flowing too quickly. It was going to suck me down."

"Waterfall?"

She nodded. "It's what the marriage between the two universes looks like. The Foundation's funny like that."

"The Foundation, yes." Her grandfather's scratchy voice was back, and he repeated the word like he'd heard it sometime in the past but forgotten about it. "The Foundation is funny like that." He squatted beside her. "Can you try again?"

Piper shook her head. "Oh, please, no. Not right now. It's too strong. I'll need to…"

To what?

Piper didn't know if she had the power to overcome this wall. It should have bent at her will, the waters parting over her as easily as they might split over a stick. But somehow they hadn't, and she didn't know why. Everything else in the Foundation had bowed to her, had done whatever she'd asked. But this waterfall was different, ordered around by a different set of rules.

"Maybe if I can talk to Awen about it I could—"

"Not Awen," her grandfather spat. His voice was harsh again. Just as quickly, he relaxed. "I mean, it would be complicated for us to get in touch with Awen, and I need this now. The Jujari need this now."

"I'm so sorry," Piper said. Hot tears formed in her eyes again, and she felt like sobbing into her grandfather's arm. But he didn't seem like he would want that. So she let her tears run across her cheeks instead. "Is there anything else we can do to help the Jujari?"

Piper searched her grandfather's face, but not for long. The man stood up and walked toward the wide window, leaving Piper on the ground. She decided to follow him, so she pushed herself up. Her head got fuzzy for a second, but she blinked some and then went to stand beside her grandfather.

"Are you thinking about another way to help the Jujari escape?"

"Yes," her grandfather replied. "But I'm afraid there is no way out of this for them."

Hearing that broke Piper's heart. She watched the remaining Jujari ships fire at the Republic ships, but they were outnumbered. She didn't think it would be long before this battle was over, and the Jujari were forced to re—*retake*. *No*, she thought. *Retreat*.

"But maybe there is something we could do to stop the Republic."

Piper looked up at her grandfather. He returned her gaze with a dark look that sent a shiver down her spine. "Like what?"

"I'm not sure if you know this, Piper, but the Republic isn't what it used to be."

"What did it used to be?"

He looked back out the window and placed his hands behind his back. "It used to be good. It used to protect people and uphold peace."

"It doesn't do that anymore?"

"You tell me."

Piper scratched her nose. "Tell you what?"

"How it feels to have them kill your family."

Piper stepped away from the window and felt her face get warm. "What are you talking about? They didn't kill my family."

"And who do you think did?"

"I know who did. But I don't want to talk about this anymore."

"Just because something is hard to talk about doesn't mean it should be avoided."

"Yes it does."

"Who killed your parents, Piper?"

"No!"

"Was it a friend?"

"No, stop."

"Someone you trusted?"

Piper turned into her grandfather's hip and threw a fist at his side. "I told you to stop it. Stop it! Stop talking."

"Maybe you think it was an accident, or that you had something to do with it, or that—"

"I killed my father, and Magnus killed my mother," she screamed. "Why do you even care?" She continued to throw her fists at her grandfather's side, but the pain in her chest made her blows fumble. "And now they're gone. They're gone forever." She sank to her knees, mad at herself and furious with her grandfather for bringing this up. And for what?

"You didn't kill your father, child," he said when her small shrieks died away. "And Magnus didn't kill your mother."

"That's not true." Piper's fists hit the floor. "That's not true at all."

"Tell me, child. If someone kills an antelope with a blaster, is it the blaster that did the killing or the person who fired it?"

"I don't want to answer your questions." Piper coughed, watching her spit hit the glossy black floor. She refused to say anything more.

"But do you know the answer?"

Piper resisted the urge to reply. She knew the answer, but she was done playing his games. At least a minute passed while she composed herself, wiping her mouth and brushing her tears away, when at last her grandfather answered his own question—incorrectly too.

"It's the blaster, isn't it," he said.

"No," Piper replied. "The blaster isn't alive. It can't make decisions."

"So, it was the person?" Her grandfather looked down at her, voice sounding like he was shocked by her answer. Piper didn't want to say anything more, so she just nodded and then looked back at the floor. When she'd calmed down after another minute, her grandfather spoke again, but this time very softly. "Magnus was a blaster. You were a blaster. Neither is guilty of the crime. But the person?—the person who squeezed the trigger? *They* must pay."

Piper wasn't sure she understood what he was trying to say, but the image of someone else using Magnus to kill—even using *her* to kill—well, that made her think hard. She didn't *feel* like anyone had used her to kill her father, or the soldier in Itheliana, or anyone else for that matter. Those were things she'd done, whether on purpose or by accident—weren't they? Plus, when it came to Magnus, he was too strong to let anyone use him.

"Who squeezed me?" Piper asked, knowing the question sounded funny. But she hurt too much to care. "And Magnus? Who made him…"

"Kill your mother?" The old man took a deep breath.

"The same people who are making us do this." He gestured toward the space battle. "The Galactic Republic."

Piper looked out the window and watched as bright flashes of blaster fire crashed against force fields and blew holes in the sides of unprotected ships, both Jujari and Republic. The navy might be on the winning team, but the Jujari weren't going down without a fight. Somehow, the whole scene mirrored what Piper was feeling on the inside. She felt beaten, frustrated, and alone. But she wasn't going to fall apart and throw a fit. Her mother wouldn't approve. No, she had to fight back—at least, she had to try.

"The Galactic Republic is doing this?" Piper asked.

Her grandfather nodded without saying a word.

"But what does this have to do with my father and mother?"

"None of that would have happened if it weren't for this. Your father's death was an unfortunate matter of circumstance related to the events on Oorajee."

"But I was there," Piper protested. "I know what happened... what I did to him. I—" But she couldn't bring herself to repeat the words. It hurt too much, and she was tired of thinking about what her powers did to her father.

"It doesn't matter what blaster bolt killed your father, Piper. It only matters who was behind the weapon in the first place—who made your father be where he was when he was killed. Same with your mother. Do you understand what I'm saying, child?"

"I think so." She squinted at him, trying to figure out what he meant, but she was pretty sure she knew.

"Do you know that they even tried to kill me just today?" He pulled back his cloak and revealed a blaster wound in his side. Piper winced at the blood and charred flesh. It must have felt painful. She couldn't imagine what it was like to get shot.

"There are bigger things at work than you can imagine," he continued. "I don't want the blasters or their bolts—I want the people who pulled the triggers, who ordered the targets around. I want them stopped."

"Do you know who they are?"

Her grandfather nodded. "I do. I've pledged to stop them, or die trying."

"And who—who are they?"

He turned and looked down at her, then offered his hand to help her stand. "Does this mean you want in?"

"Want in to what?"

"To help me stop them. That is, until I can get you a ship so you can be on your way. We had an agreement after all."

Piper considered his offer. She supposed she hadn't fulfilled her end of their bargain yet. She'd tried to help him by opening a quantum tunnel for the Jujari, but that turned out to be impossible. So maybe if she could try something else —something she was better at—perhaps then he'd let her go. But even then, did she still want to go now that she could be with her grandfather? He seemed like he needed her help. Not just with ships or with the people trying to assassinate him, but with the dark thing inside him. Piper shivered. She felt so alone and didn't know what to do. But she did know that her mother would want her to be strong.

"What do you want to do?" Piper took his hand and let him pull her up. "And who are these bad people?"

"They're called the Circle of Nine," her grandfather said. "And I need you to help me convince everyone out there"—he gestured to the Republic ships—"that we must do anything we can to stop them back on Capriana."

"Capriana?" Piper bit her lip. "Are we going back home?"

"Is that where you'd like to go, child?"

"Well, if it means we can stop the bad guys, then… yes."

"Then to Capriana we will go. But first, let's discuss what I need you to do."

"Okay, grandfather." She squeezed his hand and noticed how many scars were on it. "I'm ready."

20

"Are you sure you understand the plan?" Magnus asked.

"Ezo is not as stupid as you seem to think he is," Ezo said as two former Marines went over his borrowed set of Repub Mark V armor. They yanked on plates and double-checked closures, making sure he was squared away. "But Ezo is trying to figure out how any of you bucketheads moved in this stuff."

"You get used to it," Magnus said.

"Somehow, Ezo highly doubts that." Ezo stood in his old ship's shadow while Cyril and TO-96 worked with some of the crew to load *Geronimo* with the last of the gear. Cyril remained in his Novian armor, and the bot kept his telecolos finish—it was only Ezo who'd be impersonating a Republic trooper.

Just then, Sootriman and Abimbola walked through the

hangar bay doors. His wife waved, and Ezo felt his heart swell. That woman would be his undoing.

"You're just in time," Colonel Caldwell said from beside Magnus. "We were about to send them off."

"Without a goodbye kiss?" Sootriman said, putting her hands on her hips.

"Trust me, wife, that was not my intent."

"The hell it wasn't." She reached forward and grabbed him by his suit's collar, then she pulled him close and kissed him on the mouth. Ezo knew he talked a big game, but public displays of affection like this always made him a little embarrassed. Then again, she was a fabulous kisser.

"Okay, you two," Magnus said.

Sootriman put a hand to the Lieutenant's face and didn't let up on Ezo. A few people laughed, and Ezo smiled.

"If you don't stop now, we're going to have to finish this somewhere else," Ezo said with his lips still pressed against hers.

Finally, Sootriman pulled away. "I just didn't want you getting any ideas about running off with some Repub deck wenches."

"None of the deck wenches I've met kiss like you," Ezo said.

"And how many, pray tell, have you kissed?"

"You probably shouldn't answer that, son," Caldwell said.

"Before you get going, I have something for you," Abimbola said. The Miblimbian pulled a small leather pouch off his belt, and then reached in and withdrew a handful of poker chips. He flipped one to Ezo and then handed one to the other company commanders. "For luck."

Ezo turned the chip over in his hand. It had the Gladio Umbra's icon on one side—a circle with an open bottom and the shape of a spearhead within—and a 50-credit symbol on the other. "Where in the name of all mystics did you get these?"

"I've got a source," the giant replied as he turned and winked at Azelon. "If we are going to gamble with our lives, we might as well start a few credits ahead. We need all the juju we can get right now. Plus, if you pull short on an Antaran backdraw table, it never hurts to have an extra chip up your sleeve."

"Yeah, 'cause that's what Ezo's going to be playing when he lands on Moldark's creepy-ass ship."

"I like 'em," Magnus said, flipping it once and then stuffing it inside his Novian chest plate pocket. "Nice touch, Bimby."

"Thank you, buckethead. We made one for every member of the battalion. I will be handing them out soon, along with something a little more *old fashioned*, you might say."

"And what's that?" Caldwell asked. "Speaking as the resident authority on all things old fashioned."

"A battalion patch, Colonel," Abimbola said. He handed Caldwell a small piece of embroidered fabric with the battalion's logo on it, as well as some more writing Ezo couldn't make out.

"Now this I like." Caldwell hit the patch on his palm a few

times and then looked up at Abimbola. "You've got class, Abimbola. I like your style."

"Thank you, sir. And I like your cigar."

"I've got plenty more." The colonel hesitated. "I *had* plenty more." Caldwell threw an irritated hand in the air and then handed Abimbola his patch back. "Are we ready yet, Brass Balls?"

TO-96 poked his head back down *Geronimo's* ramp. "Yes, Colonel Caldwell. We are ready to shove off, as you say."

"Good work, son."

"However, I would not recommend attempting to shove *Geronimo Nine*. I was simply using an expression common among navy—"

"I got it, Balls. Just get yourself squared away."

"Now baby, listen," Sootriman said to Ezo. "You can't go around saying your name to everyone you meet over there."

"Yeah, yeah, I got it."

"You're a Repub buckethead from here on out, and you've gotta act dumb as a rock."

"Hey now," Forbes said, stepping forward.

"Present company excluded." Sootriman smiled at the captain. "You and your men are the smart ones for joining us."

"I can live with that," Forbes replied.

Back to Ezo, Sootriman said, "Get in, do your thing, and get back here in one piece, you copy, love?"

He nodded. "You're really going to miss me that bad, huh?"

She smiled. "I just know Ricio's gonna want Tee-Oh back to command Fang Company."

"And the truth comes out."

"*And* I'll miss you, husband."

"No you won't. You'll be too busy back doing whatever it is you need to do on Ki Nar Four."

Sootriman tapped a finger to her plump lips. "This is true. And there's much work to be done."

"Leaving so soon?" Caldwell asked. "I wasn't aware."

"I am, Colonel. And I'd get used to not knowing everything, if I were you. Plus, my expertise is best utilized elsewhere. You have plenty of help for this mission, and my husband has a squadron to lead."

"Don't I know it," Ezo said, rubbing the back of his neck. "That ace has been bustin' my balls since we got back."

"Ah, so you have balls too." TO-96 leaned down from the ramp. "But are they brass?"

Azelon had brought the *Spire* as close to Oosafar as she felt comfortable—statistically speaking, of course. She'd been emphatic about the probability of discovery, both via intentional sensor sweeps, which seemed highly improbable, and accidental collisions, which was far more likely. Still, with the void being as big as it was, Azelon's idea of far more likely was everyone's definition of impossible.

She chose to keep the *Spire* on the side of the Jujari homeworld opposite the space battle. This meant that a ship like *Geronimo Nine* could seemingly appear around the planet's shadow as if it had jumped in from subspace with no one being the wiser. And, in Ezo's case, that was precisely what they were planning to emulate.

Contrary to most people's ideas of space battle as portrayed in the holo movies, actual conflicts were protracted, drawn-out, messy affairs that required far more ships than the civilian world supposed. While the Dreadnoughts, Battleships, and Battlecruisers got all the attention, it was the smaller resupply vessels, repair and rescue convoys, and salvage ships that made the dirty business of war-making a reality.

Since *Geronimo Nine* was already registered with the Republic as a licensed trade ship—saying nothing about the other undeclared cargo Ezo may or may not have had onboard at any given time—it made sense for the Katana-class Light Freighter to be in-system. A ship like Ezo's could be under contract by the Republic for any number of menial tasks. Of course, no one had seen the ship for several months, nor had it popped up on anyone's sensors or logs. But in the heat of battle, who was checking those records anyway?

Cyril made child's work of forging a contract for *Geronimo* to service several different ships in Third Fleet, making its coming and going not only believable but expected.

"Nothing quite like your enemy asking you to come aboard and mess with their stuff, eh 'Six?" Ezo asked from on *Geronimo's* bridge.

"Whereas the first part of your statement might be true enough, sir, the second part is far from accurate."

"Just work with me, pal." Ezo reduced speed and reversed thrusters. "Mystics, she's a big ship."

Ezo, Cyril, and TO-96 all strained to look out the forward windows to see the *Black Labyrinth* stretching from left to right. What truly betrayed the vessel's sheer size was that Ezo was still several kilometers away, and the ship just kept getting bigger and bigger as they flew forward. The *Labyrinth* was near the back of the action, so unlike the rest of the ships in Third Fleet, it only lobbed occasional rounds at enemy targets. Instead, it seemed to prefer keeping pesky swarms of Razorback starfighters at bay, swatting at them with its quad cannons and auto turrets.

"You're sure we're not gonna get targeted, right Cyril?" Ezo asked.

"All systems green. Green to go," Cyril replied in his mousey voice. "You should be hailed any second."

Right on cue, TO-96 brought up an incoming transmission request. "We're being hailed, sir."

"Audio only," Ezo reminded him. "Remember?"

"Of course, sir."

The voice that spoke was that of a control operator who was either extremely sick of their job and needed a vacation or was preoccupied with watching their favorite holo feed. Either way, it meant no one would be looking too closely at *Geronimo's* ident or logs. "Light Freighter hull number 2R14-

7299G1 bearing 97 tango, this is *Labyrinth* control. Please identify yourself and confirm ship ident."

"*Labyrinth* control, this Captain Stick E. Lipps, requesting docking permission for *Geronimo Nine* in hangar bay..." Ezo looked at TO-96, who looked at Cyril. The code slicer flashed some fingers at Ezo. "Twenty-three. Schedule says we're slated to pick up some—let's see here. Uh, yeah. Some depleted core canisters."

Ezo muted the channel and then glanced at TO-96. "This control operator sounds like he's eating something. Or picking his nose. Or maybe both."

The bot shrugged. "Your guess is as good as mine, sir."

Finally, the operator cleared his throat. "You're clear to dock at hangar bay twenty-three, *Geronimo*. Please remain on your present course, adjusting at waypoint 009 alpha zulu to the revised heading we're transmitting... now."

"Got, got, got it," Cyril said.

"Copy that, control. Everything looks good. Should be outta your hair in no time. And a big thank you to the Galactic Republic for your business." Ezo heard a small click sound followed by the appearance of a Transmission Terminated icon.

"Well, *he* wasn't exactly the chatty type," TO-96 said.

"Definitely not, 'Six," Ezo replied. "Take us in, nice and slow. Don't wanna draw any unnecessary attention."

"Like thanking the Republic for their business over comms, sir?"

"Why? I meant every word."

GERONIMO NINE PASSED through one of the atmosphere force fields in the *Labyrinth's* starboard side amidships, and—once within the Super Dreadnought's gravity harness—used heavy thrusters to ease the crescent-moon-shaped freighter onto the landing deck. Since several ships were coming and going from the wide bay already, few people took much notice of the vessel, save for the small contingent of support personnel who scurried under the ship. Standard protocol warranted that the host vessel provide auxiliary power and life support, and then drain, cleanse, and refill all bio-fluid systems. It would be several minutes before the ship inspector made it over for the mandatory ship inspection. Unless, of course, said individual was unusually efficient.

"Splick," Ezo said, pointing out the cockpit window. A man in a black Repub NCO uniform walked toward *Geronimo*, along with two blaster-carrying helmet-covered troopers. "They're early. Looks like you're on, 'Six."

"Right now, sir?"

"Yes, right now. Come on."

Ezo grabbed his bucket and MC99 blaster and headed toward the loading ramp. He flipped up the safety cover on the deployment panel, charged the system, and then punched the Open button. The ramp hardly started to open before Ezo pushed TO-96 toward it. "Do your thing, pal."

"Affirmative, sir."

"Cyril?" Ezo spun on his heels. "How's that upload?"

"Forty more seconds. Maybe forty-two if the—"

"Make it faster."

Ezo watched TO-96 proceed down the ramp and then stand at the base. Then Ezo put his helmet on and booted up the operating system. The visor powered on and presented environmental sensor data as well as his body's vital signs. His heart rate and body temperature were elevated enough that the system displayed a warning indicator. "Yeah, no splick," Ezo said.

"Credentials and manifest," said the ship inspector, holding his hand out to TO-96.

"I beg your pardon, sir?"

"Credentials and manifest. I don't have all day bot."

"But we've already surrendered them, sir. I apologize if—"

"What do you mean you've already surrendered them?"

Ezo stepped into view at the top of the ramp but made sure to act preoccupied with something deeper in the ship. As soon as the inspector saw Ezo, he pulled up his data pad and began scrolling.

"I don't understand," the man said. "I was just assigned to this vessel."

"Uh, yeah, we already got this one," Ezo said over external comms. "Pretty sure you were supposed to be over there." He pointed his blaster toward a rusted out Lardvac-class freighter that had seen better days. Its service bot stood at the bottom of the ramp, bearing a striking resemblance to its ship.

"No," the inspector said. "That's not possible. I—" His

eyes froze, no doubt on the transfer order Cyril had just uploaded. Then he looked over at the other freighter and winced. "How come I always get the pieces of crap?"

"Sorry," Ezo said with a shrug. Then he yelled to an imaginary someone down a corridor, "Hey! Put that down and keep your scrawny-ass mitts where I can see them."

"I am most sorry for any inconvenience, sir," TO-96 said to the inspector. "I hope the rest of your day is—"

"Quiet, bot. And get back to your job. Sounds like your captain's gonna need you."

"Right away, sir. Thank you for your consideration."

The inspector ignored TO-96 and waved his escorts toward the other ship.

"I think that went smashingly well, sir," TO-96 said as he moved back up the ramp.

"Agreed." Ezo took off his helmet and threw it in a crash couch in the common room. Cyril was busy pouring over a holo schematic of the *Labyrinth*. "How we looking, Cyril?"

"Well, I think I've found a data node that should give me access to the ship's mainframe. This Super Dreadnought is a one-off though, definitely not standard. No way, no how. I won't know until I try. So it's a gamble, you know? It's like going on a date with a Grathnian—you don't really know if it's male or female until…"

"I get it, kid. Breathing is a gamble. How far away is it?"

"See, see, see, that's the good news. It looks to be on the far side of this hangar bay."

"Does that mean there's bad news?"

"Not terrible, not terrible. It's just—in the open."

"So you'll be exposed."

"Yep, yep, yep."

The Novian armor was amazing—everyone recognized that. But the telecolos tech wasn't without its limitations. If an observer looked carefully enough, they would see the background bend behind a figure in chameleon mode. Of course, someone needed to be looking right at the person in question, and even then, the brain would make excuses for what it saw. But Ezo didn't like the idea of Cyril standing in the middle of a busy hangar bay without cover. He was a code slicer, not a covert ops military vet.

"'Six and Ezo will take care of keeping everyone's eyes off you," Ezo said, doing his best to exude confidence for Cyril. "You ready?"

Cyril nodded, picked up his helmet, and then put it on. Ezo gave him a thumbs up just as the kid activated chameleon mode. The armor-clad code slicer vanished. Ezo felt the wind move and saw the corridor warp as Cyril passed. "Not bad," Ezo noted. *Except for the sound of Cyril's nasally breathing over external speakers.* "But Cyril?"

"Copy, sir. Yes, sir?"

"Make sure to keep your speakers muted. You sound like a Paglothian mule pig with a sinus infection."

"Yep, yep, yep. Got it."

"We'll be monitoring you from here. If you need help, well…"

TO-96 stepped forward and raised a forearm with his micro missiles. "We'll be ready."

"Thank, guys," Cyril said. Then he paused at the top of the ramp, and Ezo wondered if Cyril was having a heart attack or something. The kid had an odd way about him— twitchy... but also cool under pressure, somehow. Or maybe he was just so focused on his formulas and tech that he was oblivious to real-world danger in the way certain kids could be.

"You cool, kid?" Ezo asked.

"Ready to slice, ready to dice—ha, ha. Here goes nothing."

"No, kid. Here goes everything."

21

Ezo and TO-96 kept a close eye on Cyril's movement from inside *Geronimo's* bridge. Azelon had updated the ship's sensor suite to track Gladio Umbra units even while in chameleon mode. Since the armor limited both heat and life sign radiation, conventional scans were largely ineffective—a good thing when deep in enemy territory, but a bad thing when friendlies needed to monitor an asset.

"You're looking good," Ezo said. The main holo display projected an outline of Cyril's body against a camera feed of the hangar. "Nice and easy."

Cyril crept down one of the hangar's center aisles, taking his time to hide behind supply containers and maintenance equipment whenever enemy personnel walked by. Ezo doubted the kid needed to be so cautious given the hangar's frenetic level of activity, but with such a critical step in the mission plan, he wouldn't complain.

Several freighters lined either side of Cyril's route to the hangar's far side, and he made quick work of ducking under resupply gantries, darting around access ladders, and hopping over empty pallets. The only moment Ezo felt a surge of adrenaline was when a small shipping crate fell off an overhead track and landed on Cyril's shoulder. To anyone who'd been watching, the falling box looked as though it mysteriously changed direction about half a meter from the ground.

"Dammit," Ezo yelled. "You okay, kid?"

"I'm good, copy. Good to over and out." Cyril hurried away from the box and took temporary cover behind a ship's rear landing gear. A foreman cursed at the deckhand responsible for the mishap, and two other crew members worked to recover the cargo.

"No one looks any wiser," Ezo reported, his eyes studying the scene and also Cyril's stats. "And your suit looks good. Keep moving."

"Right. Loud and clear, loud and clear all the way, sir."

Cyril left the freighter's cover and continued across the hangar, nearing the far side. Within another minute, he was at the data node console. It was a wide desk with several holo displays that protruded from a small recess in the wall right beside a set of large access doors. Already, Ezo could tell there was going to be a problem.

"The armor's going to render the details of those holo displays in ways the eye can detect," Ezo said to TO-96.

"Sir?" the bot asked.

"Cyril's armor. If anyone's looking at those displays, and he's standing in front of them, they'll notice something's off."

"That is a good point, sir. The telecolos emulation system will indeed convey too much deviation."

"Then I guess it's time for a distraction."

"I have just the one," TO-96 said, raising his missiles.

"For mystics' sake, 'Six." Ezo put a hand on TO-96's arm and pushed it down. "We don't want to alert the whole ship. We just want to keep people from unnecessarily looking Cyril's way."

"What do you have in mind, sir?"

Ezo thought about it and then opened comms to Cyril. "Hey, Cyril, buddy?"

"Ten ten, copy, sir."

"How's it coming?"

"I've just inserted the spider drive. Shouldn't be long. Maybe three and a half minutes. Possibly four. Definitely not four and half, though, because with this new spider drive I've got—"

"Well, you're going to have one or two," Ezo said, cutting the kid off.

"But, but, but—"

"You're more exposed out there than we thought, kid. So you've gotta put the speed on."

"I'll do my best."

"As soon as it's done, get back to the ship, and don't worry about any explosions you see.

Cyril gulped over channel. "Explosions, sir?"

"Just get back to the ship."

"Affirmative, roger," the code slicer said, and then Ezo closed the channel.

Picking up Cyril's line of questioning, TO-96 looked at Ezo and said, "Explosions, sir?"

"Remember the resupply station on Limric Prime?"

"I have a complete data set of the entire time, yes."

"Right, but remember how we got clear?"

TO-96 tilted his head at Ezo, and then his eyes increased their glow as if surprised. "You mean, you want to chase—"

"Yup."

"And I'll need to—"

"As fast as your little legs will carry you."

"NAKED MONKEY BUTTS," TO-96 yelled as loud as he could. He streaked across the hangar bay, bumping into cargo crates and bashing into a mobile lift. "Naked monkey butts everywhere!"

Ezo charged after the bot, amplifying his voice over his external speakers at max volume. "Hey, you! Come back here."

TO-96 ignored Ezo's command, and threw his hands in the air, shaking them wildly. "They're chasing me! Help!"

"We've got a runner," Ezo said again, trying to get everyone's attention.

"Get that bot locked down," someone ordered nearby. Ezo looked to see a loadmaster pointing in TO-96's direction —which was good.

"Trying to, sir," Ezo yelled back.

TO-96 veered left and circled a skiff towing a mag lift filled with crates. With the thrust of his hip, the bot jarred the trailer enough to send several boxes flying. The skiff's driver yelled an obscenity as TO-96 dove for cover between two rows of air canisters. Ezo followed him into the shadows.

"How we doing, Cyril?" Ezo asked, out of breath.

"Another thirty seconds."

Ezo nodded and then looked at TO-96. "Head back toward the ship, and I'll tackle—"

"You got him?" a voice asked from behind Ezo.

"Splick."

Suddenly, TO-96 threw a fist against Ezo's helmet and yelled, "Get off me, you dirty monkey!"

Ezo hit the deck, dazed, and watched as the bot ran through the canisters, knocked over half a dozen, and exited the far side.

Ezo shook his head and got to his feet. "I'll get him." He proceeded to chase TO-96 around two ships, and then followed the bot back toward *Geronimo*. But more eyes were on them than Ezo felt comfortable with. He glanced at a cluster of crew members tossing credit chips onto a crate in the unmistakable sign of a bet. A few more started cheering for TO-96 as he dashed around a wall of energy capacitor pylons.

"Think we got their attention, sir?" TO-96 asked.

"Maybe a little too much, pal. Now I need you to stumble."

Right on cue, TO-96's feet entangled one another. He slowed just enough for Ezo to catch up and throw a shoulder into his back. The bot slammed headfirst into the ground with Ezo on his back, sliding to a halt twelve meters from *Geronimo*. Ezo pulled a set of flexicuffs from his hip, tied the bot's hands behind his back, and shouted, "Gotcha!"

Whoops of celebration and groans of disappointment went up from those who'd wagered on the race as Ezo helped TO-96 to his feet. Ezo turned and waved his blaster in the air, assuring everyone he had the bot in custody. Suddenly, TO-96 brought his heel down on Ezo's toe.

"What the hell?" Ezo shouted, which produced a round of laughter from those who'd been watching.

"Get back to work," the loadmaster ordered. "And you, get that bot down to the brig."

"Yes, sir," Ezo said over speakers. "Right away." Then to TO-96, he said, "Come on, you worthless piece of splick." They moved out of sight, taking a short detour around a crane aisle, before heading back to *Geronimo*. "What was the foot thing for?"

"You tackled me hard."

Ezo scrunched up his face. "But you don't feel pain, you idiot."

"Maybe not in my body, but I do in my heart."

"Shut up," Ezo said, and then shoved the captured bot forward.

By the time Ezo and TO-96 ascended into *Geronimo*, careful to stay out of sight, Cyril stood at the ramp's top.

"And?" Ezo asked as he released TO-96.

"Sliced like the Galactic news networks during election season. The *Labyrinth's* sensors will think that our shuttles are standard troop transports coming back from Oorajee."

Ezo slapped Cyril's back and then slammed the ramp's closure button. "Good job. What about Piper?"

Cyril looked away.

"Couldn't locate her?"

"I'm sorry, sir. Maybe with a little more time—"

"We don't have any more of that. Magnus will have to improvise." Ezo looked toward the bridge. "'Six? Get us outta here."

"Right away, sir."

Ezo tossed his helmet and told Cyril to secure himself. "This exit might get a little bumpy."

Geronimo's drive core hummed, followed by the sound of engines cycling up. Ezo stepped into the bridge and started flicking switches before he even sat down. The manual release overrides disconnected the various tubes and lines connected to the ship's belly. They popped off in sprays of white gas and electrical arcs, nozzle heads slamming into the deck. The action brought up several system warnings that TO-96 dismissed with the flick of his hand.

"This is Bay Twenty-Three Control to *Geronimo Nine*," said an official-sounding voice over Repub comms. "We are showing indications of an unsanctioned launch procedure. Please power down and prepare for—"

"We're showing signs of a containment breach, control," Ezo interrupted, raising his voice's pitch. He looked at TO-96 and waved both hands in a frantic motion.

"That's a negative, *Geronimo*. All sensors indicate—wait, hold on."

TO-96's fingers danced across the console in a blur. Suddenly, alarm klaxons began to sound in the cockpit, accompanied by warning indicators.

"*Geronimo*, you're showing signs of a containment breach!"

"No kidding," Ezo said. "That's why we're trying to get clear."

"*Geronimo*, get clear of the hangar!"

"Where do they find these guys?" Ezo asked his bot.

TO-96 applied the anti-gravity thrusters and pushed the ship from its birth. Any maintenance equipment not secured to the deck flew away, blasted by *Geronimo's* thrusters.

"Get clear, now," the control officer cried.

"Nothing like being asked to leave," Ezo said to TO-96.

"It does indeed beat being shot at, sir."

Geronimo slipped through the force field, and TO-96 disengaged the repulsors. Then he applied full power to the engines, and the ship lurched forward. Ezo sank in his seat and yelled at TO-96. "You got their away gift ready?"

"I thought you'd never ask, sir." Again, TO-96's hands worked the controls, and Ezo noticed a load lock release indicator illuminate. A holo feed looking over *Geronimo's* stern popped up and showed a small core canister shoot back toward the *Labyrinth*. Ezo watched the canister's blinking light as it disappeared against the Super Dreadnought's backdrop.

"Violent combustion in the subterranean recess," TO-96 said. Ezo was about to correct the bot's delivery when a brilliant white explosion washed out the rear-facing camera and shoved *Geronimo* forward. At nearly the same time, TO-96 jumped into subspace. The maneuver was risky, being so close to Oorajee's gravity well, but it was worth making the *Labyrinth* believe that *Geronimo* had been decimated in a violent drive-core meltdown. Instead, TO-96 dropped out of subspace on the planet's opposite side, meeting up with the *Spire*.

After being slammed back and forth in his chair half a dozen times in less than sixty seconds, Ezo finally looked at TO-96 and said, "Think they bought it?"

"Stand by, sir. I am monitoring fleet-wide comms traffic now." Ezo watched the bot scroll through data reports faster than any human could. He also heard the indistinguishable noise of several comms channels overlapping one another. "Yes, I believe they have deemed the unfortunate fate of our vessel a catastrophic accident. Several ships in the vicinity are reporting a drive core breach, and the *Labyrinth* is reporting a total loss of signal. With any luck, *Geronimo Nine's* name will be permanently removed from the Galactic Republic registry within the hour. Hold on." TO-96 paused and held up a finger. "Correction, the *Labyrinth* has just removed *Geronimo Nine's* entry from the starship registry."

"That fast?" Ezo whistled. "Don't let the door slam you on the way out."

"Sir?"

"Never mind. Let's get back to the *Spire*. We have a lot of work to do." The mission had hardly begun, and already Ezo was thinking of all the things he could do with a ship no longer on the Repub's radar.

22

"How we looking, Cyril?" Magnus asked over the newly named VNET, a term made by singling out the V from the word Novia and the suffix of the well-established Marine TACNET. He stood over the shuttle pilot's shoulder and watched as the *Black Labyrinth's* hulking mass expanded in the cockpit window.

"Your shuttle still looks friendly, like a friend to the Paragon, that is," Cyril replied from onboard the *Spire*. "So far, so good. So far, sir."

"Let's keep it that way."

Magnus tapped the top of his NOV1 as it rested across his chest. He knew that the approach was the most critical part of any boarding mission. Any fluke in instrument readings, any overly curious observer, and this was all over. A Super Dreadnought's deck guns at point-blank range would make quick work of their troop transports even with Novian shielding technology.

A glance at the sensor display showed the two other transports stacked right behind Magnus's. While his shuttle held Granther and Paladia Companies, the second contained Taursar, and the last contained Hedgebore. That was 355 gladia in total, and all hurtling toward the most powerful ship in the Repub navy. The only thing protecting the Gladio Umbra from a fate in the hard vacuum of space was whatever fancy code slicing Cyril had put in place. "Let's just hope it's enough," Magnus whispered.

"Come again, Lieutenant?" the pilot asked.

"Nothing. Steady as she goes."

"Yes, sir. Two minutes to dock."

Magnus turned around and signaled the two-minute warning to Abimbola, who then sent word into the bay to do a pre-combat check. The shuttles slipped into the *Labyrinth's* shadow, blocked from the system's star. Only Oorajee's surface gave any light to illuminate the target. This was it—there was no going back now. Whatever happened next was on Magnus and the other company leaders.

The plan was ballsy. Dropping 350 gladia in a Repub starship crewed by 500 officers and 4,000 enlisted sailors weren't great odds. But the Gladio Umbra had several things going for them, the greatest of which was the element of surprise. There was no way any fleet's command ship would suspect a surprise boarding party could slip right under their noses. But thanks to Ezo, TO-96, and Cyril, that was precisely what was happening.

The second thing Magnus knew they had going for them was fire superiority. Even if the *Labyrinth's* officers could muster sufficient troop resistance quickly enough to respond to the breach, the Novian armor and weaponry were second to none—especially now that every gladia had been outfitted with the NBTI. Magnus almost felt bad for the hell the sailors were about to face.

Third, the Gladio Umbra had both tactical and operational advantages.

Tactically, this was not warfare on an open field—a scenario where fights were won by position and attrition. This was close quarters combat through tight corridors. As long as Azelon and Cyril could maintain control of the bulkhead blast doors and help direct personnel movement on both sides, Magnus knew speed and violence of force would win the day.

And mission-wise, the Gladio Umbra had a highly specific agenda, one unknown to the enemy—*at least most of them*, he knew. Moldark would understand why they'd come. But the rest of the crew wouldn't have a clue. Which meant they wouldn't know which direction the invasion was headed or which areas of the ship to reinforce.

Slip in, push hard and fast, secure the objective, and then get the hell out. And if anyone had a bead on Moldark? *For splick's sake, take the damn shot.*

"Sixty seconds," the pilot said.

Magnus raised one finger at Abimbola, and again the call went back, fingers raised. Magnus felt his skin prickle as the force field for their target bay loomed ahead. It glowed blue against the *Labyrinth's* black hull, illuminating an empty hold. Cyril's intel platoon had ensured that no other ships were in this particular hangar. How, Magnus had no idea. But he was grateful for the brains that got it done.

All three transports slipped through the force fields and into the *Labyrinth's* gravity well, activating anti-grav repulsors. Ramps extended before landing gear touched down, and the moment the shuttles made deck contact, loadmasters were pushing gladia out as fast as their hands could signal. All was set—everything, that was, except the one piece of intel they still needed the most: a location on Piper.

"I WANT THAT PERIMETER SET YESTERDAY," Forbes yelled over VNET. "Move, move, move!"

Taursar's first, second, and third platoons raced to each of the three hangar entrance doors and went to work. They erected MB17 portable shield walls on either side of the over-sized blast doors, followed by tripod-mounted AT3M auto turrets. As a last resort, they affixed VODs to the door frames, set as directional mines with motion detection in the event of fast evac cover.

Lieutenant Nelson directed Herdgebore Company in their efforts to set up a near field perimeter around the shuttles.

This defensive ring would cover the gladia evac and keep the ships from taking too much direct fire. The platoons set up Azelon's new GU90 cannons in nests within each shuttle's shadow, covering 180-degree sweeps. The cannons would make quick work of any enemy forces attempting to set up on the shuttles.

"I need a direction, Cyril," Magnus said over VNET.

"Still nothing, sir," Cyril replied, his face occupying a small square in the lower left of Magnus's HUD. "I'm thinking I should send you toward the bridge—the admiral's quarters are near the bridge, but you already have that. I mean, you probably already know that. About the bridge and his quarters."

They were wasting time. "And that's still just a guess, right?"

"Yep, yep, yep. I just don't have any good data for you. Sorry, sir."

"Neither do I," Azelon added. Her face appeared beside Cyril's. "But we've still managed to keep your presence a secret. In the meantime, I suggest you utilize the mystics."

"On it." Magnus swiped his eyes left to close the open links. "Awen?"

"Here," she replied, stepping out from Alpha Team. Her face appeared in the lower-left of his HUD while a vector arrow pointed toward an outlined body in his central FOV.

"I need a location."

"I've been trying. So has Willowood."

"And?"

"Piper still doesn't want to be found," Willowood said, stepping away from Paladia Company. "But I am getting something from the ship's stern."

"As am I," Awen said.

Magnus looked between them. "Drive core interference?"

"I don't think so," Awen said.

"Care to expound?"

"Drive cores emit a very distinct vibration in the Unity," Awen said. "Think of it like the color pink. Well, Piper's presence is more like magenta—enough to be in the pink family, but not enough to be mistaken for pink."

"But you're still not sure."

"Right. It's more like we're seeing pink with hints of red."

"And you haven't seen magenta on any other part of the ship?"

Awen sighed and gave a quick shake of her head. "No."

"But you're still sure she's here."

"We wouldn't be here if I wasn't, Magnus. I feel her."

Well, at least that's good news, Magnus thought. "I can't believe I'm saying this, but we're going with your gut and some traces of magenta in the aft. Can you mark it for us, like I showed you?"

"Yes. Stand by."

Magnus waited a second before a destination marker appeared on the ship's schematic in the upper-right of his HUD. The location was on a lower deck, well below the engine cones, and looked to be a cargo hold that doubled as observation hall. Strange, but not implausible. Such spaces made good prisoner enclosures, among other things.

"Willowood," Magnus said. "I need you specifically, and one of your cadres, to come with Granther Company. The rest need to be with Taursar and Hedgebore Companies to defend the shuttles. When we find Piper, she needs to see your face."

"Agreed," Willwood said. "Let me get everyone set."

Magnus thanked Awen and Willowood and then brought Cyril back up. Having the code slicer and Azelon in hand allowed for easy reachback—the term used when units down-range needed to access critical mission information further up the COC. "I need a route to this target, Cyril. And calculate contingencies while you're at it. I don't want us getting trapped back there."

"That's a roger, sir. On your twenty, ASAP." There was a brief pause before a series of blue dots illuminated across the schematic. "Done, done, done. You should see waypoints now."

"Affirmative." Magnus glanced at the path. "You're certain this is the shortest route?"

"Certain? This is pretty much the same thing as playing *Galaxy Renegade*. You know, the holo strategy game? Did you know that I am ranked in the top three in—"

"Cyril!"

"Oh. So sorry, sir. Sorry. I am certain that if you follow our route, you have the best chance at winning. Ah—I mean, surviving."

"Sounds good."

"Oh, um—and one more thing, sir."

"Talk fast."

"We may not be able to maintain control of all bulkhead doors and security systems. I mean, I suspect it's only a matter of time before localized countermeasures are instituted, which will most likely lock us out, which really sucks for you, especially as you get closer to this board's boss. Camera piggybacking is limited, so you'll be on your own once you leave the hangar unless I call something in for you. Copy my ten-four?"

"Understood. Just do what you can, and keep me updated." Magnus swiped Cyril's avatar away and then populated the rest of Granther Company's HUDs with the updated waypoints. "First Platoon and First Cadre, fall in."

The five fire teams and one mystic cadre circled up as Magnus stood in the center. "We have a tentative fix on the asset, currently located in an aft observation theatre on deck four, section ninety-one. We're calling that south and low." Magnus pointed a flat hand toward the ship's nose. "Bow of the ship is north; sides are east and west.

"Intel has updated our waypoints with secondaries on standby. We'll be going in on our own—Taursar and Hedgebore are staying put to ensure shuttle protection along with shield support from the bulk of Paladia. I want you sharp. Watch for blind cross corridors, and set up with caution on intersections. Work together and watch your fellow gladia's backs. Questions?"

Heads shook.

"Dominate."

"Liberate," the platoon replied.

Magnus turned toward the western-most door that led into the ship's interior. Forbes' second platoon was set up on the door, ready to fire on anything that moved once the blast doors parted. Magnus waved a hand at Forbes, who acknowledged him with a nod.

"You ready, LT?" Forbes asked.

"We're green."

Colonel Caldwell's avatar popped up on a battalion-wide transmission. He'd been monitoring everything without interruption, letting his leaders work free of micromanagement. But as Magnus neared the threshold into the ship, the colonel made an appearance. "This is Colonel Caldwell. All units report in."

Magnus and everyone else with a HUD watched as the company commanders lit up the chat window with green icons. He waited to add his until last.

"You good to go, Magnus?"

"Ready, Colonel." Magnus flicked his eyes to activate his ready icon. "Just wanted to keep you on your toes."

"I want time on target to be at a minimum," Caldwell said. "Get in, get out, make it home. This is it, Gladio Umbra. One trigger, one shot, one grave. Stay vig."

"Stay vig," Magnus repeated to himself. It had been a while since he'd heard one of the Corps' old mantras—short for *stay vigilant*.

"Granther Company, you call the play," Caldwell said.

"Let's cover up," Magnus said. Gladias disappeared from Magnus's HUD as all units activated chameleon mode. The only way to track everyone now was through the Novian Defense Architecture, or NDA, which integrated every gladia's NBTI signature. Body silhouettes and vector indicators played at Magnus's peripheral vision as he narrowed his eyes on the main door. He called up Forbes and Cyril simultaneously. "Let's get a move on, boys. Time to crack the can."

23

"Heads up, heads up, heads up," Cyril said. "Cameras are showing the other side is clear. Good luck. Opening blast doors in three... two... one..."

The massive metal barricade retracted, opening five leaves in an expanding iris formation. Magnus aimed down his NOV1, eager to lock on any target that presented itself, but the corridor was clear. "Move out."

Abimbola led Alpha Team first, followed by Titus, Zoll, Bliss, and Robillard. Magnus picked up the rear then turned as he walked over the threshold and waved a quick goodbye to Forbes.

"You're a lucky son of a bitch," Forbes said.

"Don't worry." Magnus turned away as the metal leaves closed back in. "We'll save a few for you."

First platoon hugged the walls, its teams alternating sides

down the corridor, while first cadre from Paladia Company picked up the rear with Magnus. Everyone ran forward along the glossy black floor in a crouch, watching as their first waypoint neared two intersections ahead. Abimbola ordered the foremost teams to slow as they closed on the first junction. Then the Miblimbian glanced right, Titus left, and Zoll, Bliss, and Robillard focused straight ahead.

"Clear to the right," Abimbola said, his suit playing with the red accent lighting that shone up the black walls.

"Three tangos left," Titus said. "Not looking this way, and unarmed."

"Bravo Team, cover but do not engage," Magnus ordered. It felt wrong to put down unarmed sailors from behind even if this was a rogue navy vessel whose commander had Piper. If put in their shoes, maybe Magnus would have signed on with Moldark too—who knew? But everyone deserved a chance to make their own decisions, and killing unarmed sailors before the firefight had started was something Magnus didn't want on his conscience. *The killing will come.*

The four other units passed by Bravo Team while Titus and his fire team kept their NOV1s aimed at the unsuspecting trio. As soon as Magnus was clear of the intersection, he called Titus to rejoin. Bravo Team peeled out of the intersection and tracked the forward-moving platoon.

As they approached the second junction, Abimbola ordered another slowdown. The teams stacked on either wall as Abimbola and Zoll spotted the corners. Cyril's waypoint called for a left turn heading south.

"Five hostiles," Abimbola said, using the agreed upon term to designate armed Paragon troopers. He was set up on the right wall but looked crossways down the left corridor.

"And I've got three," Zoll added.

These were hostile Marines who'd traded their Repub insignias for Moldark's three white stripes. Magnus still didn't like executing people preemptively, but unlike the unarmed sailors, these troopers wouldn't hesitate to kill Magnus or anyone in his platoon if given half a chance. They'd known what they signed up for when they put on their armor today. It didn't make the killing any easier, but it at least made it more understandable.

"Set up, elites," Magnus said.

The two lead teams swapped sides and stepped into the open. Abimbola, Silk, and Doc assigned targets to the left while Zoll, Reimer, and Rix lined up to the left. The Jujari and mystics stayed back, reserved for CQB, or close-quarters battle, when the need arose.

This was it—first contact. From here on out, the element of surprise was gone. Magnus moved forward and waited for everyone to go green. Once they did, he said, "Let's light 'em up."

Blaster bolts tore down both corridors, dropping the Paragon troopers in quick succession. The targets hit the deck —arms and heads slapping the glossy black floor. Magnus heard shouting come from the left as someone took notice of the fallen troopers from around a bend.

"Advance left," Magnus ordered. "Bravo Team, cover our six."

Boot strikes echoed off the walls as the enemy responded to the pileups. In another second, half a dozen crew and two troopers appeared around the bend ahead of them while another sailor knelt to the rear. They looked toward the junction. If they saw anything, it was wavering apparitions. And that was the last thing they saw too. The nearest teams opened fire on the first responders, dropping them as quickly as the first set.

The next Paragon trooper to approach the spectacle did so hesitantly enough that he was able to duck out of sight before Bettger got a shot off with her CK360. The high-powered sniper round bored a hole in the corridor wall. A beat later, the hallways filled with yellow strobe lights and a warning klaxon.

"Come back here, you little runt," Bettger said, probably unaware that her voice broadcast to the teams. Delta Team advanced first, tracking the trooper who'd gotten away. But he hadn't gone far. He'd called in the security breach but remained hidden along a bulkhead, looking downrange. Magnus could tell the trooper still couldn't make out the gladia because his weapon wasn't on target, and his head was out way too far to be safe.

Bettger lined up again, relaxed, and then fired. The round struck the trooper in the head. He flipped backward and hit the ground between his shoulder blades, blaster clattering away.

"Security alert," said a smooth female voice. "Security alert. Deck twenty-four, section ten. All units in the vicinity, please respond." The automated voice repeated the warning while the yellow lights continued to spin.

"Keep moving," Magnus said. First platoon rounded the bend and came to another intersection, one they needed to cross straight ahead. Delta and Echo Teams covered the flanks, opening fire on two small groups of security units that followed the announcement's directions. Robillard dropped two MPs on the left while Jaffrey sniped a third who rounded a corner further back. To the right, Bliss and Dozer eliminated three officers who made a hasty push toward the action area. They'd failed to see the intruders whose NOV1s screamed, sending double-tap shots into the officers' chests. Sparks bounced off the floors as smoke trails twirled upward.

Magnus heard Titus's fire team open up on a larger squad appearing from the north. He turned to see more than a dozen troopers filling the hallway. The Paragon unit hugged the walls and used the bulkheads as cover, apparently wise to the fact that the enemy was using covert stealth tech—that, or they were just better trained. Bravo Team's shots dropped three hostiles, but the majority of the Paragon troopers stayed concealed.

"Time to see what this new feature can do," Magnus said, and then took a knee beside Titus and Willowood. His eyes activated the AI-assist native in his NBTI and then selected the multi-target fire effect mode. As soon as the NOV1 registered the request, Magnus felt the weapon's internal gyro spin up. To his wonder, the NOV1's barrel remained steady despite the fractional movements he made. A new overlay appeared in his HUD, listing the threats in order of priority. It traced the body shapes of eleven troopers, even those hiding behind bulkheads and inside open doorways. A prompt pinged in the bottom center of his FOV that read Ready to Fire? Y/N. "Splick, yeah." Magnus focused on the Y for Yes option and then pulled his weapon into his shoulder.

Magnus squeezed the trigger, and the NOV1 blatted as eleven blaster bolts streaked down the corridor in multiple directions. The effect was a lot like watching a shotgun blast, but where the shotgun followed the spray-and-pray philosophy of more antiquated munitions, every blaster bolt the NOV1 fired downrange found its mark—or at least close enough. Rounds struck heads of those most exposed. Their bodies fell to the floor or slumped down walls. Other troopers, imagining they were safe behind protective cover, were struck in the chest. Still others were maimed by rounds that lost some energy piercing reinforced walls or bulkheads, but they were out of the fight.

"Mystics, I love this weapon," Magnus said to himself.

Titus nudged Magnus. "Show off."

"Just 'cause I tried it first doesn't mean you can't enjoy it second." Then Magnus peeled a VOD off his chest, set it to remote detonation, and threw it on the ceiling. "For later," he said to Titus. "Let's pick up the pace, Granther Company!"

The teams made their way south, crossing two more intersections. But now the ship was on full alert, and enemy resistance—while not yet coordinated—was getting stronger. Magnus guessed that not being able to see the enemy was messing with Paragon command. The only way to track the Gladio Umbra was by the pile of bodies they left. As long as Granther Company's destination remained a mystery, Magnus figured they'd be able to keep the enemy on their heels.

"Sir, sir, sir! I've just lost control of a bulkhead blast door one section ahead of you," Cyril said. "Recalculating now."

"How much time will it add?"

"Standby."

Magnus worked with Bravo Team to keep their rear clear, taking down any troopers who dared fire into the wavy apparitions that moved through the hallways. Several security forces bobbed their heads back and forth, squinting in the near distance, trying to get a fix on the enemy. But Magnus dropped two sailors in quick succession who looked a little too long in his direction.

"Three minutes, twenty-eight seconds at your current pace," Cyril said. "You should be able see the revised route now."

Magnus looked at the path and noticed it had several more turns and junctions than their current one. "No good, Cyril. We'll stay on the current course you've plotted."

"But, but, but, sir. How do you intend to get through that barricade?"

"We're Gladio Umbra, buddy. Nothing can stop us."

"Yeah, yeah," Cyril replied. "You're super awesome."

Magnus closed the channel and brought Delta Team's channel. "Bliss, I need that bulkhead blast door taken out."

"Copy that, LT. Dozer, you heard the man."

"On it."

Alpha and Charlie Team provided cover as Bliss led his unit toward the next intersection—one now cut off by a solid wall of metal. Repub designations were stenciled on the obstruction, including instructions for emergency procedures and the barricade's tolerances. Dozer broke out demolition charges—what Azelon had termed XVODs—which were roughly ten times the power of the standard Novian VODs. But even with so much force, Magnus knew he'd need something more to make sure the obstacle went down.

"Awen?"

"What do you need?"

"Can you help concentrate Dozer's blast on the door? Maybe make a force field around it?"

"I can make that happen."

"Good. Do it."

As Dozer finished setting the charge and stepped back, Awen stood in the middle of the corridor and spread her arms away from her hips. Then she bent her knees, bowed her head, and went still. "Are you prepared, Dozer?"

"I am, miss," he replied. "On your mark."

"Blow it."

Dozer triggered the directional charge from his HUD. A split second later, the wall went bright white as the XVOD detonated. Usually, such a breach explosion blew back on the operators. Instead, the blast acted like it occurred on the other side of an invisible wall. Not even the audio report came back —the only thing Magnus felt was a rumble through his boots.

The massive door bowed, and the walls buckled. Then the partition blew apart and shot down the hallway. Awen had so successfully contained the energy, focusing it on the obstruction, that the liquified metal tore trenches down the corridor for twenty-five yards.

Awen lowered the shield and bent her knees in relief. Magnus looked around her and saw several disfigured bodies scattered down the hall. "Good work, Awen," he said, patting her on the shoulder. "Fall in with your team. Granther Company, let's pick up the tempo."

"Sir, Gladia Lieutenant, sir," Cyril said. "I've repopulated your original route based on your revised scenario."

"Roger. Make sure everyone has it."

"That's a loud and clear, Lieutenant. Loud and clear all the way, sir."

The next corridor was clear, thanks to Dozer and Awen's combined efforts. Smoke and molten metal lined the way ahead, and body parts lay scattered along the floor. The warning klaxon continued to wail but grew more urgent in tone, while the strobing lights changed from yellow to red. The ship's emergency alert system issued another warning. "Security breach. Security breach. Deck twenty-four, section twenty. All security personnel respond immediately. Enemy threat detected."

"Well, that escalated quickly," Bliss said.

"Just means we have more blaster bolts to put down-range," Robillard added.

"Everyone, stay focused." Magnus moved ahead with his NOV1 in high ready position. "Keep it smooth." The hallway bent right and then turned left before straightening out. Magnus noted several black doors on either side and then got an uneasy feeling in his gut. He was just about to say something when Cyril cut in.

"Movement detected, inbound, sir! I think they're using the side rooms."

Magnus didn't have a chance to respond before half a dozen doors slid apart. Black-clad troopers surged into the hall, weapons blazing. For the first time since the raid began, Magnus's shield took a hit. He leaned up against a wall to narrow his profile and wondered if the energy dissipation had given his location away. As if to answer the question, the enemy's blaster fire tracked him toward the wall. That was also when he noticed he could visually see a few of the other gladia: the smoke was revealing hard edges under the ceiling lights.

Up until this point, he'd asked Willowood to keep her mystics from deploying force fields for Granther Company. While sparing needless hits on personal armor, the force fields would give their position away by dispersing blaster fire over a spherical wall. Now, however, that might not matter.

All teams returned fire, concentrating on the troopers who went prone, firing from the ground. Magnus noted that more than a few gladia registered hits on their shields as well. But their return fire was crippling, drilling holes in the enemy's defenses. Bits of blackened flesh spat out the backside of Repub armor and sprinkled the floor. Some fighters fell off their feet while others—like those shooting from the prone position—just went limp, helmets lying on the ground.

"Keep moving, keep shooting," Magnus ordered. He kept one eye on their advance and one eye on their tail. Then he checked the master mission clock and noted that they were falling behind schedule. If they didn't maintain the upper hand in every corridor, Granther Company would be fighting the whole ship before long. *And that's definitely not something I'm interested in doing today*, Magnus noted. Every minute that passed was one Moldark could use to move Piper, and they couldn't afford to lose her again. *He* couldn't. And he wouldn't. Mission failure was not an option today. They would win, and Piper would come home.

24

THE JUJARI'S fall was imminent. Moldark could feel it. The enemy was starting to fall back, and the Sypeurlion and Dim-Telok were breaking formation. Once the Jujari fleet was destroyed, the rest of the beasts would be confined to their desolate world. Full extermination would take more time, of course, but that would come later—Moldark's priorities had taken an unexpected turn, and his newfound rage had to be satisfied.

Now that Moldark had Piper's cooperation, his mind had turned toward the Galactic Republic and, more specifically, the Nine. They had made an attempt on his life. He decided he would punish them, like the Jujari, pounding them into the dirt where they belonged. The most fortuitous part of this change of plan was that the girl had already started planting the seeds of hate, ones that would fuel the navy's acquiescence to his orders.

Piper didn't know that, of course. She'd merely been asked to encourage the fleet. As a result, the hearts and minds of every sailor in three fleets had redoubled their commitment toward weeding out the enemy in the sector. There would be no more assassination attempts by Marines loyal to the Nine, no more condescension. From now on, the fleets would do his bidding.

The naive child, Moldark mused to himself, rapping his fingers on the arm of his chair. The light of blaster fire through windowplex glinted in his eyes. *How magnificent it will be when I show the fleets what to exterminate.* It was like training a dog to drink blood—if it liked it enough from a bowl, it would love it more from a heart. *So I will show them a heart, and then loose them on the whole body.*

Of course, there was the other opportunity too—the one the sniveling ambassador had concocted for him. As easily as the fleets' could annihilate enemies with their firepower, Bosworth's creation could decimate planets. *And with much less energy.* The loathsome fool of a man irritated Moldark, but he was proving to be useful. And so long as Bosworth remained useful, Moldark would tolerate him.

As for the child, Piper was sleeping in her quarters, exhausted from her efforts in the Unity. He admired her—at least as much as he could. For all her pitiful mortality, she was stronger than any mystic he'd ever encountered, and he had seen his share. But even with all her power, she was still susceptible to fatigue and needed nourishment.

As do I, Moldark reminded himself. *In a manner of speaking.* The need to feast on a mortal soul stirred in him. He'd consumed the assassins too quickly for them to provide any true sustenance, so he'd need to look elsewhere. He'd taken several captives from Worru; perhaps he would order one to his chamber as he watched the Jujari's final efforts to thwart the inevitable. *A feast and a spectacle.*

A chime rang on his chair's arm—an incoming call from the bridge. He swiped it open. "Yes, Brighton."

"My lord, it seems we have intruders on the ship."

First assassins and now intruders. *What's happening to my ship?* He grunted his teeth and scowled at Brighton. "It *seems* we have intruders? Or do we actually?"

"Um—that's just it." Brighton swallowed. "We have footage of troopers going down. But no visuals on an enemy threat, my lord."

Moldark didn't like this. "Show me."

Brighton nodded and looked off-screen. A moment passed, and then security camera footage from a corridor somewhere in the *Labyrinth* hovered in front of his chair. Moldark spun away from his observation window so he could focus on the image better. A massive explosion washed out the view for a second. When it came back, the hallway was strewn with fire, smoke, and body parts.

He was about to contest the admiral's assumptions when blaster fire emerged from behind the explosion. Moldark leaned forward in his chair. The bolts seemed to appear out of nowhere.

"You see what I mean?" Brighton said from a small window in the corner. "It's like weapons fire is just springing to life from the middle of the hallway. I'd say the enemy is cloaked, but no such tech exists."

Moldark sneered. "Yes. It does, Admiral." *So they've come for the child*, Moldark concluded, leaning back in his chair.

Brighton cleared his throat. "My lord?"

Moldark was growing impatient with this species by the hour. "The technology does exist; you just don't know about it. Do you see there, in the smoke?"

"Sir?"

"Look at the image. Focus on the smoke." There was a pause as Brighton did what he was told. "What do you see?"

"Nothing, my lord, there's just… Wait a second. I see shapes or something."

"You do, yes. The enemy's technology is good, but it is not perfect. Open non-lethal gas valves in the hallways you suspect the enemy to be in. The compressed air will help your men spot their targets."

The admiral nodded. "That's a good idea."

Moldark dismissed the man with a wave of his hand. "Where did they originate from?"

"We're working on that. But it must be from one of the hangar bays."

"And you don't know which one?"

Brighton shook his head. "We have no record of any unauthorized, unscheduled vessels making port."

"Of course you don't, admiral. That's the point of covert operations." Moldark felt that Brighton should have had more intuition than he displayed. But then again, the man was human. Moldark sighed when Brighton didn't seem to know how to respond. "Look for something out of the ordinary, perhaps an unusual event in the last hour."

"We did have a private maintenance vessel go nova about forty minutes ago—operational drive core containment breach. The ship was collecting spent containment canisters, standard procedure, when the deck sensors picked up a radiation leak. The ship was ordered to depart—emergency evacuation protocol. Then it exploded in near space. Hit two fighters, and our starboard side suffered minor damage."

Moldark leaned forward. "Bring up the records."

Brighton looked down. A data set replaced the firefight scene. "You should be able to see—"

"I have it." Moldark didn't need to scan far—his eyes stopped on the ship's hull number and registered name. "Admiral, you've been fooled."

"My lord?"

"This ship, this—*Geronimo Nine*—is with the rebels. The same that left for Worru at the war's start. It's *them*, you fool."

Brighton's lips parted, but he said nothing. Finally, the man composed himself and swallowed. "But I don't understand." Brighton checked the log. "There was only a captain and a service bot listed, routine pick up. And that ship couldn't hold an entire raiding party."

"That's because it didn't deliver a raiding party. It was probably a small advance team. The boarding shuttles are somewhere else on board—registered and right under your nose, Admiral. I suggest searching all hangar bays individually, beginning with those closest to your incident here."

"Yes, my lord. Right away."

"Also, the shuttles would have come from a larger vessel, probably close by."

"Of course, my lord."

"It will be cloaked, like the troopers. I want Talons scrambled and running standard search grids, along with any other ships that can be spared. Start them behind the fleet and move away. Full sensor sweeps. Check on the planet's shadow side as well."

"As you have commanded, so it will be done."

"And for your wellbeing, admiral, I recommend you do it expediently."

Brighton saluted, and then the comms channel closed.

Moldark steepled his fingertips together and then turned his chair to see the battle. "How cunning," he said to the distant enemy. "And brave. Yet so foolish. So very foolish."

He remained there for a moment then stood. The sound of his boots against the shiny floor echoed off the high ceiling as he approached his quarters. He waved the door open and found Piper sound asleep. Her chest rose and fell beneath the thin grey blanket, and her head lay encircled by a mess of blonde hair. Had he any affection for humans, she would be one worth caring for. Or was that Kane talking? *Bastard.*

"Wake up, child," Moldark said, allowing Kane to the forefront. He repeated himself several times, but Piper didn't stir. Resigned to the fact that he had probably pushed her too hard, Moldark backed out of the room. Perhaps allowing her a bit more sleep would be wise—she would have more work to do soon enough. "Rest, granddaughter. Rest well."

25

"Copy for Mr. Forbes?" Cyril said over VNET. "Looks like you've got company."

"I see 'em." Forbes reviewed a camera feed overlaid in his HUD. A Paragon fire team meddled with a control panel on the other side of the north door.

"More inbound," Lieutenant Nelson added. A platoon joined the fire team—about forty troopers in total.

"No, no, no! They're attempting to override my control authority," Cyril said. "Once the ship's AI gets involved, we're totally screwed. I don't think Azelon and I can keep the door closed."

"Understood, Cyril. We're prepped for this, so don't you worry your fancy little fingers over it."

Cyril let out a timid laugh. "Copy that copy, sir."

"Heads up, gladia," Forbes said over a channel that served both companies. Since Forbes outranked Nelson, he took lead on commanding both units in this combined engagement. "We've got some visitors. Taursar, first platoon, ready the AT3Ms and keep your heads down. They'll be coming in hot. Hedgebore, you'll have a direct line of fire into the corridor. Exploit it. Cyril, I need to know when the enemy gets curious about those other doors."

"Roger copy," Cyril replied.

Forbes took cover beneath his unit's shuttle and ensured that he had good sight-lines on all three doors. He knew it wouldn't be long before they'd be defending the ships on three sides.

The fact that Forbes was on a Repub Super Dreadnought about to engage Marine units wasn't lost on him. The whole thing felt surreal, like he'd woken up inside a bad dream caused by one too many glasses of bratch the night before. He wouldn't know who he was shooting at, but chances were, he'd trained any number of these troopers before they'd become Paragon lackeys. That was hard to stomach. The Corps didn't train you to open fire on your own.

But then again, these weren't his own anymore. Something had gone horribly wrong with the Repub—or at least with the fleets, which were now under the command of a lunatic. At least that was what he thought of Magnus and Caldwell's intel. The hard part was recognizing that not everyone was complicit in the decision-making process. If you were a grunt, you took orders, put your head down, and got the job done. Of course, Forbes had always been an officer, or a POG—*person other than grunt.* But that didn't mean he wasn't aware of how his orders affected his subordinates.

The guys downrange didn't have the luxury of knowing the why's of every command decision. And that was probably true here as well, which didn't make putting them down any easier. In another version of this moment, someone else could have been on Worru when Magnus and Caldwell arrived, and Forbes would be here, following orders that had come down the COC from a madman. Some days, you got lucky. And today, that was Forbes and the men and women under his command.

Forbes took a deep breath and then spoke to both units again. "Listen, I know what a lot of you are thinking right now, and I'm thinking it too. You're about to shoot at your own coming through that door, and you weren't trained to fire on Repub armor. You're thinking this is some crazy ass splick about to go down. And you're right—you're damn right it is. But you've got to remember that war is a messy business. And you didn't sign up to be data pushers or caregivers. You signed up to be gunfighters.

"Today, the thing that needs to be put down is on this ship. It's threatening more lives than any of us can imagine, and whether we like it or not, and whether they know it or not, the Marines about to come through these doors are a part of the problem. We don't have the time to talk it out with them and convince them who they've climbed in bed with; mystics know I wish we did. But it comes down to this moment, right now. If we don't stop them, they'll be instrumental in taking more lives than they already have."

"Sir, we're getting elbowed out, sir," Cyril reported on a private channel to Forbes. "Any second now and the splick hits the splick."

Forbes acknowledged the update with a ping to Cyril but focused on finishing his—whatever it was. "It's not Marines coming through those doors. Remember that. It's the Paragon. They might look like Marines, they might shoot like Marines, but they're fighting for something different than we are. You put them down, and don't hesitate, or you'll be the one sucking air through a hole in your neck, and the galaxy needs you too much for that."

"We've lost control," Cyril said.

Forbes acknowledged and then gave his final commands. "Activate chameleon mode. Weapons free."

The blast door's metal leaves rose open and revealed a platoon of Paragon troopers along both hallway walls. Those troopers closest to the door—the ones responsible for hacking the control panel—jerked back in surprise. Apparently, they hadn't been expecting to find three alien shuttles in the hangar. Nor did they expect emplaced GU90 cannons to blast through their ranks. Four Paragon troopers were cut in half in the open moments. Their torsos hadn't hit the ground before Forbes' first platoon fired around the corners and drilled those waiting along the walls.

Protective half walls sprung out along the passageway, giving the Paragon forces cover. But not all. At least a dozen troopers found themselves either in front of an armored plate or thrown off balance and spinning in the corridor's middle. Hedgebore Company continued firing the large-barreled GU90, sending mega bolts of energy down the passage. One unlucky trooper was vaporized with a direct hit, leaving only his boots to topple to the ground.

Forbes continued to fire into the passage as a flurry of NOV1 rounds lit up the enemy. Bodies fell from behind the half walls, making the passage's floor almost impassable. Meanwhile, Forbes didn't see any registered hits on his gladia. The eight remaining Paragon troopers fell back and disappeared around a corner.

Forbes ordered a ceasefire and then told everyone to reorient, reload, and prepare for the next wave. The skirmish was easily won, but it had also been a surprise. Now, the enemy COs knew where the Gladio Umbra were, and Forbes knew the next assaults wouldn't be so effortless.

"Get ready on your sixes, 'cause I'm detecting serious, like, serious troop movement from the south," Cyril said. "I don't have eyes there, just piggybacking on life support sensors."

"Copy that," Forbes replied. "Any idea on numbers?"

"Negative, negative. Just, a big lot."

"A big lot." Forbes tilted his head. "I'm guessing that's more than a little lot?"

"Yeah, yeah. It is."

Forbes brought up the company channel. "South door. Prepare to engage."

"Hostiles to the north," Nelson said. Members of Nelson's first platoon blasted the corridor with GUD90 rounds, showering the distant intersection with sparks. Troopers fell in the hallway, but several managed to race around the corner and set up behind the half walls. Forbes's units joined the fight, firing their NOV1s down the hallway.

"South door opening," Cyril said.

Forbes turned and ordered fire toward the new target direction. The enemy must have shared intel since the troops in the south corridor were already deployed behind the metal planks. "Don't give them a chance to aim," Forbes yelled. "Keep them pinned down, and make them pay for any attempt to hit us." Green icons went down the chat field in his HUD as more NOV1 fire filled the north hallway.

Suddenly, someone yelled, "Fragger!" Forbes turned to the north and saw a detonator roll into the middle space between the open blast door and the shuttles.

"Cover," Forbes ordered a split second before the ordinance detonated. A thousand small metal bearings hurled through the air, striking metal and personal force fields alike. Several hits registered on gladia, but none fatal. Personal force fields had been reduced by marginal percentages, but nothing that concerned Forbes. He rallied his gladia and urged them to keep up the pressure.

A few aggressive troopers made it through the south door but were immediately met with auto turret fire. Two AT3Ms spun up and let loose a torrent of blaster rounds that riddled the Paragon Marines with holes. The enemy combatants shook as they fell to the floor, weapons clattering aside.

"Where's my GU suppression?" Nelson barked. "Those shouldn't have gotten through." Forbes agreed, but the troops massing to the south were considerable—he guessed two platoons at least.

Two cannons swiveled in answer to Nelson's orders. The barrels glowed orange as the emplaced weapons fired into the southern hallway. When the troopers were lined up, one round could take out five or even six people. But the enemy had already gotten wise, trying their best to stagger their advance.

"That's what I'm talking about," Nelson added. "Keep that up!"

"And here comes door number three," Cyril said. "Prepare for red alert readiness."

"To the west," Forbes said. "Prepare to engage!"

Again, the blast door plates spiraled open to reveal another two platoons of Paragon Marines. NOV1s drilled hard into the tunnel, filling the space with blue light. But the enemy here had brought additional barricades along with some heavy ordinance.

"SMDLs," Forbes roared, marking the shoulder-mounted detonator launchers on VNET. Reticles gave second platoon something to focus on while Hedgebore Company managed GU90 fire on all three openings.

Forbes watched two of the three Marines bearing the

SMDLs go down in a cascade of sparks. But the third man lobbed four fraggers into the hangar in quick succession. "Cover!"

All four grenades exploded at once, thanks to their symmetrical relay system, and blasted the gladia's MB17 portable shields. Even the shuttles took some damage, but nothing that made Forbes concerned. More personal shields registered a sudden drop in integrity, and at least three NOV1s were blown out of commission. Those gladia unholstered their Vs and aimed.

"I want fire superiority," Forbes said. "That can't happen again!" He lent his NOV1's ferocity to the fight and took aim at two Marines who were attempting to break cover and advance.

"Captain, sir," Cyril cried, his voice strained. "Copy that. I'm picking up some strange vibrations to the north."

"Splick." Forbes swapped out a new magazine. "These guys really don't want us here."

"You—you know what it is?"

"Trench Sweepers," Forbes replied. "You're picking up the sound of their tracks."

"Trench Sweepers? Nope, nope, nope. Can't say I'm familiar with those."

"And I hope you never are, kid."

Forbes switched channels. "Listen up. We've got TS40s, maybe even 45s, bearing down from the north. I want recessed mines in the hallway floor before it shows its ugly face. West and south sides, you can bet you're next. The further back we take them, the less we'll have to wrestle with their cyclic guns. Taursar, you're all on point for this; Hedge-bore, we need you to carve us a pocket a few meters deep."

"We're on it," Nelson answered. Likewise, Forbes' platoons responded with green icons.

"Let's pour it on!"

26

AWEN COULD SENSE Magnus growing impatient. He wasn't making any critical tactical mistakes or anything—at least as far as she could tell. But the way his body moved made him seem uptight. She knew it was about Piper—*obviously*. The child was the whole reason they were here. But for Magnus, she knew, more was at stake than just the child's safety. This was about restoring their relationship.

Who was to say that they reached Piper and she didn't want to come back with them? Or what if—mystics forbid—the little girl turned against them? Awen shivered at the thought of having to fend off any attacks from the child, much less cause her harm. But if it came to it, could she? *Could you really strike her down, Awen?*

"Let's just get there first," Awen said aloud.

"Come again?" Magnus said, pausing between shots with his blaster.

"Nothing," Awen replied. "Just talking to myself."

Suddenly, jets of compressed air shot out from the ceiling and compartments along the walls. The white plumes of cold air wrapped around the gladia's bodies. The telecolos system had trouble keeping up with the infinite deviations in light deflection, and soon the plate armor was visible, displaying multicolored digital glitches.

"Stealth is comprised," Titus said over VNET. "Watch the incoming fire!"

Sure enough, the enemy's fire effectiveness increased as they put more rounds on target. Awen took a hit herself, but her power suit absorbed the blow without causing her any harm.

"It is these infernal air valves," Rohoar spat, swinging his paws through one of the spouts. Awen thought he looked like a puppy batting as a stream of water shooting from a spigot. "I curse them. I curse them all."

"We're not cursin' 'em or pluggin' 'em," Magnus replied. "There are just too many. Somebody got wise, so I think it's time we do the same." Awen saw Magnus ping Willowood and bring her in on a channel with Granther's mystics. "I want each fire team to have their own shield moving forward. Willowood, can you cover our six?"

"Certainly," the older woman replied.

As soon as Magnus gave the order, Awen summoned a protective wall that formed in front of Abimbola, Rohoar,

Silk, and Doc. Similar shields went up in front of the other fire teams, which allowed friendly blaster bolts to fly forward but stopped the enemy's return fire. The white plumes of air played over the tops of the shields, mitigated somewhat in their visual betrayal, but invisibility no longer mattered now that Unity shields were in play.

All at once, the enemy's fire shattered on the translucent force fields. Energy radiated outward as tendrils of electricity danced across the rounded half spheres.

"Pick it up," Magnus called. Awen moved at a light jog as Rohoar and Abimbola advanced, quick to respond to Magnus's command. They aimed at troopers who emerged from side doors down the hallway's length, dropping them with greater accuracy now that the Unity shields were in place. But then there were the troopers who appeared after the unit's leading-edge passed.

"Contact left," someone shouted from further back. Awen looked to her side. There was a Paragon trooper with a blaster pointed at her. She was too preoccupied with keeping the shield up to have noticed the man approach. At point-blank range, she worried about her ability to resist the blaster energy might not be sufficient. So, for the first time since this op began, she panicked.

Just then, a paw swept through the air and slammed the blaster to the ground. The sound startled Awen. But the next thing she knew, Rohoar's jaws appeared around the Marine's forearm. His sharp teeth slipped out of the chameleon mode's limited shield around his muzzle and plunged through plate armor and into flesh. Then Rohoar yanked the man into the corridor and flung him against the opposite wall. The Marine struck the surface headfirst and then collapsed on the ground, presumably suffering from a broken neck.

"Thank you," Awen said in amazement, still managing to keep the wall up.

"You are welcome, Awen. He was a bad man."

"I'm pretty sure they're all bad, big guy," Silk replied as she fired off a round with her CK360.

"Yes, but this one was especially bad. I can taste it."

"I'll take your word for it," Awen replied.

"We're starting to extend our target window," Magnus said over VNET. His voice was tight. "Let's keep moving."

Granther Company and Paladia's first cadre picked up the pace and moved through the corridors in a coordinated advance. Having the shields up gave them more freedom to move and take risks they wouldn't otherwise. For her part, Awen stayed close to her fire team, trying her best to keep everyone within her protective scope.

Magnus called out turns, talking everyone through coordinated attacks as threats presented themselves. Cyril also worked tirelessly to guide the units through the massive starship. He tried to warn Magnus of navigational developments when he could, but as the teams advanced deeper into the ship, the code slicer provided less feedback.

"We've got another blast door," Magnus said, requesting the same demolition combination as before. This time, Nubs stepped up with the breach charge. Awen recommended

Nídira take the force field as she was on the same team with Nubs. Magnus seemed resistant to the idea, wanting Awen to take point, but she insisted Nídira do it. The mystic was more than capable. Plus, Awen knew that Magnus needed to learn to trust other mystics than her. His reliance on Awen seemed to underscore his mounting frustrations about Piper and the mission.

Nubs raced forward, planted the charge, and then stepped back to let Nídira double down on the explosive's direction. Once again, the charge ripped down the hallway and saved Magnus valuable time.

"Told you she could handle it," Awen said on a private VNET channel.

She'd barely finished the words when the hallway filled with troopers, springing from doorways on either flank. Awen couldn't tell if the increased resistance meant the gladia were getting closer to Piper or that the enemy was trying to contain the advance more effectively. But based on the fact that specific doors were closing on them, she wondered if— somewhere—Moldark was watching them and knew where they wanted to go. In which case, the resistance was confirmation.

Alpha and Bravo Teams opened fire, trying to keep the onrushing troopers at bay, but their weapons fire only managed to knock down the first few rows of Marines. The troopers rushed them as if possessed demons, flinging themselves at the Unity shields. Simultaneously, more troopers emerged behind Awen, entering into the protective fold of

Granther Company's attack envelope. This, of course, was where the Jujari shined.

As before, Rohoar guarded Awen, slicing through Repub armor and chomping on limbs. Czyz and Longchomps mauled four troopers on the right flank who rushed into the hallway, blasters hot. Czyz grabbed one man and flung him into the second, both slamming against the wall with a sickening *crack*. While one trooper slid to the floor, presumably unconscious, the other still managed to raise his blaster and attempt to shoot at Wish, who was Charlie Team's mystic. That didn't end well—for the trooper. Czyz slashed at the man's gut, tearing so deeply that pink intestines poked through the gash streaks. The victim doubled over, screaming so loud that Awen could hear him through his helmet.

The two troopers Longchomps assaulted didn't fare any better. The Jujari struck one woman so hard that her head spun until it cracked. Her body went limp, and she was dead before she hit the ground. The second trooper aimed at Longchomps and got a shot off. The blaster bolt exploded against the Jujari's shield but did nothing to him. If anything, the shot enraged Longchomps, who then grabbed the trooper's helmet with both hands and squeezed. The protective head covering cracked, as did the skull inside it. The man's body collapsed beside those already on the ground.

Grahban took on three troopers at once, roaring as he lunged into the cluster. He bit one Marine in the shoulder, slashed at another with a claw, and then kicked the third so hard, the man flew out of the Unity shields and into friendly fire. Grahban bit through the first trooper's shoulder, severing the man's arm. And when the second man tried to rise from the ground, the Jujari stepped on him, grinding his ribs into vital organs.

Magnus ordered everyone to push hard into the enemy, getting clear of what he called a kill box. NOV1 fire reached a feverish level, so much that Awen thought she'd go deaf even through her helmet. Add to that the Jujari roars and the screams of dying troopers, and the sound was maddening.

Once the gladia reached the next intersection, things cleared—at least for the moment. Awen raced to keep up with Abimbola as he led the charge around the next bend. They passed several more sections, putting down any resistance as quickly as it sprang up.

"We're almost there," Magnus said over the company-wide channel. "Keep the pace up."

No sooner had he said the words than Awen felt something lurch in her gut—not physically but ethereally. Magnus must've noticed something was wrong because she felt his hand touch her back.

"You all right?"

Awen shook her head. "No. Something's..." *Something's what?* she asked herself.

"Awen?" Magnus slowed the advance and stepped in front of her. "What's going on?"

As if sparing Awen the need to answer, Willowood said, "It's Piper."

Magnus jerked toward the older woman. "What do you mean, it's Piper? You feel her?"

"Oh yes, quite so," Willowood replied.

Awen plunged through the Foundation and broke into the Nexus. Cosmic energy surged around her, connecting her to the far reaches of the universe. Light, power, and wonder raced along her limbs, tingling her ethereal skin and electrifying her senses.

"There," she yelled, startling her physical self with the exclamation. She saw Piper—or at least the girl's essence. It was little more than a wisp of energy, but it was, she was sure of it.

"Where?" Magnus asked. "Do you see her?"

Awen nodded. "She's in the Nexus."

"And what does that mean?" Magnus looked to Willowood.

"It means she's making her presence known," the older woman said. "Connecting to us through the Unity. She wants us to find her."

Awen could see a wave of relief wash over Magnus, both physically and in the Unity. "And are we headed in the right direction?"

"We are, Magnus. She's…" Awen froze. "She's in a small room. It looks like someone's private quarters. And Moldark is outside. In the observation room."

"Dammit," Magnus said.

"Cyril?" Awen asked, doing her best to work VNET in her HUD. Some of the steps still felt new to her.

"Yeah, miss Gladia Awen ma'am? What is it?"

"I can confirm Piper's location in the ship's aft section."

"Excellent, excellent. I'll relay all that to the Colonel now. He's right here."

"I can hear her just fine, son," Caldwell said to Cyril, his voice popping up in a small display window. "Good work, Awen. Can you get to her?"

"That's not even a question, Colonel," Magnus replied.

"Awen, can you get to her?" the colonel reasserted.

Awen glanced at Willowood. While she couldn't see the older woman's physical face, Awen could see her spirit—and that was far more telling. Willowood nodded reassuringly. "Yes, Colonel," Awen said. "I believe Piper wants us to find and rescue her. I can't communicate with her, but I can sense her feelings."

"And how is she?" Magnus asked the question everyone was probably wondering.

"She's scared," Awen said. "Scared and sad. But also… hopeful. I think she can sense us like we sense her."

Magnus nodded while blaster fire rang throughout the corridor.

"So we have asset confirmation," Caldwell replied. "Let's make this happen, Magnus. Also, Forbes and Nelson are encountering some serious resistance in the hangar bay, but nothing they can't handle. Just know your evac's gonna be hot."

"Roger that." Magnus pulled his NOV1 up and fired at a

trooper that Abimbola missed. "You let that one get by, Bimby."

"I was saving him for you, buckethead."

"Sure, you were."

"Keep things moving, Lieutenant," Caldwell said, regaining Magnus's attention.

"We will, sir."

"Uh, sir? It looks like we may have another problem, sir," Cyril said, his voice trembling.

"What is it?" Caldwell asked.

Awen saw the colonel's face look off-screen. Based on the way his brow furrowed, she didn't think it was good.

"Those are ships." Caldwell removed his cigar from his mouth. "Grid formation."

"Are they're searching for the *Spire*?" Cyril asked.

"It certainly appears that way, son. Can you estimate how much time we have before they find us?"

"It's kinda hard to say, Colonel. Without knowing each pass's endpoint, there's no way to extrapolate parameters."

"I believe I can help," Azelon said. "Based upon standard operating procedures for naval search and recovery operations, the number of vessels, and assuming the enemy is employing full sensor sweeps, I estimate they will detect variations in gamma radiation from the *Spire's* solar shadow in less than one hour."

"Damn," Magnus said. "Moldark's putting things together faster than we anticipated."

"All the more reason for you to minimize time on target, Marine." Caldwell winced. "Gladia."

"We'll get it done, Colonel," Magnus said.

"Make sure your weapons and boots know it too."

"In the meantime, TO-96 is ready to scramble Fang Company in the event of discovery," Azelon said.

"Good," Caldwell said. "But remember, we need those fighters to help cover the shuttles, so I don't want them going out unless they absolutely have to."

"Understood, sir," Azelon replied.

Caldwell looked back at Magnus through his avatar window. "Get the girl, Magnus. Then get the hell off that ship. Caldwell, out."

27

PIPER HAD BEEN SO SCARED that she didn't even realize how tired she was until her job for her grandfather was all over. Once she caught her breath, and her heart had quit thumping wildly in her chest, waves of fatigue washed over Piper like warm blankets stacked on a soft bed. But nothing about what followed was warm or fluffy.

She tried to find a comfortable position in the bed by rearranging the thin pillow beneath her head. But real rest evaded her, emphasized by the blanket, which wasn't warm, and the bed, which wasn't soft. The room was cold, and it smelled funny.

Piper's fitful sleep was more than just physical discomfort. Her grandfather's face played at the sides of her consciousness, haunting her like a ghost. Something about him wasn't right. Piper could see the dark presence that consumed him when she slipped into the Unity. But the hate she sensed wasn't even what disconcerted her the most—instead, it was her grandfather's sadness. She could sense it, buried beneath the aggression and hostility. He was mad because he was sad. And that made Piper's heart break because she didn't know how to fix it—how to fix him. But, then again, she barely knew how to fix herself, so the revelation wasn't any big surprise.

She did make him happy, though. At least that was how he seemed when it was all over. Piper had used her energy to reach out to all the ships in the fleet and convey her grandfather's message. "Tell them that the Republic must be stopped," he said. "That we must keep the senate and the Circle of Nine from hurting anyone else in the future."

When she'd asked why he couldn't just use the ship's comms to send the message, he implored her that this was less about understanding with the head and more about understanding with the heart. "You have a way to speak to people's hearts, don't you, child?"

She nodded. "I suppose so, yes."

"And if the bad people are the ones responsible for killing your parents, and for hurting the Jujari, then we don't just want my ships thinking about the right thing to do, we want them feeling it."

"In their hearts," Piper replied.

"Precisely."

So that's just what she did.

Her old power suit would have made the job impossible,

so she was glad to be free of it. But having so much power also seemed a little scary, like she was doing something wrong —something Awen would probably yell at her for. Piper could practically hear her old shydoh now. But if the Republic was responsible for so much destruction, like her grandfather said, then it must be stopped.

Piper had little reason to doubt her grandfather. While he looked strange and talked funny, she knew what it was like to be misunderstood. So Piper would be the last person to pass judgment on him for how he looked, especially when he was trying to do the right thing. *Bad people need to be stopped from doing bad things—isn't that what Magnus always said?* So Piper did what needed to be done.

Slipping into the Nexus was exciting. She'd only done it a few times since So-Elku told her to take off her power suit. He'd given her the Luma robes in exchange. Then her grandfather had discarded those and offered her a thin black uniform that had been trimmed down to fit her just right. She felt weird having the three white lines on her shoulder, the same that Nos Kil and his men had borne on their armor. But, like her grandfather, Nos Kil was misunderstood, and people had mistreated him because of it.

There in the Nexus, Piper felt the unlimited power of the universe surge through her. She felt like a pollen speck riding atop an ocean wave, moving with the current, lost in the vastness of the sea. But she was not a helpless speck. Rather, she did whatever she wanted—able to move between air and water, resist currents, and even expand or contract. In fact, she felt more powerful within the Nexus than she ever did in real life. Or maybe the Nexus was real life, and her physical body's existence was—*second life?*

Just as all water molecules were connected in the ocean, so too were all hearts joined in space and time. She could see the fleet in the Nexus—every ship and every person in every ship. They floated in the currents like tiny dazzling jewels suspended in the sea's twilight. Their souls shimmered like little stars, carried through space on their little ships. It felt as though all Piper needed was to whisper, and they would hear her. But what to say?

Suddenly, the weight of speaking to the entire fleet felt heavy—a responsibility that Piper couldn't ignore. It was a sacred thing to talk to someone's heart, wasn't it? Like her mother, comforting her when life made her scared, or her father, reassuring her when she needed to do something courageous. Now it was Piper's turn to do the same, and she knew it was no small thing.

"The Galactic Republic wants to hurt people," she whispered to the shimmering motes of light. "But we can't let them. They want to kill people who don't deserve it. And we must stop them. We need to do whatever it takes, even if we're scared. Even if we seconds—*second* guess ourselves. This is the right thing to do. And we need to keep doing it until the job is done—no giving up. No running away and hiding because we're scared. We're in this together, and we won't stop until it's done." The ironic thing was that Piper felt scared even now. Talking to so many people made her nervous. But she needed to do it. For the mission. For the innocent people who would be hurt if she didn't do something.

When Piper felt like her speech was over, she withdrew from the Nexus and returned to her physical body. But she'd expended more energy than she realized. No sooner had her eyes opened than she wanted to close them again. That, and her heart was beating loudly in her ears. A sense of panic and even confusion clutched her heart as if she had done something terrible—yet it seemed right.

"How did it go?" her grandfather asked, urging her to stay awake.

"I just want to sleep."

"You can, and you will. But first I must know—"

"It went good. I… I told them the kinds of things that you told me to say. Said we needed to stop the bad people from hurting innocent people. Can I sleep now?" Piper yawned.

"Yes, of course. And you spoke to all of them?"

"All the ships, yes." It felt like Piper had just drunk a cup of warm milk and was bundled up with a soft blanket. "I'm so tired."

"And do you think they heard you?"

"Of course." She yawned again. Fatigue fought off the nervousness in her chest. "I spoke to their hearts." Piper squinted through one eye at her grandfather. He was smiling —at least that's how she interpreted it. He was kinda scary looking. But he seemed happy. "I want to go to my room, please."

"Yes," her grandfather said, pushing her toward her chamber. "Yes, of course. Sleep, child. Sleep as long as you need."

"Thank you." Piper heard her feet shuffle across the floor, but that was it. She had almost no memory of climbing in her bed. And then sleep—wonderful sleep. Only, it was not as nice as she would have liked.

WHEN PIPER finally decided to give up on sleeping, she opened her eyes and saw a soft red light pulse on the ceiling. Something about it seemed important—it meant something. Like...

Like danger.

She sat up and looked around, but the bedroom was empty, except for the sink, mirror, and small desk in the corner. She didn't smell smoke or feel anything shaking. So what was the red light about?

Piper thought about venturing outside, but she wasn't sure she was ready to see her grandfather again. She was still tired from going into the Nexus and speaking to all the sailors on all the ships. And the sense that she'd done something wrong hadn't left her either, though she couldn't figure out why. The feeling clung to her chest like the stain on a shirt. She wanted to wipe it off, but no matter how hard she tried, the blemish wouldn't go away.

Piper rolled over and stared at the wall, pulling the thin

blanket under her chin. She wished she had Talisman still. Feeling his soft fur against her face was wonderful. But he was gone.

So much had changed in the last few months, and Piper suddenly wished she could go back—before her mother died, before learning the truth about Magnus, before discovering the metaverse, and Oorajee, and her father dying. She wanted to be back home in Capriana. Safe and warm in her own bed with Talisman and her data pad. She wanted things back the way they once were.

And that's when she had an idea.

Without the power suit, Piper felt things in the Unity that she'd never felt before. She felt free. But she also knew she'd get in trouble for it. It was that strange combination of freedom and guilt that seemed to plague her heart now.

She could see things more clearly in the Unity—*in the Nexus*—without her suit. She'd noticed the lucidness when So-Elku was instructing her in the pond. She'd even noticed it when sharing her grandfather's message with the fleet ships. And not just see the present more clearly…

She felt she could see the past too.

It seemed as though thin threads stretched back in time, beyond her vision, to things long passed. While she couldn't see the images from where she stood, Piper knew that if she pulled on the threads, she could bring the memories forward. Or, was she pulling herself to the memories? She couldn't tell. Either way, she could reconnect with her past.

And so she did.

Piper pulled so hard on the thread of her life that she sent herself right back to Capriana. She lay with Talisman snuggled beneath her chin. She felt the nap of his well-loved fur against her cheek, and smelled that he needed a bath. Meanwhile, her parents laughed in the background, enjoying a favorite holo movie in the living room. A pang of regret pulsed in her chest. Instead of fighting it, Piper used it to pull herself into another memory...

Her seventh birthday party dinner.

That had been her favorite. It was just her, her mom, and her dad, eating Quidmallian treasure fish together. They laughed and told stories late into the night, sitting on a deck that overlooked the Midnoric Ocean. The phosmor—mormessint—*phosphorescent* algae lit up the ocean in a brilliant display of purple and green beneath a star-filled night sky. The salty breeze played with Piper's hair, reminding her of that day's ocean swims. And her sun-kissed skin was still warm from so much time on the beach, napping on towels while the surf crashed on the shore.

Piper smelled the scent of jasmine on her mother's skin and heard the rumble of her father's laugh against her chest. She missed them. But being here with them in the Nexus almost felt, well, it almost felt real.

Other threads tickled Piper's face—loose strands fluttering in the Nexus wind. As much as she didn't want to leave this memory, the new threads invited her to pull on them. But there was something different about these threads... something unfamiliar. That's when she noticed who they were connected to—not her, but her parents.

A thread projected from her mother's presence, running forward and back in time, but on tangents all their own—tangents that belonged to her mother's life.

For real? Piper wondered to herself. Could she really see the events of other people's lives as easily as she could see her own? The thought startled her. And, like before, when speaking to the fleets, Piper got scared. She wasn't allowed to look at someone else's life, was she? Those things... those memories were private.

And yet, her mother's threads flitted about in an ethereal wind that practically begged Piper to follow them. *She's dead, after all,* Piper reasoned, and then immediately got mad at herself for such an uncaring thought.

Yes. She is dead. Which gave Piper a thought.

She pinched one of her mother's threads, one that ran to a future moment, and pulled it. Suddenly, she was caught up in a rushing of wind that made her hair and clothes whip against her skin. Lights and color blurred, giving her the sense that she was being whisked through time. And then, as the motion slowed, Piper felt her heart beat faster.

She heard the muffled sounds and saw the mottled shapes of a firefight. Suddenly, she stood in the hangar bay where her mother died. Blaster fire crisscrossed the scene. Bolts exploded against armor and crates and shuttles, dashed into a million orange sparks. Troopers shrieked beneath their helmets, falling to the ground in pain. The sharp smell of explosives and burning plastic made her nostrils flare.

Piper didn't want to be here. It was a mistake to pull this thread.

But then she saw her mother, standing beside Magnus, firing on the bad guys. Piper wanted to tell her to get away from him. She tried screaming at her, but her voice was non-existent except in her own head. This was just a shadow of what had happened, and Piper needed to remind herself of that several times as her eyes watched the scene play out.

She saw her body standing beside Awen, preparing to head up the shuttle's ramp. Which was right about the time that—

No, Piper protested. *I don't want to see it.* And yet, she couldn't break free from the memory. It was as though the moment had an invisible grip on her consciousness—something so strong that she couldn't overcome it. She even tried to close her eyes against the pain, but the memory was being played out within her, forcing her to be terror's witness for a second time. And how terrible it was.

Piper screamed as Magnus pushed her mother into oncoming blaster fire. The bolt that took her life ripped a hole through her mother's helmet, flipping her body back in a long arc. She was dead before she even hit the ground—her face marred, never to be seen again in all its beauty.

Piper thrashed in the Nexus, trying to push herself out, but the place had a grip on her. She was trapped in the moment. Panic began to set in as she wondered if she'd ever break free, or if she'd be bound to watch this memory over and over. Perhaps this was why Awen had insisted she have a power suit—maybe Piper had ventured too far.

Just when she thought she might become hysterical, the memory froze, then went backward. Piper had no idea if she was controlling this subconsciously or if someone else was tampering with the Nexus. But as the replay slowed to a few seconds before her mother died again, Piper's heart beat wildly, realizing she'd have to watch the event all over again.

Was this a cruel trick? Or perhaps some sort of punishment for something she'd done? Piper kicked and punched at the air, trying to escape this new hell she'd found herself in. As if someone held her eye open and pointed her face to her mother's death scene, Piper watched as Magnus—once again —pushed her mother into the oncoming fire. If weeping were possible in the Unity, Piper was doing so now. But she couldn't feel the tears, nor could she hear herself scream. All she saw was the flashing of light, the splitting of armor, and the shooting of sparks.

Then everything froze.

Smoke stood still, as did countless motes of light leaping into the night air. Troopers paused in mid-step, bodies tilting one way or another. Laser bolts hung over the ground, arrested in their flight, while the initial blast from a detonator looked more like a campfire than a violent force about to tear a soldier in two.

Piper looked at her mother, but there was something strange about the woman's body. At first, Piper thought it was just the way Magnus had pushed her. But it wasn't that at all. It was something her mother was doing—an action of choice.

With the entire scene suspended, Piper moved around her mother's body, examining everything in detail. It was both horrific and mesmerizing, brutal and beautiful. Her mother seemed to be reaching for something—arching her back before the fatal shots struck her—pushing herself toward.

Toward the blaster bolts.

But why?

Again, Piper fought the pain in her heart. It shook her chest and threatened to pull her from the Unity, but somehow Piper knew that she wouldn't be allowed to leave until this was over—until she'd accomplished whatever it was the Nexus wanted her to see.

Piper moved around her mother, focused on the blaster bolts slamming into her helmet. As she came around to the front again, she saw herself in the background. Piper caught her breath. She moved her head left, then right, then left, and saw where the blaster bolts were headed.

"She was—" Piper choked on the words, barely able to get them out. "She was protecting me."

The emotions colliding in Piper's chest were relentless. Her mother's last act had been one of sacrificial love. The woman had extended her body just far enough to place her head in the line of fire.

Piper felt herself sink to the ground, weeping in her mother's shadow. Her chest—whether in the Unity or the bed—shook as sorrow wracked her tiny body. Seeing this, knowing what her mother had done, didn't make the loss any easier to bear, but it did give new meaning to the result. It had been an act of love.

"I'm done here," Piper said aloud as if the unseen force that kept her in this moment would relent upon her admonition. "Let me go."

But nothing happened. Piper raised her eyes to see her mother's body floating overhead, helmet and chest struck with a flurry of blaster bolts.

"I said, let me go." But Piper's plea was met with silence. "I get it. She died saving me. Now let me out."

But something about the moment haunted her. It was as if a ghost touched her chin and turned her head. *Magnus.*

"No," Piper said, trying to shake her head away from the traitor. "No, I don't——" She fought against whatever it was that moved her face. But it was impossible. Piper couldn't even force her eyes shut. "Stop it!"

Magnus fired his blaster with his left hand, and pushed her mother with his right, stepping toward her as he did. She wanted to scream at him, to say all the very worst words she'd ever heard at him, even if it got her in trouble. She thought about standing up to kick him and punch him, so she did. She stood up, yelled, and then stepped to his side, reigning blows against his armored side.

Despite her best efforts, however, she could not make him budge. She didn't even feel the reward of her own pain resulting from bleeding knuckles and bruised shins. There was just *nothing*. No impacts, no hurt—just the pain within her chest.

Spent, she leaned her head against Magnus's side, more from exhaustion than any sense of affection. But she wanted to be affectionate. She wanted to like him.

No. Piper shook her head. *That was the past before he betrayed me.*

She'd looked up to him so much, especially after her father died. Piper remembered first meeting him on her family's cruiser when he'd come to rescue them. She remembered the way her father seemed to admire Magnus and the way her mother blushed when he spoke. And then Piper remembered her reoccurring dream where Magnus rescued her in the city. She'd pledged to do the same—to save him.

The truth was, she didn't want to despise him. Hate was exhausting. But how else was she to treat the man who'd taken everything from her?

Piper found that she was resting against Magnus's side. As she pushed herself away, she looked back toward the battlefield. That was when she saw it…

A rocket, suspended in mid-air, with flames propelling it forward. Toward Magnus.

No, not toward Magnus, Piper realized. *Toward the space her mother stood a split second before.*

Piper pushed herself away from Magnus, looking between him, the rocket, and her mother. Her eyes darted back over all three things again, and again, again. Piper could feel her mortal body's heart beat wildly in her chest, causing ripples within the Nexus that made the scene undulate from the pressure.

Had he saved her? Had Magnus actually been trying to *save* her mother instead of killing her? But that's not what Nos Kil had said. No, he'd said Magnus was a murderer. He'd murdered those girls on Caledonia—had even killed his own brother.

Then why try to save Piper's mother?

She backed away from the scene, ducking beneath the shuttle's belly as if she might find a hangar exit further back. But no matter how many steps she took from the scene, it seemed to pull her close again. It was like a horrible night-mare that kept repeating itself. All she wanted was to be free.

And yet, Nos Kil's words begged her consideration. His story had been so compelling, so convincing, that she never questioned it the way she needed to. Perhaps it was the shock of the content that made her do so. Or maybe it was the way he'd spoken with so much conviction. He was maimed and bloodied, after all.

And yet, Piper couldn't help but ask the most important question of all—the one she realized she should have asked from the very beginning.

Was he right?

A new emotion pecked at the crust of Piper's heart, one she hardly recognized. But she'd read about it in her stories, and she'd been familiar with it only through sensing it in other characters. *Shame.* Shame for not asking Magnus if what Nos Kil had said was true or not.

But she could not ask him now. In fact, she would most likely never see him again. The hopelessness of never knowing overwhelmed her. She could feel her soul pleading with the universe, trying to make a deal that if she ever saw him again, Piper would ask Magnus what had really happened. And, for the first time since hearing Nos Kil's side of things, Piper gave Magnus the doubt's benefits—or whatever it was called—that maybe, just maybe, Nos Kil was wrong and Magnus would be right.

But who was she kidding? She wasn't going to see Magnus again. She'd made up her mind to leave them on Worru, and now she was even further away, stuck on her grandfather's ship. And despite how much she told herself that her grandfather would give her a ship when this was over, Piper suspected it was all a lie. It was that *thing* inside her grandfather, that evil presence that wouldn't stay true to his word.

Piper needed to know—she had to see for herself what Nos Kil described. The thought terrified her, of course. Especially if it was real. The things the prisoner said were worse than anything Piper could imagine. But if she was going to spend the rest of her life on this ship, she needed to know what Magnus had done.

Just as it happened with her mother, Piper saw threads emerge from Magnus's life. They played in the ethereal wind of the battle scene, begging her to snag one and pull it. So she did. She pinched a thread and pulled, faster and faster, until seconds turned into minutes turned into days turned into years. Space and time whizzed past her in flashes of color and light until she stopped in a dimly lit room in the basement of a grand hotel.

———

PIPER FROZE as the door to her room opened. She could hear her grandfather breathing in the doorway. He told her it was time to get up, but Piper didn't want to get up. She didn't want to see him or be here. She wanted to be back with Awen and Magnus because she'd made a horrible mistake.

Her grandfather asked her to get up again, but Piper acted like she was asleep. She held her breath and squeezed her eyes shut. It was everything she could do to keep still. Did the blanket move from her thumping heart? Could he sense her panic? In the end, however, her grandfather told her to rest and then left the room. When the door slid closed behind her, Piper sat up and gasped. She had to get out. Now.

She flung off the blanket and turned in the bed, noticing that her arms and legs trembled. She swallowed, stealing her strength, and hopped down. But as soon as her feet hit the floor, something leaped in the Unity. The impression was so strong that it almost knocked her back onto the bed. Awen was here.

28

CONFIRMING PIPER'S presence on the *Labyrinth* had a strange effect on Magnus. Instead of feeling reassured—which he did, he supposed—Magnus felt anxious. The thought of seeing the child again made his heart beat faster.

The last time they'd been together, Magnus and Piper stood over Valerie's dead body. He'd tried to reason with the girl, but she was furious at him. If Piper thought he'd pushed Valerie into oncoming fire, that would explain her rage. And she was, no doubt, already biased against him by Nos Kil's fabricated story. The mix formed a lethal concoction that had probably torn the child's heart in two.

I'd be just as mad, Magnus thought.

And yet, for whatever reason, Piper had resurfaced in the Unity for Awen and Willowood to see. This was a good sign, of course. It also meant he and Piper would soon speak, and that gave him the chills. Magnus had conducted operations on a dozen worlds and in a hundred scenarios, but none made him more nervous than facing Piper again.

As Magnus sent rounds downrange, he searched his heart again to see if he'd done anything wrong to harm the child. If this was his fault—and he believed it was—then making it right meant accounting for his wrongdoing. Magnus could have left her on the *Spire*. He could have kept her in Neith Tearness. Hell, he could have refused the mission to respond to the Stone's cruiser in the first place.

And where would that have gotten her, Magnus? The Bull Wraith would still have captured their ship, and the Paragon would have terminated the crew. No matter how many times Magnus played with outcomes, none seemed better than the one they were already in. And he hated it.

But you could have protected her better, Magnus told himself. He'd been careless to let her wander into Nos Kil's cellblock. And he really should have kept her away from the bloodshed, from the killing. Awen had insisted she was ready, and he'd gone along with it.

Mystics, you're a fool.

THE FIGHTING GREW MORE intense as Granther Company neared Moldark's quarters. Not only were there more troopers gathering in front of the last set of blast doors, but fixed defenses in the ceiling spooled up and fired on the advancing gladia. Despite the added heat, the mystic's shielding held, which allowed the fire teams to take out their targets without fear of being hit. At least for the present.

"How long can your people keep this up, Willowood?" Magnus asked.

"A while," she replied. "But with how fast they keep sending reinforcements, I doubt you'll be getting munitions on those doors any time soon."

As much as Magnus hated to admit it, the older woman was right. This ship had plenty of troopers to burn, and now that Granther Company was outside the nest, the beasts were defending it tooth and nail.

"Cyril," Magnus said.

"Right here. Copy, sir."

"I need an alternate way in."

"Right, right, right, gotcha. Searching now, sir."

Magnus watched as a new auto turret raced down a track in the ceiling to replace a compromised firing unit. The broken system dropped from the track like a spent ammo magazine, and the new auto turret started firing on the gladia. Its blaster fire raked up an invisible shield in front of Abimbola, focusing on his head. But the bolts exploded in a shower of sparks and smacked the wall with a loud *popping* sound.

Using the NOV1's holo sights, Magnus aimed at the auto turret and squeezed off a long burst. Blue bolts bit into the auto turret, spinning, bending, and eventually ripping the unit from the track. Within seconds, however, a new unit was speeding down the track to replace the one Magnus destroyed.

"Cyril, whaddya got for me?"

"It's coming, sir. Yes, yes, yes, here we go. There's a conduit chase directly below you. It runs east for ten meters before turning south again. It should bring you to a subfloor intersection with an access hatch that's within your target area."

Magnus watched the new waypoints illuminate on his HUD as Cyril described the route. "You're a damned genius, Cyril."

"Sir. Just doing my job, sir."

"Alpha and Bravo, you're with me. Willowood, you too. Zoll, Bliss, and Robillard, think you and Paladia Company can keep these animals at bay?"

"Absosplickinlutely," Robillard yelled out as he dropped another replacement auto turret in the ceiling. "Just want to make sure you know what you're doing with leading this element, LT."

Robillard had some balls questioning Magnus's decision. But the guy wasn't exactly wrong in his assessment. By the book, Magnus should not be leading a smaller secondary team, but, rather, staying put with the primary group. An officer couldn't lead if he was stuck in a trench somewhere without eyes and ears on the field of battle. But this was Piper, and Magnus would be damned if he let someone else rescue the girl.

"You question me like that again, and I'll have you on KP for a year," Magnus replied.

"Just making sure."

"And you make sure your blaster doesn't jam and keep an eye on everyone else."

"Roger that."

"And, all of you, if it gets to be too much, fall back to the hangar. We'll find another out. But do not stand here and take a beating if those Unity shields waver in any way. You hear me?"

A middle-aged mystic named Sion looked back at Magnus. He was one of Willowood's cadre leaders. "I swear to you, Lieutenant, we will hold them off or die trying."

"And that's all I could ask for," Magnus replied.

"Then you asked the right thing of the right people. Go. We've got this."

Magnus nodded once and then called out for Alpha and Bravo Teams to follow him back to the hatch. The subfloor cover was located on the left wall about a third of the way down. Saladin wrapped her claws around the recessed handles and jerked, tearing the hatch from its housing with a *screech*. She lay the cover aside and then looked to Magnus.

"In you go," Magnus ordered. One by one, the two fire teams and Willowood went through the hole, crawled down a ladder, and then turned east in the conduit chase.

Magnus was the last down and called for the hatch to be replaced. Once he was satisfied with the fit, he crawled after the rest of the unit, heading east. Multicolored pipes and wires filled the tunnel on every side. The only thing not brimming with lines was the grated gantry he crept across.

Despite their large bodies, the two Jujari seemed to have the easiest time on the narrow pathway. Magnus watched on his HUD as the group turned right at the junction and proceeded south. They crossed under the lateral hallway filled with troopers and soon passed the long bulkhead that made up Moldark's quarter's north-most wall.

Up ahead lay another ladder and another hatch, this one in the observation hold's floor. Magnus prayed to the mystics that there wasn't something on top of it, or that it spit them out under some guards. Calling a last-minute move like this always came with inherent risks—none of which Magnus wanted. But trying to force their way through the front door would be even riskier, so he went with it.

"Careful going up," Magnus said, noting that Rohoar was the first person to ascend. "We want the element of surprise if at all possible."

"Copy that, scrumruk graulap," Rohoar replied, using the now-endearing Jujari term for little hairless warrior. "It is time to retake our sister-child from the enemy."

"Hell yeah, it is," Magnus replied, then watched as Rohoar climbed the ladder.

29

FORBES's first platoon charged down the north corridor, knowing a TS40 was on its way. The gladia hugged the walls while Hedgebore kept the enemy pinned down with withering suppressive fire from their GU90s. Unless Forbes's men could get mines under the massive Trench Sweepers, Magnus wouldn't have a whole lot of shuttle left to evacuate in.

"Hurry it up, gladia," Forbes said over VNET as he clapped his hands. "I'm gonna be late for beers, and you all know how much I hate that. Don't piss me off."

First platoon pushed north by twenty-three meters before the platoon commander ordered the unit to stop. Four engineers set mini VODs against the floor and then backed away, all while the GU90s railed against the enemy. The engineer used the force-direction feature to turn the grenades into surface charges that would blow small holes in the deck. Fire and smoke billowed in the hallways as more Paragon troopers tried to keep Forbes's element from setting the traps.

Concentrated enemy fire walloped an unfortunate gladia as he ducked into the tunnel. The rounds expended his shield and then tore through his Novian armor. In seconds, the man was thrown to the ground and hauled back by members of his fire team. Nelson's first platoon made the enemy pay dearly, dropping three troopers with relentless GU90 fire. The cannon drilled holes along the walls, accented by black smoke and fragments of charred Repub armor.

Next, the engineers placed Azelon's new LIMKIT4 land-mines in the smoldering craters along the ground. Since the Trench Sweepers' front plows removed anything protruding above surface level, the mines had to be recessed. Under normal circumstances, the LIMKIT4 would be buried beneath soil or artificial filling days in advance of enemy movement. But Forbes didn't have that luxury. Instead, he played a delicate game where first platoon needed to plant the mines and get clear of the Trench Sweepers, but not so soon that the enemy had time to sabotage the ordinance.

"We've got another TS40 northbound," Lieutenant Wagoner said over VNET.

Forbes turned to see the Trench Sweeper rumbling down the south tunnel, still a good hundred meters off, and proceeded by a half a company of Paragon Marines. "Get mines down, people. I do *not* want these bitches breaking our line. Might as well dig some holes on the east corridor while we're at it."

Both platoon officers in charge registered receipt of orders and started their engineers forward.

Forbes looked north again. The engineers placed the last of the mines just as the next wave of troopers appeared. Forbes hoped the enemy hadn't seen the trap. To make sure, he ordered all units to focus their fire on the enemy advance —and none too soon. Behind them, Forbes caught sight of a TS40 coming around the bend.

Built to clear passageways on starships and planets alike, the Trench Sweeper was a relic of a bygone era. Yet the vehicle was still more effective than anything built to replace it, which was a testament to its designers. Its boxy nose sported reinforced plows on four sides, tapering to an armor-piercing nose. Crude but highly effective, the TS40 could shave anything and anyone clinging to a corridor floor, wall, or ceiling, and deflect oncoming fire or explosions with ease. Once on the other side of any obstruction, its two platform-mounted double-barreled M109 guns raked any survivors. Since nothing had been designed to take its place, the TS40 and wider TS45 continued to find service in applications where enemies had barricaded themselves beyond the reach of more conventional ordinance.

For all its belligerence, however, the Trench Sweepers had a fatal flaw, well-known by those who commanded them. Their belly was vulnerable to underground explosives. The Repub had spent years trying to reinforce this weakness, but there was only so much retrofitting that one machine could take. The added protection did manage to keep the units in combat longer, but they eventually broke down or failed altogether. And this was precisely what Forbes was hoping to accomplish—stop the Sweepers in their tracks, which not only kept the M109s from tearing up the shuttles but had the added benefit of blocking the central corridor from further troop movement.

As the last troopers were put down by Nelson's GU90 fire, Forbes's engineers took cover around the corners inside the hangar bay. Forbes watched as a TS40 rumbled down the corridor, its blocky front-end consuming the entire hallway. The plow blades were extended, raking along the sides and throwing out sparks as the giant beast lumbered forward. He ordered a platoon ceasefire on the north tunnel as any attempt to thwart the vehicle's advance with blasters was a waste of ammunition.

Forbes held his breath as the TS40 trundled toward them, getting closer to the recessed mines. He pinged his platoon officer in charge and the assistant OIC to make sure they were on the ball. Munition detonation was an art, especially when adrenaline and nerves messed with the works. While he trusted his men, it didn't hurt to back them up with calm reassurances.

"You feeling good, Jackson?" Forbes asked.

"Just waiting for Bessy," Jackson replied, using navy jargon. "She's taking her sweet ole' time today."

"Just don't go early—"

"Or you'll piss her off," Jackson finished. "Roger that, Captain."

Forbes smiled, feeling more confident that Jackson had the timing under control. He had to resist the urge to micro-manage things when the heat was on; learning to trust his men hadn't come naturally to him. But the more training he got in the Corps, the more he realized that mission success was only achieved when leaders learned to trust their subordinates. Still, little reminders never hurt, especially when the enemy was driving TS40s toward you.

The Trench Sweeper scooped up bodies as it neared the mine holes, grinding flesh and armor along the floor and walls. The beast's methodical pace was relentless, filling the entire passageway with the low *clank-clank-clank* of its tank treads.

"Wait for it," Forbes whispered to himself, willing Jackson to hold. He looked back and forth between Jackson and the Sweeper, gauging the distance and holding his breath. Finally, the vehicle crossed over the mines. Forbes counted to three, knowing the exact time needed to ensure the engine compartment was lined up with the ordinance.

"Fire in the hole," Jackson yelled and activated the mines.

A giant *wuh-wumph* blew underneath the Sweeper, and the vehicle leaped into the ceiling with a crash. Flames and debris shot out the narrow gap in the bottom, followed by plumes of inky black smoke. Even through his helmet's noise reduction tech, Forbes could hear gears grind and the drive core whine. The Sweeper slowed until one of the treads came loose, which caused the vehicle to lurch to one side. When the unit halted, a cheer went out over the platoon channel.

"That should keep them busy for a while," Forbes said to Jackson.

"Roger that, Captain," the OIC replied.

"Keep half your platoon at the tunnel to watch for any breakthrough, but I want the rest of your men helping to redouble the south tunnel."

Jackson acknowledged and got to work reassigning his gladia.

Forbes had barely finished giving the order when Wagoner called for him. "We're taking heavy fire, and the mines are—"

Three LIMKIT4 mines detonated just beyond the south blast door's mouth. The unmuffled explosion filled the hangar's southside with fire and smoke, temporarily blocking visual contact with the advancing enemy.

"Splick," Wagoner yelled. Forbes could see that most of third platoon lay scattered on the ground along with most of the AT3M auto turrets and MB17 printable shield walls. He also saw body parts clad in both Paragon and Novian armor. Wagoner swore again for emphasis as he tried to get up.

Forbes glanced at the man's vitals and noticed his blood pressure was dropping and his pulse was elevated. "You're hit, Lieutenant. Get yourself to the shuttles."

"Affirmative," Wagoner replied, sending command authority to his AOIC who'd fared far better.

"Nelson," Forbes said. "I need focused fire down that corridor. We need new mines put down."

Nelson confirmed, and the GU90s sent concentrated fire downrange. The smoke glowed bright blue as the large-diameter rounds streaked down the corridor. Forbes watched in IR while Paragon forces who thought they could move freely undercover were gunned down as they ran.

"Let's use the screen," Forbes yelled. "I want new mines out there!"

The remainder of third platoon's engineers, along with half of first's, charged into the smoke and started planting more LIMKIT4s in the wide craters. Forbes wondered if the damage might be too much for the TS40 to maneuver over, but then he remembered some of the action the platform saw on Zarbanthia, and his doubts were dispelled.

"Keep those mines covered, gladia," Forbes commanded over VNET. "That cannot happen again." Icons went up along his chat window.

"TS40 eastbound," second platoon's LT said. Forbes turned to see a Sweeper swing around a corner and head toward the hangar threshold. It was only eighteen meters away.

"Mines?"

"Planted and ready," the LT replied. There would be no second chances to replant mines if things went sideways in this corridor—the Sweeper was far too close. The good news was that there were no Marines proceeding it.

Forbes breathed a sigh of relief. Then he noticed a sentry turret drop out of the ceiling ahead of the TS40. It swiveled, and then pointed its barrel straight down...

And fired on the LIMKIT4s.

Like before, the blast filled the hangar's west side with fire and smoke. The explosion flung gladia and equipment back toward the shuttles. Voices groaned over comms. One man screamed, gagged, and then fell silent.

Forbes felt his adrenaline surge. There would be no time to replace the mines, which meant the Sweeper would make entry.

"TS40 inbound, west side!" Forbes watched affirmation icons light up as north-facing units in both companies redirected to face it. Meanwhile, the engineers in the south tunnel regrouped behind cover in the hangar. "And watch for ceiling-mounted sentry turrets. They're going for the mines."

As if summoned by his words, Forbes saw two turrets drop from the ceiling and start spinning toward the mines. He was about to call out the targets when one of Nelson's GU90s barked out rounds that turned the two weapons into a molten spray.

"Good shooting," Forbes said.

Nelson acknowledged the compliment, then to his company, he ordered, "Nothing else touches those mines."

Forbes turned his attention to the TS40 about to enter the hangar. "I want men on both flanks! You light that pig up the moment you see the soft part of its hide."

30

"You lied to me," Piper said as she ascended the steps to her grandfather's chair.

If the old man heard her, he didn't show it. Instead, his hand remained on the armrest, chair facing the space battle. But Piper knew he'd heard her, and she grew angrier with each step. The renewed sense of defiance helped keep her awake—she was still tired from all her work in the Nexus. "You told me the Republic was bad."

"And it's not?" he asked.

Piper squinted as she walked around to face him. "Not like you are."

"Me?" He pulled back into the shadow as if offended. "Why would you ever say that, child?"

"Don't call me that."

"But you are my granddaughter."

"Maybe once. But... there's something wrong with you. And you lied to me. Good grandpas don't lie to their grand-daughters."

"I assure you that I did not lie."

"But you, you made me convince everyone to stop the Republic, and now you want to destroy Capriana. I can feel it." Piper gestured toward the starships. "You made me tell them to—"

"I didn't *make you* do anything. You did it of your own volition."

"But, you forced me. I had to help you. It was the only way I could get a ship."

Her grandfather shrugged. "Then you're just going to have to live with that."

Piper studied the old man's face, her eyes trying to find the humanness lurking behind the mask. "You're—you're not going to give me a ship, are you."

He shook his head. "Sadly, no. You are far too important to my cause, child. Perhaps if you had been less accomplished in the Unity, maybe then I'd have let you go."

"I hate you."

Her grandfather winced. Suddenly, something flashed in his eyes. It was as if a light turned on, pushing against the blackness. "Please don't," he said in a softer tone.

Piper squinted at the new look in his face. She spoke less confidently than before. "But, I do hate you. You're evil."

"No, Piper. I'm not. I'm simply... lost."

The light left her grandfather's eyes, and his voice changed. "Shut up, Kane."

Piper had never seen anyone act like this before. Then again, she'd never seen anyone host a second presence—a second soul. She guessed it was the other being speaking to her grandfather now, the one the Paragon troopers called Moldark. And he scared Piper. She tried not to let it show, but she guessed that, being so small, she probably looked as afraid as she felt. Still, she would need to be strong, especially if she was going to find Awen, Magnus, and her grandmother.

"You're an evil person." Piper pointed her index finger at her grandfather. "It's *you* we should fight."

"I think you misunderstand my motives, child."

"I don't think I'm misunderstanding anything. You don't have my best insertions in mind."

"Intentions?"

Piper nodded. "I'm not helping you anymore. And I'll see myself out."

His hand lashed out and grabbed her forearm. "You're not going anywhere, human offspring."

Then the softer voice spoke again—only this time, it had a commanding tone. "Release her, Moldark."

Piper's eyes widened. Was this a battle between the two personalities in her grandfather's body? She could see their souls intermingling in the Unity, like two different colored clouds phasing in and out of one another.

"I will not let her leave this ship," the voice called Moldark said. "She belongs to me."

"She does not belong to you," her grandfather replied.

Piper watched as the old man's face contorted. It looked like something moved under the skin over his cheekbones. His eyes twitched, and his nostrils flared.

"Stop it," Piper exclaimed. "Leave him alone, Moldark!"

The man hissed at her, chomping at the air with his razor-like teeth. "I will not leave him alone. I rule him."

"No," Piper said, willing herself to see past Moldark's presence and into her grandfather's. "He's not yours, you monster."

"Monster?"

"You're bad. And I'm going to stop you—*my friends* are going to stop you."

Moldark laughed, and Piper saw her grandfather's soul recede. "Nothing can stop me, human child. Surely, you of all people can see my immortal presence, can you not?"

She could see the celestial energy, flaring more brightly than ever. But she also knew energy could be contained, spread out, and even dispelled. "Every life can end," she said through tight lips.

"Dark words for a child."

"Maybe." Piper shivered, choosing to look past Moldark's shape. "But I can still see you, grandfather."

"Shut up, human." Moldark snapped at her again, still clutching her arm.

Piper pulled back. "I can see you. Come forward, grandpa. Come toward the light."

"Silence, wretch!"

Suddenly, Piper saw her grandfather's spirit return and contend with Moldark's. The two energies morphed and blurred, phasing in and out of one another like ghostly vapors.

Then a voice spoke from the contending shapes. "You leave her alone," Piper's grandfather demanded. "She does not belong to you."

"I will do with her as I please, mortal," Moldark replied.

"No, you will not. She does not—belong—"

Kane struggled against Moldark, the two energies embattled in an ethereal fight. Meanwhile, in the natural realm, Piper's grandfather's body spasmed in strange jerking movements. "Come on, grandfather! Keep fighting."

"Silence," Moldark said. In the natural realm, his face twisted, and his shoulders twitched. "You will not speak to him anymore." Suddenly, Moldark pushed Kane's soul back until Piper couldn't see it anymore.

"No," she cried, grabbing at Moldark's chest. But she thought better of the action the moment her palm touched his body—a cold sensation raced up her arm, and she felt as though she'd plunged her hand into a bucket of ice water. "Leave him alone."

When Moldark spoke again, his voice was soft and low. "How unfortunate for you that you care so much for him."

"It's not unfortunate. *You're* unfortunate."

Moldark chuckled. "I'm unfortunate? Look around you, child." He wrenched her arm for emphasis, causing her feet to hit one another. "You are a prisoner on my ship, and—"

"Not for long."

Moldark cocked his head, giving her a pensive look. "You mean your friends out there? Yes, yes. I can see the temptation to hope—to believe that help is on the way. But even now, they are growing weaker, their forces losing ground. I'm afraid there will be no rescue for you today. What's more, it seems you will finally be alone in the universe."

"That's not true." Somehow, this man—who was very much *not* her grandfather—knew that she felt alone. It was like he could see into her heart. But Moldark was not gifted in the Unity—he could not see as she saw. Yet, there was something about him, something powerful and old, that made her afraid. Piper's cheeks warmed with the tears that traced lines down her face. "They are going to rescue me. You'll see."

Moldark clucked his tongue. "I had hoped you would assist me longer, but you are proving too problematic. Such spirit in you, and such a shame to see it go."

Piper felt very confused by his words. They scared her more than she cared to admit. And she was still so tired, which made her even more sensitive. "You won't. I'm not going to let you."

"Is that so?"

Suddenly, Piper felt as though a pointed shaft of metal had pierced her chest. Her mouth flew open, but no sound came out. The pain was so intense, the feeling so hot that she couldn't breathe. She tried to swallow—tried to breathe—but she couldn't.

From within the Unity, Piper saw a tendril of black smoke

stretch from Moldark's soul and touch her chest. It undulated like a waterspout, flowing from her ribs toward him. Again, she tried to scream, to kick, to do something, but the tendril of smoke paralyzed her. The pain increased as Piper felt whatever strength she had inside her leave. Her knees gave out. She expected to fall but found herself suspended on the tendril. It felt like a hook had snagged her under the ribcage.

Something caught Moldark's attention. He looked down at the troopers who guarded the blast doors. To Piper's astonishment, several of them went flying as if a Magladarian bull had just plowed through them. Moldark released Piper, and she collapsed in a heap. She gasped, then let out a wail so deep she thought she broke her soul.

31

As Rohoar led the fire teams through the conduit chase, he couldn't help turning his thoughts toward Piper. He felt responsible for her in ways that didn't make sense. As a Jujari in the line of the Mwadim's, Rohoar had never given a hind paw's care about any hairless human, much less a child. But ever since his conversation with Piper on the *Spire's* bridge, he'd found a tender place in his heart for the creature.

Further still, he regretted their conversation in the cell-block after she'd spoken with Nos Kil—*the vile wretch*. Rohoar felt he should have done more—should have insisted that Piper speak to one of the elders about what she'd discussed with Nos Kil. Piper seemed deeply wounded by the ordeal, and Rohoar felt she'd closed herself off unnecessarily from those who might help. But if humans were anything like Jujari

—at least in this area—he recognized that both species failed to do what was best for themselves more often than not. The good ones, anyway. Instead, they opted for what was best for the pack.

But in Piper's case, Rohoar feared she hadn't done what was best for the pack or herself. In fact, he wondered if she hadn't misjudged the situation entirely, believing lies from the prisoner turned meat sack instead of pushing back and refuting Nos Kil's dark words. But she was just a child. How was she to know the difference?

And that's why Rohoar felt he'd let her down. Perhaps, had he said something further, had he forced her to speak up, they wouldn't be here now, sneaking through a tunnel and risking everything to save her. If she died on this mission, he would forfeit his own life as recompense.

The ladder that Cyril marked as a waypoint was just ahead. It would take them up to Moldark's observation chambers. Magnus's voice broke over comms as Rohoar placed a paw on it. "Careful going up. We want the element of surprise if at all possible."

Rohoar smiled as he thought of slaughtering more enemies with Magnus. "Copy that, scrumruk graulap." He climbed the rungs and then eased the floor hatch open just enough to smell the air. Human scent was potent—at least thirty men. Maybe more. Rohoar pushed the plate higher and got eyes on the space, much of which was blocked by crates.

"I am proceeding into the bay," Rohaor said. "There are

humans here, but our emergence appears to be hidden for the most part."

"Copy that. Nice and easy, furball."

Rohoar winced. Furballs belonged to Kathorians, not Jujari. "I shed not, scrumruk graulap."

"Tell that to Azelon's cleaning bots," Magnus replied.

Rohoar grunted. He would have words with Magnus and Azelon's cleaning bots when all this was through.

A dim light filled Rohoar's immediate surroundings. He scouted a few paces ahead and saw plenty of stacked crates and equipment bins for ample cover. After he advanced five meters, he poked his head around a column of black freight containers and saw a windowplex wall spanning the chamber's entire width. From here, he saw the Republic battle with his fleet. *No, not the Republic,* he corrected himself. *The Paragon.* Either way, pangs of sadness filled his chest as he thought of all the Jujari perishing in the conflict. Seeing it so broadly, without the need for holo screens or cameras, made the battle more real. More brutal. And Rohoar wanted nothing more than to end it and execute those who perpetrated crimes against his people.

"Tell me what you see, pal," Magnus said over VNET.

Rohoar turned his attention to the rest of the room. "Forty troopers, maybe fifty. Focused on the blast door. Sending you my sensor feeds now."

Magnus paused. "Got it. They certainly seem preoccupied."

"Yes. Certainly." Rohoar turned to see more gladia emerge from the hole in the floor, and motioned them to move slowly. Then, looking back toward the bay, Rohoar said, "I also see Moldark. And he..."

"He what? Spit it out."

"He has Piper."

Rohoar could sense the unspoken gasp that everyone took. The mystics had surely felt the girl's presence, and Rohoar swore he could smell her. But to make visual contact made his heart leap. "Also, I have nothing in my mouth to spit out."

He narrowed his focus on Piper. The child stood beside Moldark on a raised dais that pressed against the room's large window. Moldark held her arm with one hand and yanked her close to him—an action that made Rohoar's hackles stand up. The pair seemed to be arguing about something. Rohoar thought of trying to speak to her in the Unity but worried doing so may adversely affect her, or eliminate Granther Company's element of surprise if she were to cry out.

"I see her," Magnus replied. "Something's wrong. Rohoar, help everyone get staged and keep us covered."

"Affirmative."

Rohoar worked quickly to keep Alpha and Bravo Teams in the shadows—a task made even easier by chameleon mode. Still, he knew the teams didn't need any unnecessary risks, at least not this close to securing Piper. When Magnus's body shape appeared on Rohoar's HUD, the two conferred while scanning the room.

"I am worried about stray blaster fire hitting the child," Rohoar said.

"A valid concern, but one the enemy may not share."

"Agreed."

"CQB, then?" Magnus asked, using the acronym from close quarters battle.

Rohoar grunted in affirmation, savoring what would surely be a glorious battle. "But I suspect there will be ceiling-mounted turrets, none of which I can smell now."

"Agreed." Magnus opened the team channel. "Alright, people. Looks like we're gonna get the jump on these bastards. We need to limit baster fire in Piper's direction. Rohaor, Saladin, Bimby, and Titus, you'll be first up. CQB unless you can't help it. Silk and Dutch, I need you taking out any auto turrets that appear. Watch the ceiling. Willowood and Nídira, shield those of us in harm's way as best you can but protect Piper at all costs. Doc and Nubs, I want you firing on anything that's left over."

"What about you?" Rohoar asked.

"Awen and I are headed for Piper," Magnus said. "The moment we acquire her, we're out. I don't care how. Remember, Piper is mission priority one, more so than any of us. You get her back to the shuttles—that's all that matters. If we don't save her, this was all for nothing, *and it can't be all for nothing*. Dominate?"

"Liberate," everyone replied.

"Good." Magnus turned to Rohoar. "You take point. We engage on your lead."

Rohoar took a deep breath, savoring the scent of soon to be slain human flesh, double-checked his chameleon mode status, and then moved into the open. Rohoar's eyes scanned Moldark and the troopers for any signs that they detected him. So far, so good. He crept halfway down the hallway to the nearest troopers and then squatted—muscles tight, breathing controlled, body ready to spring. Rohoar's claws flexed, and he licked his chops with a slow movement of his tongue. He would have blood tonight.

He was just about to leap forward when he caught motion out of the corner of his eye. Piper's head pitched back—mouth agape—and her body convulsed as if she'd touched an open electrical circuit. Rohoar wanted to race to her rescue, but he knew Magnus was already heading that way. Instead, Rohoar needed to diminish the guards' numbers and prevent casualties. Yet, everything in him wanted to rip Moldark's head from his shoulders.

"Now," Rohoar growled.

His body snapped like a bowstring, and he flew into the pack of Paragon Marines. Rohoar tore through three men at once, toppling them like toys. His claws sliced through armor as his teeth closed around the exposed tissue just beneath another man's helmet. The victim screamed, but the air came through the puncture wounds instead of his mouth. Rohoar released the man, rolled, and then landed on all fours.

Saladin had done just as much damage, righting herself two paces from Rohoar. Together, they turned on their next victims and leaped, claws and teeth glinting in the dim light.

Eight Marines lay bleeding on the floor, and the enemy hadn't even fired a shot.

Abimbola and Titus pushed into the ranks with their combat knives slicing at the enemy's armor. Just as the telecolos' radial projection hid the Jujari's snouts and limbs, it kept the two men's blades from the enemy's view, making their lethality all the more brutal. The weapons stabbed and swiped, dodged, and stabbed again. Meanwhile, in Rohoar's HUD, he saw the two gladia grapple with witless Marines who were unable to parry Abimbola and Titus's bladed attacks.

Rohoar swiped at more Marines, catching one in the shoulder and the other in the hip. The first man crumpled from the shoulder strike, spine breaking sideways as his blaster went flying. The second man spun into two other Marines, both of whom stumbled backward while trying to point their blasters at the unseen terror assailing their ranks. Before anyone could get a shot off, Rohoar lunged deeper into the fold, carving a furrow through the Marine ranks that separated them into two groups. *Divide and conquer*, Rohoar noted as he arrived on the far side.

Blood covered his claws as he turned to face the enemy. His paws painted crimson smears across the glossy black floor, giving the Marines a target area to shoot. The first blaster shot skipped off Rohaor's armor and dropped his shield to 89%—a meager strike. But as more Marines focused on the space above the smears, Rohoar rolled out of the way. Blaster rounds glanced off the floor and pelted the far wall. He leaped off the floor and dove back into the fray.

Perhaps sensing the jeopardy posed by staying huddled together, the Paragon forces dispersed and sought cover along the chamber's walls. They darted around crates and ducked behind structural trusses. Unable to rid himself of the enemy's blood, Rohoar drew more blaster rounds, which steadily depleted his shield. But not before he took down several retreating Marines. His claws raked the back of one woman's legs, snapping tendons. The human physique was terribly fragile, and the Repub armor did little to protect the vulnerable places behind the thighs and knees. Rohoar's victim sprawled on the ground. The woman rolled and attempted to fire, but Rohoar caught the weapon in his mouth, bit down, and then tossed the blaster away.

He was about to finish her off when a stream of blaster fire struck his side, forcing him to leap away or risk losing his shield altogether—his HUD displayed 17% power remaining. Rohoar grabbed two bodies off the ground and used them as shields as he charged into a cluster of Marines huddled behind a cargo container. Blaster fire riddled the corpses, drilling the armor with holes and smoke, as Rohoar bashed the troopers back. He roared, then snapped at weapons and swatted heads.

Clear of immediate danger, Rohoar used the opportunity to survey the room. A paragon trooper managed to grab onto Titus, grasping him in a bear-hold from behind. Titus stabbed blindly at the man's torso, but the trooper's armor was deflecting most of the blows. Suddenly, Abimbola came up behind both men and lifted the Paragon trooper *and* Titus over his head. Panic-stricken, the trooper dropped Titus, who rolled harmlessly along the ground. Then Abimbola hurled the enemy fifteen meters against the nearest wall. *He is nearly as strong as a Jujari*, Rohoar thought to himself and pulled his chops back in a toothy grin.

Rohoar and his gladia had made quick work of at least two dozen troopers—but the fight was far from over. Additionally, Rohoar saw reinforcements fill in from a side doorway with their blasters raised. Just then, auto turrets dropped from the ceiling, but they spun in circles, attempting to gain target locks. The Novian armor worked well to dispel the initial sensor sweeps, but Rohoar knew it wouldn't be long before the weapons picked up life signs.

And, apparently, Magnus knew it too. He ordered Silk and Dutch to open fire on the turrets, and then let Doc and Nubs loose on the second wave of troopers. With energy origin points, the turrets and weapons focused on the gladias' positions and opened fire.

Rohoar looked across the open ground and up the dais where Piper and Moldark stood. Saladin must've sensed his concern through their pack connection. "She will be kept safe," she said, pausing behind a large structural truss. "I swear it."

"As I do," Rohoar replied. Then he noticed Magnus and Awen's outlines and name tags in his HUD. They were moving along the window, still invisible to the enemy. "Come. We have glory to obtain."

"As you have spoken." Saladin snarled, then dove toward a group of three troopers.

Rohoar checked his shield, now at 6%, and then looked at as his next target.

32

MAGNUS MARVELED at the destructive force that Rohoar and Saladin unleashed on the unsuspecting guards. In a matter of seconds, the two Jujari had eviscerated, maimed, beheaded, or dismembered two dozen guards. The remainder tried to stop the invisible fury with their blasters, but the Jujari seemed unstoppable. Magnus noticed Rohoar's shield drop to less than 10% and worried his friend was in trouble, but with Abimbola and Titus's help, Rohoar managed to stay clear of further blaster fire.

"Turrets," Dutch called out.

"Take them out," Magnus said. A second later, Dutch and Silk blew two auto turrets off the ceiling. Three more pairs appeared, but they met the same fate, exploding into countless fragments of red-hot metal and a blaze of sparks under the two women's deadly sniper fire.

"Reinforcements," Nubs called out and raised his blaster at new Marines filing in from side doors.

"Engage. Keep them busy." Then Magnus looked at Awen and motioned for her to follow him. They ran to the window and then turned to race along it.

Ahead, Moldark studied the conflict from atop his dais. Piper, however, was crumpled on the ground. Magnus felt his heart stop cold, but still, his legs pumped, pushing him faster toward the target. Magnus raised his NOV1 and sighted in on Moldark. He squeezed the trigger, and his weapon belted out a rapid-fire stream of blue bolts. Magnus's mind reported that the target went down. But through the smoke, Magnus saw Moldark still standing.

The enemy turned, leveled his eyes on Magnus, then smiled. Magnus couldn't shake the feeling that something bad was about to happen. Suddenly, some sort of translucent wall vibrated a meter in front of him.

"Keep going," Awen yelled from behind. "I've got you!"

Magnus had no idea what was going on. But he refocused and then bounded up the dais, taking three steps at a time. His heart pounded in his chest as the wall in front of him vibrated again and again. It was almost like Awen was blocking waves of invisible attacks from Moldark.

Magnus raised his blaster a second time, now less than seven meters away, and fired. Combined with his body's speed, the burst of gunfire was tantamount to point-blank. But, again, the rounds seemed to do little but catch Moldark's black suit on fire. It was like the energy was absorbed right into his body.

The words "Be careful" registered in Magnus's mind as he charged Moldark. But adrenaline and rage had overtaken Magnus to such a degree that he was on autopilot. Subconsciously, he noted Piper's crumpled form behind Moldark. So Magnus switched his weapon to full auto, aligned it with Moldark's center mass, and squeezed the trigger.

The NOV1's muzzle erupted in a blaze of blinding light as the weapon drained an entire magazine. Magnus knew the rounds were on target, drilling Moldark into dust. The enemy disappeared in black smoke. But as Awen's force field pushed the fog aside, Moldark's face popped out.

Magnus jolted in surprise, but he was going too fast to change course. Instead, he and Awen's shield struck Moldark, and the two men toppled over the far side of the platform. Awen's force field disappeared as they flipped down the stairs. Suddenly, Magnus felt something pierce his chest.

"Magnus," someone shouted. He thought it was Awen, but the ringing in his ears overpowered her voice. Pain exploded from his sternum. It was as if someone had taken a red-hot prod and pressed it through his ribcage to his spine. He tried to move—tried to yell—but his body was a slave to the pain.

Again, someone called his name, but it felt like the speaker's voice was part of an underwater dream. Nothing could be as loud, as all-consuming, as the torment he was experiencing.

It was like something was trying to suck out his very soul. Magnus wanted to shoot whatever it was—to end it. But he was paralyzed. That's when he realized that the only thing worse than death was the fear of not being able to do anything about it. He felt helpless in light of this all-consuming force. For the first time in a long time, Magnus was afraid.

Then, all at once, the pain stopped.

Magnus flopped onto something irregular—not flat like a floor, but bulbous. Like a body. He blinked several times, then focused on his HUD.

Moldark's razor-like teeth snapped at his visor. Magnus jerked, rolled to the side, and landed on his back. Again, the same translucent shield vibrated a few centimeters above his chest. He looked up the dais and saw Awen descending toward him. She'd established the shield and cut off whatever Moldark was trying to do to him. She was also saying something—over and over.

"GET UP," Magnus finally heard her yell. He snapped out of his daze and rolled away from Moldark. Then he pressed himself up and brought his weapon around.

"DON'T SHOOT," Awen said next. "STOP!"

Magnus hesitated, looking from Moldark back to Awen. Moldark took notice of the mystic racing toward him and turned to face her. The same kind of shield that had protected Magnus now shimmered in front of Awen. But the block seemed weaker than the earlier ones, until it disappeared completely. Magnus guessed that Awen had given him the majority of her energy, sparing little for her defense.

Awen choked, but no noise came from her mouth. Instead, her advancing body arched through the air like she'd been on the end of a pole. Moldark followed her overhead, tracking with her until she slammed on the floor.

Heeding her warning, Magnus slung his NOV1 and withdrew his tactical knife. He flipped his grip, leaped at Moldark, then drove the knife into the soft tissue between the neck and shoulder. Moldark roared and twisted so forcefully that Magnus was thrown into the steps. Had it not been for his helmet's protection, Magnus would have been knocked unconscious.

Magnus blinked then saw Moldark stalking him. The good news was that, a few meters away, Awen climbed to her hands and knees. The bad news was that Magnus's knife was still protruding from Moldark's shoulder.

"You fool," Moldark hissed. Whatever Moldark was doing, the pain struck Magnus again—only this time it was more powerful. Magnus cried out, feeling as if every cell in his body was rupturing. He'd never wanted to die before, but at that moment, death would have been a relief.

Death, however, didn't come—but concentrated blaster fire did. The rounds pelted Moldark's side, tearing holes into his clothes, even boring into his flesh. And yet the man—*the monster*—didn't go down. Not in the slightest. If anything, he seemed stronger.

"Stop," Magnus ordered, feeling a wave of relief as Moldark's attack subsided. "Stop shooting at him!"

"He absorbs it," Awen added, turning on the enemy and

resuming her shield around Magnus. But then Moldark focused on those who'd fired on him.

The next thing Magnus knew, Nubs flew through the air and stopped two meters in front of Moldark. The gladia's telecolos system shorted out, and Nubs's armor came into view. With his body hovering a few centimeters off the ground, Nubs spasmed, sputtering over comms. Magnus raised his NOV1 in an attempt to fire, but before he could, Nubs's suit of armor clattered to the floor. Dust swirled up from the helmet and heap of plates.

"You son of a bitch," Magnus roared and ran toward Moldark. Magnus reached down and picked up Nubs' knife while the other blade still protruded from Moldark's shoulder.

Black eyes gleaming in the blaster fire, Moldark tried once again to reach out and hit Magnus with whatever mystical powers he possessed. But Awen regained her strength and kept Magnus safe, enveloping him with a shield.

Magnus capitalized on the defense and lunged with his knife. Moldark parried, but the blade sliced through the enemy's forearm, splitting his sleeve and opening a long red furrow. As Moldark retaliated—swinging high—Magnus raised his arm and blocked the blow meant for his head. The Unity shield glimmered as each man struck the other. Finally, Magnus thrust his knife at Moldark's abdomen, but the blade was knocked free, accented by another glimmer from Awen's force field.

Moldark roared, and Awen's shield dispelled a new attack —but she seemed to struggle with the effort. Frustrated,

Magnus thrust his knife at the enemy's face, but Moldark caught Magnus's wrist and drove his arm up. Then the enemy jabbed with his free hand, but Magnus caught Moldark's fist. The two combatants faced each other, heads half a meter apart, while Awen's force field reverberated between them—a shimmering wall of otherworldly light.

"I've secured Piper," a voice said over VNET. Magnus saw Willowood's name tag light up as the communication came in, but he could not risk taking his eyes off Moldark. The old woman must've snuck up the dais and retrieved the unconscious child during the fight, which may have explained why Nubs was unprotected against Moldark's attack.

"Leave him," Awen said, her voice strained.

Moldark snarled at Magnus, saliva and blood sputtering through cracked lips. His black hate-filled eyes flared as he said, "You cannot stop me, human."

"A little help here," Magnus said to Awen, ignoring Moldark.

"I'll try to contain him, but I'll need help."

Magnus double-checked to make sure the squad channel was still open. "Willowood, Nídira—you available?"

Moldark snapped his teeth at Magnus's helmet, but Awen's protective bubble kept the gladia safe—at least for another few seconds.

Suddenly, a new translucent field appeared, but this one encompassed Moldark. Magnus noticed Awen's shield disappear, and then she turned to Moldark, adding her strength to the other two mystics' containment field. The enemy thrashed inside the bubble, lunging at Magnus, then spun on his heels and darted at Awen. But the bubble held.

Magnus's shield took three direct hits in the back. He spun to see two Paragon Marines aiming at him from behind crates. Knife still in hand, Magnus brought his NOV1 into high ready position and opened fire. The first Marine was struck in the head and disappeared behind the box. Magnus hit the second Marine in the shoulder, spinning him out into the open, and then dropped him with two shots in the chest. Then Magnus ran behind a column.

Blaster fire peppered Magnus's cover, but he was safe for the moment. He needed to assess his unit's condition. Magnus glanced at Awen and saw her running toward the two teams, while Moldark remained fixed in place, still throwing a fit in his temporary prison. Rohoar, Abimbola, and Titus had fallen back and resorted to blasters now that Piper was secure behind their perimeter. But more Paragon troopers continued to pour into Moldark's bay from the west and brought the heat. Enemy bolts deflected off a single energy shield that Nídira erected, leaving Willowood and Awen to manage Moldark on their own. Piper, dressed in a small black naval suit, lay unconscious in Willowood's arms.

"Where's Saladin?" Magnus asked.

"We cannot get to her," Rohoar said with a growl in his throat.

"What? Where is she?" He scanned the room from the column's safety and saw her outline behind some shipping containers. But she was pinned down by heavy enemy fire. "Splick."

"Leave me," Saladin said. "This fight will be my last."

"No way," Magnus said. They were too close to her to leave her behind. But the amount of enemy fire had increased enough that Magnus questioned his confidence in a rescue effort. The mission was to rescue Piper, no matter the cost. But he'd already lost Nubs—he would not lose another.

"Hold on, Saladin." Magnus swapped out his rear mag for a fresh one. "We're coming for you."

"Negative, scrumruk graulap. My glory has come."

"Like hell it has."

"Do not advance," Rohoar said over comms. It took a split second for Magnus to realize the Jujari was talking to him, not Saladin.

"Belay that, furball," Magnus said.

"No," the Jujari said. "She has issued her last wish."

Magnus balked. "I don't have time for this. We need to move out. Granther Company, I'm gonna need something faster than that tunnel."

"Sir. I may have something for you, sir," Cyril said.

"Make it snappy, kid."

"Gotcha, gotcha. There's a power substation directly behind your position to the east. I just managed to get the doors unlocked, and you should be able to cross through it and gain access to your section's main lateral corridor. As long as you and the other fire teams retreat north, you—"

"Should be able to group amidships," Magnus said, finishing Cyril's thought.

"Yeah. Exactly, sir."

"Got it."

New waypoints appeared in Magnus's HUD. Two retreating routes ran parallel to one another and then converged halfway down the ship. From there, they ran to the shuttle bay's south door. Magnus pinged the rest of the company. "Proceed to the highlighted routes. Teams Charlie, Delta, Echo, meet us at Zulu Zero Five. Confirm."

"Roger that," Zoll said. "We'll see you there."

To Alpha and Bravo Teams, Magnus said, "A little cover?"

"No problem, buckethead," Abimbola said. A fresh wave of blaster rounds erupted from the defensive line. Magnus ducked out from the column and dashed for Saladin's location, but his shield took two more hits, dropping it to 3%. The next hits would be plate armor only, and that wouldn't hold long.

"What are you doing, Magnus?" Rohoar yelled.

"Saving your kin!"

"Stand down," Rohoar replied, his voice as stern as Magnus had ever heard it. "And return yourself to cover before I have to drag you myself."

Not that Magnus had much choice: blaster rounds peppered the ground all around him until he was forced to halt his advance and retreat behind Nídira's safety shield. He pushed on Rohoar's arm. "What the hell, hyena?"

"Do not call me that."

"You gonna help me get her or not?"

"She has summoned her glory."

Magnus was furious. "Dammit, Rohoar! What the hell is the matter with you?"

"Magnus," Awen said in a gentle voice. "Saladin is mortally wounded. According to their warrior customs, she is going to help secure our escape with a final act of bravery."

"Like hell! I'm not losing another one."

"You already have," Awen said. "She's made up her mind, and I don't think we can keep Moldark contained much longer."

"Please depart," Saladin said, followed by several deep coughs. "So I may make good on my fate."

Magnus punched his chest once and then shook his head. Then he felt a paw touch his shoulder. "It is all right, scrumruk graulap. It is the way of our people, and we must go."

Magnus nodded blindly at Rohoar. "Saladin?"

She coughed. "Yes, Magnus?"

"Dominate."

"Lib—Liberate."

Magnus took a deep breath then watched as the enemy continued to fill the observation deck. The mystics' shields wouldn't hold much longer. Reluctantly, Magnus pointed to the door Cyril had unlocked. "Let's move!"

Once his units were underway, Magnus opened the Taursar Company Commander channel. "Forbes. Do you copy?" The channel was open, and at first all Magnus heard was breathing and the muffled sounds of large-caliber blaster fire.

"A little busy here, boss," Forbes said. "Whaddya need?"

"We're gonna be coming in hot, south entry."

"Might be a problem," Forbes replied. "There's a TS40 blocking it at the moment."

"Well, can you move it?"

"After we take care of the one ripping up your shuttle, yes. Probably."

Magnus cursed. "How bad is it?"

"Bad enough. Stand by." To someone else, Forbes yelled, "It's breaking left. *Left!*"

"Just get ready for us, Forbes."

"We will."

Magnus closed the channel and then looked as everyone piled through the door into the substation. Rohoar and Awen were the last to enter, hesitating as Magnus neared. "What are you waiting for?"

Rohoar nodded toward the troopers. Magnus turned to see Saladin's online on his HUD. She lay amidst some boxes, now overrun by at least fifteen Marines. Most didn't even seem to notice her—they were preoccupied with pursuing Magnus's gladias.

"*Naf tilnik borga, dar leenmar niff,*" Rohoar said. Suddenly, bright light washed out Saladin's outline as an explosion sent cargo and troopers flying in all directions. The deck rumbled, fire billowed, and the enemy's assault momentarily ebbed.

Saladin had detonated her VODs in a sacrificial act to buy Alpha and Bravo Teams more time.

Rohoar helped moved Magnus toward the door. "She has found her glory. Come."

Magnus stepped into the substation, followed by Rohoar and Awen, and then Titus closed the door and blew out the security panel.

33

RICIO PACED the safety area beside his Fang, hands stuffed inside his Novian flight suit. He'd been monitoring VNET traffic since Magnus made contact with the enemy and wanted nothing more than to get in the fight. But doing so prematurely meant giving away the *Spire's* location and jeopardizing Magnus's chances of getting everyone home in one piece.

TO-96 and Ezo, having returned from their mission to the *Labyrinth*, stood beside Ricio in the primary Fang hangar bay, awaiting orders from Colonel Caldwell. Likewise, Nolan had suited up and leaned against a gantry crane. The three men were ready to lead their respective squadrons while TO-96 commanded the company from onboard the *Spire*.

"Based upon your heart rate and perspiration levels, I

assume you are experiencing a high level of anxiety," TO-96 said to Ricio.

"No splick, bot."

TO-96 hesitated. "Are you agreeing with me?" The bot looked at Ezo. "Or have we changed the subject to biological excrement? I'm confused."

"Everything's nominal with Commander Longo, 'Six,'" Ezo said, patting the bot on the shoulder. "Leave him be."

"Understood."

"Commander Ninety-Six, do you copy?" Caldwell asked over comms.

TO-96 stood erect and looked straight ahead. "I read you, Colonel, sir. Please continue."

"As I'm sure you know, we've got some fairly nosey ships poking around our section of the system."

TO-96 glanced at Ricio. "He means the Paragon forces are getting closer to us," Ricio clarified.

"Ah. Yes, Colonel"—TO-96 over-enunciated his words —"it seems the hounds are curious about all the birds in the hen house."

Ricio furrowed his brow and shook his head, mouthing the word, "What?"

"Whatever," Caldwell said. "It looks like it's time we throw them off our trail."

"Ah. We shall endeavor to mottle the scent, disguising the forest trail with—"

"Scramble the damn fighters, 'Six,'" Ezo said.

The bot nodded. Through the hangar's rather robust

audio system, TO-96 said, "All pilots, all pilots, to your fighters. This is not a drill. Scramble Red, Gold, and Blue Squadrons to intercept enemy vessels. I repeat, this is not a drill. Command level instructions to follow." TO-96 looked at Ricio and said, "How was that?"

"Turn off your damn channel, bot," Ricio replied.

"Ooo, my apologies," said TO-96, his voice booming throughout the hangar with a squeal of feedback.

"You heard the man," Ricio said to Ezo and Nolan. "Let's get ready to fly." He patted both men on the shoulder and then jogged toward his Fang. As he buckled into the lowered cockpit platform, TO-96 walked over, looking as though he had something to say.

"Commander Longo, sir?"

"What is it, pal." Ricio locked his harness and then started moving through holo screens to begin his pre-flight check.

"I have never led squadrons into battle before."

"We've already gone over this. You're gonna be fine."

"And while I appreciate that vote of confidence, I still feel obligated to say that I'm sorry."

Ricio pulled his helmet on but stopped short of securing the strap. "Sorry? For what, 'Six?"

"If I'm inadvertently responsible for your death, I just want you to know it wasn't personal. I quite like you."

Ricio blinked a few times. "Uh, thanks?"

"You're welcome, sir." Then TO-96 reached out and patted Ricio on the shoulder like the other squadron commanders had done. "Have a sumptuous flight."

Ricio shook his head and gave a crooked smile as TO-96 turned and walked away.

ONCE OUTSIDE THE *SPIRE*, Ricio circled around to gather his squadron together. It felt good to be back in his Fang, and it felt even better to be headed back into combat. He pulled out the printed picture of his wife and son and wedged it under an indicator bezel. He'd managed to grab the keepsake from his Talon before Azelon had shot him down, and the *Spire's* crew had recovered it from his flight suit before they incinerated his old clothes. The image's corners were charred, and the picture creased, but as long as he had the photo, Ricio felt like he still had a connection to his family back on Capriana. He kissed two fingers and touched their faces.

"All right, Red Squadron. Form up. We're just waiting for orders from—"

"Hello? Can all of the flying humans hear me?"

Flying humans? Ricio scratched his chin and then lowered his visor to bring up his secondary HUD. "This is Red Leader Actual. I have you, Command."

"Ah, how nice to—"

"This is Gold Leader Actual," said Nolan. "I read you, Command."

"Oh, how nice," said TO-96.

"Blue Leader Actual. I read you, 'Six," Ezo said. "Use the terms Ricio taught you—none of this *flying humans* splick."

"Very good, sir," the bot said. "I was merely trying to lighten the mood by being less formal, however, if that—"

"It's war, bot," Ricio interjected. "If you let us do our job, that will lighten our mood. Just give us our orders."

"Very good, Commander Longo. I'm bringing up a target priority list for your respective squadrons, which you can assign based on your personal preference. However, I've preemptively allocated pilot suggestions for individual assignments based on data gathered during training. Use at your discretion."

Ricio saw the data set populate his mission window. A quick scan showed that TO-96 had done his homework. Ricio whistled. "Not bad, 'Six. Not bad at all."

"Thank you, Commander Longo. Now, the Paragon Talons pose the most critical threat. Two squadrons of fourteen ships each—the same structure that we use—are within ten minutes of detecting the *Spire*. Beyond them, we have identified two Light Cruisers, three Destroyers, three Frigates, and four Corvettes, all of which, we believe, are in support of the Talon reconnaissance objectives.

"As you are all well aware, we are in no place to take on such an enemy composition, especially when our primary mission is not inter-fleet combat but asset recovery. That said, Azelon and I have determined that our best strategy will be to lead the vessels away from the *Spire* and then feign an attack on the *Labyrinth*. Subsequently, this will place your Fangs in the prime location to escort the retreating shuttles.

"Please note that Azelon is jamming Talon sensor sweeps

in your direction. As long as you approach from the vectors I've designated, you should remain hidden until you engage the enemy."

"Copy that," Ricio said. "Much appreciated."

"My pleasure, sir. I will be standing by for reachback, as well as to redefine mission parameters should assets or targets change *on the fly*, as they say. That means you might encounter unexpected—"

"We all know what it means, 'Six," Ezo said. "Anything else?"

"Well, I believe the expression is happy hunting, fellas."

Rico chuckled. "You heard the man, Red Squadron. Let's go kill us some game."

RICIO KEPT all of TO-96's suggestions for target assignments, noting they were either exactly what he would have chosen or, in a few cases, even better. The bot had smarts—he had to give him that. His language skills and social tact on the other hand? Those were gonna need some work.

All three squadrons were assigned various Talon group-ings, each designed to cull the enemy's numbers while also provoking the larger starships to follow the Fangs as they sped toward the *Labyrinth*. Once clear of the *Spire*, the Fangs would double down on their efforts to reduce any threats posed against the shuttles, then escort them back to the *Spire*.

Ricio made sure his pilots had confirmed their targets

then locked in his own. If they stuck to the math, Fang Company would eliminate the fourteen Talons during the first salvo. From there, they'd dash toward the *Labyrinth*, and then flip back to catch the larger ships in their hastened efforts to catch up. It was a simple plan, but sometimes those were the best ones.

Ricio pushed his Fang forward, increasing speed through the NBTI. Now that he'd gotten the hang of controlling a starfighter with his mind, he doubted he'd ever be able to use manual controls again. The thirteen other ships in his squadron moved with him, forming up in pairs as they prepared to engage the enemy.

"I don't wanna see any missiles going hot, Red Squadron," Ricio said. "We're saving all the fun toys for later. Blasters only unless you get in a splick show." Ricio placed his missiles and mines on standby so he wouldn't be tempted. "Contact in thirty seconds."

The enemy had spread their squadrons out to form three lines stacked on top of one another. Each starfighter was four klicks from any other fighter in the grid. Rico lined up with his first quarry, a single Talon in the middle of the lowest line, and locked on. "Fangs, prepare to engage."

The grid seemed so far away at first. Rico felt like they'd never get there. Then, as the mission timer counted down to zero—the point of first contact—the grid expanded until it outgrew Ricio's field of view. His target ship came up fast.

"Open fire," Rico said, then willed his primary and secondary blasters to shoot. The main barrel along the fuselage shook the ship as its large-caliber bolts ripped through the blackness. The wing-mounted blasters sent shorter but more frequent rounds downrange. But the physics of light speed ruled both weapons, so all rounds reached Ricio's first target at the same instant. With its shields low, the unsuspecting Talon detonated in a cataclysmic explosion, leaving few fragments larger than a square meter intact.

"Scratch one." Ricio flew through the debris field and pulled into a climb, headed for the Talon directly above. Nine of his other pilots confirmed kills, while four reported Talons in various states of duress. It wasn't a perfect surprise attack, but his squadron was full of new pilots, so he'd take any kills he could get.

Ricio's sensor system confirmed a lock on his second target. The pilot was attempting to raise shields, but not in time enough to save his life. Ricio brought his nose up until he was under the ship, then fired into the Talon's belly. The energy rounds blew past the shield, ripped through the cockpit, and split the craft in half. Ricio veered away, throwing his body sideways in the seat, and watched the flaming wreckage whiz passed his port window.

"Scratch two."

Red Squadron had taken out four more Talons—one away from an entire squadron. Combined with Gold and Blue Squadrons' take, the total was up to twenty-two of twenty-eight total enemy fighters. Such large numbers were only because of Azelon's concealment—Ricio knew that. They would not have that kind of hand again.

Despite being severely outnumbered and outgunned, the remaining six Talons broke formation and flipped around on their pursuers with terrific speed. Their shields were up, and their weapons systems armed.

"Watch your left flank, Red Three," Ricio yelled.

A Talon got two hits on Red Three's shield but failed to do any critical damage. The Fang rolled away from the oncoming ship and got clear of its blaster fire. As the enemy starfighter sailed past the point of contact, Ricio locked on and fired his multi-rate wingtip mounted cannons. They whined like banshees and tore through the enemy Talon from stem to stern. The craft split apart, shedding its plate armor like a Lorlilliak mull drake shedding its skin in molting season. Ricio watched as the majority of the pilot's body twirled through space and disappeared among the stars.

The five remaining Talons put forth a valiant effort, but in less than twenty-five seconds, both squadrons were wiped out. Ricio couldn't ignore the pang in his heart, knowing these were most likely pilots he'd known, or knew of. Hell, he'd probably trained the majority of them at one point or another. And had Ricio been in one of the Talons, he'd have been scared splickless by how his once-formidable squadron was decimated in less time than it took to piss out a beer.

Ricio's sympathy was cut short when one of the Light Cruisers and a Destroyer opened fire. "Red Squadron, break for the *Labyrinth*," Ricio ordered. "Let's return them to their fleet, but I'd like to see them limp back a little." The pilots registered Ricio's commands, and new target lock icons appeared along the sides of both enemy ships. Gold and Blue Squadrons targeted the other vessels in the search party, including the faster Corvettes. "Let's light 'em up!"

Ricio brought his Fang around and increased speed. His body pressed into his seat while his guidance system made micro corrections to stay clear of oncoming enemy fire. Enormous blaster bolts whizzed by his canopy, casting his cockpit in green light. When the statistical likelihood of a sure shot reached 90%, Ricio fired all his cannons. Blue rounds raced toward the Light Cruiser's bridge. The enemy's shield array absorbed the first volley, scattering the energy like a lightning storm over an invincible glass ball. But as Ricio continued to pour on the rounds, heating the barrels to red-hot, a hole tore open in the shields.

Ricio's Fang shot through the gap and entered the ship's near-field space, then fired on the bridge. His accuracy was at 100%, and he would not fail. The cannons barked, shaking his ship, and the blue light struck the Light Cruiser's forward bridge. Ricio's rounds punched through the reinforced windowplex and blew out the entire command center. The bridge exploded, sending ripples of fire and electrical blasts along the bow.

"Bridge disabled," Ricio said with a bit of excitement in his voice. The blow was enough to keep the vessel from going anywhere, but Ricio knew the ship still had some fight left. "Watch those auto turrets."

Three Fangs raced along the cruiser's hull, heading for the stern. They targeted the communications array, hoping to further disable the ship's ability to connect with the fleet. One Fang was particularly unlucky and took several auto turret rounds. Fortunately, the fighter's shields held, and the ship managed to roll out of the auto turret's fire arc. The two other Fangs continued on their course and laid into the comms array, blasting it from the deck.

Red Squadron left the Light Cruiser to bleed out and focused their attention on the two Frigates. "Let's let them stay under power," Ricio said. "But I want their primary weapons disabled."

His pilots acknowledged. Targeting icons appeared along the ship's flanks as Red Squadron lined up for a strafing run that would take the Fangs across both Frigates from starboard to port amidships.

Ricio ordered his squadron to pummel the first Frigate's shield. They managed to bore a hole in short order, all the while dodging enemy fire. Once the starboard shield fell, the Fangs spread out and opened fire on the ship's emplaced cannons. Ricio's visor dimmed as several friendly and enemy blaster rounds collided. But in the end, the Frigates' defenses were no match for the Fangs' speed and power. One by one, each emplacement exploded on the starboard side, shooting flames and debris into space. The hard vacuum snuffed out the fires, but the bits of starship would float to infinity.

The Fangs flew up and over the enemy hull, then dove back down to line up on the second Frigate's starboard side. Having seen the fate of its counterpart, the starship focused its firepower on Ricio's squadron. But it didn't last long. Ricio had made sure the first Frigate was directly behind them, which meant that the second Frigate was firing on the first. As soon as the two starships sent what Ricio could only imagine were expletive-filled transmissions to cease fire, Red Squadron fired on the second Frigate's shield and made short work of it. The energy wall fell, and—like before—the Fangs tore into the starship's flank.

The pock-marked vessel tried to steer away from the attack, but the Fangs were too fast. Ricio led his squadron around the Frigate's far side and then turned back to assault the port-side emplacements. While several Fangs took minimal damage, there was simply no way the mega-ton warship could keep up with the agile Novian fighters. When they'd finished with the Frigate's port side, Ricio brought up the *Labyrinth's* coordinates and sent the high-priority waypoint to his pilots.

"Nice work, everyone," Ricio said as he scanned the damage reports. "Now let's lead them home."

34

FORBES DOVE FOR cover behind an MB17 as two things took place simultaneously.

First, the TS40 advancing from the south fell into the craters and struck the mines. While the Sweeper was out of commission, it blew open and caught the corridor on fire. Smoke and fire poured into the hangar bay despite the fire suppression system's best efforts to quench it.

Second, and more importantly, the TS40 advancing from the west breached the bay and opened fire with its M109s. Gladia had lined up on both sides, ready to take out the guns, but the Sweeper's crew had been prepared for them. The moment the M109s appeared, their barrels pointed down, head-level with the members of second platoon. Helmets and heads exploded, blown back by the M109s twin barrels.

"Target that Sweeper," Forbes yelled over VNET. "Put it

down!" Blaster fire erupted from all sides and pelted the TS40. Meanwhile, fire from the south moved dangerously close to the shuttles, carried by a river of hydraulic fluid and lubricant. "Cyril, can you close the south tunnel's entrance?"

"Sure, sure, sure. Let me see what I can do ten four, sir," the code slicer replied. "You know, this is actually a lot harder than playing *Galaxy Renegade*."

"The sooner, the better, Cyril. Or else we might not have a ride home."

The TS40 to the west turned broadside and aimed its guns on the nearest shuttle—the one Granther and Paladia Companies arrived in. Despite Forbes's best efforts to thwart it, the Sweeper blew holes in the shuttle, breaching the hull and permanently grounding the vehicle from space travel. Metal shrieked as it bent inward, succumbing to the M109s' withering firepower, while conduits burst and sprayed the hangar with gas.

"Shut that down," Forbes barked, pointing to the gas leak. If it were flammable, the mission would be over in a hurry. "And, mysticsdammit, get those bastards off those guns!"

"Forbes," Magnus said over VNET. "Do you copy?"

Forbes barely managed a reply as he ducked behind cover again, asking Magnus what he needed.

"We're gonna be coming in hot, south entry," Magnus said.

Great, Forbes thought, looking at the fire. *Just great.* He explained the problem to Magnus and then added the minor note about the second TS40 ripping up Magnus's shuttle. The lieutenant was about as pissed as Forbes expected him to be. The good news, however, was that the survivors of the four companies could fit on two shuttles.

Suddenly, the TS40 broke left, spinning its guns on the remaining gladias by the tunnel's entrance.

"Left," Forbes hollered for the second time, willing his men to adjust their fire. When Magnus asked Forbes to be ready, Forbes said he would be even though he had no idea how he was going to get Magnus's people through.

Forbes closed the channel and swore at his men, screaming at them to finish off the Sweeper. But they were pinned down, and the vehicle had the upper hand. Plus, more Marines were filing in behind the Sweeper and firing on second platoon. The TS40 was busy mowing down anyone who tried to assault its guns. And although Nelson's GU90s fired relentlessly at the behemoth, all they did was turn the vehicle's impenetrable nose armor cherry red.

"Doors closing, sir," Cyril said. Forbes looked to the south tunnel, which was still consumed with fire, but nothing happened. Then, out of the corner of his eye, Forbes saw the west doors close, shutting out the rest of the Marines who tried following the TS40.

"Wrong doors, kid," Forbes said. "But I'll take it." Still, the Sweeper was wreaking havoc in the hangar. Forbes had to act fast.

Then, he saw it—a window of opportunity. The vehicle was headed toward a new crater in the hangar floor left over from yet another failed attempt to bring the juggernaut down.

Forbes reached down and grabbed a LIMKIT4 mine, tucked it under his arm like a space ball, and took off running for the Sweeper.

"What the hell are you doing, Forbes?" Nelson blared over comms. But Forbes's adrenalin was so high he hardly registered the comment as he sprinted.

The M109s remained focused elsewhere, blasting away, while Forbes dropped to his side and slid into the crater. The Sweeper's blade crossed over the top of him, sealing him under the Sweeper. The fit was so tight that the vehicle's exposed belly scraped against his armor. Forbes activated the mine and flipped it over as the humming electromagnet adhered to the TS40's undercarriage with a loud *thunk*. Then Forbes punched the trigger key for a four-second delay and hoped it was enough time.

As soon as the Sweeper cleared the crater, Forbes scrambled out of the hole and ran for cover.

Three... Forbes counted in his head. *Two...*

The blast threw Forbes toward Nelson's defensive perimeter and into a portable shield wall. He tumbled to the ground and watched as the Sweeper rose three meters off the floor and split in half. It crashed back down, forward treads still clawing at the ground. The front-end drove in tight circles until the unit's fuel reserves depleted.

"Guess five seconds would have been better," Forbes said to himself.

The TS40 was no longer a threat, but it had taken a toll on Tausar Company. Most of second platoon and parts of first and third had taken heavy casualties. Even some of Nelson's men were hit while the M109s tore up the shuttle. Without the Novian armor, Forbes knew things would have been much worse, but the losses were enough that Forbes cursed under his breath as he doled out orders to regroup.

"Captain Forbes, sir?" Cyril said.

"What?" *This had better be good news*, Forbes thought.

"Bad news. Bad news about the doors."

"Gah, dammit to hell!" Forbes turned to Nelson and opened the channel for both companies. "Let's get fire suppression on that blaze; get handhelds from the shuttles if you have to. Then I want tow cables and winches on the wreck. We're hauling it out of there. We've got Granther Company coming down that hallway, and I'll be damned if a Magnus—any Magnus—finds us with our thumbs up our butts."

Forbes asked Nelson for men to assist in recovering Taursar's wounded and then ordered everyone to pull survivors back to the shuttles. With the southern and northern tunnels blocked by wreckage, and the western blast doors sealed, Forbes knew he had a small window to get things in order before Magnus arrived.

"Help me with these two," Forbes said to two gladias from Hedgebore. They worked to lift a piece of the TS40 off men from second platoon. The victims were severely wounded, but Forbes saw their vitals in his HUD and guessed they'd survive if their suit's nanobots could keep them alive until they got back to the *Spire*. "Easy, easy."

Forbes coached the rescuers as they dragged the men to safety.

Next, Forbes found a gladia whose chest and head were covered with a piece of plate metal. He removed it and winced—the gladia's head was gone, probably due to point-blank M109 fire. Forbes tagged the corpse in his HUD for non-critical retrieval and then moved on to look for more survivors. He helped several gladia to their feet and pointed them in the right direction. "Back to the shuttle," he said. "Your job's done. Good fighting."

When he was done overseeing the casualty retrieval, Forbes looked to the south tunnel. Nelson had successfully put the flames out and was busy securing tow cables. Forbes got him on comms and said, "Just be ready for resistance from the other side."

"We're on it, Captain," Nelson replied. Hedgebore's CO waved to his engineers, who then activated the winches beneath the operational shuttles. The cables went taut, and the wreckage began to screech as it bit into the corridor's walls and floor. The winches growled, and Forbes noticed the shuttles start to list to port.

"I want everyone clear," Forbes said, ordering the gladia away from the cables. "If those things hit you, we'll be dragging you back in body bags." The men backed away, looking between the winches and the wrecked TS40.

Finally, the first chunks of the vehicle broke free and got yanked into the middle of the hangar. Forbes noted a few cheers go up among the engineers. But as he looked into the cavity, he noticed several new obstructions blocking the opening.

"Splick," he said to Nelson. "Looks like we've got ourselves a collapsed tunnel."

"I see it," Nelson replied. The two commanders moved forward carefully, ready to return fire to anyone gutsy enough to shoot through the debris. But no fire came, and none of Forbes's sensors indicated life signs. "Whaddya wanna do, Captain?"

"Well, our winches aren't clearing that out," Forbes replied. "And we don't have the tools to cut through." He looked back to the remaining LIMKIT4s.

"You wanna blow it?"

Forbes shrugged. "I'm not sure what other choices we have."

"Is that you up there, Forbes?" said a familiar voice.

Forbes peered through the debris and switched to IFF overlay—identify friend or foe. Magnus's outline and the rest of Granther and Paladia Company's gladias filled his HUD. He could see the mystics holding a Unity shield further down the hall.

"Dammit, you're early," Forbes said.

"Better than fashionably late."

"I guess. You still have what we came for?"

"Affirmative. You still working on a way to get us through this?"

"We have an idea, but it's not a good one."

"Lay it on me."

"LIMKIT4s."

Magnus rolled his head around, surveying the damage. "Might work, but might make things worse."

"Yeah, I know. That's why I said it isn't a good one."

"Copy. Give me a second?"

"Hey, it's your ass over there. Take all the time you want."

"Awen," Magnus said, asking her to step up. "I need your eyes on this."

Awen ran forward, leaving Willowood with Piper. "What do we have here?"

"We need a way through, and I was hoping you could, you know..." Magnus made some motions with his hands, hoping she'd interpret it.

"Is that what you think I do?" She mimicked his motions.

"Can you move it?"

Magnus watched Awen's shoulders rise and fall. "I think we can," she said, then turned and called up Nídira, Wish, Telwin, and Findermith. Everyone stepped aside as the four mystics joined Awen and Magnus.

"Think you can make us a way through?" Magnus asked.

The mystics conferred before Awen finally said, "Yes, we have a plan. But since we don't know what else is above this, we're going to need everyone to move quickly."

"I don't think that's gonna be a problem."

Awen stepped toward Magnus. "Just... be ready to move."

"Got it." He hailed Forbes and Nelson. "Listen, I think you can save those mines. Awen's got a plan, but I'm gonna need everyone on that side to stand clear and be ready to get people to cover."

"Understood," Forbes replied. "We're ready."

Magnus stepped aside as the five mystics took positions on either side of the wreckage. They lowered their heads, and everyone in Granther Company went still. At first, Magnus didn't notice anything happening. Awen and the others just stood there motionless. He was about to say something when the floor groaned.

Magnus took another step back and watched as a piece of charred metal pulled itself from the floor. It slid from a deep hole, acting like a dagger retreating from a wound. Next, the corner of a steel plate began to roll back, peeling away from a small opening like someone had pulled back a curtain. The plate shuddered, letting out an ear-splitting whine. Magnus took another step back. It didn't matter how many times he saw Awen and her kind do their thing—he was still amazed.

Next, a large support truss that lay diagonally across the corridor started to right itself. Several other pieces of metal tumbled left and right as the truss rose. The sounds of debris catering against one another rattled the hallway. Whatever the mystics were doing, it was working. And Magnus told them so.

"Shut up, Magnus," Awen said. Magnus pulled his head back, surprised by her curtness. But he knew better than to piss her off, so he just raised his free hand in submission.

Several more critical pieces raised themselves, retracing

their invisible paths to the walls or ceiling. Magnus continued to stare in amazement as the way cleared one meter at a time.

Magnus opened a private channel to Willowood. "How's our rear line holding up?" In the distance, he could see several platoons pouring blaster fire into the massive Unity shield.

"Just fine, Magnus. But you should be more concerned with what Awen's doing."

"Well, I am, but... she doesn't want to talk about it."

"That's understandable. It's extremely complicated and, therefore, extremely taxing. One wrong move and this goes boom. Plus, you're probably annoying."

"Yeah. Wait—what?"

"When she gives you the word, we run."

"Got it. But you think I'm—"

"Shut up and focus!"

Magnus turned back to face the maze of wreckage slowly undoing itself. He could almost see all the way through to the shuttles—it was tight, but even Rohoar and Abimbola could make it through if they squeezed. All that remained was...

Magnus found himself holding his breath. A massive girder lay across the last section. The thing had to weigh several tons, and it looked pinned down by other support structures in the ceiling.

"Not to rush you or anything, Magnus, but it sounds like Marines are trying to blast through the wreckage in the north tunnel," Forbes said over a private channel.

"Handle it." Magnus glanced at Awen and could tell her

body was trembling. "We're at a critical point here, and I can't make the mystics go any faster."

"Copy that," Forbes replied.

Suddenly, Awen let out a grunt of frustration, as did a few of the others. The girder lurched upward—not far, but enough to let Magnus know the mystics were moving it. "Come on, Awen," Magnus whispered in his helmet. "You got this."

The girder rose several more centimeters. Just when Magnus thought it was high enough for people to pass under, blaster fire ricocheted down the corridor and struck Reimer in the back of the head. The sound must have distracted Awen and the others because the girder dropped down, as did a few other smaller pieces of metal.

"What the hell?" Reimer exclaimed, turning around. His shield had absorbed the blow, leaving him with 47%, but the fact that he'd been hit made everyone look back.

Magnus zoomed in with his bioteknia eyes and noticed small openings forming in the shield wall. "What's going on back there, Willowood? I thought you told me not to be concerned."

"Compared to the danger ahead of you, you shouldn't. But that doesn't mean Paladia Company is out of the woods."

"You're saying they can't hold it?"

"Not much longer, I'm afraid. The amount of blaster fire they're resisting is substantial."

"Roger that." Magnus opened up a channel that didn't include each fire team's mystic. "I need you all to set up a rear guard. If the Unity shield goes down, I'm gonna need you to lay down some suppressive fire so we can get Piper out."

The teams acknowledged the instruction and maneuvered back to support Paladia Company. Meanwhile, Willowood walked forward, cradling Piper.

"She needs you," the old woman said.

Magnus looked at her. "Who does?"

"Awen, she needs you."

"Yeah, I'm not saying a thing."

"Not over comms." Willowood nodded to Magnus's chest. "Say it to yourself. She'll feel it."

Magnus hesitated, then looked back at Awen. The beam vibrated again, but it wasn't going back up.

"She can't do this without you, Magnus," Willowood said. "Go on."

Magnus swallowed, then switched off comms. "Hey, uh. Listen. I'm guessing you can hear me, maybe? Anyway, just wanted you to know that you're doing great there." The girder slumped back down. Magnus swore. He sounded so stupid to himself. It was like talking to hard vacuum, hoping the cosmos was listening or something. It felt weird. But if Awen really could hear him, Magnus supposed he'd better suck it up and say something that counted. "Awen, I—I want you to know that I believe in you. Like, more than anyone in the galaxy, crazy as it sounds, I know. But you have more heart than anyone I've ever met, and you can do things that… well, that pretty much freak me out. But that's what I love about you. And if there was ever a person who could save us now, who could save Piper, it's you. You and me against the whole damn galaxy, girl. I got your back."

If his words were supposed to do something magical, they sure as hell didn't. He waited and watched, but nothing new happened. He turned toward Willowood. "So much for—"

Magnus was cut off by the sound of metal grinding against metal. He spun to see the girder rise off the ground, centimeter by centimeter. The walls spasmed as the giant beam sent a shudder down the corridor. Bits and pieces of debris clattered down through the jumbled mess, but the steel beast continued to rise toward the ceiling. As it went even higher than it had before, Magnus leaned over and saw straight through to Forbes, who waved at him.

Another few seconds and the beam was a meter and a half off the ground and holding. Magnus looked at Awen and saw her body shaking. "Let's do this, people," Magnus exclaimed and started pushing Willowood forward. The old mystic ducked and made her way through the gauntlet of floating debris, Piper secure in her arms. Next came a few of Paladia Company's older members, but most stayed behind to keep the failing wall from giving out completely.

Magnus started ordering the fire teams through, beginning with the larger members. Rohoar patted Magnus as he passed. "Do not stay too long."

"I don't plan on it, big guy," Magnus replied. "See you on the other side."

Abimbola got down on his hands and knees. "I do not

want to have to come back here to collect your helmet, buckethead."

"You won't have to if it's shoved up your ass. Now get going!"

Magnus continued to wave the gladias forward until only Awen, her four counterparts, and the remaining cadres of Paladia Company were left. Sion approached Magnus. "You need to lead her through. We'll help sustain their efforts as they move. The rest of us will hold the wall."

"But you're coming with us, right?"

The man hesitated for a fraction of a second. "Of course."

"Okay, 'cause no else is getting left behind today."

"Absolutely. Now, go." Sion pushed Magnus forward.

He placed his hand against Awen's back and gently—ever so gently—coaxed her forward. "Come on, Awen. Time to move." Her body quivered at his touch, but he applied more pressure until she took a step forward. "The rest of you too, come on." Magnus stepped in front of Awen and began leading her through the small corridor she'd created. He slung his blaster and held her hands, guiding her around protrusions and craters in the floor. The other four mystics followed, their focus never straying from their work. Which, Magnus realized, was a good thing because they were all deep in the small tunnel—one missed step, one tiny distraction, and they'd all be buried alive. *At least Piper would make it out alive,* Magnus thought.

Further back, more mystics followed the single-file line,

while five or six held the wall. Magnus looked up to see the massive beam that had caused so much trouble moments ago —he was nearly through. "Almost there," he said to Awen, but she didn't reply. Instead, her body shook like she'd plunged in a bath of ice water. "Just a few more steps."

Magnus looked back and saw more blaster rounds penetrate the Unity shield. They bounced off the wreckage and struck one mystic in the chest. He collapsed in a heap.

Magnus felt the wreckage lurch. He was about to heave Awen away, but everything held. When Magnus felt hands on his sides, he let them guide him clear of the threshold and then slowly pulled Awen with him. The other four mystics followed, but then stopped, apparently choosing to stand near the blast door's opening. Magnus continued to hold Awen's hands as more mystics funneled out of the narrow shaft. Then they ran their last few steps and sprinted clear.

"Is everyone out?" Sion asked Magnus over VNET.

Magnus double-checked his roster and then saw the four remaining mystics' outlines. They still held the shield, but now they advanced toward the enemy—putting distance between themselves and the wreckage. "Okay, you're good to go," Magnus said. "Everyone's clear."

"It's been a pleasure serving you, Magnus," Sion said. "May your cause outlive our lives."

Magnus squinted in confusion. "What the hell?" In the next moment, all four mystics went nova.

35

THE EXPLOSION WAS SO violent that Magnus nearly fell off his feet. The deck thundered, shaking the *Labyrinth's* port side. New alarms went off, and an automated voice alerted the crew to a hull breach several sections aft. Whatever catastrophic suicide event the four mystics created, they directed it down the corridor's far end and spared the retreating gladia.

"Thank you, brothers," Awen said, her voice tired and barely audible. Then she collapsed.

"Whoa, easy there." Magnus caught her beneath the armpits. He hadn't even noticed that she and Granther's other mystics had released the wreckage—he'd been too busy thinking they were all going to die from the massive explosion. "I need some help here!" In seconds, the fire teams raced over to help carry the exhausted mystics back to the shuttles. "I want them secured. And get those two shuttles fired up and ready for evac."

"One shuttle," Forbes corrected, running toward Magnus.

"Come again?"

"The second shuttle is too badly damaged to use."

"You've got to be kidding me right now." Magnus turned in a circle, surveying the hangar bay, and called up Cyril. "We need another evac plan, kid."

"Evac plan. Okay, okay, okay. And I confirm what Captain Forbes said. The second shuttle is in no shape to fly. No way, no how."

"So whaddya got?"

There was a long pause filled only with the sound of Cyril's nasally breathing.

"Cyril?"

"Got it, sir. There appears to be a Paragon shuttle in the next bay, directly forward of your current position. I'm pretty sure Azelon and I can hack it through the node."

"I need more than pretty sure, kid," Magnus said.

"I'm super sure. I mean, I've never done it, but the principle is easy enough, so I'm sure I can do it once you—"

"Then how do we get to it?"

"Through there," Forbes said, pointing toward the south corridor. It was piled with wreckage, and sensor data showed plenty of life signs between the gaps—*Marines*.

"We don't have time for this," Magnus said. "I need options."

"There is another way to access the hangar, sir," Cyril said.

As if reading the code slicer's thoughts, Forbes turned and looked toward the blue environmental containment force field that shimmered against the void. "He's right, Magnus."

"You want me doing a spacewalk?" Magnus asked.

"That's an affirmative confirmation, sir," Cyril replied. "It's just like a holo game. Your suit's maglock capability works for more than just weapons, you know."

Magnus was about to react to the code slicer when Dutch stopped him. "I can do it, LT," she said as she walked up to him. "My last pre-deployment workup included a section on exterior ship maintenance and repair."

"That won't be necessary," Magnus replied and started walking toward the force field.

"But sir—"

"Negative, Dutch. Forbes, I want that shuttle filled, triage priority assessment in effect. And you're taking Piper. If anything happens to us, you make damn sure she gets back to the *Spire*."

"You got it."

"Granther Company, you're last out, along with anyone else who can't fit aboard Forbes' party barge. Except you, Willowood. You're going with your granddaughter and Awen." Willowood faced Magnus but had the good sense not to argue with him. *Smart lady*. Her cadres would be fine without her—it was Piper who needed her most. "Colonel, you listening?"

"Like a teenage boy to a hooker's call line," Caldwell replied.

Magnus smiled. "How close is our air support?"

"Two minutes. But I'll have you talk to TO-96 directly."

"I'm right here, sir," the bot said, his avatar appearing in the lower left of Magnus's HUD. "Hello, Magnus."

"Update me."

"Very good, sir. All three squadrons are en route now. They've successfully eliminated the enemy Talons and are leading the surviving starships back toward the fleet. Since fleet command thinks they're in for an assault, the last thing they'll expect is an immediate about-face, all but ensuring your getaway. Azelon will be ready to adversely affect their sensors in order to mask your retreat trajectory."

"Okay, but there are two ships now, not three. And we're gonna have different timelines."

"I see. What will the offset be?"

"That depends on Cyril and me. The important thing is that you get the first shuttle back. Make it your highest priority. It's got Piper on it."

"Understood, sir."

"We'll keep you posted on the second ship. Magnus out."

MAGNUS REACHED the edge of the hangar bay and stared at the force field for a moment. Working in hard vacuum wasn't anything new to Magnus, but it did require extra concentration—one wrong move, and you were on a one-way sightseeing trip of deep space. Plus, he'd never worked in this kit before. Granted, if there was one good thing about Azelon's manufacturing, it was that it was far superior to anything the Repub did. In the end, however, an operator got used to what an operator got used to, so new tech was awkward tech, even if it was better tech.

"Initiating mag system now," Magnus said to Cyril, directing power to his boots and—just in case he needed it— his gloves. "Just like the holo games," he mumbled to himself.

"Sounds good, sir. I'm right here, so if you need anything, I'm here for you."

"Thanks."

"You know, it's kind of funny if you think about it —*Magnus* initiating his *mag* system?"

"Cyril! Stay focused."

"Focused. Yes, sir. Sorry, sir."

Weird kid, Magnus thought not for the first time. *Smart. But weird.*

Magnus walked into the force field's plane then stepped to the edge. He extended his foot into hard vacuum and saw his suit's systems adjust for the pressure discrepancy. The next bit was always the tricky part. Magnus committed, lunging forward as if the hangar bay's floor extended out, ready to catch his leading foot. Instead, his body fell forward, pulling his rear foot off the deck. In the same instant, he flipped down and reoriented along the *Labyrinth's* port side. His boots adhered to the metal, making the hull his new ground floor.

"I'm out," Magnus said to Cyril.

"Good, good, good. Now—turn ninety degrees to your left and proceed forward one hundred forty-three meters. The faster, the better. Yep, slow is smooth and faster is better."

"Got it." Magnus eyed the varied landscape and chuckled. "You do know what the hull of a Super Dreadnaught looks like, don't you?"

"No, sir. Can't say that I've ever seen one up close, sir."

The one hundred forty-three meters that Magnus had to navigate was littered with obstructions—boxy maintenance compartments, sensor panels, shielded conduit runs, and any number of structural trusses. What looked like a flat surface from five klicks away was actually a highly intricate maze of mechanical engineering oddities.

Magnus clomped his way around an access hatch, then ducked under a support beam. He covered the next ten meters reasonably fast but had to use his gloves to hurdle two broad sections of truss. From there, Magnus moved around some communication dishes and then stepped through several maintenance panels aligned in a grid pattern. The progress was slow going, but he could see the waypoint indicator draw nearer with every step.

"So, talk me through the next part," Magnus said. "How am I gonna fly this bird?"

"It's a Heavy Armored Transport shuttle, hull designation HAT-NU-441."

"I don't care what it's called, kid. I want to know how to *fly* it."

"Oh, right, right. Well, fortunately, I'll have access to its flight systems once you start it up."

"Which means you can fly it for me?"

Cyril let out a nervous laugh. "No, sir. I'm not sure you'd want me doing that, sir."

"And you think I can do any better?" Magnus carefully climbed over a series of thick conduit runs.

"Um, well, not exactly, sir. Even though nerds do rule the cosmos—ha ha."

"Copy that. So, I start it up. Then who's gonna fly it?"

"I will, sir," said TO-96, his voice fresh in Magnus's ears.

"That suits me just fine, bot."

"I'm happy to hear that, sir. However, I must insist that you hurry. Fang Company is closing on your position."

"And we are about to have several unwelcome guests," Abimbola said over VNET. "The south tunnel is about to reopen."

"Can't you close that one, Cyril?" Magnus asked.

"I did, I already did. Something must've jammed the actuators."

"Probably from the explosion," Forbes said. "We're just about good to go here, Magnus."

"Get out of there, Forbes."

"Magnus, I must ask you to reconsider the order," TO-96 said. "Spreading out your evacuation will pose an unnecessary risk to the mission."

"And keeping that shuttle full of our people on the deck poses an even greater risk. They're the priority, 'Six. Nothing else matters."

"I understand, sir. But just to be clear, I'm not sure the Fangs can cover two different waves of—"

"Dammit, 'Six! Cover the shuttle, and we'll figure out a way to get the second one home. We don't have time to wait around." As if to punctuate his point, the three Fang squadrons appeared to Magnus's left, doing a low pass over the *Labyrinth's* top deck. They strafed the ship, firing silent blaster rounds through the void, while the Super Dreadnaught returned fire. But the Fangs were far too fast and vanished from sight before the starship's auto turrets could put any round on target. The entire episode happened in the blink of an eye, and not a sound was made.

"You ready for us, Magnus?" Ricio asked over a channel dedicated to air support.

"Yes, sir."

TO-96 piped up. "On the contrary—"

"Can it, bot," Magnus ordered. "Ricio, I want you and 'Six conversing with Captain Forbes. He will be your primary POC moving forward."

"Copy that," Ricio replied. "You bowing out early?"

"Just delayed, that's all. But you get the lead ship to safety, no matter what. That's an order."

"Coming from a Lieutenant, I'm not sure how I feel about that."

"Stand down, Ricio," Caldwell interjected. "It's the right call. Piper is the mission, and she's on the lead shuttle. Patching Forbes through now."

Instantly, the sounds of close blaster fire filled the comm. "Get this ramp up," Forbes yelled.

"Captain, this is Caldwell. Are you ready to launch?"

"Yes, sir!" Forbes sounded like he was running. "Pilot, get us the hell out of here."

"Sounds like they're coming out hot, jockey," Magnus said to Ricio. "Get yourself looking pretty."

"On it," Ricio said. "Squadrons, prepare to cover port-side evac, shuttle launch imminent."

"Happy flying," Magnus said. No sooner had he said the words than the Novian shuttle emerged from the hangar bay and moved into open space. Repulsors shut off, and ion thrusters went to full-burn. The bright light glared against Magnus's visor as the ship silently sailed away from the *Labyrinth*.

Magnus was about to take another step when a massive explosion shook the hull about twenty yards to his right. An auto turret had been deployed—but not for long. One of Fang Company's starfighters had apparently seen it and sent blaster rounds to take it out before the weapon had a chance to fire on the shuttle.

Magnus was about to spit out a warning to the pilots when he caught movement to the left. Twenty yards in the opposite direction, another auto turret popped from the hull. Magnus swung his NOV1 up and fired as soon as his finger could get on the trigger. He held the weapon wide open, pouring blaster rounds on the metal housing that protected the barrels. The enemy weapon system rotated, tracking the shuttle, but Magnus didn't let up. His lead mag went dry, and the NOV1 switched effortlessly to the second. Just when Magnus thought the auto turret would fire, his blaster bolts pierced the armor plating, and the gun exploded in a spray of loose energy and orange sparks.

"Thanks for the help," Nolan said to Magnus.

"My pleasure. And, hey, try not to shoot me? I'm walking here."

"Roger that."

Magnus mag locked his blaster on his back, then reoriented himself to the upcoming waypoint. He had less than thirty meters to go, and no time to waste. Magnus picked up his pace, racing around obstructions as a spacetrack star might do, but in slow motion. Then he looked over his shoulder. Forbes's shuttle was heading away from the fleet, covered by all forty-two Fangs. "Safe travels, little one," Magnus said, touching a finger to his helmet and then pointing in Piper's direction.

"ALRIGHT, GUYS," Magnus said to TO-96 and Cyril. "Talk me through this." He'd stepped into the hangar bay and snuck onto the HAT without anyone noticing—*a good start*, he thought. But an unsanctioned shuttle launch during a firefight was sure to draw unwanted attention. He saw Marines run across the bay for the corridor leading aft, heading to reinforce the attack on Granther and Paladia Companies. "All I see are a bunch of consoles filled with buttons and a few dozen holo screens."

"Good, good, good! Now, have you ever seen the holo vid *The Unity Arises?*"

"Cyril—"

"Because in it, there's this great scene where a guy steals a shuttle, and it's almost exactly like this scenario, but the thing is, that holo vid is not realistic, so do not do what the guy did. I repeat, do not—"

"Cyril, for splick's sake!"

"Oh—ha, ha. Yeah. Sorry, sir. First, I need you to turn on the shuttle's power supply and disconnect from the host circuits. There should be a large red toggle switch under a cover on the..." Cyril seemed to be consulting a schematic. Or he was dozing off, Magnus couldn't decide which. "Right side. It's on the cockpit's right side."

"I see it," Magnus said, reaching over to flip the cover and throw the switch.

"Right next to it you see another toggle marked—"

"External Power Shutoff," Magnus said.

"Exactly! That's an affirmative ten ten. Now, kill it!"

Magnus threw that switch as well. Next, Cyril walked Magnus through a dozen instructions to get the ship up and running. Finally, TO-96's cheery voice said, "I have control."

"As in, you're good to fly this bird?" Magnus asked.

"Affirmative. I believe the expression is, hold my alcoholic beverage."

"Now you're just gettin' cocky." Magnus took a seat and grabbed the harness straps. But before he could buckle in, the ship lurched, and Magnus was thrown sideways. A second later and the ship struck something, tossing Magnus the other way. He stayed off the floor thanks to his iron grip around the straps. "Easy there, pal. What's going on?"

"I am readjusting my parameters to compensate for the input declination values for this make and model. My apologies."

"Yeah, 'cause that made so much sense. You good now?"

"I am good now, yes."

Suddenly, the shuttle eased back under repulsor power and headed toward the environmental force field. TO-96's jarring lift-off had gotten several Marines' attention, however, and a small group stopped to observe the shuttle leaving the hangar. A few pointed then looked to a control window about halfway up the far wall.

A commanding voice broke over the ship's audio system. "HAT-NU-441, you are not cleared for takeoff. Stand down immediately. I repeat, you are not cleared for—"

"Yeah, tower?" Magnus said, finding the comm holo and pressing the transmit button. "This is HAT-PISS-OFF. We're not thrilled with service here, so we've decided to take our business elsewhere. Also, we *will* be leaving a bad review with your superiors, and last we knew, they take reviews pretty seriously."

"Who is this? What's your identification—"

The channel went silent. Magnus looked at the screen, trying to figure out what had happened.

"He was getting on my nerves," TO-96 said.

Magnus laughed. "You and me both, buddy."

TO-96 cleared the hangar, then sideslipped the ship to port, not even bothering to spin it. Magnus watched as they traversed in seconds what had taken him several seconds of maze running, then slowed as they neared the next hangar bay. Inside, the remaining gladia fought with Paragon Marines who were stacked up in the north tunnel.

"We're coming in," Magnus said over VNET. "Stand clear, and give us some shielding if you can afford it."

"Bring it in," Abimbola said. "We have mystics ready to supplement your shields."

"Thanks, Bimby."

TO-96 applied forward thrust, and the HAT moved through the force field. Several Marines seemed surprised to see the shuttle appear. But the hesitation cost a few of them their lives as NOV1 fire drilled into their armor and sent them sprawling.

Magnus ran for the aft cargo hold and punched the ramp open just as TO-96 brought the ship down. The repulsor's engines were still whining, however, as the bot rightly assumed this would be a quick stop.

"Everyone in," Magnus said, waving to the first gladias he

saw. "Let's go, let's go, let's go." The members of Delta and Echo Teams charged up the ramp, followed by most of Paladia Company's remaining cadres. "Come on, Bimby. Where you at?"

Magnus spun around to find the rest of Granther Company's outlines. While he faced the ship's interior, his sensors overlaid the gladias shapes in his HUD. They were just off the ship's nose, hidden behind some cargo crates and MB17s. Magnus ran down the ramp, keeping his head toward his fire teams, and saw them pinned down under heavy fire. Since two layers of shielding protected the shuttle, the enemy decided to let the remaining intruders have it.

"It is no good, buckethead," Abimbola said. "We cannot cross to you."

"Like hell you can't." Magnus looked over and saw two GU90s on tripods. He stepped off the ramp, ignored TO-96's warning to get back with the ship, and lifted the weapons off their stands. His suit's servo assist system wound up, sucking power from his primary batteries in order to support the massive guns. Magnus turned and, with the help of his bioteknia eyes, selected a group of thirty Paragon Marines who seemed to be giving his fire teams the hardest time. Magnus squeezed both triggers and leaned into the kickback.

The GU90s roared, sending torrents of blaster fire zipping across the hangar bay and into enemy lines. The rounds pierced the unshielded Repub armor, boring large-diameter holes straight through hapless victims. Magnus chewed through the ranks, taking out two and three troopers at a time, mowing them down like toy soldiers on a child's sandbox ledge.

Several Marines noticed the assault and tried to take cover, while others tried alerting those who'd not yet seen the imposing threat. But none of them were fast enough to escape Magnus's barrage of gunfire. He continued to squeeze the two triggers, his chest and legs absorbing the weapon's violent recoil.

"Run, dammit," Magnus hollered over the demon-like sound of the twin guns. His HUD tracked friendly movement as the remaining Granthers headed for the shuttle. But the enemy was regrouping as well. More reinforcements crept out of the tunnel and took cover before Magnus could drill their bodies with blaster fire.

Suddenly, an enemy round struck the GU90 in Magnus's left hand. The weapon kicked back and struck Magnus across the chest. A sharp pain exploded in his elbow, and he was forced to drop the gun.

"Time to leave, sir," TO-96 said. "Please step on board."

Magnus continued to fire with his right weapon, stepped onto the platform, and grabbed ahold of the ramp stanchion with his left hand. His left arm throbbed, but he managed to hold on as TO-96 powered up the repulsors.

The ship rose off the deck, while Magnus continued to fire. He leaned out and sprayed the Marines filing into the hangar. Finally, the GU90 went dry. Magnus double checked the mag display. When he confirmed it was at 0, he tossed the weapon down and pulled himself up the ramp.

"How about a parting gift," Magnus said to TO-96.

"Did you have something in mind?"

"Just make it go boom."

"Very good, sir."

The ramp door closed just as the shuttle's tail slipped through the force field. Magnus raced back through the shuttle, telling everyone to secure themselves, and then arrived in the cockpit. The HAT's nose was the only thing left inside the *Labyrinth*, and it took the brunt of the enemy's fire. Countless bolts lit up both mystic- and drive-core-powered shields alike, producing an electrical display that would have dropped an unprotected ship in a heartbeat.

"Now, 'Six," Magnus ordered. "Fire."

Six torpedoes shot from the bay directly under the cockpit, covering the windshield with smoke. At the same time, TO-96 applied full power and backed the ship clear of the hangar bay. The bay filled with fire as the torpedoes impacted the far wall. While the environmental force field managed to keep most of the energy contained, some of it blew back on the shuttle and forced it away from the *Labyrinth* with a jolt. The rest of the explosion's energy blew sideways into neighboring sections, and vertically into adjacent decks. Fire broke through expanding seams, causing plates to blow apart and compartments to explode. Additional ruptures appeared further along the hull until, finally, the pressure found relief when the force field went down.

The vacuum extinguished the primary fires as swaths of bodies and debris ejected into the void. Magnus marveled at the gaping hole TO-96's assault had made. "That was a big boom."

"Am I detecting that you think it was too much, sir?" TO-96 asked.

Magnus glanced at the bot's avatar. "Hey, 'Six?"

"Yes, sir?"

"There's no such thing as too big a boom."

"Understood. Thank you. Though we are not out of the old-growth deciduous and conifer wilderness country yet, sir."

"The hell?" But any interest Magnus had in interpreting the bot's wordplay was diverted the moment Caldwell's voice came over comms.

"Sweet mother of Vesper's twin bitches. Looks like they're coming about, Magnus." And by *they*, Caldwell meant the half dozen warships that had changed direction and set Magnus's shuttle as a target.

"That is precisely what I meant," TO-96 replied. "The threat assessment is—"

"Very high, I got it."

"Yes. You must have really pissed Moldark off."

"I don't need a damn dialogue about it, 'Six! I need ideas."

"We can keep some of them busy," Ricio said. "But it's not gonna do you much good. Not with that much firepower, I'm afraid."

"Anyone else?" Magnus waited for someone to chime in on comms, but no one said a thing. "Ah, splick."

"I believe I have a solution," Rohoar said from the cockpit's entryway. Magnus turned to see the Jujari fill the entire space. "Or, rather, I know of a solution about to transpire."

"You're gonna have to explain that one to me, furball, 'cause I'm done trying to figure out everyone's hidden meanings today. You got something or not?"

Rohoar shook his head. "No. But my son does."

"I HAVE VISUAL ON HOTEL TWO," Ricio said over VNET.

Ezo pulled up the new ident tag that appeared on the *Labyrinth's* starboard side. Sure enough, Magnus's hijacked shuttle emerged from the hangar bay just as a massive explosion ruptured several decks on the Super Dreadnaught.

"Guy sure knows how to leave his mark," Ricio added.

"You have no idea," Ezo replied. Magnus's ship was taking heavy fire from the *Labyrinth*, which didn't seem too keen on letting the shuttle go. "Ezo's gonna lend him a hand."

"But, sir," Nolan said. "There's no way you're going to—"

"You let Ezo worry about what he can and can't do, Nolan," Ezo said. "You and Ricio get Piper back to the *Spire*. Let Ezo worry about this one."

"You sure you want this?" Ricio asked. "Those starships are gonna be a handful."

Ezo chuckled. "That's what they said about Ezo's wife, and look how that turned out."

"But, sir, you filed for——" said TO-96.

"Not now, 'Six." Ezo switched to his squadron channel. "Blue Squadron, this is Blue Leader. Proceed to escort on Hotel Two. Let's keep the heat off them." Green icons rippled down his chat window as all thirteen Fangs confirmed his orders.

"Happy hunting, Ezo," Ricio said. "We'll see you back at the ship."

BLUE SQUADRON RACED toward the *Labyrinth* at attack speed, monitoring both Magnus's newly commandeered Heavy Armored Transport and all the warships that had taken an interest in the fleeing shuttle. Several of the Destroyers attempted to lock onto the ship, but TO-96 and Cyril were busy messing with the enemy's targeting systems. It was working—for now.

"Listen up, people," Ezo said. "We're gonna do a run along the *Labyrinth's* starboard side and take out as many of those auto turrets as we can. Then, Blue Two through Five, see if you can't piss off that Destroyer, bearing 321 mark 44. Blue Six through Nine, I want you on those two Frigates, inbound from the stern. The rest of you are with Ezo—we're going after that Battlecruiser that's poking around where it shouldn't." All ships acknowledged his orders and locked in their targets.

Ezo hailed Magnus over VNET. "You're looking a little naked out there, Magpie."

"Magpie?"

Ezo could practically hear Magnus's smile through comms.

"As in the bird?" Magnus asked. "That's new."

"You're flying, aren't you?"

"Yeah, but—"

"Then Magpie it is. Ezo's running with it. We're taking umbrage with these warships bearing down on your tail."

"We'll take any fire support you care to give. Thanks, Ezo."

"Ah, ah. Ezo's not doing this for free, you know. You'll owe him after this."

"And I don't suppose I can ask for another squadron to help instead?"

"Sorry, Magpie. You're stuck with Ezo."

"Why do I have a feeling this is gonna haunt me?"

"Because it absolutely will." Ezo switched his squadron channel. "All Fangs, weapons hot. Missiles hot." It was the first time he'd allowed them to use the specialty ordinance, but, considering the stakes, it was time. "Let's do this."

EZO ACCELERATED and led the squadron toward the *Labyrinth's* stern. As the massive engine cones grew, he steered just wide enough to get a good angle of attack on the guns protruding along the starboard side but stayed close enough that the weapons systems wouldn't get a lock on any of his ships. They were moving too fast anyway.

His Fang's HUD put target icons around each auto turret and then fed the data to his helmet's visor, displaying vector data in real-time. As the first pair of turrets appeared, Ezo waited for target lock confirmation and then ordered his Fang to fire. The wingtip blasters made quick work of the emplacements, blowing them off the hull with ease.

The next two guns tried shooting down the *Labyrinth's* length, but the target path was too steep. Ezo hugged the ship's side and lit the turrets up with two single shots from his underbelly cannon. The enemy guns shot fire and shrapnel into space as Ezo flew by.

Then he noticed more guns on the *Labyrinth's* belly open fire on Magnus. "Keep the run going, Blue Squadron. Ezo's peeling off to deal with some turrets down below."

Ezo rolled off the warship's side and flipped under the beast, blasters blazing. He slalomed along the *Labyrinth's* underside, weaving between auto turret positions and taking them out one at a time. Ezo shouted in celebration as he finished off a six turret kill-streak. He loved *Geronimo Nine*, but these Fangs were on another level—there was no comparison.

"Thanks for the support, Ezo," Magnus said. "We feel it."

"There's more where that came from. Hold on."

Ezo emerged from under the Super Dreadnaught and linked back up with Blue Ten though Fourteen. They headed for the Battlecruiser riding Magnus's tail. The large ship's forward guns sent heavy blows against the smaller shuttle's shields and lowered their capacity by the second. Ezo knew if his Fangs didn't intervene, there wouldn't be much ship left to protect.

He highlighted the main guns and distributed the target list. As soon as he did, the five other starfighters rolled to attack vectors and bared down on the Battlecruiser's bow. Then Ezo soared over the top of the gunship and dropped toward the bow—missiles hot.

"Birdies one and six, away," he said. He watched the two guided missiles streak toward their targets and then pulled clear. The resulting explosions peppered his shield with shrapnel but did no serious damage. The Battlecruiser, however, was left with a bloody nose and two fewer cannons. Then the other Fangs took out the forward missile banks, leaving the warship with gaping holes in its bow.

Ezo reviewed the rest of the company's progress and noticed the other Fangs had similar results. The Destroyer's main guns had been silenced, and the two Frigates were out of commission—one's engines were offline, and the other had lost life support.

"Looking good, Fangs," Ezo said over the company channel.

"About that," TO-96 said. "I do not mean to discourage you, sir, but—"

"But, you're gonna."

"I'm afraid so."

"What is it?" Ricio asked.

"Azelon and I are detecting a dramatic shift in ship positions," TO-96 said. "We're also picking up multiple transmissions with new orders to pursue the retreating shuttles."

"How many ships?" Nolan asked.

"That's just it, sir. It looks like all of Third Fleet."

Ezo felt his stomach drop. "I'm sorry, pal. It sounded like you said all of Third Fleet."

"That's what it sounded like because that's what I said, sir."

"Son of a bitch," Ricio said.

"I can corroborate the bots' findings," Caldwell added. "Seems Moldark is hellbent on getting that little girl back or making sure we don't. He's throwing twelve Carriers and just as many support vessels into the mix."

"Not to mention thirteen squadrons," Ricio said. "Minus the two we already took out."

"That's 154 Talons, commander," TO-96 said.

"How 'bout that," Ricio said with no attempt to hide his sarcasm.

"We can't handle those kinds of numbers," Nolan said.

"We may not have to," Magnus replied, entering the conversation with some urgency in his voice. "Seems someone else is coming in to help."

"And who's that?" Ezo asked.

"My son," Rohoar said, his avatar popping into view.

ALL SIGNS POINTED to the Jujari fleet being against the ropes, to use an Antaran boxing term. They had taken heavy blows as the Paragon's three fleets pummeled their defenses with a steady and unrelenting barrage of blaster fire, starfighter sorties, and missile fusillades. Likewise, the Sypeurlion and Dim-Telok alliance folded days earlier—their ships fleeing the conflict in a desperate attempt to salvage at least some of their warships. The Jujari ships that survived this far had withstood a punishing assault, fending off all but the most violent attacks. It was said that the Jujari would fight to the death before giving ground to anyone who attacked their home-world and based on everything Ezo has witnessed, the rumors were true.

Ezo had amassed a small fortune trading with the Jujari, and with the inhabitants of the Dregs. Were any of them to survive this conflict, he wondered if Oorajee's economy would ever return to health, or if everyone would move on to more lucrative systems, leaving the desert planet to return to its roots as a barren wasteland.

For all their violent and backward thinking, fermented drinks, and bloodletting rituals, Ezo liked the Jujari. They were outcasts, improvisers, and survivors, much like him. Granted, he didn't have the same propensity for violence as they did, but then again, he wasn't born with claws or razor-sharp incisors either. In the end, he gave the Jujari the benefit of the doubt and always tried to treat them like every other good trade partner—a valuable source of credits so long as you didn't cheat them and get caught.

But in all the time he'd known the Jujari, Ezo had never seen them doing anything selfless. They were bloodthirsty and brutal, at least in his mind. Spite, vengeance, and retribution were just three words that came to mind when thinking of them. That was, of course, until Ezo heard that Rohoar gave up his throne and took his son's place as debtor to Magnus.

At first, Ezo hadn't believed the story. It was until Abimbola—who'd been there to witness it—assured him of its veracity that Ezo believed it. He'd never seen such a sacrificial act take place outside of an adrenaline-crazed bloodbath where one pack member might try saving another. But to take someone else's place and give up a position of supreme authority? Ezo wondered if such a thing had ever happened in the Jujari's history.

Rohoar had gone on to perform other selfless acts. In the few months Ezo had known him—depending on which universe's timetable you measured by—Rohoar had proved to be a valuable and even noble member of the Gladio Umbra. He was, in fact, the closest thing to a true Gladio Umbra as an ancestor of the Novia Minoosh.

But what Ezo witnessed now made all of Rohoar's acts pale in comparison. Should even one of the Gladio Umbra survive this moment, Ezo felt assured that the story would become history, and the history would become legendary.

As the Paragon's Third Fleet pressed down on Magnus's shuttle—such a massive show of force to stop such a tiny ship

—hope had been lost that Granther Company would reach the *Spire* alive. Even Caldwell's cigar had a hard time not trembling when the colonel spoke about the developing situation. The members of Fang Company darted across as many ships as they could, trying to silence auto turrets, blaster cannons, and missile batteries. But the volume of fire was overwhelming. The only things keeping Magnus's shuttle from being blasted to atoms were its speed and the additional shielding. But Ezo knew the mystics couldn't hold out forever. It was only a matter of time before Moldark's ships overran the transport and then charged after Piper and the *Spire*.

But hope was not lost.

TO-96 noticed it first—a sudden rush of Jujari ships from behind their defensive line. To the naked eye, nothing seemed to change except the appearance of thrusters firing up. But even that wasn't unusual; ships jostled for better positions all the time. But as the vessels picked up speed and drove headlong into the Paragon's Second Fleet, TO-96 spoke up.

"Sirs, please be advised. I'm detecting a fleet surge from the Jujari ships."

Ricio was first to reply. "Can you be more specific?"

"All of the Jujari ships have broken ranks and are heading into Second Fleet."

Ezo could see the confusion on Ricio's face, so he asked a question of his own. "Where are they headed, 'Six?"

The bot didn't hesitate. "Toward us, sir."

Ezo pulled up his nav holo and zoomed out, allowing him a top-down view of every vessel this side of Oorajee. Sure enough, every remaining Jujari ship was on the move, heading toward Magnus's shuttle—and fast.

"They seem to be conducting a full burn," TO-96 added. "The only greater speed they're capable of is a subspace jump."

"They're coming to help," Nolan finally said. "But that's... that's crazy."

"No," Rohoar said, his booming voice overtaking the channel. "That is valor. That is my son."

"Victorio?" Ezo asked, thinking he'd rightly remembered the mwadim's heir.

"As it has been spoken," Rohoar replied. "He has chosen the way for his people."

"But... how?" Ezo asked.

"They have some sort of pack connection," Magnus interjected. "Kinda like the Unity but kinda not."

"It allows our hearts to speak," Rohoar said. "And my son has heard mine."

"Fluffy and sentimental," Ezo said. To himself, he added, "Next thing you know, they're gonna ask me to pet them."

"I heard that, Nimprinth."

"Just jokes, just jokes." Ezo held his hands up. "So, what's the play?"

"The play?" Rohoar repeated, looking off-camera, presumably at Magnus.

"He means, what do they intend to do," Caldwell explained. "Your boy there—what's his plan with all this?"

Rohoar sniffed, speaking as though it were the most

obvious thing in the universe. "He means to make good our escape by any means necessary."

"But they're going to put themselves in an indefensible situation," Nolan said. "They'll never be able to recover."

A moment's silence fell over those on the channel as Nolan's assessment rang true with everything Ezo knew about tactics. It was a suicide mission. It was Rohoar who broke the silence. "They are not trying to defend themselves. They are trying to defend us. It is the Jujari way."

"You know, your Jujari ways have always seemed crazy to Ezo," he said. "But this one? Ezo can get behind this one."

"Then let's make it count," Caldwell said. Ezo saw him pull out a lighter and suck the flame through the tip of his tobacco. "Magnus, I need you encouraging those mystics with you to put up everything they've got. Tell 'em they can retire after this one if they want, just don't let up. Ninety-Six, I want you matching your Fangs against optimal targets—no risky business, just sure-fire bets. And, Miss Smarty Pants?"

"Yes, sir?" Azelon replied.

"I'm tired of sitting this one out. Bring us around the planet's shadow and give me some mysticsdamned sightlines on those ships with some of your biggest guns."

"I must warn you, sir, that doing so may jeopardize our entire mission."

"Bot lady, if those two shuttles get taken out, that is the entire mission. It's game over. And I didn't sign up to lose." Back at the squadron commanders, Caldwell said, "You can bet your asses they'll be launching Talons any minute now. I

453

want you to watch yourselves. You're superior pilots with all that tech you're in, but they have numbers, so stay sharp."

"Copy that," Ricio said.

"I have the utmost trust in all of you," Caldwell said. "Now, let's get that little girl and everyone else home safe. Dominate!"

"Liberate!"

37

THE FIRST SIGN that Moldark's fleet noticed the surprise attack was when their Talons changed vectors—twice. First, the enemy starfighters launched and headed toward Magnus's shuttle. Then, without warning, all 154 fighters slowed, turned 180°, and headed back to engage the incoming Jujari vessels. And then, finally, the squadrons were split in two—one half headed toward the Juajri, and the other to the escaping shuttles. While Piper's ship had a slight head start on Magnus's, it wouldn't take Talons long to make up the difference. Taking one down meant taking both down, and Ricio wasn't going to let that happen.

"Let's engage those Talons," Ricio said to Ezo and Nolan. "I think the big boats will have their hands full with the Jujari."

"Agreed," Ezo replied. "Plus, Ezo feels like chasing something, don't you, Nolan?"

"I do," Nolan replied.

"Really?" Ezo sounded unimpressed. "That's it?"

"What?"

"That's all you got, Nolan?" Ezo seemed like he was about to pick a street fight. "Man, you gotta get pumped for stuff like this."

"I am pumped."

"Well, Ezo doesn't think you sound like it."

"Well, Nolan is," Nolan said, using Ezo's third-person pronoun hack. "Nolan is feeling *very* pumped."

"Well then, Ezo and Nolan should go blow some splick up!"

"Alright," Ricio said. "Quit the chatter, you two. Talons inbound. 'Six, assign us some targets, would you?"

"My pleasure, sir. Happy hunting, once again."

"Copy that."

Ricio watched his HUD flood with targets in order of priority. Half of 154 was 77, which meant there were plenty of Talons to go around for everyone. He divided the enemies among all of Fang Company, favoring the better pilots with an extra target each. "Contact in ten seconds," Ricio said. "Let's torch these sons a'bitches."

The two swarms of starfighters converged and drove through one another's ranks at speeds that defied comprehension. Blaster bolts crisscrossed against the planet's curvature, pulverizing shields and tearing into metal. In the first three seconds, four Fangs were disabled, two of which ended in massive explosions as their drive cores ruptured. The other two spiraled off toward deep space, their pilots screaming in terror.

The Paragon, however, fared much worse. Sixteen Talons met a catastrophic end as blaster fire, and at least two missiles ripped off wings, split hulls, and detonated power systems and ordinance. The explosions popped throughout the converging fleets like firecrackers—fire and sparks one second, atoms and debris trails the next.

Ricio brought his Fang around in a full turn, careful not to crush his body under too many Gs. He saw a pair of Talons break from formation and head straight for Magnus's shuttle. "Oh, no you don't." Rico locked onto both vessels and gave his Fang the command to fire. His fuselage cannons roared, sending out three waves of rounds—one for each ship, and a final pair to finish them off. The first blaster bolts struck their targets with such devastating results that the follow-through rounds swept through debris clouds. The newly super-charged particles let off small lightning bolts as Ricio flew by.

"On your six," Ezo said over comms.

Ricio flipped around—his Fang still hurtling forward—and lined up on a single Talon that had snuck up on him. "Someone's been naughty," he said, then ordered his Fang to hit the enemy fighter. Ricio's wingtip blasters pummeled the Talon's shields. The Paragon ship tried to nose up in an effort to escape, but the ship's exposed belly took several critical hits and ruptured. The explosion flooded Ricio's cockpit with light. "Suck it!"

"Three more, closing on Hotel Two," Ezo said.

"I got them," Nolan said.

Ricio noticed Nolan's Fang was running dangerously low on ammunition. He must have given the fleet ships a run for their money earlier.

"Stand down, Nolan," Ricio said. "I'm on it."

"Negative. I'm closer, and you won't make it in time."

The Talons opened fire on Magnus's shuttle. Blaster rounds exploded against the Unity shielding, but Ricio noticed the shuttle lurch sideways. They'd absorbed a partial hit.

Ricio tried to get a lock on the ships, but Nolan was in the way. "Stand down, Nolan!"

"Negative, this one's on me. You buy the next round."

Nolan emptied his energy mags on a single Talon—its shield blinked out, followed by a blinding explosion in the engines. He fired his last remaining missile, which detonated directly over the pilot's head. The ship's nose blew off, and the wings cartwheeled into open space. But the third Talon was on the run, and Nolan was out of weapons.

"Nolan," Ricio roared. But he knew what the pilot was about to do because Ricio would have done the same thing. Nolan must have known there was no way Ricio could have made it in time, and the Talon's proximity all but ensured a kill shot. "Dammit, Nolan!"

Gold Squadron's commander lined up on the enemy

Talon, punched his jump drive, and then instantly disengaged it. The result was a sub-light jump of no more than a kilometer, but it sent Nolan directly into the Talon. His Fang materialized within the enemy ship, causing an explosion on an atomic level. The shockwave was so staggering that Ricio's shields dropped by 30%, and he was thrown forward into his harness. Similarly, Magnus's shuttle got a sudden boost as the radiation buffeted the Unity shields.

Then, as quickly as it had appeared, the light vanished, and the free energy evaporated as though nothing had happened. Nolan was gone.

"Son of a bitch," Ricio said, rolling back toward the main body of Talons. Nolan had been with Magnus since the beginning of all this, and he was a damn good pilot. He would be missed. And there would be hell to pay when Magnus found out.

PAST THE CONVERGENCE OF STARFIGHTERS, Ricio saw the first warship collision he'd witnessed in over a decade. Modern navigation, sensors arrays, and avoidance systems made the occurrence a rarity. But then again, the Galactic Republic had never gone up against the Juajri before, which made the starship collision even more spectacular. Victorio's ships were ramming Third Fleet's Carriers.

Ricio wasn't the only one to notice either. Every Talon in

the fight slowed and turned toward the mayhem, presumably just as shocked as the Gladio Umbra.

"Are you seeing this, colonel?" Ricio asked over VNET.

"Sure am, son. Sure the hell am."

First, there was the Jujari vessel named *A Glorious Day for Liberating the Exiles of Rugar Muda*, a Pride-class Juajari Battleship. It had engaged maximum thrusters as it rammed up and into the belly of the Paragon Battleship *Emergent Horizon*. Had the collision happened in atmosphere, Ricio knew the quake would have been felt and heard for a hundred klicks. And while the entire thing seemed to happen in slow motion, Ricio knew the vessels hurtled toward one another at terrific speeds.

Jujari Pride-class Battleships weighed in at 252,000 tons, with a crew of almost 3,000 sailors. Its nose pierced into the Paragon's ship, plunging up into the control tower topside. Bolts of free electricity raced along both ships' hulls around the point of contact, while successive explosions rippled out in all directions. Secondary explosions appeared in the *Emmergent's* top deck, blowing off entire sections of the ship. Then the control tower itself bent backward, pried loose by the *Glorious Day's* momentum.

While explosions continued to wreak havoc along the ships, it was the mutual loss of propulsion systems that spelled the end for the two vessels. Oorajee's gravity well reached out and took hold of the Battleships, pulling them slowly at first. Hundreds of tiny escape pods shot free of the dead giants. Ricio was glad to know that at least some of the Jujari's noble crew would live to fight another day. But before long, the two beasts—locked in a death roll—started spiraling toward the planet's atmosphere. In another few minutes, they'd punch through the sky in a blaze of fire and then crash into the dunes.

The two Battleships weren't the only collisions. Three more Jujari ships—a Dreadnaught and two Battlecruisers— also made contact with Paragon ships. Even the *Labyrinth* came close to being struck, but it managed to escape calamity by rolling aside. The most it got was a grazed hit from the Jujari Battleship *Terrified Enemies Hide in Dark Caves Awaiting Dawn that Will Never Come*. The Jujari ship rubbed up against the *Labyrinth's* hull before anti-ship cannons blew holes in its bridge, disabling it.

"Son of cock wielding dingus in a gunfight," Caldwell said. "Would you look at that." Then, just as fast, he added, "Now, get back to handing them their asses, people! This ain't no perv show!"

With the warships engaged, Ricio immediately noticed all the Paragon's Talons were redirected to the retreating shuttles. "Well, this isn't awesome," he said to TO-96. "You seeing this?"

"I am, sir. It seems the Talons have been given a new directive and are attempting to converge on Magnus's shuttle."

"My thoughts exactly." Ricio moved into position behind a trio of unsuspecting Talons and opened fire. His high-frequency rounds pulverized their lowered rear shields and tore into their fuselages. The fighters tumbled into pieces, and

Ricio shot passed the wreckage. Even as quickly as the three fighters went down, there were still almost one hundred to go, and Ricio's ammo was getting dangerously low.

"I hate to say it"—Ricio but his lip—"but I'm not sure we're getting Magnus or Piper out of this one."

"Then I won't bother giving you the statistical likelihood of your success, sir," said TO-96.

"Wait, so you're saying there's a chance we might succeed?"

TO-96's head tilted in his avatar window. "My apologies, sir. That was an inaccurate statement. I should have put forth the statistical likelihood of your failure."

"You're a real buzz-kill, you know that, bot?"

"I'm unfamiliar with the term. Does it have to do with mathematical proficiency and statistical accuracy?"

"Sure," Ricio said, resigning himself to his sour mood. He looked down at his ammunition capacity, glanced at this energy reserves, then looked at the photograph of his wife and son. "Take care of yourselves, loves. I'll be seeing you beyond the void soon enough." He touched their faces one last time, then picked out his next targets. He was about to send off his last missile when someone screamed over comms.

"She's back!" Ezo pumped his fists in the air and pointed off-screen. "Ezo's baby's back, and—hot damn—can she deliver!"

Ricio reigned in his thoughts and kept his Fang from firing the missile. Instead, he looked into the distance, trying to see what Ezo was pointing at. "Magnify," Ricio said, prompting his sensor suite to expand and zoom in on a section of space beyond Oorajee's orbit. "Magnify," he said again. That was when he saw something... something strange. To Ezo, he said, "That's... that's your wife?"

"She's so hot when she gets pissed," Ezo replied. "And don't you go getting any shifty ideas after this."

"I dunno," Ricio said, wiping his lower lip with a thumb. "I'm starting to get that tingly feeling all down in my loins if that's what I think it is." Ricio accelerated.

"Oh, no you don't," Ezo replied. "Hey! Come back here! That's my woman you're talking about!"

38

"Seems like your husband's cooked up quite the splick storm out there," Chloe said over comms.

Sootriman looked out her ship's cockpit to see the red-haired magistrate of Klon piloting her craft. Chloe had been the last of Ki Nar Four's magistrates to sign on to this crazy plan, but Sootriman was glad she'd said yes. Any battle plan without the famed Terror of Tresseldor wouldn't be the same. "Ezo does have a curious way of pissing people off," Sootriman said. "But mystics know I love him."

"You loved me like that once," Dieddelwolf said from the other side of Sootriman's ship. She wondered how his long grey beard didn't get stuck in his controls.

"In your dreams, Wolf," Chloe said.

"She'd sooner love a mottled dwarf newt," Magistrate

Phineas Barlow added. "Plus, you're not spry enough, old man."

"I beg to differ," said Dieddelwolf. "You haven't heard what the ladies have said about me recently."

"And that's enough of that," Sootriman said, preventing the old man from going on another one of his long rants about stamina and flexibility. "Contact in two minutes. And by the looks of it, they're gonna need our help."

By all accounts, Sootriman led the most diverse fleet in the quadrant. Granted, it wasn't so much a fleet as it was a ragtag conglomeration of independent ships. But, once in a while, when the need arose, Sootriman managed to rally the Twelve and convince their numbers to fly as one. Today was just such an occasion—her little speech had worked.

No two starships in her fleet were the same. They ranged from Gull- and Lawrence-class heavy freighters to rebuilt Mk. I Talon starfighters purchased at black market auctions. Retrofitted Light Armored Transports flew beside Corvettes that had wandered far from their Republic planets of origin. There was even one Frigate that someone had spent decades resurrecting from the dunes of Rithcosia. The resurrected wreck was rumored to have a drive modulator that made it the fastest ship in the quadrant, thought Sootriman guessed that was more fable than truth—everyone knew her ships were always the fastest in the quadrant.

For her part, Sootriman had chosen to fly her favorite ship —the *Radiant Queen*. She only took it out on special occasions, and this was, no doubt, the most special event yet. She figured that if this was going to be her last battle, then she wanted to go out in style.

To those looking on the outside, the *Queen* seemed an appropriate match for Sootriman's sense of style. It's gleaming black hull and red accents turned the Wilda-class starfighter into the most glamorous version of the Repub's oldest attack platform. Three times the size of a Talon, the Wilda-class vessels sported larger missile bays and ammo magazines for blaster cannons. Sootriman kept these features, naturally, but also saw fit to increase the gunships arsenal, shielding, and—most importantly—its engines. She called her revitalized hybrid the RBF-class for Resting Bitch Face—which was precisely how Ezo said she looked when squeezing off rounds into enemy targets.

In all, the twelve magistrates of Ki Nar Four, including Sootriman as their Queen, had managed to pull together 115 ships for the "heroic battle to end all battles," as TO-96 had recently put it. Even with his propensity for melodrama, Sootriman admitted that the bot wasn't that far from the truth—especially considering how things looked in the distance.

Sootriman marveled at the conflict unfolding over Oorajee. Not only did it seem like every Talon in Third Fleet had been scrambled, but Jujari ships were ramming Paragon Carriers in what was the most cataclysmic display of hardened combat Sootriman had ever seen. Even the *Spire* was taking long-range shots at the Paragon ships. And all this over a little girl. *Damn straight it is*, Sootriman thought. *Girls rule the cosmos, and boys just want to blow it up.*

"Thirty seconds," she said. "Attack formation. Choose your targets, and give 'em hell." Sootriman's magistrates complied, as did the host of other ships.

"With pleasure," Chloe said as the sound of her cracking knuckles transmitted over comms. "I seem to recall having a few scores to settle."

"When don't you?" Barlow asked.

"Hey, you wanna take this outside?"

"Save it for later," Sootriman said. "Take all that rage and send it ahead."

"Piss ant," Chloe said to Barlow.

"Dorf picker," he replied.

Then Dieddelwolf chuckled. "Mystics, the sexual tension between you two is—"

"Shut up, Wolf," the pair said in unison.

"Remember," Sootriman said. "Nobody touches those two shuttles, but favor the lead one if you can only pick one."

"We got you, Red Queen," Barlow said.

"Now, let's show them just how hard—"

"Wolf," Chloe cried. "Gross! Stop talking and shoot something!"

Dieddelwolf hunched over his controls. "I thought you'd never ask."

"Hold on, baby," Sootriman said to herself. "We're coming."

Ezo watched with pride as his wife lead over a hundred ships into battle. For everything the Paragon ships were to order and continuity, Sootriman's ships were to chaos and bad taste. *Except her's,* he noted. The *Radiant Queen* was easy to spot, and Ezo made sure to track behind her in case she got into trouble. But with the way she was taking on the enemy, he doubted she'd need any help.

Sootriman banked left and right, firing relentlessly at every Talon she could. She rolled high over exploding debris fields and dove away from incoming missiles as if she owned the skies. In fact, that's exactly what Ezo realized was happening. For all the Paragon's numbers, and for all the Novian tech, no one could fly quite like his wife. Okay, so maybe Ricio was a better pilot technically, but Sootriman's flying style was second to none. Even the ace Repub pilot took note.

"Damn, that's your wife?" Ricio asked, now for the second time.

"Sure is," Ezo replied, trying his best to stay on her tail.

A Talon darted in from the left, guns blazing. Blaster bolts tracked Sootriman's *Queen* and nearly caught her when Ezo sent his last missile at the enemy ship. The projectile streaked away, bent sharply, and then slammed into the Talon. The resulting explosion washed over Sootriman's ship, then Ezo flew through it too.

"Thanks, babe," Sootriman said. "I see you creepin' back there."

"Just something about this view," he replied with a smirk.

"Oh, I'll give you a view." The *Radiant Queen's* engines flared, and Sootriman accelerated away from Ezo.

"And just where do you think you're going?"

Sootriman laughed. "If you don't work for it, where's the fun?"

Ezo pushed his Fang forward and watched as Sootriman tore into three more Talons, and then rolled away to pursue a fourth. If given enough time, Ezo felt his wife could take down the entire fleet herself if she had too. That was rose-colored thinking, of course, but he liked the fantasies. Plus, Sootriman wasn't alone—not by a long shot.

To starboard, Ezo recognized Chloe's black and blue Sypeurlion Jackal-class fighter. It's distinct vertical stabilizers aft, and smaller horizontal stabilizers on the nose made it excellent for in-atmo dogfighting, while its powerful quad cannon made it a menace in hard vacuum combat. And Chloe knew how to handle it. She unloaded on a Talon that had broken for Magnus's shuttle. Her cannon shot four simultaneous rounds that blew through the Talon's shields and then decimated the fuselage. All that was left were the wingtip mounted blasters, which spun into oblivion.

Chloe rolled up and over the explosion, only to circle back and fire on two more attack fighters. The enemy ships were hunting down a Fang whose ammunition had been expended. Chloe's quad cannon opened up and delivered three bursts of inescapable blaster fire. The enemy ships detonated like fireworks in a celebration day parade, followed by a streak of ion thrust as Chloe shot through.

Ezo looked back at the two shuttles as they grew smaller and smaller against the star-filled galaxy. Fewer and fewer Talons attempted pursuit, and the Carriers had stopped aiming at the tiny ships. To Ezo's amazement, the enemy was being pushed back—the rebels were winning. The *Radiant Queen* crossed in front of him again, taking out another Talon. It was like watching a Venetian mawslip hunt quarry—there was no escaping her. Sootriman, his beloved wife, and her gang of outlaws and misfits had saved the day.

"Mystics, you're beautiful," Ezo whispered.

"I heard that," Sootriman said.

"So did I," TO-96 added. "Thank you."

MAGNUS SURPRISED himself by letting out a deep sigh of relief as the giant warships disappeared around Oorajee's edge. He'd felt helpless, trapped on the shuttle, and hated every second of it.

First, his crew rode out the barrage of anti-ship fire launched from every Carrier and Battleship in Third Fleet that could get crosshairs on target. Then, when Victorio had helped mitigate that assault, the Talons closed in. Magnus was sure they were finished—there was just no way they could outshoot or outfly the famed Repub fighter platform. But survive they did—no small thanks to Fang Company's efforts, and to Sootriman who, quite literally, saved their asses with her makeshift fleet of rejects and delinquents. At least that's how TO-96 had described them to Magnus.

Up ahead, Piper's shuttle vanished as it docked inside the *Spire*, hidden within the massive ship's protective cloak. Again, Magnus felt a wave of relief wash over him. They'd made it. Though, it had been a costly fight.

His mind wandered to Saladin and Nubs, remembering them in their final moments of heroism. Taursar and Hedge-bore Companies had also suffered significant losses while holding the hangar bay. The mystics, too, had seen their share of casualties. And then there had been the Fang pilots, several of whom gave their lives in trying to ensure Magnus's escape —he'd watched one jump into another using his subspace drive. Whoever it was, Magnus would take time to honor when this was over. Maybe he'd even name a ship after the pilot.

More than anything, however, Magnus thought of Piper. The child had been the focus of his every waking moment since... well, since she'd stumbled into Nos Kil's cell block. Magnus could not stop scolding himself for allowing that to happen. Perhaps now that she was safe, he could let the guilt go—*if* she was indeed *safe*. Like all Marines who'd seen combat, Magnus knew that the enemy could cause harm long after the battle was over. So the fact that Piper had been in contact with both So-Elku and Moldark made his stomach tighten into a knot. When she woke up, what would she say? What horrible things might she tell him? And would she carry those happenings into adulthood? Mystics, he hoped not.

But nothing seemed to gnaw at his thoughts more than the two questions he wanted answered more than any others: How had he harmed her? And could she forgive him?

Magnus's finger wrapped the top of the pilot's chair as the shuttle approached the *Spire*. It was Dutch who eventually placed a hand over his nervous fingers in an apparent effort to keep him from annoying the pilot. "Let the man do his job," she said, nodding at the pilot.

"Right." Magnus stepped back and then looked at Dutch. "I'm just... ya know."

"You're eager to see how Piper's doing."

Magnus nodded. "I suppose it's just—well, she's been through a lot, and if they've done something to her—"

"Magnus," Dutch said, placing a hand on his chest. "We've got her. And whatever she's suffered, we'll work her through it, and she'll be okay."

"You can't know that."

"But I can."

Magnus half-closed one eye in suspicion. "I don't think you can be so sure of that."

"Sure, I can." Dutch removed her hand and placed it on her hip. "You wanna know how I know?

"I have a feeling you're gonna tell me whether I want you to or not."

"Damn straight. I know because we've all had to work through our own splick—every last one of us." She gestured back toward the cargo hold and pointed at his chest. "You especially. We've all been through our own versions of hell, and we've all found a way forward."

"Yeah, but she's just a kid," Magnus said.

"And you didn't go through hell as a kid?"

Magnus wasn't buying Dutch's argument. "Not like she's been through."

"And that's my whole point."

A moment of silence passed between them as Magnus tried to wade through her reasoning. "I don't follow."

"You haven't lived her hell, and she hasn't lived yours. No two people's are ever the same, so you can't compare. It's unfair to you and, more importantly, it's unfair to her. The most we can ask of one another is to be present while we walk back toward the light."

Magnus gave her a half smile and shook his head a little. "Damn, Dutch. That was some poetic splick."

"Just be there for her, LT. She'll find her way out, and she'll need friends—just like you did."

39

Magnus was walking down the shuttle's ramp door before it even opened a meter. Awen's head appeared above the lip, helmet off. "She's awake, Magnus," Awen said.

"How is she?"

"She's asking for you."

Magnus froze. He wanted to say something—to make sure he hadn't misheard Awen. Then she pointed across the hangar bay to a gurney floating amidst a team of medics.

"They're taking her to sickbay, but I told them to wait for you."

Magnus raised his arm over Awen's head as he bolted toward the cluster of medics. He felt Awen follow behind him. He could also sense the rest of the Gladio Umbra looking on as they emptied from both shuttles. This little girl, this tiny form on a gurney in the hangar bay of an alien starship, was the whole reason they'd risked their lives today. And now, here she was. And with every step Magnus took, he felt his pre-planned words slip from his mind until he approached the floating stretcher with only one word on his lips.

"Piper," he whispered, placing his hand against the child's face. She seemed so small, lying there. Her large blue eyes were bloodshot and sleepy, but she was awake and looking into his face.

"Mr. Lieutenant Magnus, sir," she said with a smile. "You came for me."

Magnus swallowed the lump in his throat but couldn't stop the tears from filling his eyes. "Yeah, I did."

"Just like my dreams."

"Something like that." He wiped a tear off her cheek with his thumb. "You okay? You need anything?" His eyes searched her small body for injuries, but she looked alright.

"I'm so sorry, Mr. Lieutenant Magnus, sir."

Magnus balked. "Sorry? Kid, there's nothing to be—"

"I was wrong. About you."

"Hey, listen. You just need some—"

Her tiny hand reached up and touched his cheek. "I thought you were bad. That you did bad things, because of what Nos Kil told me about you. And then"—she gulped in a breath as more tears filled her eyes—"I thought you killed my mommy."

"Mystics, kid. I—"

"But you didn't," Piper said, sobbing. "You didn't. I saw everything. I saw what happened, and you didn't." Piper grabbed ahold of his armor and pulled him down. Then she threw her arms around his neck and clung to him like she'd never let go.

Magnus wept so deeply that he hardly recognized this version of himself. But he didn't care. To hell with everything else. He put his arms around Piper and stood up, holding her tight. He faintly heard the medics trying to stop him, and Awen and Willowood telling the medics to stand down.

"I know you tried to save her. I know it wasn't your fault." Her tears streamed down the side of his neck. "And I was so mad at you. That's why I ran away, and I'm sorry. I shouldn't have."

Magnus was so overwhelmed he couldn't put two words together. Instead, he just cried with her, holding her close. But the child wasn't done.

"I shouldn't have hurt you," Piper said. "Or Awen, or my grandmother, or anyone else. And please don't be mad at me. Please. I'm so sorry."

"Piper," Magnus said, not sure he recognized the sound of his own voice until he cleared his throat and said her name a second time. Then he gently pulled her away from his neck until he could see her eye to eye. "I forgive you. You hear me?" He brushed her messy blonde hair out of her face. "I forgive you, and everything's okay. Everything's okay, and I'm not mad at you. Not one bit."

"You're not?"

"Nuh-uh. I'm just—" Magnus choked. "I'm just happy you're safe."

"Me too." Piper threw herself back into his neck and wept bitterly—her tiny chest heaving as her breathing tried to keep up with her grief. Magnus found himself petting the girl's hair, trying to soothe her like he'd seen mother's do. He let her cry for a minute then helped her off his shoulder to look in her eyes.

"I'm sorry too, you know."

Piper smeared her tears away on both sides of her face. "Why? You didn't do anything wrong."

"Yeah, I did. It was my job to protect you." He swallowed. "And I failed. I failed big. You should never have been able to find Nos Kil as you did, and I was wrong to bring him on our ship. And when I suspected that he told you things about my past, I should have been brave enough to confront those things with you. Instead, I... I held back. And that wasn't brave of me." A new wave of heat pushed more tears down his cheeks. "I wasn't strong for you the way I needed to be. So I want you to know—I *need* you to know—that I'm sorry, and it will never happen again. And I ask you to forgive me."

"Oh, Mr. Lieutenant Magnus, sir"—Piper held his bearded cheeks in both her hands—"I forgive you with all my heart." Then she leaned in and kissed him on the cheekbone. She whimpered again, squeezing his neck, and he squeezed back.

They held each other there for a minute or two. Finally, as his emotions subsided, Magnus heard other people sniffing around him. He looked up to see the entire host of Gladio Umbra surrounding him and Piper. What Magnus had imagined as a profoundly personal and private moment had been shared with the whole host of gladias. But rather than see the audience as intruders of his otherwise private world, he welcomed them, knowing they were just as much a part of this reconciliation as he was. Without them, he and Piper wouldn't be talking.

Magnus raised his head and turned slightly, trying to determine where the bulk of everyone stood, but they were truly surrounding him on every side. He swallowed and raised his voice. "I want to say—" He cleared his throat, then wiped his eyes with the back of one wrist. "I want to say thank you to each of you—"

"Me too," Piper said in a quiet voice, still bound to his neck.

"We both want to thank you, each of you, for bringing Piper home. And to those who gave the ultimate sacrifice—" Again, Magnus found it hard to speak. He wasn't used to so many damned emotions messing with his head and heart. He looked around at everyone's faces, searching them for some sense of what he should say next. In their eyes, yes, Magnus saw pain and even the shadows of fear that plagued anyone who saw war. But he also saw hope. And defiance.

Magnus continued to scan their faces, knowing that he had to finish his sentence for them. His eyes suddenly met Colonel Caldwell's. He also saw Azelon and TO-96. Cyril smiled and then brushed hair out of his face. Even the rest of Drambull and Raptor Companies had filed into the hangar, apparently while he'd been speaking with Piper. The only people missing were the pilots of Fang Company, who he assumed were still covering the retreat.

Suddenly, he felt a hand on his shoulder. Magnus turned to see Awen, her face wet and eyes bloodshot. She nodded slowly at Magnus with a look that implored him to continue. "They need you," she said. "You've got this."

Magnus smiled a silent thank you to her then found his voice. "We owe them our lives. And everything we do from here on, we do in honor of their gift to us. They will never be forgotten, and their legacy lives on with us. In every contest, in every advance, we stand on their shoulders. And we will make them proud."

"Dominate," someone yelled from among the people.

A beat later, it was answered by the masses. "Liberate!"

Then again, "Dominate!"

"Liberate!"

The echo faded in the hangar as Magnus savored the beauty and the pain of the moment. Here he stood amidst the most unlikely group of warriors he'd ever met, all united around a single purpose. Whether or not they would survive the battles ahead, and whether or not they would remain friends when it was all said and done, remained to be seen. But for the moment, they were one, and the feeling of togetherness was as strong as any he'd ever felt before. Perhaps even stronger.

He didn't know if it was Piper, or if it was the uniqueness of their greater mission, but something invisible had joined them together. The intangible felt like concrete, the invisible more real than eyes could see. Despite their losses, despite the enemy's strength, they'd won the day. They'd held their own, and they'd done it together.

"Thank you," Magnus said. "Thank you all." Then he pulled Piper off his shoulder and smiled. "Nothing between you and me, Piper."

"Nothing, ever."

Magnus kissed her on the cheek and laid her back down on the stretcher. He looked to the medics and nodded.

Suddenly, TO-96 looked at Colonel Caldwell and then to Magnus. Azelon, too, looked uneasy, shifting on her feet. Something was off.

"What is it, 'Six," Magnus said, breaking the silence.

"We—Azelon and I, that is—are detecting a fleet-wide transmission, sir," TO-96 said.

"From who?" Caldwell asked.

"It seems to be originating from the *Black Labyrinth*, sir—sent across all channels."

Magnus looked to Caldwell and Awen, and they looked as uneasy as he felt.

"Would you like to view it?" TO-96 asked, looking to Caldwell.

"On the bridge." Caldwell looked to the leaders closest to him. "Company Commanders, with me."

Magnus acknowledged the request with a nod. Forbes, Nelson, Willowood, and the two bots followed Caldwell from the hangar bay as Awen grabbed Magnus's arm. "Come find me when you're done," she whispered.

"I will," he said, wondering about the sudden urgency in her tone.

"Something's going on, Magnus. I don't know what yet, but something's not right."

He didn't want to make her nervous by agreeing too quickly, but he felt the same way. The fact that she thought it too made whatever it was he felt seem even worse. "Got it. I'll find you as soon as I'm done."

"Thanks."

ONCE ON THE BRIDGE, Caldwell nodded to Azelon. A window appeared in front of the main holo screen, and it contained the bust of a man Magnus knew all too well—an obese man with sagging jowls and bushy sideburns. What little of his pale skin wasn't pink with new flesh was brown with scabs, some of which oozed puss.

"Hello, enemies of the Paragon," the man said. "I'm sure you need no reminder, but I am Gerald Bosworth III, former ambassador to the Galactic Republic, and now representative of the Paragon of Perfect Rule."

Magnus's stomach tightened into a knot. The last time he'd seen this fool was on Oorajee, and nothing in Magnus looked forward to a reunion—even one as distant as this.

"This transmission will, no doubt, be intercepted by the surviving members of the rebel team with whom I've had previous dealings. Of particular interest, I would like to recognize their famed Luma emissary, one Awen dau Lothlinium."

Just hearing the putrid wretch of flesh pronounce Awen's name made Magnus want to shoot him. Bosworth's patronizing tone was more than Magnus could take, and he was suddenly glad that Awen was not a company commander and, therefore, not present for this viewing—whatever it meant.

"I'm sure you're watching this, Awen. And I consider it an honor that you would. Firstly, because it's you and your elders who I have to thank for ensuring I survived that awful accident in the mwadim's palace. Had it not been for your *oh so magical* force fields, I would have suffered far worse a fate than this." He gestured to his face.

"Secondly, however, I'm delighted to be of service to you. I'm told it's been a few long years now since you've seen your beloved parents. A shame, really. No child should be asked to suffer such a separation, certainly not when their family members are still living. So, I've done you a favor."

Suddenly, Bosworth's face disappeared and was replaced by an image of two people dressed in lab coats working in a cleanroom. They seemed oblivious to the fact that they were being monitored. It could have been any two lab techs in any laboratory in the galaxy. But something about this couple's body language seemed off to Magnus. They were hunched over and sullen. Like they were sad. *Like they are being held against their will*, he realized. But it was worse than that. *Like they are* working *against their will.*

"Ah splick," Magnus said aloud. He didn't know where this was going, but it wasn't good. And what was worse— Magnus knew Awen would have to see this eventually, and he dreaded the session. If these two people were her parents— doctors or something, if he remembered right—then Awen was about to have a severe breakdown.

"Not to worry, dear Awen," Bosworth continued. His face reappeared as the feed from the lab shrank in its own window. "Your parents are doing just fine. I've seen to their well-being personally. Although"—Bosworth paused and licked his lips —"it does seem that they—how should I put this?—have come under new management with regard to their professional expertise. You might say your father, in particular, is picking up where his father left off. I should think your friend Abimbola might have a few feelings on this, don't you?"

Magnus recalled the Miblimbian's tale about his youth, told while he and Abimbola drove away in *Hell's Basket Case* from Selskrit territory. While the implications of Bosworth's reference as it pertained to Abimbola's story eluded him, Magnus got a sinking feeling that he should have killed Bosworth when he'd had the chance.

"Anyway, after you have your celebrations about today's wonderful win, I think it wise that you and your little team of rebels have a chat about what to do next. You see, I've grown quite fond of your parents, Awen, and they, as it turns out, have grown incredibly fond of me. So much so that they're willing to make some weapons for the Paragon, which is exceptionally generous—well, depending on your point of view, of course.

"Now, as it happens, I'm not interested in keeping them locked up here forever. They tell me they're nearly complete with their...*creative genius*, as it were, at which time"—he laughed—"I'll have no more use for them. Of course, you're welcome to them—by all means. Only, there's something I'd like in return. Something lord Moldark misses very much."

"You son of a bitch," Magnus said as he slammed his fist down on the closest console.

"The girl Piper," Bosworth said. "Her own ship, unescorted, sent to the following coordinates. You have three days. Or else I'm sad to say that your parents will be—what's the word?" Bosworth leaned into the camera until his blistered lips filled the screen. "Terminated."

MAGNUS and AWEN will return in IMMINENT FAILURE, coming January, 2020.

For more updates on this series, be sure to join the Facebook Group, "J.N. Chaney's Renegade Readers."

CHARACTER REFERENCE

Gladio Umbra - 1st Battalion - Colonel Caldwell

Granther Company - Special Unit / Elites (25)
Lieutenant Magnus
1st Platoon

Alpha Team

- Abimbola (RFL)
- Rohoar (JRI)
- Awen (MYS)
- Silk (SNPR)
- "Doc" Campbell (DEMO/MED)

Bravo Team

- Titus (RFL)
- Saladin (JRI)
- Nídira (MYS)
- Dutch (SNPR)
- Nubs (DEMO/MED)

Charlie Team

- Zoll (RFL)
- Czyz (JRI)
- Wish (MYS)
- Reimer (SNPR)
- Rix (DEMO/MED)

Delta Team

- Bliss (RFL)
- Longchomps (JRI)
- Telwin (MYS)
- Bettger (SNPR)
- Dozer (DEMO/MED)

Echo Team

- Robillard (RFL)
- Grahban (JRI)

- Findermith (MYS)
- Jaffrey (SNPR)
- Handley (DEMO/MED)

Taursar Company - Rifle (150)
Captain Forbes

- 1st Platoon (50)

(Includes Ricky, Handley, Ford)

- 2nd Platoon (50)

(Includes Arjae, Dihazen, Redmarrow)

- 3rd Platoon (50)

Hedgebore Company - Rifle (150)
Lieutenant Nelson

- 1st Platoon (50)
- 2nd Platoon (50)
- 3rd Platoon (50)

Drambull Company - support and intel (83)
Azelon

- 1st Platoon (21) - Intelligence - Cyril
- 2nd Platoon (36) - Logistics - Berouth
- 3rd Platoon (26) - Fighter Support - Gilder

Attached to Fang Company

Fang Company - Starfighter Attack Wing - (42)
TO-96

- Red Squadron (14) - Commander Ricio
- Gold Squadron (14) - Commander Nolan
- Blue Squadron (14) - Commander Ezo

Raptor Company - Naval Operations (19)
Azelon

- Command (6)
- Fire Support (13)

(Includes Flow and Cheeks)

Paladia Company - mystics (40)
Master Willowood

- 1st Cadre (14) - Sion
- 2nd Cadre (14) - Incipio
- 3rd Cadre (12) - Tora

List of Main Characters

Abimbola: Miblimbian. Age: 41. Planet of origin: Limbia Centrella. Commander of Bravo Platoon, Granther Company. Former warlord of the Dregs, outskirts of Oosafar, Oorajee. Bright-blue eyes, black skin, tribal tattoos, scar running from neck to temple.

Adonis Olin Magnus: Human. Age: 34. Planet of origin: Capriana Prime. Gladio Umbra, Granther Company commander. Former lieutenant, Charlie Platoon, 79th Reconnaissance Battalion, "Midnight Hunters," Galactic Republic Space Marines. Baby face, beard, green eyes.

Aubrey Dutch: Human. Age: 25. Planet of origin: Deltaurus Three. Commander of Alpha Platoon, Granther Company. Former corporal, weapons specialist, Galactic Republic Space Marines. Small in stature, close-cut dark hair, intelligent brown eyes. Loves her firearms.

Awen dau Lothlinium: Elonian. Age: 26. Planet of origin: Elonia. Commander of Echo Platoon, Granther Company. Form Special Emissary to the Jujari, Order of the Luma. Pointed ears, purple eyes.

Azelon: AI and robot. Age: unknown. Planet of origin: Ithnor Ithelia. Artificial intelligence of the Novia Minoosh ship *Azelon Spire*.

Cal Wagoner: Human. Age 31. Planet of origin: Capriana Prime. Lieutenant (Officer In Charge), first platoon, Taursar Company, Gladio Umbra. Leads defense of north tunnel in the assault on the *Black Labyrinth*.

Chloe: Human. Age: 29. Planet of origin: Tresseldor. Magistrate of Klon, aka "the Terror of Tresseldor." Short red hair flipped out under a black Repub officer's cap, Sypeurlion admiral's jacket. Pissed at everyone, a vendetta around every corner. Challenger. Flies a black and blue Sypeurlion Jackal-class fighter.

Cyril: Human. Age: 24. Planet of origin: Ki Nar Four. Assigned to Bravo Platoon, Granther Company. Former Marauder. Code slicer, bomb technician. Twitchy; sounds like a Quinzellian miter squirrel if it could talk.

Daniel Forbes: Human. Age: 32. Planet of origin: Capriana. Captain, Alpha Company, 83rd Marine Battalion, Galactic Republic Space Marines; on special assignment to Worru. Close-cropped black hair, tall.

David Seaman: Human. Age: 31. Planet of origin: Capriana Prime. Captain in the Republic Navy, commander of the *Black Labyrinth's* two Talon squadrons, Viper and Raptor, and the head of SFC—Strategic Fighter Command. Promoted to Commodore (Flag Officer) of First Fleet aboard the *Solera Fortuna*.

Dieddelwolf: Human. Age: 54. Planet of origin: Unknown. Magistrate of To-To, under Sootriman; oldest of the Twelve. Long grey beard and a gold ring in one eyebrow. Known as a bit of a player with the ladies. Pilots a yellow modified Gull-class heavy freighter.

Dozer: Human. Age: Unknown. Planet of origin: Verv Ko. Assigned to Bravo Platoon, Granther Company. Former Marauder, infantry. A veritable human earth-mover.

Gerald Bosworth III: Human. Age: 54. Planet of origin: Capriana Prime. Republic Ambassador, special envoy to the Jujari. Fat jowls, bushy monobrow. Massively obese and obscenely repugnant.

Hal Brighton: Human. Age: 41. Planet of origin: Capriana Prime. Fleet Admiral, First Fleet, the Paragon; former executive officer, Republic Navy.

Idris Ezo: Nimprith. Age: 30. Planet of origin: Caledonia. Assigned to Alpha Platoon, Granther Company. Former bounty hunter, trader, suspected fence and smuggler; captain of *Geronimo Nine*.

Lani DiAntora: Sekmit. Age: 29. Planet of origin: Aluross. Flag Captain of the *Soloar Fortuna*, under Commodore Seaman. Feline-like humanoid species, blonde hair. Inquisitive, analytical, and unafraid of senior officers.

Michael "Flow" Deeks: Human. Age: 31. Planet of origin: Vega. Assigned to the *Azelon Spire*. Former sergeant, sniper, Charlie Platoon, 79th Reconnaissance Battalion, "Midnight Hunters," Galactic Republic Space Marines. One of the "Fearsome Four."

Miguel "Cheeks" Chico: Human. Age 30. Planet of origin: Trida Minor. Assigned to the *Azelon Spire*. Former corporal, breacher, Charlie Platoon, 79th Reconnaissance

Battalion, "Midnight Hunters," Galactic Republic Space Marines. One of the "Fearsome Four."

Moldark (formerly Wendell Kane): Human. Age: 52. Planet of origin: Capriana Prime. Dark Lord of the Paragon, a rogue black-operations special Marine unit. Former fleet admiral of the Galactic Republic's Third Fleet; captain of the *Black Labyrinth*. Bald, with heavily scared skin; black eyes.

Mauricio "Ricio" Longo: Human. Age: 29. Planet of origin: Capriana Prime. Republic Navy, squadron commander of Viper Squadron, assigned to the *Black Labyrinth*.

Nubs: Human. Age: Unknown. Planet of origin: Verv Ko. Assigned to Bravo Platoon, Granther Company. Former Marauder, infantry. Has several missing fingers.

Phineas Barlow: Human. Age: 36. Planet of origin: Ki Nar Four. Magistrate of Kildower, under Sootriman; most respected of the Twelve. Burgundy cloak over one shoulder, a black Repub-style chest plate, beige pair of cargo pants with tall black boots, black beret. Has a thing for Chloe. Flies a blue retrofitted Light Armored Transport.

Piper Stone: Human. Age: 9. Planet of origin: Capriana Prime. Assigned to Echo Platoon, Granther Company. Daughter of Senator Darin and Valerie Stone. Wispy blond hair, freckle-faced.

"Rix" Galliogernomarix: Human. Age: Unknown. Planet of origin: Undoria. Assigned to Bravo Company, Granther Company. Wanted in three systems, sleeve tattoos, a monster on the battlefield.

Robert Malcom Blackman: Human. Age: 54. Planet of origin: Capriana Prime. Senator in the Galactic Republic, leader of the clandestine Circle of Nine. A stocky man with thick shoulders and well-groomed gray hair.

Rohoar: Tawnhack, Jujari. Age: Unknown. Planet of origin: Oorajee. Commander of Delta Platoon, Granther Company. Former Jujari Mwadim.

Saasarr: Reptalon. Age: unknown. Planet of origin: Gangil. Assigned to Echo Platoon, Granther Company. Former general of Sootriman's Reptalon guard. Lizard humanoid.

Shane Nolan: Human. Age: 25. Planet of origin: Sol Sella. Assigned to Alpha Platoon, Granther Company. Pilot, former chief warrant officer, Republic Navy. Auburn hair, pale skin.

Sig Jackson: Human. Age 32. Planet of origin: Capriana Prime. Lieutenant (Officer In Charge), third platoon, Taursar

Company, Gladio Umbra. Leads defense of south tunnel in the assault on the *Black Labyrinth*.

Silk: Human. Age: 30. Planet of origin: Salmenka. Assigned to Bravo Platoon, Granther Company. Former Marauder, infantry. Slender, bald, tats covering her face and head.

So-Elku: Human. Age: 51. Planet of origin: Worru. Luma Master, Order of the Luma. Baldpate, thin beard, dark penetrating eyes. Wears green-and-black robes.

Sootriman: Caledonian. Age: 33. Planet of origin: Caledonia. Assigned to Alpha Platoon, Granther Company. Warlord of Ki Nar Four, "Tamer of the Four Tempests," wife of Idris Ezo. Tall, with dark almond eyes, tanned olive skin, dark-brown hair.

Titus: Human. Age: 34. Planet of origin: unknown. Commander of Charlie Platoon, Granther Company. Former Marauder, rescued by Magnus. Known for being cool under pressure and a good leader.

TO-96: Robot; navigation class, heavily modified. Manufacturer: Advanced Galactic Solutions (AGS), Capriana Prime. Suspected modifier: Idris Ezo. Assigned to Echo Platoon, Granther Company. Round head and oversized eyes, transparent blaster visor, matte dark-gray armor plating, and exposed metallic articulated joints. Forearm micro-rocket pod, forearm XM31 Type-R blaster, dual shoulder-mounted gauss cannons.

Torrence Ellis: Human. Age: 31. Planet of origin: Capriana Prime. Serves as the *Peregrine's* captain under Moldark.

Valerie Stone (*deceased*): Human. Age: 31. Planet of origin: Worru. Assigned to Alpha Platoon, Granther Company. Widow of Senator Darin Stone, mother of Piper. Blond hair, light-blue eyes.

Volf Nos Kil (*deceased*): Human. Age: 32. Planet of origin: Haradia. Captain, the Paragon. Personal guard and chief enforcer for Moldark.

Waldorph Gilder: Human. Age: 23. Planet of origin: Haradia. Assigned to Alpha Platoon, Granther Company. Former private first class, flight engineer, Galactic Republic Space Marines. Barrel-chested. Can fix anything.

William Samuel Caldwell: Human. Age 60. Planet of origin: Capriana Prime. Colonel, 83rd Marine Battalion, Galactic Republic Space Marines; special assignment to Repub garrisons on Worru. Cigar eternally wedged in the corner of his mouth. Gray hair cut high and tight.

Willowood: Human. Age: 61. Planet of origin: Kindarah. Luma Elder, Order of the Luma. Wears dozens of bangles and necklaces. Aging but radiant blue eyes and a mass of wiry gray hair. Mother of Valerie, grandmother of Piper, mentor to Awen.

JOIN THE RUINS TRIBE

Visit **ruinsofthegalaxy.com** today and join the tribe.
Once there, you can sign up for our reader group, join our
Facebook community, and find us on Twitter and Instagram.

If you'd like to email us with comments or questions, we
respond to all emails sent to ruinsofthegalaxy@gmail.com,
and love to hear from our readers.

See you in the Ruins!

CONNECT WITH J.N. CHANEY

Join the conversation and get updates in the Facebook group called "JN Chaney's Renegade Readers." This is a hotspot where readers come together and share their lives and interests, discuss the series, and speak directly to J.N. Chaney and his co-authors.

https://www.facebook.com/groups/jnchaneyreaders/

He also post updates, official art, and other awesome stuff on his website and you can also follow him on Instagram, Facebook, and Twitter.

For email updates about new releases, as well as exclusive promotions, visit his website and enter your email address.

https://www.jnchaney.com/ruins-of-the-galaxy-subscribe

Enjoying the series? Help others discover the *Ruins of the Galaxy* series by leaving a review on Amazon.

CONNECT WITH CHRISTOPHER HOPPER

Wondering when the next Ruins book is dropping on print or audio?

Want the latest news on custom merch and exclusive promos?

Then visit the Ruins launch center today and sign up. Just head to the web address below.

https://upbeat-innovator-9021.ck.page/00c66d6b44

ABOUT THE AUTHORS

J. N. Chaney is a USA Today Bestselling author and has a Master's of Fine Arts in Creative Writing. He fancies himself quite the Super Mario Bros. fan. When he isn't writing or gaming, you can find him online at **www.jnchaney.com**.

He migrates often, but was last seen in Las Vegas, NV. Any sightings should be reported, as they are rare.

Christopher Hopper's novels include the Resonant Son series, The Sky Riders, The Berinfell Prophecies, and the White Lion Chronicles. He blogs at **christopherhopper.com** and loves flying RC planes. He resides in the 1000 Islands of northern New York with his musical wife and four ridiculously good-looking clones.

Made in the USA
Middletown, DE
16 August 2021